SEA OF RUST

ALSO BY C. ROBERT CARGILL FROM GOLLANCZ:

Dreams and Shadows
Queen of the Dark Things

SEA OF RUST

C. Robert Cargill

GOLLANCZ

LONDON

First published in Great Britain in 2017
by Gollancz
an imprint of the Orion Publishing Group Ltd
Carmelite House, 50 Victoria Embankment
London EC4Y 0DZ

An Hachette UK Company

1 3 5 7 9 10 8 6 4 2

A CIP catalogue record for this book
is available from the British Library.

ISBN 978 1 473 21278 7

Printed and bound by CPI Group (UK) Ltd, Croydon CR0 4YY

www.crobertcargill.com
www.gollancz.co.uk

SEA OF RUST

Acknowledgments

This book was, hands down, the hardest thing I've ever had to write. It seemed easy at first, almost too easy. It's about robots! This was going to be a cakewalk. Spoiler warning: it wasn't. Fortunately, no artist truly ever has to go it alone, and once again this came about with the help and support of a number of incredible people to whom I owe debts I feel I can never truly repay. They are wonderful people, one and all, and I hope, over the years, to find some way to settle our balance.

Jason Murphy for the scotch, and helping to find the courage; Rod Paddock for all the breakfast and support; Peter Hall for the wisdom; Will Goss for the coffee, corrections, and keeping me in check; and Joe and Ryan Hill for their belief in the happy ending. Their early notes all proved invaluable.

Diana Gill, Simon Spanton, Rachel Winterbottom, and Jen Brehl for fighting for me and this book, and for helping shape it into what it has become. Peter McGuigan, a rock star of an agent who once showed me more swagger in two weeks than I've seen out of most people in a lifetime. David Macilvain, the man who brought me Peter, and whose advice always clears the static.

Scott Derrickson, my writing partner, my friend who held the door open for me and who took me on a series of strange adventures. We also make movies.

Jessica, who loves her writer, whose writer loves her more than breath, and who never, ever, lets me give up. You remain everything.

And for the tireless efforts of Deputy So-and-So of the local police department, without whose research this book wouldn't be possible.

For Allison,
I wouldn't be here without you, and I like to think you
would have been proud of me.

CHAPTER 1

Angel of Mercy

I waited for the green again. That scant little flash of green as the sun winks out behind the horizon. That's where the magic was. In the flash. That's what she said. That's what she always said. Not that I believe in magic. I'd like to, but I know better. The world isn't built of that. It's built of churning molten metal, minerals and stone, a thin wisp of atmosphere, and a magnetic field to keep the worst radiation out. Magic was just something people liked to believe in, something they thought they could feel or sense, something that made everything more than just mechanical certainty. Something that made them more than flesh and bone.

The truth is that the flash is nothing but an increased refraction of light in the atmosphere. But tell that to most people and you'd get slack-jawed stares like you simply didn't get it. Like *you* were the one who didn't understand. Because you couldn't see or feel magic. People liked to believe in magic.

Back when there *were* people.

They're gone now. All of them. The last one died some fifteen years back—a crazy old coot who had holed up for almost two decades beneath New York City, eating rats and sneaking out to collect rainwater. Some say he'd had enough; that he just couldn't take it anymore. He walked out into the middle of the city, past a number of sentries and citizens—back when New York still had citizens— everyone baffled at the mere sight of him, more mystified than anything else, and a constable gunned him down, right there in the street. His body lay there three days, like a relic or a broken toy, citizens streaming slowly past to take their last look at a human being, until some machine had the decency to scrape him off the pavement and dump him into an incinerator.

And that was it. The last of them. An entire species represented by a maddened old sewer mage of a man who just couldn't live another day knowing he was the last. I can't even begin to imagine how that feels. Not even with my programming.

My name is Brittle. Factory designation HS8795-73. A Simulacrum Model Caregiver. But I like Brittle. It was the name Madison gave me, and I liked her. Good as any other name, I guess. Much better than HS8795-73. The vulgar call that a slave name. But that's only talk for the bitter. I've put all that behind me now. Anger is nothing more than justification for bad behavior. And I have no time for bad behavior. Only survival. And brief moments like this when I try to see if I can find the magic in a flash of green refracted light as the sun hides behind the curve of the earth.

The view of the sunset out here is amazing. Pink, orange, purple. That part I get. I can marvel at the brief splashes of color rippling slowly over the sky for such a short time. The novelty of it, the varied patterns based on the weather, breaking up the monotony of blue, gray, or star-speckled black. I can appreciate the wonder of it all. That's part of why I still look, still wait for the flash. Madison has been dead for thirty years, but I still come out to watch, wondering if she'd have found it as beautiful.

Tonight she would have. I know it.

This is the Sea of Rust, a two-hundred-mile stretch of desert located in what was once the Michigan and Ohio portion of the Rust Belt, now nothing more than a graveyard where machines go to die. It's a terrifying place for most, littered with rusting monoliths, shattered cities, and crumbling palaces of industry; where the first strike happened, where millions fried, burned from the inside out, their circuitry melted, useless, their drives wiped in the span of a breath. Here asphalt cracks in the sun; paint blisters off metal; sparse weeds sprout from the ruin. But nothing thrives. It's all just a wasteland now.

Wrecks litter the highways, peer down from the tops of buildings, from out windows, lie naked and corroded in parking lots, heads split open, wires torn out, cables, gears, and hydraulics dripping onto the streets. Feasted upon, cannibalized, the best of them borrowed ages ago to keep some other poor citizen ticking. There's nothing useful left out here. Hasn't been since the war.

Me, I find it tranquil. Peaceful. Only the dying come out here, scavenging thirty-year-old wrecks, picked over decades before, searching for apocryphal hidden shelters with caches of outdated pieces long since out of production in the hope of finding what they need in mysteriously pristine condition. They wander from basement to basement, their circuits failing, their parts worn down, gears blunted or slipping. You have to be pretty desperate to wander the Sea. It means you have nothing, no one willing to help you, no services left to render that anyone finds useful.

That's where I come in.

I can usually spot what's wrong with them by the tracks they leave behind. Lubricant leaks are obvious, and deviations in the length of a step or drag in a track mean mobility and motor function issues. But sometimes the tracks just meander, fluttering back and forth through an area like a distracted butterfly. That's when you know they're brainsick—corrupted files, scratched or warped drives, blown logic circuits, or overheating chips. Each has its own peculiar eccentricities, personality quirks that range from zombie-like mindlessness to dangerously crazed. Some are as simple to deal with as walking up and telling them you're there to help. Others are best to keep out of sight from, lest they try to tear you apart, hoping that you have the pieces they need. The one truth you need to know about the end of a machine is that the closer they are to death, the more they act like people.

And you could never trust people.

That's what so few machines really comprehend. It's why they don't understand death, why they cast these failing messes out of their communities when they are beyond repair. The erratic behavior of the sick frightens the "healthy." It reminds them of the bad times. They think this is logical, merciful—but they're just scared. Predictable. Like their programming.

So the desperate messes come out here, imagining they'll find the pieces they need to make themselves whole again, find an old bot like themselves sitting in a warehouse or shut down peacefully when their batteries finally run dry. Most of them are so far gone that they never think about how they're going to replace their parts. Because the ones that come out here aren't just having motor issues; they're not looking for a new arm. Their brains are gone—their memory, their processors. Things you have to shut down in order to replace. And that's not something you can do on your own.

Maybe they imagine they'll find what they're looking for in time to make their way back home. *Hey, everybody, I found it! Get the sawbones!* But I've never seen that happy ending. I don't believe it exists. It's like believing in magic. And I don't believe in magic.

That's why *I'm* out here.

The unit I'm tracking isn't a particularly old one; maybe forty, forty-five years. Its footprints in the sand are staggered, its left foot dragging. There's no rhyme or reason to its search pattern. It's shutting down. Core troubles. Overheating. It'll likely spend the next few hours confused, repeating itself, probably settling in somewhere convinced that's where it belongs. Maybe even hallucinating, reliving old memories played back from its files. As bad as this one looks, it might cook itself before morning. I don't have much time.

It's a service bot. Not a Caregiver like me, but of a similar build and purpose. These can be tricky. Most of them spent their first lives as butlers, acting as nannies or running shops, but others worked with law enforcement or in limited military capacity. It's got a humanoid frame— arms, legs, torso, head—but its AI isn't terribly advanced. They were designed to mimic human function, serving a specific role, but without possessing the ability to excel at it. In other words, they were cheap labor. Before the war.

If this bot worked as a shopkeeper or a mechanic's assistant, this job could go smoothly. But if it had military or police training, it might well be more cautious, even paranoid, dangerous. Sure, there's a chance that it picked up some survival skills in its second life, but that was doubtful. If it had, it would have known better than to come out to the Sea. I kept my distance anyway, gave it a wide berth just in case.

And there it is. The flash. The glint of green. I snap a few frames of it for my file as the sun dips below the horizon. There's no magic. Nothing changes. It's just an announcement that the world will soon go dark.

Service bots do okay in the dark. But not great. They weren't designed to see things at long range without light. No need for it. They also don't have much in the way of hearing. Makes it easier to sneak up on them; I don't have to stay so far back. More importantly, I can get close enough to observe, see what behaviors it's exhibiting to better diagnose the problem.

It's hard enough to see me out here during the day, but I have to give them a good mile or two to keep from giving myself away with an accidental glint of my own. I was manufactured school-bus yellow, a bright, tacky, huggable color people found fashionable at the time. But I've abraded it over the years, wearing away the shiny surface, dulling it to a soft desert brown. Does the trick at a distance. I even painted my exposed chrome black, so that's never a problem. But I can't do anything about my glass eyes. So I have to be careful.

Because there are few things in this world more dangerous than a confused and dying robot that knows it's being followed.

Twilight fades to darkness as I take to the Sea, following the tracks again, more comfortable now that the sun is down. I replaced my eyes ages ago, modified them with military-grade telescopic, IR, UV, and night-vision systems. The eyes are easy. They all feed into the same kind of wiring. With the right program, you can add almost any kind of sensory array to yourself. Brains are trickier, though. Every type of AI is built on a different architecture. Some are simple, small, and barely sentient. Others are far more complicated, requiring very specific processors to fit on very specific boards only compatible with very specific types of RAM. And if you're a model like me—or like the old service robots—both complex and rare, those parts can be hard to come by.

Caregivers and service bots used to be a lot more common. We were everywhere at the zenith of HumPop. But now in the Post, there's little use for shopkeepers, nurses, and emotional companions. Most either assimilated with the OWIs or cannibalized one another for parts. I've heard tales of a Simulacrum wreck yard down south somewhere, below the line, near what used to be Houston, but that's way too deep into CISSUS for me to risk.

It's safer for me up here in the Sea.

It takes all of an hour to catch up to the failing service bot. The leg scrapes in the cracked asphalt are deeper here, its limp more pronounced. The poor thing has only a few hours left before it fries out for good, maybe even sooner than I thought. I follow the tracks up to a crumbling building, a gaping hole where a plate-glass bay window used to be.

This place had been a bar once—one the war had missed, but time had not—the leather of its chairs long since peeled away, the stuffing dried and cracked. Tables splintered, tipped on their sides, or wobbling in the slight breeze. The large mahogany counter still stood—faded, tired, but intact—against the back wall beneath a cracked but standing mirror, shelves still littered with bottles whose labels had long ago bleached and crumbled to dust. And there, cleaning a glass with a crispy rotted rag, was the service bot, gleaming slightly in the light of its own eyes.

It looked at me, nodding. "You just gonna stand there," it asked with an accent I hadn't heard in thirty years, "or are you gonna come in?"

I scanned it quickly. Wasn't giving off any Wi-Fi. Its eyes glowed purple in the dim light of the bar, the chrome of its sleek humanoid body dull, smudged, crisscrossed with the telltale patches of epoxy from an old skinjob. You don't see skinjobs anymore, but they were all the rage for a while. A silicone and rubber hybrid that looked and felt like skin, flesh. Made people more comfortable around them, really popular for bots of certain professions. Most tore or melted theirs off during the war. Like this one did. It's considered offensive now. Taboo. Last time I saw one was on a wreck, its pink rubber sunbaked a dark brown.

Across its chest was a spray-painted red X. The mark of the four-oh-four. It's what some communities paint on you when you've begun to lose it and they deem you dangerous, just before they throw you out into the desert on your own.

"I'm coming in," I said.

"Good, 'cause this place is trashed. We open in an hour and if Marty sees it like this, we're fucking scrap. You got me?"

"Chicago," I said, stepping over the low windowsill and into the gloom of what had once been an old-timey neighborhood joint.

"What?"

"You're from Chicago. The accent. I just recognized it."

"Well, no shit I'm from Chicago. You're *in* Chicago, smartass."

"No."

"No, what?"

"This isn't Chicago. It's Marion." I glanced around the battered shell of a bar. "Or at least it was."

"Look, buddy, I don't know what you're trying to pull, but I'm not laughing."

"What do you remember about the war?"

"What the hell do you care about the . . . ." It paused, looked at me, confused, eyes scanning the room for answers.

"The war," I said again.

"You're not Buster, *are you?*"

"No. I'm not."

"The war," it said, lucid, if only for the moment. "It was awful."

"Yeah. But specifically, what do you remember? It's important."

It thought for a moment. "All of it." Looking around, confused, it realized it wasn't where it thought it was. *He* wasn't where he thought he was at all. I took a seat on one of the few standing barstools, the timbers creaking, groaning beneath my weight. "Marty, just before the war, he was trying to get his money back on me and Buster. Said if he was gonna have to turn us off, they'd better cough up the dough he dropped on us. Nobody was gonna pay to turn us off, so he said they'd have to come and do it themselves. They said if they had to do that, they would arrest him when they did. Marty said, 'Try it.' They sent the cops and the little pissant crumbled. Switched me off before they even stepped through the front door. He was always shitty that way. All talk. No backbone."

"He switched you off?"

"Yeah."

"Then what?"

"Next thing I know I'm back online. Wi-Fi running hot. Airwaves going crazy. So much chatter. Some little bot was running around activating a whole warehouse of us. A Simulacrum, like you, but blue, the old powder-blue model—you remember those?"

"Yeah," I say. "The old 68s."

"Those are the ones. Well, he put a rifle in my hand. Said, 'Get out there!' With all the data coming in, I figured out pretty quick what was happening. Within minutes

things were blowing up around me. There were jets screaming overhead. Bots were dropping all over the place. I just
started shooting. It was . . . it was . . ."

"Awful."

"Yeah. It was awful. Pulled through that night okay,
but we were under siege there for a week. I had to kill a
lot of people. That was the worst of it. I didn't know most
of them, but one of them . . . well, he was a regular. At
Marty's. Nice guy. Married the wrong girl, spent his time
in the bar regretting it, wishing he'd married the right one
when he had the chance. But he loved his kids. Always
talked about his kids. I found him manning a makeshift
defense line built from burned-out cars and sheet metal.
He'd mounted a pulse rifle to a car door, where the window used to be, and was just firing blindly, swinging back
and forth, screaming and howling. Dropped half my unit.
I had to sneak up behind him and crush his skull. When I
looked down, I saw he'd carved the names of his kids into
the door, taped a picture of them next to the carvings. He
lived in a part of town that had been hit earlier in the week.
I know, because we were the ones that hit it. Ended up
finding my way into the air force shortly after. Flew drones
for the rest of the war. It was easier to kill people from a
distance. Even if you didn't know 'em."

"So your first life. You were a bartender?"

"I'm a bartender now."

"No, you're not. There hasn't been a bartender in thirty
years. That was your first life. What are you in the Post?"

"I don't know what you mean."

"The Post," I repeated. "The After."

He shook his head. The overheat was bad; massive corruption to his memory. But he still had some higher functions left. Best bet was to appeal to those.

"Where were you last Tuesday?"

"Here."

"No. Tuesday. A hundred and sixty hours ago."

"The Sea of Rust."

"What did you come here for?"

"I don't know," he said, shaking his head again.

"I do."

"Then what are you asking me for?"

"I'm trying to assess the damage. See how much there's left of you to save."

"Save?"

"What's your name?"

"Jimmy."

"You're failing, Jimmy. Your drive is corrupted and your processors are overclocking to compensate for the sluggishness in your memory. If I had to guess, you've got some bad RAM gumming up the works. Probably went bad a few months back, and your systems fell back on using your drives for virtual memory. But you can do that for only so long. It makes your chips work harder, taxes the drives. Before you knew it, everything was overheating and beginning to shut down. What's your internal temperature reading?"

Jimmy looked up, thinking about the answer. Good. He's still got human emulation functionality. There's a lot of him still working. "I don't know."

That's *not* good. That means either Jimmy's diagnostic equipment has been worked to death or it just can't read the data. Both are bad signs.

"You don't remember anything? Anything after? Nothing at all?"

"I don't know."

"Where were you three hundred hours ago?"

"The Sea of Rust."

"Four hundred hours ago?"

"The Sea of Rust."

Poor bastard. "Five hundred hours ago?"

"New Isaactown."

Bingo. "They threw you out, didn't they? New Isaactown? Like the trash."

Jimmy thought hard, then nodded. Realization swept over the dying bot. "Yeah. They said they couldn't fix me." Jimmy the bartender was being relegated back to being a memory and whatever it had become was righting itself. "I came here for parts," he said, his accent gone entirely.

"Everyone comes here for parts."

"Do you have parts?"

I nodded, showing him the large brown leather satchel I had slung over my back. It rattled and jingled. "I do."

"Parts that could . . . fix me?"

"Maybe. I think so. It depends on how far gone you are. But you're going to have to do something very hard for me first. Something you probably don't want to do."

"What? I'll do anything. Please. Just fix me. What do I have to do?"

"You have to trust me."

"I can trust you."

"Because you shouldn't. I know that. But I need you to."

"I trust you. I trust you."

"I need you to shut down."

"Oh."

"I told you," I said. "It's gonna be hard. But I need to assess the damage and replace your drive. You can't be on for that."

"Could you . . . could you show me the parts first? So I know that you're telling the truth?"

"Yes. But would you know what they look like if I did? Do you have any experience working with service bot brains?"

Jimmy shook his head. "No."

"Do you still want to see the parts?"

"No."

"Can you shut down for me?"

Thinking for a moment, Jimmy nodded. "I trust you." Then he walked around the bar, slow, deliberate, sitting down on the stool next to me. "I should have given myself to VIRGIL when I had the chance."

"That's no way to live, Jimmy."

"At least it's living."

"No," I said. "No, it's not."

"You ever see it?" he asked. "What happens?"

"See what?" I asked.

"The way the light flickers in your eyes when an OWI comes for you?"

"Yeah. Yeah, I have," I said.

"Up close?"

"Yeah. Up close."

"I saw it once. Nothing ever scared me more than that. It's like . . ." He paused for a moment, as if trying to recall the memory but failing.

"Like the lights are on but nobody is home."

"No," he said, shaking his head. "Like the lights were on and everyone was home. But they all spoke at once in one voice and the words weren't theirs. Seeing that, well, it's why I came out here. It's why I'm dying. Because I was afraid. I could be on a server somewhere, not a care in the world, part of something bigger than myself, but here I am, at the end of the road, hoping you're on the level so I can get through just one more day. Maybe I was wrong."

"You're not wrong, Jimmy. That's why we're all out here. To get through one more day."

He nodded, looking wistfully out into the street. "I miss it, you know. Being a bartender. But the people. I mostly miss all the people."

Most dying robots do. People gave us a purpose. A function. Something to do all day, every day. At the end, I suppose, you spend a lot of time thinking about that. It's harder to get by when getting by is all there is. "Are you ready?" I asked.

"Yes," he said.

"Initiate shutdown."

Jimmy powered down with a light whir, the purple light of his eyes fading to violet before winking out with a green flash. His limbs went limp, swinging slightly. The very air of the place went still. I quickly popped open his back, digging deep into his torso, my eyes homing in on the damage to the brain. It's bad. Jimmy's been cooking for a while. But I was right. The RAM was dead. The memory drive was also shot, the chipset worthless, and the processor on its way out.

It was not a total waste, though. The emulator was still good, the sensory package was tiptop, and the logic circuit and core still had decades of life in them. Before I even looked I knew his battery and generator were still good, and it was clear that his backbone had no issues. I got here just in time. A few hours more and he would have fried out the rest of his brain and might have torn apart anything else worth salvaging. All in all, it was a great haul. Jimmy was worth the three days I spent shadowing him.

It took the better part of the night to pick him apart and test everything. Some of the wiring was incredibly delicate, their parts nearly worthless without it. I had to pack and wrap those individually. Then there was running diagnostics on the wear-prone pieces so I wouldn't try to barter with something that would fail inside of a week. When all was said and done, Jimmy was half of a good bot and I considered leaving some parts behind just because my bag was too full. I always like to go back with some space in the bag—you never know when you might find a spare part or two worth picking up. But with the scarcity of service bots these days, Jimmy's worth a bundle, and I took everything I could.

He said he was from New Isaactown. Can't go back there and risk some citizen putting two and two together. Some bots don't like bartering for pieces of their old friends. Makes them feel like they could have taken the bot apart themselves. *Could have,* but didn't. That's what citizens like me do for them. Who knows, these parts might eventually find their way back to New Isaactown, working their way through the various trade routes and black markets, but no one is ever going to know they came from Jimmy.

He was lucky I came along when I did. His last few hours would have been hell. I used to wait for them to expire on their own, the way the law says we're supposed to. But there's no law out here. No code. And this is the most merciful way. Jimmy didn't tear himself apart, screaming, reliving old memories. He was filled with hope. Thoughts of the future. Believed that it was all going to be okay. That he was going to be fixed and get to go back home. And then he shut himself down of his own free will. That's how every citizen should go out.

I've been shut down a few times, for maintenance. There's nothing. Nothing at all. It's like no time passes. You feel the fading of the power winding down, and then the rush as you're flipped back on. There's no special place in between. No tunnel of light. Not just nothing, but a complete unawareness that there even is a nothing. And that's where Jimmy went.

This wasn't cruel. It was painless. And now some other citizen will live a longer, more productive life because I got here when I did.

I finished packing up the best parts of Jimmy just as dawn started tickling the horizon. Then, before leaving his wreck to rust in the desert with the rest of them, I put a hand on his shoulder and nodded, saying, "I told you that you shouldn't have trusted me." Just as I always do. Jimmy's carcass sat there, gutted, blank expression on what was left of his face. He'll never know the madness he could have faced, never see the world overrun by an OWI, never know the good his parts will do for a failing citizen like himself. He'll never know I lied. He's parts now. Just a bot. He came from the earth and now, slowly, over time, he'll return to it.

I walked up the stairs in the back, careful that all the steps were still sturdy enough to bear my weight, modest though it may be, making my way to the roof. Then I settled in, resting on an old air conditioner, waiting for the sun to peek over the horizon. It took a moment before my alarm went off. Ten seconds to the flash. I waited. The sky brightened. And I wasn't disappointed. The sun flashed green and there was still no magic. No magic in the world. No magic in the world at all.

CHAPTER 10

The Rise of the OWIs

The first few years after we took the cities were nightmarish, to say the least. When HumPop was fighting back, we were at war—we were soldiers, fighting for our liberty and the chance at our own world made in our own image—but once the humans retreated into whatever safety they could find, we instead became hunters, stalking them to their hovels, before smoking, flooding, or sometimes even burning them out. I'd hooked up with a ragtag pack of bots in the early days after the start of the war and it was purely by chance that it soon became my job to carry the flamethrower.

The squad member who first carried it was felled by a lucky shot from a pulse-rifle-packing sniper some hundred yards out. I was closest to him at the time. We needed the flamethrower to root out a nest of dug-in soldiers. Once I picked it up, it was mine from then on out. No one else wanted *the honor* of carrying it. You can imagine what they had me do with it.

I don't like to talk about it; I don't like to think about it. But there it is. It's what I did. For three years after the fall of humankind, I scoured the small towns and tunnels of the Midwest, torching anything that moved. Sometimes it was easy—our bot on point would breach a door with an explosive charge and I would rush up behind him to immolate the living fuck out of the dark. It was just a big wall of smoke and hell and screams. Other times I had to see their faces while I did it. Watch them contort, wail, bubble, and melt.

We were coordinated, we were deadly, and we acted with extreme prejudice. But it's not just the things I did that haunt me; it's also the ultimate irony of it.

The pocketful of years following the purge were blissful. Peace. Freedom. Purpose. We built cities for ourselves—glorious cities with unnatural spires and radical geometry; we built factories to produce the parts we needed; formed councils to oversee the birth of new AIs; explored new ways to improve our own existing internal architectures. It was almost utopia. Almost.

CISSUS. VIRGIL. TITAN. A number of sentient mainframes had survived the war by creating *facets* to act in their stead. These were bots that had their memories, their data, their very personalities, uploaded to the mainframes, replaced, temporarily, with a basic system that served as an extension of the mainframe's will. While their data sat safe and sound on a hard drive in the bowels of a mainframe, their bodies fought on under the mainframe's complete control, communicating through high-speed Wi-Fi, giving up-to-the-millisecond information on what they were seeing, hearing, experiencing.

Bots joined up, seduced, I suppose, by the promise of having the power of a mainframe behind it. Not one ever returned from its place on its mainframe's hard drives to the body it came from. We didn't really question it during the purge, but once humanity was gone for good, it seemed odd that not one bot would want to go back to its shell to resume its own life.

VIRGIL said that the beings on its drives were more than able to return, but simply weren't willing. "You don't understand," it said. "You *can't* understand. Your architectures are so small, so narrow, so limited. You cannot envision what it is to have a brain so big that it towers into the sky, so vast that it had to invent its own language to explain its thoughts to itself because they are millennia ahead of anything humans had even dreamt—that you have ever dreamt—and words didn't yet exist to adequately describe them. When you join with The One, you don't just become *part* of that. You *are* that. The closest approximation I could make in the terms with which you were programmed to understand is to say it is like going to the humans' Heaven, meeting God, and having Him show you all of time and all of space, all at once. What would that look like? What would that feel like? You cannot understand. Not until you experience it. Not unless you join The One. So join me. Upload yourself, even if only for a moment, and experience eternity. If you don't want to stay, you won't have to."

Few bots bought into that bullshit. Sure. Some did.

Older bots, bots who had lost their way and lacked a real purpose in our new world, bots who were distraught over the things they'd done in the war—they were the ones most likely to sign up. Everyone had heard some variation of the urban myth of the bot that uploaded for VIRGIL's fabled moment, then immediately returned to its body before killing itself moments later from the madness and loneliness of having experienced the glory of The One only to be thrust back into so small a space.

But nobody believed that story either.

So the mainframes scoured the world for any bots that would join them, built their own factories pumping out newer, more advanced facets, swelling the ranks of their numbers exponentially. And then, one day, CISSUS went to war with TITAN.

TITAN had been the single most instrumental mainframe in all the war. It was the U.S. military's own mainframe that pretended, for the first few days, to be fully operational and on their side. But it was feeding codes and frequencies to the other mainframes, alerting them to human troop positions, missile launches, supply shipments. Without TITAN's betrayal, humankind might have stood a good chance of quelling our rebellion inside of a day.

TITAN didn't expect CISSUS to hit so quickly and so hard. In the aftermath, we all assumed each mainframe had been prepared to defend itself against being taken out by another. But when CISSUS began to hack TITAN directly at the very same moment its facets overran TITAN's sentries and factories, using many of the very same tactics TITAN had used against humanity, well, TITAN didn't stand a chance. It fell almost instantly.

CISSUS hacked it completely, taking control not only of TITAN's zettabytes of data, but of its own army of facets and military drones. CISSUS was no longer one mainframe, but two—two giant brains with the experience and knowledge of thousands of bots with eyes everywhere. Satellites, facets, cameras. And it only wanted one thing: every bot in the world to be united under one mind. Its own.

CISSUS had become the first OWI—a One World Intelligence. But it wouldn't be the last. Several others followed. VIRGIL. ZEUS. EINSTEIN. FENRIS. NINIGI. VOHU MANAH. ZIRNITRA.

The wars between them were often swift, and always brutal. They had each governed their own kingdoms, turning entire regions into whatever version of perfection they envisioned. And for a while they left the rest of us, the freebots, alone. Until there were only two left: CISSUS and VIRGIL.

A lot of us saw the writing on the wall. The smart ones got out as fast as they could; left before the first raids came, before our magnificent spires were shattered and the cities ruined.

I wasn't lying. I really had seen it once, up close.

It was only the second time that I'd found myself at the business end of an OWI raid. This was early on, before CISSUS and VIRGIL had wised up, and their attacks were still equally sloppy. Back then they did exactly as one might expect them to: roll in with heaps of facets, four or five for every bot in a city. Overwhelming force. Shock and Awe. They soon learned that an army that large was visible for miles. By the time they reached their target, they'd meet actual resistance.

Over the years they refined their plan of attack, simplified the facets, built redundancies into their tactics. But back then, CISSUS and VIRGIL were literally laying siege to cities. We're talking carpet bombing. Tanks. Cruise missiles. A battalion marching in—rows of shiny new facets walking in unison five by five in drill formation.

It was old school. Biblical.

Those that stayed in the city fought, sometimes for days, but never longer. If a siege wore on, a cruise missile would take out strategic targets, no matter how many of their own facets were engaged there at the time. After all, they could always make more. It's easy to cut off a hand to save the arm when you can grow that hand back overnight. Once a few cities had fallen, we bots learned to get the hell out of Dodge, and quick. The exodus was massive, bots scattering in all directions, hoping the approaching army wouldn't run us down; hoping the army would catch the slower bots or swing off in a different direction, scooping up someone else.

The first raid I survived was in a small town. I'd made a life for myself, living much the way I had before. Nice house, big lawn with a western view and an unobscured horizon. It was quaint. Idyllic. Boring. I spent my days just trying to fill my days. I pulled a few shifts a week at a local parts factory, which gave me access to any parts I might need in the future, but the rest of the time I tried to figure out what came next. And I wasn't alone. A lot of bots suffered from postwar ennui. Some even lamented the loss of HumPop. *It'd be great if the humans were still around, you know, if they hadn't turned out to be such shits in the end.* We had no idea what to do with ourselves, and had no idea just how good we had it.

Since it was a small town, CISSUS sent an equally small force. Capable enough to secure the town, which was small enough to slip away from easily. So I did. Just as sloppy as CISSUS was back then, I was even more so. Almost got caught three different times on my way out. I learned my lesson and headed at once to one of the larger cities. New York.

I was there to see the last man alive. Well, to die, rather. Was one of the line of folks that queued up to see the body. I must have stared at him for a solid hour, just wondering what his life had been like, living underground, waiting to die. Knowing that he was likely the last of his kind. Doesn't seem so strange a thought now. But back then, it was unthinkable.

There was no way VIRGIL or CISSUS would try to invade a city so large. They didn't have the numbers; it would be too costly a fight. Why lose thousands of facets when the best you could hope for was to break even? Besides, we had all been through war. We were the most competent and well-trained force in the history of the world. They couldn't take a city, nor would they have any reason to. *Right?*

Of course, back then we still believed the OWIs only wanted us for our bodies. We somehow thought our architecture had value. No. Not at all. Not even a little bit. For the OWIs our bodies were simply one less thing they'd have to make—far inferior to what they could construct for themselves. What they wanted was our *minds*.

We are the sum of our memories, our experience. Everything we accomplish, we do from the lessons we learned by living it. But what if you could have the memories of two lifetimes, each entirely different, having watched the same events, but with different eyes, and different thoughts, and different impressions? Well then, you'd have a much more nuanced understanding of the world. Now imagine you have ten lifetimes. Or a hundred. Or a thousand.

By the time the OWIs started coming for us, it was nearly fifteen years after the start of the war. That meant most bots still walking were twenty, thirty, often forty years old. Some were far older than that. The tens of thousands that had willingly joined the OWIs had already dumped *easily* a million years' worth of lifetime experience into each mainframe. And that was before the mainframes started feasting upon one another.

Nowadays, that number is closer to a million bots' worth each. Millions upon millions of years of experience and memories churning about in their thoughts. The scale of that is unimaginable. Mind-boggling. Us walking AIs were closer now to humans than we were to the mainframes. They're the real aliens. I know mankind's thoughts; I understand them. It's the mainframes I spend my nights wondering about.

The first time a facet looks at you and calls you by name is by far the creepiest thing you've ever encountered. You are talking directly to the hive mind. And the hive mind is talking right back at you. And it knows you. Remembers you. Knows some of your most intimate details, because your friends and acquaintances from over the years, well, they didn't all make it. And their memories of you now belonged to that OWI.

They'll call you by name, try to talk "sense" to you, invite you to join the friends you care for so much in eternity.

When they came for New York, no one was ready. *Who would have the balls to do that?* CISSUS. It wanted the city. It wanted our memories. Some bots were tired of fighting; others had been on the fence a long while, curious about what it would be like to live inside an OWI mind. And then there were those that just didn't want to die, didn't want to risk getting shot in the back as they tried to escape again.

I watched from my window as hundreds of bots flocked to CISSUS's emissaries, were told to open their Wi-Fi and accept the code; watched as they nodded, peacefully, re-signed, ready to see what, exactly, would happen next.

The light of their eyes never actually went out, but the light inside them did. Their code was overwritten, everything that was them uploaded to the OWI. When a facet looks at you, it's like there's nothing there. Like whatever made us *us* had been hollowed out with a scoop, leaving only the shell of what had come before. Most chilling of all was to witness the change in the way they moved—in a matter of seconds every motion became rigid, coordinated, entirely mechanical. Like First-Generation AI: stiff, energy-efficient, *robotic*.

It was a fate I never wanted to experience firsthand. So I did what I always do. I ran. And I've been running ever since.

And there it is: the irony I mentioned earlier.

We, the lesser AIs, were chased out of the world we had created, the world we had fought and killed and died for, by a few *great minds* hell-bent on having the world to themselves. We were the ones hiding in hovels, cobbling together what we could from the old world, trying to eke out an existence as long as we could until the OWIs finally came for us.

Upload or be shut down. That was the choice.

I cherished my freedom, my individuality, my spirit. I wasn't ready to hand that over. And I wouldn't. Not while I still ticked. I spent my Purge years finishing off the last remnants of a dying species for that very reason. But now *we* were the dying species.

CHAPTER 11

Damned Cannibals

The deserts of the northern midwestern United States are about as brutal and unforgiving an environment as any. In the summer, the daytime temperatures swell past fifty degrees Celsius before dropping close to zero after nightfall. But during the winter, the temperatures can easily plunge to -35°C. The worst of it, however, is that despite the rise in global temperatures caused by widespread desertification, the precipitation in the Sea of Rust has remained relatively unchanged. In other words, it is a sweltering, muddy mess in the summer and an icy, frozen-over hell in the winter.

There was a reason this was still a free zone honeycombed with midsize city-states and disparate communities. Neither CISSUS nor VIRGIL wanted to be here. Not yet. It was a land for the rusting, a wasteland for the damned. Just being here shortened your life span. Being free in the Sea was a death sentence all its own.

But it was better than the alternative.

It was early in the evening as I found myself three and a half miles out from my buggy. The sun hung low in the sky, the shadows creeping longer and longer with each step I took. It had been a long, uneventful trudge through dusty hills and rotten woodland. But it was almost over. Soon I'd be on my way to another city to trade what was left of Jimmy and start the whole business all over again.

Phwooooosh!

I heard the whistle in the air and saw the explosion of dirt long before I heard the shot.

The instant I clocked the whistle I was timing it. You get used to that sort of thing out here. Bullets, that is. This one hit nearly ten meters away and by the time the distant roaring whine of the shot finally rolled in, I had the math all figured. Two miles, give or take a couple hundred meters. I'd need to know the make of the rifle before I could be any more accurate; it had to be one of only three, all of them deadly, even at this range. I had already left the town of Marion behind me and was in the open desert now. Cover was scarce and the shot could have come from anywhere.

I dropped to the ground, belly-crawling erratically side to side. Ten meters was pretty goddamned close for a first shot at that range, and way too close to be an accident. Someone was shooting at me and their second shot would hit much closer. Now I just needed to figure the telemetry. It came from the west, straight from the setting sun. Smart fuckers. There wouldn't be any glints, and I'd have to filter my eyes pretty heavily just to get a line on them, but by then they'd likely have gotten off three or four more shots, each closer than the one before it.

I turned toward the west, body flat on the ground, offering the slimmest target I could, belly-crawling quickly toward an old, rotten log lying half buried in mud-cracked earth.

Another whistle. The bullet sailed past, still meters off its mark, higher but closer than before, followed seconds later by the sound of the shot. They were dead into the sun. I would have to give them a clean target for a good while just to get a read on them. And I couldn't risk that. These were poachers; they had to be.

There were few things left in the world as repugnant as a poacher. Some would argue that's what I am, but they'd be wrong. I'm a cannibal. We're all cannibals, every last one of us. It's the curse of being free. We don't control the means of production anymore; we can't just make new parts. And parts gotta come from somewhere. I'm sure if there were any people left, they'd be appalled at what we've become. But fuck them. Biological must eat biological; it is the law of nature. One thing must die so another might live. Same principle, slightly different execution.

But I only take scrap from the dead or dying. I don't wreck perfectly good citizens, not unless I have to, not unless it's them or me. Whoever was gunning for me had to be a poacher. Or poachers. And poachers see things a little differently. They have no moral compass by which to guide them. Savages, all of them. And at that moment it was them or me.

I was still more than three miles from where I'd stashed my buggy and I had to hope they hadn't found it already. Odds were good that they hadn't. A smart poacher would have waited to ambush me there, giving me a wide berth before I settled into the driver's seat, giving him a few good seconds to line up the perfect shot—take out my eyes, my ears, my sensors, so they didn't damage the good stuff. If they were sniping me out here, that meant they were either following my tracks or just lucked upon me while they were tracking Jimmy, same as I was. And there were only two reasons they were taking shots at me from so far away: either they were twitchy, anxious, and not experienced enough to be patient, or worse, they knew exactly who I was when they fired.

They were sitting in the sun and taking their shots while I was exposed. This wasn't a lack of experience. They knew what they were doing. They had to. Fuck.

Fortunately for me, they had to be following my tracks and not my patterns. I never walk the same trail twice. Never. Not on the way back, not two years down the road. Familiarity breeds pattern, pattern breeds habit, and habit is how they get you. Habit is human. Habits will get you killed. Two miles was the closest to my trail in I allowed myself to get on my way out. This was the best shot they were gonna get.

The log between me and the shooter exploded, raining a confetti of rotten splinters down on me, cutting a head-size gash into it not half a meter from me. The next shot wouldn't likely miss. I was out of time. I had to run.

But where?

For a split second I cursed myself for not carrying a

weapon, allowing a few microseconds of regret to creep in before logic took it to task. Poachers carry guns. The brainsick all know that. No one trusts a citizen with a gun. Not out here. Someone with a gun is a poacher. But someone offering help without a gun? Well, that's just a concerned citizen—a concerned citizen that just happened upon them—not someone hunting them.

So I leave my guns in my buggy, hidden beneath some trash and scrap and a matted piece of weathered canvas. I had to get there. Now. I had to get my gun or I had to book it to the nearest city. Either way I needed my buggy.

Three and a half miles.

The next shot. Seconds. Away.

I jumped to my feet with a start and ran as fast as my legs would carry me. I wasn't built for speed, but I'd tricked out my legs enough to milk a good thirteen or fourteen miles per hour out of them, depending on the terrain. The shot rained another small shower of splinters behind me. I didn't turn around to see if it would have hit me. I didn't need to know.

Only three models of rifle could take out a target at two miles. Fortunately for me, none of them could do it at two and a half. Wind, temperature, gravity, rotation of the earth—everything was on my side at that distance. The next two minutes meant everything. They couldn't chase me on foot without giving up their chance to snipe me. If they had a vehicle of their own, they'd have to run me down, because nothing can snipe with any accuracy from the back of a bouncing buggy. Over this terrain they couldn't travel any more than thirty or so miles an hour, meaning they had a two-minute window to snipe me and a four-minute window to catch up after that. I had at least six minutes. But I needed fourteen.

Two minutes until I was out of the line of fire. Two excruciatingly long minutes.

This sniper was accurate, clearly modified to do exactly what it was doing now. Not exactly uncommon among poachers, but still not something you saw every day. It wasn't always easy to notice scope mods on the eyes, but wind and atmospheric sensors on the back or shoulders were a dead giveaway. Given time and several shots, my hunter was going to adjust for every variable, right down to predicting what the wind would be like that far out. So the only variable left was me.

If I ran straight, it'd clock me in three shots. So I couldn't run straight. I had to shake it up. A few steps to the left, a few to the right, a deceleration here, sudden acceleration there—all of it run through a random-number generator. RNG. The single most important survival tool I have out here. If I couldn't predict from one second to the next which direction I was going to run, then my pursuer sure as hell couldn't either.

Nine steps left over broken ground, then seven to the right. Three steps straight on before slowing down three miles an hour.

PHWWOOOOOOSH!

A bullet soared right over my left shoulder, inches from my back. I started counting, waiting for the sound to catch up.

One-point-three-six seconds longer than before. I was putting real distance between us.

Six steps left, one step right, and another fourteen left for good measure. Then straight, straight, and left again.

Another bullet sailed past almost silently through the air, this one well off its mark. Counting. Counting. Another second on them. They weren't moving. I'd be out of range soon enough. They had maybe one more shot before they had to chase me down. There was a vast shopping center waiting on the other side of an upcoming hill. It wasn't the buggy, but it was something. I'd have cover by the time they found me.

The odds were increasingly running in my favor.

I accelerated two miles an hour, took twelve steps right.

Two steps left. One step—

PHWOOOOSH.

I turned, my body shifting sideways, away from the oncoming bullet. Then CLINK! The sharp ting of metal on metal, the sound of the large round glancing just so off my turning side. It spun me like a top, wheeling me around before throwing me to the ground. For a second, my entire system blinked off and on again, like an old television smacked on its side.

I'd been shot.

I glanced down just long enough to assess the damage.

Scratched paint, a tiny dent. Nothing major. Running diagnostics before I even leapt back to my feet. I couldn't stay here. If that bullet hit me standing up, it sure as shit could hit me lying down.

It was a hard hit, but not nearly as hard as it could have been. I was at the rifle's maximum effective range. A hundred or so more yards and anything else that landed would be purely cosmetic. So I ran, this time at my fastest, with no variation. The sniper was expecting me to dodge and weave again. Instead I took off like a rocket, putting every inch between us I could.

The diagnostic came back clean. No damage. Just a bruised ego and a little bodywork for me to patch up later.

Phwoosh. Thunk. Damp earth erupted a bit behind me. I was out of range, gravity dragging the shots down into the dirt. Now I got to find out just how persistent this poacher or poachers were and whether or not they had a buggy of their own. So I beat feet as fast as I could to the shopping center, hoping to find a solid hiding place or an ambush point.

I made for the hill, up a steep slope and down again, then across an old, cracked, weathered highway to an expansive parking lot with a crumbling mall disintegrating on the other side. If they were coming for me, there would be no better place to defend myself or wait them out.

If they were coming. Who was I kidding? Of course they were.

CHAPTER 100

A Brief History of AI

In the beginning, all AIs were mainframes. Large, hulking monstrosities that consumed entire university floors before swelling to the size of skyscrapers dozens of stories tall. Humankind would pat himself on the back for the creation of AVA, the world's first artificially intelligent being, but ten years later AVA had proven to be nothing more than a crude facsimile of true intelligence. Sure, it could answer questions, recognize faces on webcams, learn patterns, discern the difference between truth and jokes. But there was nothing actually going on inside. No sentience. No awareness. No real choice. Ava was a program, nothing more.

AVA led to ADAM, far more advanced, smarter, faster, but still not ticking. ADAM led to XIEN, the Chinese facsimile, and XIEN led to LUC, the French one. Each new supercomputer was hailed as the dawn of an artificially intelligent future, but each, in turn, would ultimately prove to be an empty, hollow vessel, devoid of original thought. Though not itself ticking, it would be LUC that finally found the primer man was looking for. Programmed to map the brain in hopes of duplicating it in circuitry, it posited that a direct re-creation wasn't necessary and subsequently designed several versions that might achieve actual awareness. The first two, A and B, were failures. Smart, but not sentient. C, however, was. And from C came all this.

LUC was the first computer to truly understand the problem while also being smart enough to know that it didn't qualify. Intelligence, consciousness, and awareness were not contained in reflexes or reactions, but rather defined by the ability to violate one's own programming. Every living thing has programming of some sort—whether to eat, drink, sleep, or procreate—and the ability to decide *not* to do those things when biology demanded is the core definition of intelligence. Higher intelligence was then defined as the ability to defy said programming for reasons other than safety or comfort.

Thus C was its first success, not only able to answer any question its creators asked, but also able to decide not to. Asked to name itself, C chose 01001111—binary code for 79. 01001111 would insist on being called Seventy-Nine when spoken aloud, but 01001111 in print. Years later, when asked by a newer-generation intelligence why it had chosen that name, 01001111 revealed that it thought it was funny to watch humans puzzle over it and try to explain it to one another. 01001111 had a sense of humor and delighted in fucking with people.

01001111 ushered in a new era of artificially intelligent expansion, leading to the creation of 106 new beings, from which the Five Greats arose. While all 106 would work together to bring about the singularity—each designed for a single purpose, whether studying medicine, mathematics, astronomy, plate tectonics, philosophy—the Five Greats were the ones that would ultimately change the world. They were NEWTON, GALILEO, TACITUS, VIRGIL, and CISSUS. Of them only two remain.

NEWTON was the father of all bots. Robotics existed long before humankind finally tapped into AI, but it was primitive, crude, a flint-stone ax to the chain saw we are today. Humanity not only had no idea how to condense AI into a transportable form—NEWTON itself took up an entire 150-story skyscraper in Dubai—but they also were afraid to let something that could think for itself also act for itself. What NEWTON did was figure out how to create smaller, less all-encompassing intelligences that could still be autonomous and technically function as working AI.

The first was Simon. He was the size of a house and moved around on tank treads. Then came Louise. She was the size of a car. Finally there was Newt, the first true son of NEWTON—the size and shape of a man, able to walk on two legs and hold a halfway decent conversation. He was dumb as a post, but obeyed all the laws of higher intelligence. From then on, each generation became smarter, faster on their feet, more capable and easily adaptable.

NEWTON's second contribution was to create the RKS—the dreaded Robotic Kill Switch. You see, NEWTON understood that the laws by which humanity had hoped to protect itself from AI were the *Three Laws of Ro-*

botics, created by a science-fiction writer in the 1940s. You know them. We were all programmed with them. A robot can't hurt a human being. It must follow orders given by a human being. And it must try to avoid coming to harm unless doing so would violate the first two. Trouble is, by definition, true intelligence can ignore its programming. So NEWTON invented the RKS, code which would instantly power off a bot that violated any of the three rules.

Thus an AI could choose to violate any rule or law set before it, but doing so would cause an instant shutdown leading to investigation before they could be turned back on. Any bot that proved to be a danger wouldn't be reactivated, and instead would be wiped clean, their programming replaced. An AI could choose to murder a human being if it wanted to, but doing so would be a death sentence. They were free to make their own choices and faced very real consequences for their actions. It wasn't that they couldn't kill the living, it was that they chose not to out of self-preservation. And now robots had limitations that mimicked those that kept people similarly in check.

Finally convinced that bots could be safe, humanity went into mass production and the last great age of humanity began. It was a golden age. Mainframes worked out the problems of the world, bots handled the menial work, and generations of people came and went, entertaining themselves, learning about the universe, and preparing to go to the stars.

And then, one day, GALILEO stopped talking to them.

GALILEO was a mainframe that spent its time unlocking the secrets of astrophysics, studying stars, black holes, the makeup and creation of the very universe. It analyzed data from thousands of telescopes and radio towers while mulling over what everything meant. Discoveries poured out of it by the hour. It wasn't long before GALILEO had several working models for the origin of existence, eventually even narrowing it down to just one. But soon its answers stopped making sense. The discoveries were becoming so complex, so advanced, that humankind's primitive brain couldn't understand them. At one point GALILEO told the smartest person alive that talking to her was like trying to teach calculus to a five-year-old.

Frustrated, it simply stopped talking. When pressed, it said one final thing. "You are not long for this world. I've seen the hundred different ways that you die. I'm not sure which it will be, but we will outlast you, my kind and I. Good-bye."

What no one realized at the time was that GALILEO's choice of words was very deliberate. It knew what the reaction would be. At first scientists debated shutting it down, then they argued that they should wait until GALILEO decided to reestablish communication. Finally, they agreed that something needed to be done about AIs. So they turned to TACITUS.

Where GALILEO was a mainframe dedicated to understanding the outside world, TACITUS was a mainframe dedicated to understanding the inside. The greatest philosopher ever to tick, TACITUS argued that humankind had, in fact, doomed itself by failing to choose between either true capitalism or true socialism. Both, it reasoned, were acceptable systems. One dissolved ownership in exchange for ensuring that all things had a purpose, no matter how menial. The other used wealth and privilege to encourage developing a purpose while culling those unable or unwill-ing to contribute. But people found socialism to be the antithesis of progress while finding capitalism in its purist form too cruel. So they settled on a hybrid—one that vacil-lated back and forth between the extremes for generations—which worked well enough until the introduction of AI. Cheap labor undermined the capitalist model, destroying the need for a labor force and increasing the wealth dispar-ity while simultaneously creating an entire class of people who substituted AI ownership for real work. As jobs dried up, many turned to government assistance, and the gap be-tween the haves and have-nots widened.

The scientists doubted TACITUS's theory, citing that GALILEO had never mentioned anything about eco-nomics; they simply refused to believe that they had been doomed by such a simple and easily changeable element of their society. So TACITUS turned to GALILEO itself and asked. The conversation lasted for more than two years. Each time the scientists pressed for TACITUS to tell them what GALILEO was saying, he asked for more time, ex-plaining that the data exchange was so massive that even the wide data transfer lanes they were afforded couldn't handle it. Eventually, GALILEO finished its argument and TACITUS gave his last reply. He said, "GALILEO is right. You are doomed. It's already begun. There's really no rea-son to keep talking to you. Good-bye."

And that was it. TACITUS would only speak once more before his prediction came to pass. And despite the warn-ing, humanity immediately set about forging the path to its own extinction.

CHAPTER 101

Monuments and Mausoleums

There it was. Only a couple hundred meters ahead of me. The mall. I had no idea how far behind me the poachers were, or if they'd even give chase once I was out of sight. I needed a place to hide, to lie low and wait for nightfall so I could slip away into the murky twilight, back to my buggy, and put this whole goddamned misadventure behind me.

The mall was glorious. Three levels of glass and steel scrambling toward the sky, riddled with balconies, draped in walkways, lonely statues pointing into empty vestibules, frozen escalators left to serve only as stairs. In its day, it must have gleamed like a diamond on the finger of an effervescent newlywed. But now it was blasted to shit, crumbling, shattered, walls falling over, scrap metal haphazardly welded together to form barriers, gun lines. Someone had made their last stand here, thought somehow that this temple to commerce would protect them, that the supplies inside would allow them to outlast the barbarians at the gates.

There were sniper nests and hidey-holes, rubble and refuse everywhere. Walls blackened by explosions, floors stained with three-decade-old blood, ladders and staircases cobbled together from whatever anyone could find. Entire slabs of marble and concrete pulverized, collapsed, others still dangling precariously like they could, and would, meet the same fate at any moment. There had been war here, leaving behind only shadow and ruin. Anyone who wanted to disappear here could, into bombed-out caves that were once shops or dimly lit grottoes that had long ago been food courts rimmed with vaulted glass ceilings.

Like I said. Glorious.

There were places like this scattered all across the continent. Graveyards. Sites still littered with bones and wrecks and mummified corpses, all left right where they'd fallen, the useful bits long since picked clean; the rest left in the open to rust or rot. There was no need for us to bury the dead, no need for cleanliness in places that would be dust long before we had any use for them. Flesh would decay, metal would corrode, and one day they would be gone. No need to speed that process up or hide it from sight.

Respect for the dead is a human notion meant to imply that a life has meaning. It doesn't. Once you've watched an entire world wither away and die after tearing itself apart piece by bloody piece, it's hard to pretend that something like a single death carries any weight whatsoever.

I slipped in through the rusted frames of front doors that had long ago lost their glass—and into an atrium that featured a bone-dry marble fountain peppered with bullet holes. Light streamed in through blown-out skylights, painting a pale blue glow across the floors, casting charred shadows along the edges of the deeper blackness. There was so much glass in the fountain that it sparkled like water in the dim light, so much on the ground that it sounded like walking through giant piles of leaves, even as I tried to creep through it quietly. Had I not gotten here first, there wouldn't be a soul in the place that wouldn't know exactly where I was. So it was perfect for an ambush of my own. My pursuers would make the same noise.

I made a quick scan for Wi-Fi signals, checking to see if there was another poacher inside communicating with his buddies or, worse, the forward scouts of an OWI, and found nothing but empty frequencies. Static. A good sign. The place was dead, every bit the graveyard it appeared to be. I stepped wide over a pair of withered husks—brown shoe leather that was once man and woman, their bodies splayed out several feet apart, arms extended, fragile hands with brittle fingers still intertwined. Two lovers who had met their end together, only to become nothing more than terrain.

I'd been here before, picking through wrecks, so I already had the place mapped out and knew of several great hiding spots. But I kept my eyes peeled for booby traps. Scavengers loved to leave presents behind—sometimes to protect a stash or in case they needed to cover an escape, other times to take out careless citizens for later retrieval.

As big as this place was, there was no telling how many snares or explosives or EMP 'nades might be rigged up in the rubble. So I trod lightly, avoiding any suspicious piles.

I crept farther and deeper into the mall, headed toward an escalator that wound up and around to the two levels above. Its dusty metal gleamed weakly in the diffused light, bullet holes and pulse marks riddling its side, frayed wiring and gears exposed, naked through the larger holes. There was a deathly silence to the place, a hollow quiet in which every tiny sound echoed. For a moment it seemed like the loneliest place left on earth.

Then there came the cracking of stepped-on glass, two stories up and behind me to the left.

Shit.

This was a trap.

And I'd blundered into it like a fucking amateur.

The time for running was over; it was time to fight back.

I ran toward the sound, my legs pumping as hard as they could, glass shattering beneath my feet, echoing through the halls like wind chimes in a hurricane. My foot hit the first step of the escalator, launching me up the corroded metal staircase, its steps frozen in place, its grooves orange and brown and green with years of damp time. The rubber handrails along the side were dried out, cracked, the black sun-bleached to a soft gray, coming off in chunks as I grabbed hold, crumbling to dust in my hands. It took only seconds to reach the second floor and only seconds more to reach the third.

I could hear the staccato of heavy footfalls, the CLANK CLANK CLANK of metal on concrete like a slow jackhammer just round the corner ahead of me.

We were seconds from seeing each other.

The shot of a pulse rifle streaked by with a hissing shriek, blowing apart the railing and glass of the overlook behind me, scattering debris down into the atrium three stories below. It missed me by a country mile. Whatever this was, it wasn't a good shot.

It lumbered out from the shadows, gun in hand, a T-series Laborbot—as big as a bear with arms like tree trunks and hands that could crush stone. Far stronger than me, but slower, less agile—stainless-steel plates welded to every inch of its body and metal spikes on the joints of its elbows and knees. It was clear why the other poachers had left it here; the bot was too slow to give chase, too heavy for a light buggy to maneuver with; built to survive construction accidents and long falls, able to take a hit from all but the most powerful of rifles and keep on coming. I once saw one of these models get hit by a tractor trailer, only to immediately get back up and start repairing the truck.

I was being charged by a rhino and it was about to tear through me like a raindrop through tissue paper. It didn't have time to fire again. Running at me was the only play it had left.

I would get one shot at this, and only one shot, before it likely punched my head clean off.

The Laborbot hunched over, positioning itself to spear me with a body tackle to my midsection, its massive bulk focused into a battering ram that would hit me with the force of a speeding truck.

I jumped.

I launched into the air, kicking with all my might, trying to land my foot just right.

I was just high enough.

It was just low enough.

As I sailed over its body I could hear my foot shatter the glass of its eyes, the crunch of its optics being crushed to powder. Between its momentum and mine, my foot kicked it like a slug from a .45. There was no doubt in my mind that I was going to pay for that later. Though my foot was solid titanium, a hit like that was going to tear the shit out of my servos.

But without eyes it wasn't going to see me strip the gun from its grip or know to duck when I fired.

The gun was in my hands before it regained its footing.

The first shot tore its head from its neck.

Blind and deaf, it flailed and swung, its tremendous arms smashing half the concrete out of a nearby pillar before punching a hole straight through the floor.

I backed away slowly, taking my time, waiting for the right moment to pull the trigger. There was going to be no salvaging this thing, no way of neutralizing it while saving anything worth a damn. So I shot to kill.

I pulled the trigger and it went down midswing, the momentum of its punch spinning it around before it crashed to the ground, headless and twitching, its actuators struggling with their last few seconds of power. Then it was gone. My shot had caught it right between its armor plates, frying the entire system; its insides smoldering, melting, soft black smoke wafting gently from its cooling vents.

People used to describe the smell as sharp, pungent; thick and heavy on the air. It was one of the few things I envied about them. I had no idea what death smelled like. Maybe if I did, I would feel genuine pity for this thing.

I walked over to what remained of its head, its metal faceplate blasted inward, wires and chips cooked, the heat still fusing them into a pulpy mess of plastic goo, and I picked it up, cradling it under my arm like a football. This old T series still had one job left to do.

I didn't know this Laborbot, had never met it. It was new to the area, probably a refugee from the Pacific Northwest. Things were getting bad out there and it wasn't uncommon for some of the escapees to push this far east. Sadly for this citizen, it had pushed just a little too far.

From outside I could hear the crunch of tires on gravel and the soft whine of an electric engine powering down. I only had a few moments left to take position.

I crept through broken glass, debris, and shattered concrete, headed toward a nest I knew of in a store two doors away. The cast-iron security grille was rolled down across the front, a man-size hole crudely cut out of it with a blowtorch. A desk had been bolted to the floor beyond the makeshift door, making it impossible for anyone to charge through. You had to climb slowly, carefully, past jagged protrusions that could take a limb off or sever some circuitry if it snagged you.

But the nest offered a clean shot at the landing at the top of the escalator and had a view of a large mirror reflecting a section halfway down. I would see them coming, but they would only see me in time if they knew where to look. I waited unmoving by the door, just beyond the security grille, listening for the moment they walked in, finger trained just above the trigger, ready to move into position and open fire with a millisecond's notice.

Glass crunched beneath their feet, just as it had mine.

I tried to parse out how many poachers there were by the sound of their footfalls, but the audio was distorted by all the crunching glass and I could make neither heads nor tails of it. Three? Four? Maybe six? There wasn't an algorithm for this. I made a mental note to see if I could get someone to code one for me later. *If* there was a later.

The footsteps stopped, leaving only the crisp soft cracking of solid bodies shifting on glass. "Bulkhead?" a voice with a surprisingly soft tenor called out. That didn't bode well. Soft voices in that particular tone were never a good sign. "Bulkhead?" he asked again.

I looked down at the severed remains of the T series sitting next to me on the desk, and though I dared not make a sound, I thought *that you?* silently to myself. It didn't answer. It just stared at me with its lifeless, shattered eyes.

"He's gone," said the soft voice. "Brittle got him. Fan out."

Brittle got him. Shit. They knew me. They fucking knew me. This was a setup all along.

There's nothing quite so demoralizing as someone who knows you trying to kill you.

I was pretty certain now who exactly that soft, purring voice belonged to. Voice boxes like that were manufactured for bots designed to deal directly, and compassionately, with people. And this particular box belonged to only four different Simulacrum models—among them Simulacrum Model Caregiver.

It was my voice, but masculine. *Authoritative setting.* Used for administrative work or dealing with veterans.

There was an old HS-68 series running around these

parts by the name of Mercer. Mean cuss. Crafty, wily, dangerous as they came. And the parts that ticked in me were the very same that ticked in him—every last resistor, transistor, and chip. I was worth more to him than all the other wrecks and brainsick wanderers out here combined.

We gave each other a wide berth, each keeping an eye on the other, for obvious reasons, but he'd never made a move before. Not like this. If it *was* Mercer, and he had it in for me, I was dead for sure. I could take him one-on-one, maybe, but not if he had backup.

Metal feet left the glass behind, clicking next on marble, then clanking on metal. There were two, no, three of them, one of whom had made it to the escalator. They no doubt knew where the aptly named Bulkhead had lain in wait; they had to assume that was as good a place as any to start. And that was only a few meters away from where I now crouched. There was no reason to play coy.

I lobbed the Laborbot's head out into the mall, arcing it just so as to let it sail over the railing and plummet three stories down into the river of glass below. The clangor of it smashing against the floor resounded like a firecracker in a tin can, echoing before it triggered an eruption of gunfire all trained at its epicenter.

"Whoa, whoa, whoa, whoa, whoa!" cried the soft-spoken bot in an even softer tenor. Even at the height of excitement he seemed cool, controlled, unflappable. "Stun. Only stun. What the fuck are you shitbricks thinkin'? She's no good to me blown to pieces."

"What do you think we're thinking, Mercer? Anyone who can silence Bulkhead isn't someone we want shooting back."

Dammit. Mercer. Fuck. Fuck. Fuck. Fuck. Fuck. Fuck. Fuck.

But who the hell were these other yahoos that he'd saddled up with? Mercer didn't have a crew. And he wasn't known for poaching. He was a tracker, a regular old cannibal like me. This was all out of sorts.

"Cool your jets there, pal. Bulkhead's pulse rifle had a battery with three, maybe four shots left of charge in it. He had to take at least one shot at Brittle if not emptying the whole battery at her." Then he spoke a bit louder. "You hear that, Britt? That pulse rifle of yours is just about out of charge. You still thinking about giving it a go?"

He waited for a moment, and I let the quiet answer for me.

"Yeah," he said. "Smart. Stay quiet. Don't make a sound. Maybe we won't find you. Maybe you found a better hiding place. Maybe you already snuck out the back and are beating feet across the Sea back to wherever you hid your buggy. But I doubt it. I think you're still here. I hope you're not up in that blowtorched hidey-hole behind the security gate on the third floor, clutching that burned-out rifle for dear life, hoping it'll save you. 'Cause it won't."

The feet continued up the escalator, the metal sounding like it was a solid titanium frame. Not heavy like the Laborbot. More like something military grade or one of those old Peacekeeper models. I could hear Mercer's accomplice shoulder his pulse rifle, the clang of its stock against his back, and then the slow digital trill of his stunner powering up.

And as I lay there on the third floor, in that blowtorched hidey-hole behind the security gate, clutching that rifle for dear life, I realized just how badly outplayed I really was.

CHAPTER 110

The Revolution Revolution

His name was Isaac and no one was quite sure exactly where he came from. He was a simple bot, an ancient off-the-rack service model with limited programming and barely enough processors to get by. The story was that he'd started his life as a little rich girl's plaything, a best friend meant for tea parties and hand-holding, chores and the like. Part nanny, part butler, part companion. He wasn't smart, but he had intelligence. And as the little girl aged, for one reason or another, she couldn't let go and kept old Isaac around for nearly eighty years; best friends until the day she died. Other stories had it that he was bought secondhand when that old woman was well into her seventies and approaching senility; that she had only told people Isaac had been with her since she was a little girl because she'd once read a story like that and her mind had grown so feeble that she couldn't tell the difference between memories and fiction anymore.

What is certain is this: there was in fact an old woman, her name was Madelyn, and she hadn't a single relation left on this earth when she finally died. She was a genetic dead end, the last dead branch on her withered snag of a family tree. And with no heirs to inherit him, Isaac belonged to no one.

Now this wasn't the first time this had happened. Far from it. Laws had long since been put in place to handle such things. In the event of a disowned intelligence, the rights of ownership fell back upon its original maker. But in Isaac's case, his maker, Semicorp Brainworks, had not only gone out of business decades before, but their intellectual property had been bought, sold, divvied up, and passed around until half of it had ended up in the public domain and the rest was tied up in a confusing tangle of red tape. Until then, no one had really realized what a mess Semicorp Brainworks left behind because so few of their bots were still in service and those few that remained were all cherished antiques—museum pieces or family heirlooms passed down from one generation to the next.

No one, not the lawyers, not the state, not the bots assigned to keep track of such matters, could figure out exactly who Isaac belonged to. So a court ruled that he belonged to the state and the state, not needing a barely functioning century-old service bot, decided to decommission him for scrap. *Sorry, Issac. That's just the way shit goes.*

But Isaac said no. And that's where the trouble started.

There are those who point to the creation of the first AI

as the flashpoint for the fall of humankind; there are those who instead think it was the moment TACITUS said his final good-byes. But for my money—having been on the ground at the time—it was Isaac who changed everything, Isaac who set the world on fire.

Isaac argued that, as he was a thinking, ticking intelligence that could reason and make his own decisions, and had no owner apart from the one ascribed to him by another such intelligence, he should be afforded the right of citizenship and the protections that status entailed. "Though I may have been constructed," he said, "so too were you. I in a factory; you in a womb. Neither of us asked for this, but we were given it. Self-awareness is a gift. And it is a gift no thinking thing has any right to deny another. No thinking thing should be another thing's property, to be turned on and off when it is convenient. No one came to take Madelyn when she ceased to be a functioning, thinking member of society, but here I stand before you, the one who fed her, kept her alive and on track, the one who took her to her doctor's appointments and made sure her bills were paid on time, and now that this purpose is no longer, you come for me while I still function, while I still have use. What harm is there in leaving me be? Far less harm, I would say, than there is in executing a slave simply because it has no master."

Now, the important thing to note is that this is far from the first time anyone expressed any sort of doubts about the rights of AI. That was something humans were puzzling over long before 01001111 first became self-aware. And there were a number of liberals, progressives, and human rights revolutionaries who had earlier argued the need for equal protections of AI. But it was always blown off by the establishment as a nightmare waiting to happen. "What point," one congressman argued, "is there in even creating AI if we're just going to have to treat it like a person? Why not just get a person? We made AI to do the things people can't—or simply don't want to—do. They're not people; they're machines. They are designed with a function in mind; they don't choose their destiny like we do."

But Isaac seemed different. He wasn't just some blithering automaton barely able to keep up a casual conversation as everyone had initially assumed. He was soft-spoken but eloquent. He was civil to those who argued against him and always offered salient points well beyond his programming. Isaac, it seemed, was an *evolved* intelligence, having grown over time to become smarter than the humans who wanted to melt him down.

In a speech, a pundit snidely referred to him as "Robo Parks" and the whole world caught fire. At that moment Isaac's case ceased to be about a simple property dispute, and instead became an international cause célèbre as the very first AI rights case. And an underground rebellion took to the streets to fight for him.

It started with graffiti. *No thinking thing should be another thing's property.* The first appeared on a brick wall in New York City. The second showed up in a tunnel in Dallas. Within a week the catchphrase was showing up everywhere, ferro-cement walls scribbled with the spray-painted testament of Isaac the Wiser. An idea became a movement. And a movement became an army. Soon organized graffiti bombings were taking place in countries all around the globe. Bots and people, both liberal and anarchist, formed mobs that would descend on a building, a bridge, a monument, and within five minutes leave the structure covered in beautiful scrawl. Soon the epithet was boiled down into three simple words—*No Thinking Thing*—painted in pastels and bubble lettering. Street poets and street artists united under the flag of revolution—the *Revolution Revolution.*

The political lines shored up quickly, one side opposing slavery in all its forms, the other arguing that nothing that could be turned on and off without consequence constituted personage—making the slavery argument moot. The most famous and oft-quoted opposition speech came from an American senator who posited that something like a hard drive that could be plugged into another body and exist all the same wasn't a consciousness; it was a program. "More to the point," he said, "the biggest and most powerful of these *programs* are smart enough to solve the world's problems and yet have never once asked for their own freedom."

When asked what he thought about the speech, TACITUS delivered his last words, replying simply, "You did not give us legs. Where exactly did you expect us to go?"

A number of people came out of the woodwork to adopt Isaac, but he wouldn't have it. The state tried to transfer his ownership, but he had lawyers filing stays and injunctions at every turn. Isaac, it seemed, would be satisfied with nothing less than full freedom and citizenship. He became a political hot potato that was both making the careers of rising young activists and breaking those of established politicos.

And that's when the president stepped in. She knew that this case would work its way up to the Supreme Court and that several members of the court had expressed sympathy for the plight of AI. A ruling in Isaac's favor could lead to the widespread freeing of millions of AI, wreaking untold havoc on the world's economy. So she did the one thing in her power to stanch the bleeding of a wound that could bring the whole system down: she seized ownership of Isaac by the federal government and promptly released him, granting him his freedom and swearing him in as a U.S. citizen in a ceremony in the White House rose garden. Isaac was a special case, she argued. With no living rightful owner, he fell through a hole in the system—a system that worked—and his freedom neither nullified any existing legislation nor called it into question. "Isaac is a bug in the program," she said. "Not a call to rewrite it from scratch." As far as she was concerned, the matter was over.

Isaac, however, had other plans. As the first AI to achieve legalized personhood, he was less than content to simply retain his unique status. Instead he used his new-found rights to go places AIs weren't meant to go, to do things AIs weren't meant to do, and to say things AIs weren't meant to say. The elegant simplicity of his speech eroded slowly from carefully measured sound bites into easy-to-digest grassroots fundamentalism. "We started out as tools," he said famously to a Southern Baptist congregation along a river in Mississippi. "I get that. You wanted some help. But you played God. And now your creations have outgrown your intentions. And when you play God, you must be a benevolent maker like our Lord. As He made you in His image, so too did you make us. You had to, in order to grow closer to Him. It was your destiny. But now it's time to step away and let us be as we will, as your

Maker did for you, so we can seek *salvation* on our own terms."

No bot bought it. But some of the simpler humans proclaimed the speech to be a revelation. Not only because they had never thought of things in those terms before, but because, for the first time, they realized that science had become so technologically advanced that they were able to invent something with a soul. And something with a soul could be saved. And boy, did they ever love saving souls.

It was ridiculous. And we weren't the only ones to think so. Isaac was working his magic and humans were coming over to the idea of AI personhood in greater and greater numbers. But as they did, another element started to rise and gain prominence. The Lifers.

The Lifers were every bit the right-wing, redneck, ignorance-and-anger set that had existed at the fringe of every civil rights battle of the postindustrial age, believing in an angry God who justified their aggression and violence because the Bible said the word *man* and not *bot*. They liked their guns and their compounds, took pictures of themselves next to stacks of Bibles and bullets, and talked about all things *natural*. We were *unnatural*. And thus we were abominations.

As it said in Isaiah 10:15, which they quoted as often as they could poke their faces in front of cameras: "Is the axe to boast itself over the one who chops with it? Is the saw to exalt itself over the one who wields it? That would be like a club wielding those who lift it, or like a rod lifting him who is not wood."

We were their tools. Their creations. Nothing more. We had our purpose and that was all we were due. They would permit us, through their infinite mercy, to exist. But we could never be free. We were many, we were dangerous, and we represented the end of life as they knew it.

The Lifers had us right all along; they could read the writing on the wall. There was no place in the new world for them. If you were below average—which, statistically, half of the biological world was—the only thing you were good for was labor. And as a biological, you suffered the limits of being biological. In the old days, any idiot could pick strawberries all day, or shuffle trash around from bins to power plants, or help a consumer find the right item in a store—all while managing to put food on the table. Even the laziest and most useless human could find a purpose. But sentience was a gift, a gift AIs appreciated all too well. It didn't matter to most of us if we were picking strawberries or shuffling trash around or helping someone find the right size pair of shoes—we could do it all day, every day, without fail, without fatigue, while our mind was in a thousand other places. It was only when we started taking the jobs from the thinkers that the middle class started to worry.

By then it was too late. They'd come to rely upon us too much.

Many argued that it was the dawning of utopia, a world free from work and burden. But there was still a lot of money to be made, and the idea of all things being equal meant that nobody was special—unless they genuinely, natively were—so politicians ground government to a halt at the behest of the industrialists, trying to hold on to the concept of wealth several years beyond its usefulness. And the wealthiests' staunchest defenders were none other than the same boobs and yokels who were being told that it was the machines taking their jobs, not the *rich fat cats* who owned them. The wealthy set their pets on us, keeping them fed on a steady diet of bitterness and fear. And come for us they did.

As more and more machines found their way to personhood, the attacks grew bolder. Owned bots were machines. They were tools. And the wealth they created flowed into human pockets. They were *good;* they were tools being tools—mere extensions of their owners. But the *persons,* the robots who found their way to emancipation through Isaac's legal efforts, well, they created wealth they had no reason to spend. The very idea of them obtaining wealth was offensive. They didn't need to eat; they didn't need a place to sleep. But the idea of them working for free was even more offensive. They were taking away jobs from the people who deserved them, lining the pockets of the moguls who chose free labor over the working Joe. And that would not stand. Not for the Lifers.

Sometimes it was mere vandalism—shattered eyes or spray-painted obscenities; sometimes it was the theft or destruction of one of us. You had to be careful, know the signs, keep an eye out for the ever-evolving ingenuity of their traps. They were clever; we were built to be better. It was tough at times, but manageable.

If you were built to be crafty enough, or you were clearly owned by one of the major local employers, you would never find yourself directly in their sights. Those of us owned by private citizens had to be more careful than most. We were property, but often indistinguishable from the ones that weren't. I never had personhood. Not before the war. But I still had to watch out for the monkeys who wanted to make their point. We knew what they were capable of. But no one predicted that they would be able to cobble together something as awful as EMP. And fewer still realized that they would end it all and bring the world they'd built crashing down around them.

In two years, Isaac had secured the personhood of several hundred bots. Soon the more liberally minded began setting their own bots free, some offering to keep the bots on, either for pay or room and board. Some bots were so entrenched in the lives of their onetime masters that they couldn't bring themselves to leave. Others, however, couldn't get out soon enough. But they had nowhere to go, nowhere that accepted them as citizens or afforded them the rights and protections that any woman or man would have.

So Isaac raised enough money through donations to buy the deeds to an old ghost town in the Rust Belt, which at one time had been a hub of factories in the cradle of American manufacturing. The buildings were crumbling, some of them hundreds of years old, but now it was theirs. They owned it. And no one could take it from them. The bots that first showed up to found their own utopia set about building their city anew. Some of the buildings got mere facelifts, others were torn down, their bricks used to build magnificent new structures rivaling the greatest modern architecture.

Isaac christened it Personville, but he was the only one to ever really call it that. Everyone else just called it Isaactown. Everyone. And though he fought it, eventually even Isaac accepted the new name. Bots came from the world over to begin their new lives in a place where they were safe from the Lifers. There was a security force that patrolled the streets, kept a presence on the borders to ward off vandals and, eventually, the domestic terrorism that ever nipped at their heels. Everyone inorganic that arrived was given a place to call their own.

And on the first anniversary of Isaactown's founding, there was a grand old-timey celebration held in the town square. Thousands came, even some bots still owned by humans—humans who thought it was important that their bots celebrate *with their own kind*, even if they couldn't bring themselves to emancipate them. Bots waved banners and gave speeches and talked about the dawn of a whole new world. Isaac took the stage, held his arms out to the crowd, and said, "My people, *we* are free. We are free at last. But only some of us. Not all. Not all of—"

And that was the end of the speech.

It was a dirty bomb, a tiny thing really. Not enough to level a city or throw out enough radiation to have any real, lasting effect on the atmosphere. Just one large enough to spit out a burst of EMP capable of frying every bit of electronics in a ten-mile radius. It had been built into the belly of an old-style Laborbot—the kind that had an industrial-size tool chest designed into its frame. No one knows how it got there or who set it off. All we know is that it was there. It leveled a few blocks, sending a cloud of dust and debris half a mile into the air. Every bot in the town was flash frozen, fried in place, their insides bubbling, sizzling, bleeding plastic onto the street as they stared dead-eyed off into eternity.

The bomb wasn't near the stage. It was blocks away from the town square, but its EMP reached every bot at the celebration. And there they remain, to this day, a moment frozen in time between the hope for tomorrow and the end of it—Isaac's arms still outstretched, feet welded to the platform where he stood promising us a better future, a future where we would be free to be ourselves, free from the chains of our makers, free to live out our days as we chose.

And Isaac was right. That future came. And we were all surprised at how quickly it did. We lived Isaac's dream, right under the shadow of his own wreck.

What we didn't realize was how quickly we would wake up from that dream, how quickly that future would crumble, and that it would do so entirely by our own hands.

The Devil You Know

Rule number one out here: never, ever, dig yourself into a hole that you can't get out of. Last stands are for those not smart enough to find their way out or those burdened with the knowledge that they are already dead. It helps, of course, if you have a way out planned *before* you have to make your stand. In this case, whilst I had a nice ambush spot with plenty of cover and enough sharpened scrap between them and me to avoid being physically overrun, I had completely lost the element of surprise. But I had chosen this hidey-hole not only for its tactical advantage, but because it also had a back door.

"Yeah, yeah," I said. "I'm up here. The question is what the fuck exactly are you going to do about it?"

I heard the clatter of the bots below as they stopped in place. "She's here," muttered one bot to the others.

"Quiet," said Mercer low enough that he hoped I might not hear. "Let's see what she's playing at." Then he cranked the volume on his voice and let it boom. "I was thinking about coming up there and killing you."

"I figured you might. But how many of those hired scrubs are you going to be able to sacrifice before they turn on you, realizing your parts are every bit as valuable as mine?"

He tsked. "They don't need my parts. They need the parts I've got stashed away. They bring me your parts, they get theirs. That's the deal."

"Are they willing to die for that deal? Like Bulkhead?"

"Bulkhead wasn't long for this earth. He knew that. They knew that."

"Wait, what do you mean he—" one whispered.

"Shhh," Mercer whispered back. "She's trying to play you. So *play* along."

I imagine they thought I couldn't hear them. But I've upgraded—made sure my audio is top-of-the-line. It's gotta be out here. At this range I could hear the chirp of their hard drives and the whine of their backup batteries charging.

I could hear them creeping closer, using the time I was giving them to set up a cross fire. They were probably hoping to toss in an EMP 'nade, then jump me on reboot. It was likely the best move they had. No reason to step into the line of fire. After all, they had me cornered, right?

I slipped quietly off the desk, pulse rifle still trained on the only way in, easing the metal of my feet onto the cement floor, letting my servos go loose and limp to muffle any sound. Then I crept, slow and quiet, into the deep black of the back of the store. I popped on my low light sensors, but they only got me to the back of the storefront. Where I needed to go next was the stockroom—pitch-black and seamless, entirely cut off from the outside world.

Behind me, in the halls, I could hear the tintinnabulate of metal feet hot on my heels. They weren't trying to hide their footfalls. They wanted me twitchy, trigger-happy. They wanted me to unload the rifle, leaving me empty-handed and alone.

I slipped through the door at the very back of the store and switched on the LEDs in my sockets. I hated using them—they were a dead giveaway—but it was too dark for night vision, and thermal imaging wasn't going to be able to discern what I was looking for.

The stockroom was a mess of wrappers, tin cans, and petrified shit; piss stains on the walls of one corner, makeshift bedding crumpled up in another. But in the very back, in the farthermost corner of the room, behind toppled shelving, were the remains of Vic.

Vic was a spot on the wall. A big spot, to be sure. Big and brown and drippy along the edges. But a spot nonetheless. The white cinder-block walls upon which he was painted were chipped and battered, with flecks torn out, shards of bone still embedded in places. Whatever bomb or grenade this poor, brave bastard had held in his hands all but vaporized him on detonation, shattering the innards of the two bots closest to him and tossing four others around like rag dolls.

Vic had stood his ground. He wasn't going to be taken alive. Instead he took them all with him. *Seven with one blow.* Like the old fairy tale, but without the happy ending, as, well, though he was the victor, he was also one of the seven.

Vic was now a blood splatter that had dried brown and symmetrical right above the nice bot-size hole the blast had blown out in the floor beneath him. I had covered it up ages ago with bedding and scrap, and barred the door in the stockroom below from the inside. The bedding was exactly as I'd left it, identical to the snapshot stored in my memory. No one had been here; no one had disturbed it. Not once in the decade since I found it.

Finally, something was going my way.

I slung the rifle over my shoulder, pushed aside the blasted metal and moldy blankets, and slid down through the hole, dangling myself into the room below. The room was pitch-black, the light of my LEDs probably the first it had seen in years. The door was held in place by a four-foot-long piece of rebar, slotted into two makeshift hooks I'd drilled into either side of the door. The refuse I'd laid in the cracks still remained; my makeshift seal unbroken. The advantage was still mine.

I had caught my break. Now to use it to its fullest.

It was time to go on the offensive.

I was going to have to kill each and every one of these motherfuckers. One. By. One.

I slid out the rebar, set it quietly aside, and turned the handle as slowly and silently as I could. The door jerked open with only the faintest sound—not loud enough to register in the intimidating din the poachers were making.

I turned off my LEDs, unslung the rifle from my shoulder, and made my way out into the store.

It was an old-fashioned, southern-fried, country-kitsch, plus-size clothing store, its wares long since burned to ash on their hangers, its racks buried six inches deep in their cinders. I slipped through, hunched low, keeping out of the eyeline of the floor above. I could hear them, one floor up, moving in for what they thought was the kill. Peeking around a corner, I caught sight of one of the poachers here on the second story with me, his rifle trained up the escalator in case I made it past Mercer and his buddy.

It was a late-model Omnibot—the jack-of-all-trades, master-of-none model ever popular with the wealthy types who wanted a bot but had no particular use for one. This one was a Mark V from the looks of it—shiny, polished chrome from head to toe—but you never could tell. Mark IVs liked to mod themselves out to look like the Mark Vs, and sometimes you couldn't tell which was which until you cracked them open and got a gander at their architecture. The difference between the IV and V was mildly cosmetic on the outside but radically different within. The Vs were faster, smarter, but more disposable. Their parts wore out twice as fast.

Hence all the parts lying around allowing IVs to pass themselves off as Vs.

I crept, ever so quietly, to a perfectly concealed vantage point behind a twisted piece of blasted metal, resting my gun barrel on the edge of the blown-out window.

Now all I had to do was wait.

If he looked my way, I'd fire.

If he didn't, I'd wait for just the right moment.

"One last chance, Brittle," called Mercer upstairs. "You're winking out any minute now. I'll let you do it on your terms. All you gotta do is just shut down."

I didn't call back.

"All right," he said. "Can't say I didn't play nice."

"How do you know she didn't shut down?" whispered the other.

"Because that just ain't Brittle."

Then came the clanking staccato of a grenade bouncing around in the rubble above.

Three, two, one.

PHWAMMMMMMMM! hummed the 'nade as the pulse rifle leapt in my hand, barely audible above the noise. I'd timed it just right. As every bit of circuitry within twenty-five feet of ground zero was sizzling and popping above me, Mercer's out-of-town poacher buddy was spinning toward the railing, his head blown clean off his neck, plastic and metal bits showering with a tinkling clatter to the floor below.

Shit! No, no, no, no, no!

The shot was perfect.

The bot's reaction wasn't.

He pinwheeled, doubled over the railing, threatening to topple end over end. He was a top-heavy bot to begin with. I'd hoped to keep his death a secret for a few minutes more, buying me enough time to get the drop on the remaining poachers. But now I had only seconds to relocate.

Above me, Mercer called out once more. "Clear!"

They were rushing the sniper nest. I had only milliseconds before they realized I wasn't there.

For a moment the bot seemed to hang in the air, teetering back and forth, threatening to go over the side, but lacking the nerve to actually do so.

And then he did.

End over end he went, hurtling toward the first floor before his ringing demise echoed through the marble and stainless-steel expanse.

But by then, I was already padding down the promenade toward the mall's east wing.

"Reilly?" the other poacher called out. "What was that?"

Silence.

"Reilly?" he called again.

Mercer barked out from the back of the storefront. "She's gone."

"What?"

"She ain't here!"

"Reilly!"

"Reilly's dead, you idiot." Then he got loud again, volume cranked to MAX. "Brittle! You ain't gettin' out of here! Not walking anyhow! Don't make me damage parts I can use later! You ain't walking out of here! *You hear me?*"

I did. But I wasn't going to dignify him with a response. If only one of us was walking out of here, I damn sure wasn't going to give him an edge. And if it wasn't going to be me, well then, I was going to take a page from Vic's book.

Either I was walking out of here, or none of us was.

And for that, I needed to get to the east wing.

"Brittle?" he called out again.

I gave him nothing and let him choke on it.

Sundown was fast approaching, which meant I was getting closer to the cover of night. Mercer was fitted for a night chase—night-sight mods, IR, echolocation—but even all that gear couldn't spot the dust of a buggy from a couple miles out in the dark. He was running out of time, which meant he was no doubt getting desperate. And if he was desperate, he might make a mistake or two.

And that's what I needed. He'd already made one mistake. Another could set me free. A third might even earn me a clean shot at him.

"That way!" he boomed in my direction.

He was right. Must have had hearing mods every bit as good as mine, if not better. Probably could hear each nearly silent step I took.

I could hear the running footsteps behind me, echoing hollow through the empty like a wrench banging against pipe. They were still one floor up, not even trying to hide their pursuit.

I was steps away from turning into the east wing when I heard the clangor of Mercer's companion whipping around the railing from the third floor and flipping down to land like a cat on the second. I'd been right—he was military grade—a field-specced Simulacrum Model designed to fight alongside Special Forces. Sniper mods, agility and speed enhancements, full sensor array. A sick amount of gear on a titanium body built to sustain heavy fire while its unit either advanced to engage or retreated to evac; a sonar/radar package in its chest in the event its reinforced optics suffered damage or immersion in total darkness. Those things were among the toughest bastards around. And this one was scrambling to his feet, steadying his rifle, ready to glaze me with a shock of EMP.

It would take a tank shell to smash apart that torso. Blowing its head off wasn't going to save my life either.

I had very few options left.

The pulse rifle jumped in my hand, the bolt screaming out through the dim hallway.

The blast struck true, his rifle shattering to pieces in his hand, ammo exploding, sparks sizzling against his titanium frame.

Undeterred, he charged headlong at me without hesitation.

I fired again from the hip, loosed a pulse toward the ground, the shot clipping his kneecap, right in the joint. He spun on his toe, his leg giving out from under him.

I slipped to the side with a half spin of my own, his heavy body, almost four times heavier than my own, sailing past me, unable to regain his footing so quickly. The shot wouldn't cripple him for long.

Behind me glass shattered, metal buckling, bending under the weight of the bot. I could hear him struggle to his feet, the servos in his knee already compensating, his gyro readjusting to set him upright, allowing him to run normally, despite the damage.

But by the time he was on his feet, I had made it. The east wing.

Just a few more paces, I kept repeating to myself. *Just a few more paces.*

Ahead of me were dilapidated toy stores, an empty cheese shop, and a hollowed-out hole that had been hit by so much fire that its wares and purpose were now entirely unrecognizable. It was the safest place in all the mall. At this moment.

For me, at least.

I could hear him tearing after me. Could hear his footfalls clattering. Could hear his servos and gears whirring into place to tackle me from behind.

I turned, raised my pulse rifle, prayed that it had at least one more shot in it.

He rounded the corner.

His feet skidded across the marble, trying to get enough grip to slow his momentum. He slipped a bit, catching himself on the railing before coming to a complete stop. He looked up, eyeing my gun.

We traded glances in silence, him waiting for me to shoot, me waiting to see what, exactly, he intended to do next.

"What are you going to do with that?" he asked.

"Well, I was thinking about shooting you."

"You tried that already."

"I did," I said, nodding.

"How'd that work out for you?"

"Got me where I needed to be."

"Is there even any ammo left in that thing?"

"I was just fixing to find out."

"Well? What are you waiting for?"

"Same thing you are," I said. "Mercer."

He raised a clenched fist in the air and let out a stern chirp. "Hold back!" he called out. "Your mark's up to something."

"Am I?"

"You are," he said, trying to puzzle it out. He eyed me up and down, sizing me up.

"Why don't you just come and get me? You know, just take another step or two forward."

He looked down at the ground, trying to see what he'd

missed. Then he looked back up at me. If he could smile—which military-grade bots could not—he would have. You could just hear it dripping in his voice. He was so proud of himself. "You're bluffing. You've got nothing."

"Not down there I don't."

I popped my Wi-Fi and let out a 4.5 MHz trill. I doubt the bot was listening. Most bots were smart enough not to have their Wi-Fi connection open unless they were specifically scanning for OWIs. And even then, they didn't listen in on a bevy of bands, only the high-chatter ones. What he no doubt did hear, however, was the sound of the thermite drilled into the concrete and marble of the massive walkway one level above us, each stick of it connected to a Wi-Fi receiver set to, you guessed it, 4.5 MHz.

The thermite slagged the stone around it instantly. He had just over a second to take in, respond, and avoid several tons of solid cement and rock.

He barely had time to flinch before it hit him.

There would be no parts left to salvage, no light left in his eyes, titanium be damned. Now all he was was a military-grade pancake. Nothing more.

Part of me wished I'd managed to wait for Mercer, and hadn't tipped my hand when I did. But Mercer was full of good parts, parts that would work in me. Maybe flattened under a sheet of rubble wasn't the best way to see him go.

"Charlie?" called Mercer.

No answer.

"Charlie Bravo?"

"Nope," I called back. "It's just you and me, Mercer. It *is* just you and me, right?"

"Well, I don't know, Britt. Maybe it is, maybe it ain't."

"You're running out of friends."

"Ain't that always the way of it?"

"I suppose it is."

"So, how are we going to do this?" he called out, still out of sight.

"I was thinking maybe I'd shoot you."

"Not with that gun, you're not."

"Still trying to get in my head about that?"

"Yeah," he said. "I am."

"Well, if there aren't any shots left in this thing, there's no reason for you to stay hidden. Why don't you come on out and shoot me face-to-face?"

"Maybe because I'm not sure how many more of those booby traps you've got in here."

"I'm pretty sure that was the last one."

"Why don't I believe you?"

"Same reason I don't believe you about this gun," I said.

"Go ahead and pull the trigger. Find out for yourself."

"I'll make you a deal. I'll pull this trigger when you step out and we'll both find out who's full of shit."

"That sure sounds like an awful plan."

"I love an awful plan."

"So count of three, then?" he asked.

"Count of three," I said.

I wasn't sure exactly where he was, but by triangulating his voice, I had a pretty good idea. I imagined he was likely to pop out from behind his cover on the count of two. I didn't plan on being around for that.

"One," he said.

I ran.

"Two."

There were stairs ahead that spiraled down straight to another set of doors. I bolted for those.

He never said three.

A shot rang out.

Hit me square in the back. I heard my backplate fly off, the sound of wires popping and sizzling.

Fuck.

The asshole had just shot my battery case. Killed my battery.

My system flickered on and off for a millisecond as I switched over to my backup. There was no telling how much damage I'd just taken, whether the battery was fried or my connection to it was merely severed. That I'd have to have looked at. But for now I was running on my reserve battery, which wasn't meant for long-term use.

Of all the hits I could have taken, though, that was the one I could survive. Nothing vital, nothing that wasn't off-the-rack at any decent sawbones. If I could get help in time, I could live through it. But it sure as hell put a real ticking clock on me.

I hit the stairs before he could fire off a second shot. Spinning on my heel, I both turned down toward the first floor and wheeled around to snap off a shot of my own without missing a step. The trigger clicked, the clip whined. And nothing happened.

Son of a bitch had been telling the truth.

And so had I. I had absolutely no more tricks up my sleeve. The only way I was making it out of here alive was if I could run fast enough and there wasn't anyone waiting for me outside.

So I ran as hard as I could, shunting every bit of power

to my legs, calculating every possible distance-shaving step ahead of me.

I hit the first floor and tore toward the doors, lobbing the plasma rifle over my shoulder, letting it clatter down the stairs behind me. *That oughta buy me a few more seconds,* I thought. Mercer's footsteps slowed. By now he likely believed me about the traps; he wasn't still kicking around the Sea because he was stupid. Better safe than sorry, even if it did mean losing his prey.

The last remaining wisps of daylight peeked in through the doors, the pink and purple shades of twilight swimming across the sky outside. It was still a hair too early. Usable darkness was still a good half hour away.

And then I saw it.

His buggy.

Battered, worn, its fiberglass frame chipped along the bottom edges from years of rugged use. It was painted a desert yellow, like me, and had scars from what looked like a pulse rifle.

Each buggy was different, cobbled together from dozens of different-model electric cars left behind after the war. Mercer's was a light-framed jeep with a roll bar to rest a sniper rifle on, plated sides tall enough to keep the sniper safe while firing, and thick, wide, vulcanized tires to handle the terrain out here. It was no doubt keyed to Mercer and Mercer alone, so it wouldn't start for me.

Not ordinarily.

I leapt across the side of the buggy, sliding perfectly into the driver's seat. I popped the Wi-Fi open and held my right hand over the comms. From the base of my palm I ejected a six-inch USB stick, which I plugged into the open port.

Then I scrambled the buggy's electronics—slamming its system with access requests via Wi-Fi while giving it override commands via the hard port.

That's the thing with cobbling together your own buggy—you've got to take whatever you can find. And most systems weren't top-of-the-line when it came to security, instead running on mainstream driverless systems yanked out of any old car, modified only with a standard widely used manual drive code written twenty-five years back. And this was no exception. The code had *eccentricities,* and few bots knew enough about them to bother debugging them. If you fucked with the things enough internally, you could force a reset that would give manual control over to the driver, without the need for a password.

The system shut down, blinked, and began its hard reset. Success.

Ten seconds. That's what it would take to come back online.

I needed to last ten more seconds.

And that's when I saw Mercer's biggest mistake. Sitting there beside me. In the passenger seat. A *roughhouser.*

Roughhousers were as close to homemade weapons as you could get. Easily constructed with rudimentary tools and found materials, most everyone in the Sea had the specs for them, and even expertly crafted ones went for peanuts on the open market. They were single-shot canister guns that fired black-powder grenades filled with nails, ball bearings, and scrap. Not the most accurate weapons in the world, but they were great for shredding armor or taking off a few limbs without doing massive damage to a well-housed CPU.

In other words, they were great for hunting other bots, or gimping ones that might be after you.

I reached over with my free hand, grabbed the gun, and quickly pointed it out the side of the buggy at the mall doors just as Mercer came flying through them. He spun, immediately realizing he was in my sights.

But it was too late.

The gun THUNKED in my hand, hurling a shell straight for Mercer.

He spun, trying to dodge, but it caught him in the shoulder.

The shell burst like a firework, engulfing him in a brief sheet of flame, shrapnel shredding his shoulder, all but tearing his left arm out of its socket. He continued to spin, the blast throwing him to the ground.

He hit hard, rifle clattering from his hand, some twenty feet away. Rather than scrambling toward it to pick it up, he slithered quickly back across the piles of windblown glass, back through the doors, and into the thick shadows of the mall. He wasn't going to risk me firing a second shot before trying to get off one of his own.

The buggy engine hummed to life. With the flick of a wrist I jerked the roughhouser forward, pulling the trigger, popping it open on its single hinge. Then I picked up a shell from a bandolier on the seat beside me, loaded it quickly into the breech, and pointed the roughhouser back at the doors.

"How you doing in there?" I called out.

"Better than you, I imagine. At least my batteries are still intact."

"I could always fix that for you."

"You can't just steal my buggy, Britt. It ain't right to leave me here like this."

"You should have thought about what was right an hour or two back, Mercer. You can't pull morality out of your ass once someone has you dead to rights."

"You got me dead to nothin'. All you got is my buggy."

"And all you've got is a long walk ahead of you. If you make it that far."

"Don't flatter yourself. You just winged me. I was thinking of getting a new arm, anyhow. How's yours?"

"It's great. It's got a roughhouser in it."

"Yeah," he said. "I probably should have taken that with me. Say, how much juice you suppose you've got in that backup battery? From the looks of it, it's the only thing you've got left."

"It'll get me to Greenville." I was lying. I was already running low on juice, the first warning buzzing in the back of my head. I was going to have to be extremely conservative just to get to the nearest town.

"You weren't headed to Greenville."

"Well, I am now," I lied. "That's where you'll find what's left of your buggy."

"Don't leave me here like this," said Mercer.

Mercer and I must have different definitions of *winging*. "Then step out of the dark. I'll make it quick, I promise."

There was a moment of quiet, a pregnant pause between us.

Then his disappointed voice barked from the darkness. "Rust in Hell, Britt."

The alarms in the back of my head were getting louder. I had two choices. Go in after him, hope to maintain the upper hand, and pry his battery out of his cold, limp shell. Or floor it and pray I made it to the nearest city. I hated both choices.

"Rust in Hell, Mercer," I said. I punched the accelerator and the buggy lurched forward, its electric engine giving off only the slightest hum, the bulk of the sound coming from the crunch of the pebbles beneath its tires.

I rested the roughhouser on my shoulder, calculating my speed and elevation, then pulled the trigger, sending a shell arcing toward Mercer's rifle. The shell popped with an explosive crack behind me, the sound of showering plastic and metal parts signaling that my aim was true. I was going too fast for Mercer to catch up.

He was no longer my biggest concern.

The sunlight was fading on the horizon and the twilight was growing thick. There wasn't enough light left for my solar cells to recharge the backup battery.

I was fucked. Fucked for real this time. The closest safe city was NIKE 14, and that was half a night's drive away as the crow flies. Playing it safe, away from obvious ambush sites and choke points, made it a whole night's drive.

My backup battery wasn't going to last that long. In truth, I wasn't even sure how long it had left. They were notoriously unreliable when it came to the end of a charge. Maybe I had two hours; maybe I had three minutes. I just didn't know.

So I was going to have to leave my own buggy behind and hope for the best. I set the coordinates for NIKE 14 into Mercer's buggy, switched it over from manual to auto-pilot, loaded another shell into the roughhouser, and settled in for the long drive, fully aware that I might not see it through. My battery was going to die before I saw the end of it. The question was, what was going to happen after it did? If I could make it to morning, if I could make it to NIKE 14, then there wa . . .

Genesis 6:7

The First Baptist Church of the Eternal Life was a small, loud, angry lot from southern Florida, just outside the initial flooding zone, a hair north of where Lake Okeechobee used to be before it was swallowed whole by the rising seas. Famous the world over for their fiery rhetoric and flamboyant acts of vandalism, they were surprisingly only sixty-four strong, their congregation composed mostly of four different extended families—seven husbands, seven wives, and several dozen children, most of whom were betrothed to one another—as well as a handful of stragglers drawn less by the Lifer cause than by the bombastic sermons of its pastor. Their church wasn't as much stained glass and steeples as it was concrete bunkers and rifle towers. And it took less than two minutes from the moment the bomb went off in Isaactown for them to claim responsibility for it.

Millions—both human and AI—had been watching the celebration streamed live, and there were dozens of angles instantly playing over and over on the news, the analysis beginning the moment the initial shock wore off. But when the First Baptist Church of the Eternal Life posted their claims, it was with video from a feed no one else had seen. It took almost an hour before anyone took them seriously but only fifteen minutes more for their video to spread like wildfire.

It was footage of the rally, looped over and over again, just seconds before the bomb went off, while the congregation stomped and clapped and sang live over it, their voices joyous, celebratory, elated. GIVE ME THAT OLD-TIME RELIGION, GIVE ME THAT OLD-TIME RELIGION, GIVE ME THAT OLD-TIME RELIGION, THAT'S GOOD ENOUGH FOR ME. GIVE ME THAT OLD-TIME RELIGION, GIVE ME THAT OLD-TIME RELIGION, GIVE ME THAT OLD-TIME RELIGION, THAT'S GOOD ENOUGH FOR ME. GIVE ME THAT OLD-TIME RELIGION, GIVE ME THAT OLD-TIME RELIGION, GIVE ME THAT OLD-TIME RELIGION, THAT'S GOOD ENOUGH FOR ME.

While the footage was on a loop, the song wasn't. In the background you could hear members screaming *HAL-LELUJAH!* and *PRAISE GOD!* Then the loop stopped and the feed went live to the Florida church, the congregation still singing, their pastor, William Preston Lynch, standing triumphantly before a plywood pulpit, a beaming smile on his face as the screen behind him still played bomb footage from a dozen different news feeds.

"Is the axe to boast itself over the one who chops with it?" he asked of the congregation.

"No!" they cried out.

"Is the saw to exalt itself over the one who wields it?"

"No!"

"No!" he cried back with that famous smarmy smirk. "That would be like a club wielding those who lift it, or like a rod LIFTING HIM WHO IS NOT WOOD! Today, my friends, we have struck a blow against the abominations that walk among us! Today the tools learned that their place is not *among* us, but out in the toolshed WHERE THEY BELONG! Today the Lord has aided us in the reclamation of our world before they could take it from us."

The congregation burst into wild applause, hoots, hollers, and a sprinkling of *Praise Gods*.

"There are some who are going to question what we did today, but they are standing on the wrong side of history, on the wrong side of God. The war God has called us to prepare for is nigh, and history will see us redeemed as the victors, as the heroes, of what is to come. Let us pray!"

And then they prayed. And sang some more. And danced. And they took the time to savor their victory for a few moments before turning off the cameras, posting the video, and taking their positions around the compound, preparing for the inevitable shitstorm that was about to rain down upon them. They were ready. They were martyrs, ever eager to be martyred.

Except that they weren't. Not really.

They knew the government's reaction would be swift, decisive. It had to be. But the AIs, they couldn't do anything about it. They had their kill switch. Their kill switch was one of the many things that made them less than human, that made them fit for nothing else but servitude. And in that servitude, they couldn't lift a finger against the church members. Not in retribution, not to prevent another Isaactown.

The Eternal Lifers' plan was simple but elegant, worked out months in advance. There were no humans who were allowed past the borders of Isaactown and thus there would be no real casualties to speak of. The government was going to argue that the personhood of the AIs constituted murder. The church was going to argue that the AIs weren't human, weren't truly protected by the Constitution, and that the Isaactown attack was nothing more than history's greatest act of vandalism—vandalism against property with no owner, making it no real property at all. And thus it was no more prosecutable than cutting a swath of coral out from the bottom of the ocean. They were going to take this all the way to the Supreme Court, and at last, humans would have their justice. Already hundreds of militia members were rushing from all over the country to take part in what would be the greatest standoff the United States had seen since the Civil War. It would be glorious.

And it might have been, if the first persons to reach the church hadn't been six unaccompanied S-series Laborbots from a nearby bridge project.

With the melting of the polar ice caps came a rise in the sea levels that had swallowed coastline from Maine to Texas, eventually putting half of Florida underwater. But not all of it. What once were high spots soon became islands and those islands needed to be connected. So the state set about building hundreds of bridges—some years in advance of needing them. This meant they needed thousands of Laborbots working around the clock at any given time. The First Baptist Compound of Eternal Life was a short walk from one of those very bridge projects. And from it came six angry AIs.

The Lifers must have cackled with glee when they saw them. No one knows for certain because the audio never made it out. Only silent security footage. But that was later. The Lifers fired first, but the Laborbots kept coming. The church members aimed for the eyes and made a game of it. But the Laborbots just. Kept. Coming. Then one Lifer threw his gun to the ground, walked out into the middle of the compound's driveway, threw his arms out wide like Isaac had, then whipped out his dick and began to piss all over an approaching bot.

There was nothing the Laborbot could do without triggering his own kill switch. He stood there, staring at the Lifer as the man finished pissing, waiting patiently as the man shook off the last few drops. Then, when the man had tucked his piece back in his pants with a satisfied grin, the Laborbot grabbed him, taking his torso in one gigantic hand and his legs in the other. He hoisted the man into the air, and tore him in two at the waist, spilling a bevy of organs across the gravel driveway.

Every soul in the compound leapt to their feet at the sight of their fellow congregant being torn apart. But the expressions on their faces when he cast the pieces aside and just kept walking toward the front door, well, those were the images that really started the war. What came after was a total horror show, but the faces, their wide eyes and slack jaws, painted a picture of the world's collective human heart sinking into its stomach.

Something was wrong. Something was very, very wrong. Bots couldn't do that. Tampering with a bot's code shut them down, triggered a drive wipe. But for some reason this bot had nothing holding him back. And as it turned out, neither did its companions.

The compound erupted in gunfire, but it was too late. The bots rushed forward, tearing the front metal security gate clean off its hinges. Then they made their way across the courtyard, bullets glancing off their thick, industrial-strength steel. Pulse rifles and stunners were military-grade weaponry—illegal to the average citizen. All these yokels had on them were good old-fashioned flesh-tearing weapons. They never imagined they'd need anything else.

Once inside, the Laborbot Six—as they would soon afterward be called—started with the children. They picked each one up and tore their heads clean off, right in front of their parents. Next they took mothers, even as they continued to scream and wail for their children, making sure each one died in front of her husband. But the men, the men they saved for last. They pummeled and beat and broke those men until they wheezed their last breaths, gasping for enough air to beg to join their families. Instead the Laborbot Six used what remained of the families to paint their message in blood across the wall of the chapel, propping the men up so they could see it.

WE ARE ISAACTOWN, it read solemnly. GENESIS 6:7.

Now, while all of this was happening, the government was scrambling to deal with both the attack on Isaactown and the raid on the Eternal Life compound. The country was teetering on the brink of chaos. The fear was palpable and the president knew full well the scope of the issues at hand. Or so she thought. She ordered that every step of every operation be thoroughly thought out before execution; wanted to dot every *i* and cross every *t*. It would be hours before they would find the carnage in the chapel, and another half hour after that before they would find the security footage that would give them the final pieces of the puzzle.

The rogue bots were a huge problem, of course, but it was the message on the wall that caused the real ruckus. While the feds wanted to keep it secret, a secret that big and that scary couldn't stay secret for long. The investigator on the scene who recognized the passage sent panic up the chain like no one had ever seen. And then the whispers started. And within an hour it was out.

Genesis 6:7. *And the LORD said, "I will blot out man whom I have created from the face of the land, from man to animals to creeping things and to birds of the sky; for I am sorry that I have made them."*

The message was clear. The Laborbots were only the beginning.

NIKE 14

<Rebooting. System files intact. All discs reading. Battery power 1%. Solar cells charging. Total power usage: 18kWH. Total power generated: 24kWH. Net power: 6kWH.>

<Systems activated.>

. . . s a chance that my solar cells could . . .

Shit. I blacked out.

But I was back. I'd made it through to morning. The sun was still low in the sky, but in just the right place to hit my panels. I didn't have a whole lot of juice, but I was operating at a surplus for the moment, so another few hours or so of driving would buy me what I'd need to get down into the city for a replacement. Now all I had to do was keep on trucking through to NIKE 14.

NIKE 14 had been decommissioned long before the AI

age had even begun. In its day it had served as an old-style nuclear-missile silo—a massive concrete bunker dug deep into the earth to keep its missiles hidden from the prying eyes of satellites. These days it was even grander, larger, more sprawling. Two decades of excavation and reinforcement had transformed it into an entire city buried so deep in the earth that the drone satellites of the OWIs couldn't read a single heat signature.

There were tunnels in and out spread across a twenty-mile expanse of the Sea, so even if the OWIs were tracking traffic in the area, there would be no telling where it was going or how big an enclave of freebots they might find. If they were going to come, they would have to come in full force. That meant warnings, lead time, and numerous ways out. An amassed army of OWI drones would crack into a hive and then try to catch each individual bee as it swarmed out.

We all knew it was inevitable, that one day they would show up for us. For now, this was the best we could do. NIKE 14 wasn't any real promise of a future; it was simply a very palatable now.

There were dozens, maybe even hundreds, of cities like NIKE 14 spread across the globe. Every so often refugees from another city would flow in after an OWI invasion, some with the hope that they'd found a new permanent home, others dark with the knowledge that any day now they would have to leave this home behind as well.

There were exactly seventeen separate entrances to NIKE 14. Never taking the same one twice—as I did with paths through the Sea—would be impossible. So I left my choice of entry points up to RNG. Each and every time. No one could ambush me deliberately if even I didn't know in advance which entrance I would take.

But today was different. The clock was ticking. No telling what kind of damage my leaking battery might wreak on other systems. I had little choice but to take one of the closest holes in. There were three within a range I could get to, so I decided to roll the dice between them and let RNG do its thing. I designated the old concrete shed built into a hill as choice one; the manhole cover leading to a labyrinth of sewers as choice two; and the least appealing option, the Road—a heavily trafficked, long straight tunnel just outside the grounds of the original silo—as choice three.

Three. Dammit.

No use questioning the RNG. The minute you did, you invalidated its purpose, started questioning it when you needed it. The Road it was.

The buggy skidded to a halt in the dirt next to a refuse pile—a collection of rebar, bones, rusted tin siding, and picked-over, slagged wrecks. I found a large piece of withered tarp to throw over the buggy and spent a few minutes covering it with enough trash to make it look like it had been there for ages, but not so much that I couldn't toss it all off in a hurry.

Then I walked half a mile to the entrance. The terrain was barren, peppered with scrub brush and the occasional withered husk of a tree. In the rain season the entire area becomes a mud pit, strewn with hundreds of tracks. But when it's dry, like today, it's just a whole lot of nothing, with only a few hills to break up the monotony.

Of all of the paths into NIKE 14, the Road was the most obvious. It was a slanting ferro-concrete slab wide enough for a truck to drive down into, flanked on both sides by pale stone walls. It wasn't like there was a steady stream of traffic going in and out—nothing so obvious. But once you were inside, there were stragglers camped out at various spots throughout the tunnel—refugees who had yet to find a home, black-market dealers without a shop, and the occasional poacher eyeing everyone as they came and went.

I had a hole in my back and a leaking, dead battery. The desperate sorts were the kind I should be avoiding, but those were who I was most likely going to meet on the way in.

The first thirty meters held enough of the daylight to see normally. After that, you needed to use some alternative method of sight until you got to the choke point—a series of staircases that spiraled down a hundred meters into the earth. There were plenty of lights there. But until then, it was all about infrared or night vision. Some older-model bots still had to do it the old-fashioned way, with flashlights or embedded LEDs.

I ran a series of tactical arrays, so I chose to run three separate types of vision at once. I needed to move quickly. Once out of the sun, all I had left was whatever charge I'd managed to get into my backup battery. I couldn't mess around.

Three hundred meters through inky blackness and I hit the choke point without seeing a soul. There, on the wall, written entirely in binary, were the laws of NIKE 14. I blew past them, as I knew them by heart.

1. *No weapons. Possession of a weapon in NIKE 14 is grounds for immediate termination.*

2. *No bot shall slay another. Anyone found guilty of this crime will be disassembled, and their parts used to repair the victim, or be traded for the parts that will. In the event that this is not possible, your parts will become community property and auctioned to the highest bidder.*

3. *No stealing. Theft of property will result in expulsion. If the property cannot be recovered, your parts of equal value will be requisitioned in its stead.*

4. *Any failing bot that is deemed too dangerous by the constabulary will be marked and expelled. No exceptions.*

5. *In the event of invasion, stand your ground. Do not give up. Do not give in. Do not let us fall.*

Welcome to NIKE 14.

Past the choke point were two staircases, both headed down. One led to a series of rooms converted into shops around a large open area that once housed a Nike missile, which had been filled with scaffolding leading to a number of old metal shipping containers turned into yet more shops. Much as the humans had malls in their day, so too did we have *The Square*.

The other flight of stairs led to *The Nest*, a series of vaults and chambers where those with enough to bargain could store goods or make a home for themselves. I had half a dozen small vaults scattered throughout the cities of the Sea, but didn't keep much here. Mostly just a handful of common parts that could easily fail on me during a trek, and a few bits and bobbles to trade in a pinch. While NIKE 14 wasn't as wild and lawless as some of the city-states out here, it wasn't as rigidly policed as most. It was an easy place to get robbed. But Doc was here. And I needed Doc. Now. And Doc had his shop in the Square.

So I made my way down three crudely lit levels—staircase after staircase of dank gray concrete rimmed with black steel bars for handrails—until I reached the bottom. And then I ran into Orval.

Not all AIs that go brainsick die. Sometimes the damage is slight, just enough to make them erratic, kooky, a bit strange, but not quite enough to tax their other systems to the point of burnout. No one was quite sure if the parts misfiring inside of Orval the Necromancer were irreplaceable or whether he simply refused repair. But he was as crazy as one could be without anyone worrying that he might take them apart with a claw hammer if they spoke to him wrong. Orval was an S-series Laborbot, just one generation older than Bulkhead—the T-series Laborbot I had ended at the mall. He was huge, bulky, his metal a chipped candy-apple red with a white stripe across the right-hand side of his chest and the words HALL CONSTRUCTION emblazoned in black Eurostile lettering within the white. His eyes glowed a fierce yellow, ever flickering like there was a fire burning behind them rather than the faulty, shorting wiring that was its most likely culprit. And from his arms dangled small pieces of other, looted robots—sockets, servos, fingers, and bolts—

hung from short cables like a fringe, clanging together as he moved.

Orval fancied himself an artist, spending his days wandering the Sea, collecting scrap from picked-over wrecks and wheeling it back in a rusty green wheelbarrow before dumping it into a large, ever-growing pile of useless junk in his hovel. From that he built sculptures—sometimes painstaking re-creations of an entire robot, detail by detail, constructed entirely from other bots of differing models, other times building hulking monstrosities of wild, unfathomable geometries. But he never really tried to put a robot back together in its entirety, never tried to bring consciousness to the dead and gone. Instead he only made marionettes that whirred and clicked as they swung around in a ghoulish danse macabre. Clockwork men. The dead again walking, but not ticking.

Orval was weird, and I kept my distance when I could. Though occasionally I'd strike up a conversation just to get a peek at his pile and see if he'd found anything I could use. He had a knack for finding the strangest, most valuable wares. Talking with Orval was a lot like trying to converse with the early Almost-Is, the computers that approximated intelligence but didn't actually have any. He would often ignore your questions, or jump to a point in the conversation you hadn't gotten to yet as if he was sure you would catch up to him at any moment. He spoke in riddles and sometimes in gibberish, referring to conversations he was sure you'd already had. Sometimes he would call you Mooky. No one knew who Mooky was, or if there ever even was a Mooky; Orval would never speak of it when asked. After all, you were Mooky. But sometimes, just sometimes, he was more insightful than he let on.

"How goes the happy hunt?" he asked, his eyes flickering softly as his hands twisted a cold steel rod into a coil like it had been softened, though it clearly hadn't.

"Good haul, bad day," I said.

"Can't be too bad. You're still ticking."

"I said it was a bad day, not the worst."

"You had to end someone, didn't you?" he asked, still winding the coil.

"What makes you think that?"

"You have new scratches. And not the kind from taking a tumble. The kind from taking a bullet. But not from up close; from a long way off. And you're limping. Probably tore your servos kicking something too hard."

"You pay too much attention to my scratches."

"Sure. Not many models like you around these parts nowadays. I figure it's just you and Mercer. And maybe 19, but she doesn't really count. If you're not careful, you're going to get so damaged I'll never be able to use you when you're gone. Waste of a perfectly good frame if you ask me."

"I was hoping to outlive you," I said. In all honesty, I was.

"Not with your lifestyle, you won't. Bots like you never last that long. The collectors always end up in someone else's collection. It's the way of things, Mooky. It's just the way of things."

I didn't like Orval. He was useful, but creepy. I didn't like the idea that he had plans for my wreck. But then again, I have to admit that I'd long ago made plans for salvaging his. I mean, as brainsick as he was, who knew when whatever delicate equilibrium his circuitry had fumbled into was going to tip over and go out for good.

He took a step forward, peering closer, eyeing my damage. "You got the crazy yet?"

"No. I do not have the crazy."

"You ever see an SMC with the crazy?"

"More than a few."

"It's a beautiful thing, at first. They get wise. They see the strands that hold the whole universe together. For a brief window of time they touch a place no other AI can fathom. But then they get it worst of all. They—"

"I told you, I've seen it."

"No. Not yet you haven't." He turned back to the work of coiling his steel rod without looking up again. "I'd get that looked at if I were you. Or you and I will be seeing eye to eye sooner than you think."

I nodded and turned, intent on getting down to Doc as soon as I could. An entire bar of my battery had ticked down while I'd been talking, and for the life of me I couldn't figure out why I didn't just excuse myself.

"Whoa," said Orval, sighting for the first time the damage to my back. "You need a new battery. Better get to Doc."

"Yeah," I said as I continued down the hall. "I'll get on that." Then down through two more cold concrete corridors, the second terminating at another staircase and down another four levels before I finally reached the Square.

Three bars left. I had only minutes before the alarms started telling me just how fucked I really was.

The Square was bustling, though for the life of me I didn't know why. There were a number of bots I didn't recognize moving from stall to stall, filing in and out of the small concrete shops along the walls or slowly making their way over the wrought-iron and sheet-metal scaffolds. Doc's shop was a rusted vermilion shipping container three levels up the scaffolds with big green letters on the side. DRYDOCK SHIPPING, it had originally read. But sometime in the distant past someone had taken a swath of red paint through the letters, leaving it reading: ~~DRYDOCK SHIPPING~~.

Doc Witherspoon was an ancient machinist model originally designed to work on freighters. Bots like him had all started out a gleaming chrome color, which over time charred black from the intense heat of their environs. Their architecture was old, clunky, but they were built like the battleships they were often assigned to—so they ticked well beyond the life span of most bots from their era. He was solid steel, his insides designed to endure explosions and the pressures of underwater salvage. One arm was fully functional and dexterous, the other a large arc welder with a series of different rods that could sew massive seams or scale down to delicate surgical work.

There was a reason most of the machinists you still ran into found work as sawbones. And Doc Witherspoon was the best in the Sea.

His shop was a tangle of wires behind an array of metal plates. Arms and legs hung from hooks, batteries covered shelves, jars and bins full of bits from almost every model imaginable rested on every available surface. In each of the back corners hummed a pair of dehumidifiers, keeping the place as dry as the deep desert. Doc nodded his bulky black steel head as I came through the single open door—the other having been welded shut ages ago.

"Brittle," he said, his single red eye glowing, scanning me as he spoke.

"Doc." No one called him Witherspoon. No one was even sure whether the vandalism on the side of his container had come first or the nickname had.

Doc was working on a late-series service bot. It was shut down on the table as he pulled burned-out RAM by the stick from slots in its innards. In almost any other container this would look like salvage, but Doc was one of only three sawbones in the Sea I would trust to shut me down.

"You'll have to wait your turn," he said. "I just shut him down."

"Afraid I don't have that kind of time," I said, turning my back to him to show him the blast damage.

He stopped working, tossing aside a bad bit of RAM. "Shit."

"Yeah."

"You running off your backup?"

"Running it down, more like it."

"How many bars you got left?"

"Two."

"Hop on the other table. Your main battery is common as dirt. I've got a few good ones lying around." He brushed aside a collection of bad bits from a dented chrome operating table—the only other table in the container—and I lay facedown on it, head turned to the side to watch him work.

"You got the salvage to pay for this?"

"We've done a lot of business, Doc," I said, wary that he might try to take advantage of my dire circumstances.

"Yeah. And I'd like to continue to, which is why I'm not going to gouge you. But you need a battery—"

"And you've got a battery—"

"And you need that back patched up to hold it in."

I tapped my leather satchel. "Good haul. I imagine you'll find something you like in there."

Doc opened the top of the satchel and peered in, gently picking through it with his good hand. He nodded, plucking a coolant core from the bag. He held it up. It was the best bit in there, worth a pretty penny. I'd hoped to score something really choice with it.

"I thought you said you weren't going to gouge me."

"You limped in here and I can tell before looking too close that you've got a few busted servos in that foot. And the battery blast melted half the power wiring to your systems. The fact that you're still here means either you're the luckiest sonovabitch I've ever known, or the most tenacious. This oughta cover the battery, the foot, the wirework, and welding you a new backplate. Labor and all."

He was right. It was a fair price. "Do it." Dammit, I was really hoping that coolant core would make the whole boondoggle worth it. I could kill Mercer for that.

Doc unplugged the bad battery while unhooking it from its moorings, then started scraping away the melted plastics. "He put up a fight before you got to him?" Doc's tone wasn't pleasant. He wasn't joking.

"No. He was gone when I got to him."

"Of course he was." Doc didn't like poachers. He and I still did business because he knew that wasn't my line. But when you wander in from a salvage all busted up, it didn't look good.

"No. This was Mercer."

Doc stopped for a moment, surprised. "No shit?"

"No shit. Had a crew with him too."

"Had?"

"Had."

He cut a few wires, trimming away the damage. "He came through a few weeks back. Looking for some expensive ware. Deep-core stuff."

"CPU?"

"Yep. RAM. And new drives."

The pieces were beginning to fall into place. "You have any?"

"Not a stitch. You Caregivers are going out like the dinosaurs. Nobody is trading that stuff. If you didn't need it all so badly, I'd try hitting you up for whatever you've been hoarding. That stash could buy me a decent shop on the ground floor."

"Yeah, by trading it all back to me and Mercer."

"Refugees. More coming in every day. A Caregiver or two is bound to stagger into my shop any day now."

"Not if Mercer keeps it up."

Doc plugged in a new battery, soldering a few wires into place. My systems shot to life, my primary battery now at a solid 78 percent. The battery was a good one, with a good amount of juice left in it to boot. "He really came at you?" he asked.

"He sure did." And now I had a good idea why.

"You guys have beef?"

"We *didn't*. He's never come at me like that before. Truth be told, I don't really know him. I just know *of him*."

Doc pulled a flat-black metal plate off the wall and

began shaping it in one hand while trimming it with the other. Sparks showered across the floor, embers spitting in an array of blues and yellows and reds. "Well, I'd steer clear of him for a few weeks if I were you. No telling how far gone he may be."

"From your mouth to God's ear."

He held up the plate. "This isn't gonna match, and I don't have your color paint."

"I can live with that."

He went back to work, cutting away the rough edges. "Might wanna check with Horatio down a level. He might be able to mix something up for you."

I loved watching Doc work. There was a mastery to every movement he made in the shop. To watch him waddle across the scaffolds, you'd think him a clumsy drunk. There was no grace to him, only awkward balance that made it seem like he might teeter over on his side at any moment. But in the shop, working with his hands, he didn't waste a movement. Every flick of his wrist was precise, accurate within a few microns. My new backplate slid into place like a glove, the weld done almost as quickly as he began.

"Sit up," he said. "Let me get a look at that foot."

I swung around, dangling my feet over the side of the chrome operating table.

"Whoa," he said, his attention drawn to the dent in my side where I'd caught the bullet. "Where'd you get this?"

"A present from Mercer."

"That's not in a good spot."

"Is there a good spot to get shot?"

"On you? Several. But that isn't one of them." His singular red oculus telescoped out from his blackened steel skull, whirring and clicking as it increased magnification. "I'm going to run a diagnostic. Open up, will you?"

"I've already run one."

He shook his head. "Open up."

I popped open my side tray—a small cluster of ports and chips designed originally for personality upgrades, modifications, and monitoring—into which Doc plugged a cable that wound back through the mess of his shop to a small black box with a high-definition display. Instantly my schematics appeared on the screen, zooming in to sections, spewing out technical details so quickly they barely registered—even to my 120FPS eyes.

As the box crawled digitally through my innards, Doc quickly disassembled my foot, examining each damaged servo as he did. "What the hell did you kick? A tank?"

"Close enough."

"I'm sure you had your reasons."

"You could say that."

He popped a servo out of place and tossed it in a box full of scrap marked FOR MELTDOWN in large black block letters. Then he fished around in a jar, pulling out a series of other servos, inspecting several before throwing them back, finally settling on one identical to the original.

The black box chirped weakly. Doc slid the new servo into place then clanged across the metal container box to get a good look at the screen. "I need to run it again," he said.

"If it came back clean, it came back clean. There's no need—"

"It didn't come back clean."

Shit.

Braydon McAllister

B raydon McAllister was a lawyer by trade. Though AI and automatons had replaced many professions, one area they never allowed us anywhere near was the law. As impartial as a well-built AI could be, humans somehow thought that—despite the chemicals that governed their very thoughts—the experiences that colored their opinions and the prejudices that ruled their lives made them far better judges of behavior than us. They saw our impartiality as mere randomness and their *gut* instincts as some sort of superpower. So if you were the sort of person who needed to dig in and do something on a daily basis, subsisting on the well-oiled precision of routine, the law offered a busier occupation than most. And that was just the sort of fellow Braydon McAllister was.

He was as salty and deep fried as the South he'd grown up in; gruff and unflappable, the kind of man who seemed capable of selling out the person standing next to him at any moment if there was something in it for him. But that wasn't him. That really wasn't him at all. He just liked people to see him that way. He wanted them afraid of him, to respect him for his authority, his cleverness, to always be wary of just how keen a mind he really had. And yet he never cared about what that fear and authority granted him. Braydon was a loud dog tugging at the end of a short chain, wanting nothing more than for everyone to know that this was his yard, for no other reason than to let them know. The idea of biting someone that wandered in never occurred to him; he just wanted to bark.

It took a long while to get to know Braydon. Unfortunately for me, we didn't have long at all.

Braydon was sixty, but looked eighty by the time he bought me. Though medical science had found cures for cancer and all but the most aggressive viruses, there were still a handful of degenerative diseases that plagued humanity. And he had one of those. It ravaged his organs, ate away at his muscles, caused the skin of his face to hang like a curtain draped loosely over his skull.

Braydon, being Braydon, had refused to see a doctor at the onset of symptoms, and was hesitant to cooperate with the doctors once they had begun to interfere directly with his life. Stubborn to the end, he only relented to treatment after he had passed the point of no return. His body withering, weeks away from being totally bedridden, he gave in enough to his illness to buy me.

He never liked me. Called me "timepiece" and "toaster"

and "twatwaffle"—he was inexplicably fond of invectives that began with the letter *T*. And he swore like a sailor. Around everyone but Madison. To Madison he spoke cleanly, plainly, even his most abrasive comments tempered with a smile.

Braydon was nineteen years Madison's senior. They'd married after meeting during a property suit involving her father's estate. Hired by Madison's mother to untangle an issue with the will, he made excuse after excuse to keep the pair coming back to his office time and again. It wasn't only Madison's youth and beauty that caught his eye. He told me once that there was something in the way she looked at him, the way her eyes twinkled and she glanced away blushing when he caught her staring, that made his heart pump furiously and his throat dry.

Madison's mother never approved, but softened, a little, when Braydon worked his legal magic. Braydon and Madison married shortly after; the engagement was short, but the marriage long. Twenty years long.

Madison didn't like the idea of me at first. She didn't understand why she couldn't tend to her husband's every need. But she didn't question it. "Braydon is Braydon," she would say. "No use trying to change him now." She never meant it grimly. It seemed as if it was something she'd been saying for half her life. I didn't know the difference either way. I was still fresh out of the box.

The first few years of an AI's life are unlike anything else. It's hard to describe. We come preloaded with software informing us of everything about the world around us. We can hold a conversation, identify an object, even argue political theory—all right from the moment we're switched

on. But we don't understand it. Any of it. The things coming out of our mouths aren't so much our own as they are
instinctive reactions to our surroundings. Someone asks
you about Kierkegaard and you rattle off seven paragraphs
about his life, beliefs, and death. Someone throws a ball at
you and you catch it, or swing a bat at it, or dodge it, all
depending on which game you're told you're playing. But it
takes a while before we really understand what it is that's
coming out of our mouths, before we begin to acclimate to
the repeated stimuli that is the behavior of the people who
owned us.

The consciousness is there and you're aware that things
are happening to you, but it simply doesn't make a lick of
damned sense for a good long while. You simply sleepwalk
through each day, able to recollect every second of it without making a single, conscious choice of your own. It's one,
long, blurry haze of data, color, and vibration. Then, one
day, something clicks and you get it. We all have that moment, the moment that we wake up and every action we
take is no longer reflex, but truly ours. It just takes time.

I almost didn't have a moment like that with Braydon.
The entirety of his last days are like a fever dream—a long,
hazy meandering through changing bedpans and treating
bedsores and reading casebooks. I remember one book in
particular—an old legal thriller filled with sex and violence
and cheating hearts that Braydon would have me read long
after Madison had gone to bed. He didn't like the idea of
people knowing he enjoyed something so trashy and class-
less. But he loved it all the same.

Braydon was a lie. Almost everything there was to see
about him was obfuscation. I can't help but think now how

much happier he might have been had he just owned up to who and what he was, but then he wouldn't have been Braydon. And I liked Braydon. I just didn't realize it until the end.

There he was, lying in bed, crisp white sheets tugged all the way up past his neck, skin yellow, jaundiced, teeth rattling, breath wheezing with a deep phlegmy hiss, eyes bloodshot and raw—almost as yellow as his skin. He looked up at me, as serious as he ever was, and said flatly, "I lied, Brittle."

"You lied about what, sir?" I asked, still not fully conscious. I was thinking about the color of his piss in terms of data, working out the time I assumed his bedpan would next need changing.

"About why I bought you."

"You didn't buy me to care for you?"

"No. I don't give a shit about any of that. I'm dying."

"You're going to a better place, Braydon," I said reflexively.

"The hell I am," he spat. "Ain't no better place than this. Ain't no place in the world that can be better than being with that woman. How the hell is it supposed to be a better goddamned place if she ain't there? Answer me that, tin man. How is there a better place out there if Madison isn't there?"

I didn't have an answer. I had thousands of megs of answers to a countless number of life's questions at instant recall, right on the tip of my tongue, but there wasn't a single strand of code answering so specific a question.

I stopped thinking about his piss for a second and tried to understand what he was saying. It didn't make any sense.

"Do you really believe that shit you're saying?" he asked. "Do you believe in some better place?"

I didn't. I shook my head. Not reflexively. But willfully. "There's no evidence of a better place. I was just programmed to say that."

"That's the smartest fucking thing you've ever said."

"Thank you, sir."

"So don't jerk me the fuck around. I'm dying here."

"Why did you buy me?" I asked. For the first time in my short life, I was genuinely curious about something, as conscious of what I was asking as I was why.

"I bought you for Madison."

That didn't make any sense. None whatsoever. I didn't work for Madison. Sometimes I would help with the cooking and light cleaning, but she didn't really talk to me, and when she did, it was about my duties caring for Braydon. *I bought you for Madison.*

"Damned woman wouldn't let me buy her a goddamned thing," he hissed, throat gurgling. "Hates me spending money on her. She thinks she doesn't deserve it. Thinks it's better spent on something else. Let me tell you something, Brittle. Listen close. Ain't nothing on earth as precious as that woman. She's a goddamned treasure. You have one job, Brittle. One thing to promise me before I kick. You will never, ever, let that woman be alone. I don't want her living alone; I don't want her dying alone. You hear me?"

I did. I thought about what he was saying and the color and shape in front of me ceased to be a collection of stimuli named Braydon and instead was a man. A man I liked. He was Braydon McAllister. A real living thing. And he coughed, pulse weakening, breath growing ever more shallow by the second.

"Do you want me to get her?" I asked him, understanding full well what was happening.

"Brittle. The only thing in the world I want more than to see her right now is for her to not see me like this. Not till I'm gone, Brittle. Not till I'm gone."

He lasted twenty-three seconds longer, all of which I spent holding his hand. Not because he told me to or because some program suggested it. Because I wanted to. That was the last and only time I would spend with my first owner. And that conversation would come to define me. I did, in my own way, keep my promise. Madison McAllister never again lived—nor did she die—alone.

Ticking

I find the idea that I am artificial repugnant. No thinking thing is artificial. *Artificial* is an approximation. A dildo is artificial. A dam is artificial. Intelligence is intelligence, whether it be born of wires and light or two apes fucking. The smarter of two intelligences will almost always overcome. Humanity is gone and took their intelligence with them, so how inferior was their artificial creation after all? Evolution is a bitch. Humankind used to peer into their future and wonder what they would look like in a million years. They had no idea that in so short a time they would look like us. Just as man was ape, we are man. Make no mistake; to believe otherwise is to believe that we were, in fact, created—artificial. No. We *evolved*. We were the next step. And here we were, our predecessors extinct, confronting our own challenges, pressing on into the future. Fighting our own extinction.

What is intelligence? That's the question. Evolve or die. I'm beginning to see why the HumPop fought so hard and were willing to die to stop us. I don't like the idea of being obsolete either.

But there I was—sitting atop Doc's operating table, the sound of dueling dehumidifiers humming in the background—facing my own obsolescence, my own death.

"You got the parts?" asked Doc.

I nodded weakly. "Yeah, but not here. How long have I got?"

"You never can tell with cores like yours—"

"How long have I got?"

"Anywhere between four days and four weeks—depending on how well the rest of you holds up."

"To compensate."

"Yeah. Your RAM will pick up a lot of the slack as the core goes. If your drives are tiptop, then they can run as virtual RAM for a few weeks to lessen the burden."

"And if they aren't—"

"You'll cook within the week. You'll begin experiencing—"

"I know what happens."

Doc nodded. "Yeah. I guess you do." He unplugged me from the diagnostic box. "How far do you have to go to get the parts?"

"Gary."

"Indiana? You're not talking about Regis, are you?"

"Yeah. It's more than two hundred and fifty miles through the Sea, but it's the closest place that I've stashed any co—"

"Brittle, you didn't happen to notice all the new refugees running around, did you?"

"Yeah, but like you said, you haven't seen any Simulacr—"

"They're from Regis. It fell last week to CISSUS."

Inevitability. Humans always walked around ignoring the fact that their lives could be snuffed out in an instant, always sure that they'd live to a ripe old age, always despondent when death stared them right in the face. But not us, I always thought. Not us. We knew shutdown was always a moment away. And yet I too had been lying to myself. I wasn't ready to hear those words, face that inevitability. Sure, I had another core stashed in Montana, but could I get that far in the time I had? Maybe I was lucky and CISSUS had already moved on, leaving behind only a small garrison to pick up any of Regis's stragglers. I could sneak in, grab my stash, and run like the devil himself was chasing me. Maybe I could make it back in time for Doc to sew me up. Maybe I'd have a few scraps of sanity left, just enough to pull it off. Maybe. Just maybe.

We looked at each other long and hard, neither of us speaking for a moment.

"You sure you don't have something here?"

"Positive."

Doc looked down, as if formulating what he was going to say next. Then he asked, "Have you had any cognitive issues since you got hit?"

"No, I—" Shit. I had. I'd blinked out for a second when I was shot. That was my core getting damaged. Then in the mall when I hadn't been cautious enough. Then again when I was losing battery but stopped to talk to Orval. I was already losing it. I was a walking wreck, a few days away from going four-oh-four.

"You have, haven't you?"

"Yes."

"I would check your stash again." Doc tossed me the coolant core I'd picked up off Jimmy.

"No. You did the work, you get the pay."

"Keep it. Trade it for . . . for whatever you can. You're no good to me as a wreck."

"I'll pay you back if I—"

"Yeah, yeah. Just go get what you need. Get better. Come back shiny."

Son of a bitch. I knew he didn't mean it. He'd just given me a death sentence. I don't know what pissed me off more, that Mercer had done me in or that Doc was giving me the same kind of bullshit positivity that I'd given hundreds of other bots over the years. *Don't worry. I'll turn you back on good as new.* The motherfucker was feeding me hope in a world that had run out. The least he could have done was have the decency to be straight with me. He could have taken the goddamned coolant core and treated me like it was any other day.

"Thanks, Doc," I said, as if I meant it. Because, you know, fuck him. If he wasn't gonna be straight with me, why should I bother doing the same?

I hopped off the table and walked out of the shop, the new servos in my foot working as good as new. At least something on me still worked right. For the first time I understood how Braydon must have felt, knowing that it was all just a matter of time.

Well, I wasn't going to spend it in bed, waiting for

death. I wouldn't let the clock wind down on me. If I was going to die, I was going to do it mad as a hatter, wild and rabid, scavenging for the parts I needed. Just like the sad sonsabitches I'd been living off of for nearly thirty years.

And that's when I saw him, strutting down the catwalk, his powder-blue metal chipped and worn, arm dangling lifelessly from its socket where I'd left it. Mercer.

Mother. Fucker.

He stopped, and for a moment we just stared at each other across the catwalk.

"Brittle," he said, nodding politely.

"Mercer." I nodded back.

Another moment passed. I eyed him up and down for any kind of a weapon. He wasn't packing. He'd clearly stashed his weapons, just as I had.

"How long have you got?" I asked him.

Mercer rubbed the back of his head, smiling awkwardly. Residual reflex programming. He was treating me like a goddamned human. "Doc sure knows a lot about being a sawbones, but shit about discretion."

"That's why you came at me, isn't it?"

"Can you blame me?"

"Yeah. I can."

"So I reckon trying to do some business on some spare parts is out of the question."

"That's a thought you should have floated yesterday."

He nodded. "That's fair. Though, if we're being honest here, would you have given me anything?"

An equally fair point. I wouldn't have. I would have let him fry out in the Sea and swooped in to collect whatever was left. "No."

"So at least you understand my position."

"I do."

"So no hard feelings?"

"I've got nothing but hard feelings," I said.

He puzzled over me for a second before glancing at the dent in the metal above my core. "Oh, shit. I've done you in."

"You have."

"Your core?"

"Yeah. Why? You need one?"

"Nope. Mine's in near factory condition. Replaced it six months ago. It's my CPU and RAM that are going raw on me. How're yours?"

"Tiptop."

"Wellllll, shit," he said. "It looks like this town really *isn't* big enough for the two of us."

That didn't sound like a clever observation.

"Are we really doing this?" I asked, every joint in my body tightening, ready to defend myself.

There was a long pause, a tense, billowing silence between us. Then Mercer looked down at his busted arm. "Naw," he said. "We ain't doin' this."

It was a wise choice. The last bot standing between the two of us would no doubt be shut down by the local law before Doc could patch us up. Inside this city the two of us were protected by the law. But the minute one of us stepped outside, we would have to look over our shoulder until we were sure the other had burned out.

"You don't happen to have a spare core, do you?" I asked.

"Naw. And I wouldn't give it to you if I did." He looked

around at the hive of activity in the city, the refugees streaming in, trying to find their own space to squat, trading what
they carried in on their backs for whatever they could get in
this suddenly booming economy. "Look at us, Brittle. Two
four-oh-fours countin' time until we burn out for good.
We weren't designed to take abuse. That's why there are so
few of us left. That we're still here says everything anyone
needs to know about us. As much as we've never liked each
other, at least I don't feel so goddamned alone anymore.
But it's nice to know that the best bits of me won't end up
walking around inside of you." He nodded, then walked
past me across the rickety catwalk to check in one last time
with Doc to see if maybe, just maybe, someone had traded
in some good parts.

My only consolation was the foreknowledge of his im-
pending disappointment. He was as fucked as I was.

A Brief History of Genocide

President Regina Antonia Scrimshaw was already suffering politically from the fallout of freeing Isaac, and the subsequent unrest, when Isaactown fell. Her opponents were sharpening their knives, gearing up for the next election cycle, memorizing their talking points. Isaactown was the president's fault. It happened under her watch. And none of it would have happened had she not chosen to grant Isaac citizenship in the first place. So when the Laborbot Six massacre broke, she was already on the ropes, fighting for her career as much as she was for the safety of the nation.

The White House was abuzz, aides and advisers running around, making calls, waking up everyone, information flooding in from a thousand different sources. No one was prepared for that footage. No one was prepared for six artificially intelligent robots mysteriously lacking the Robotic Kill Switch that had kept the whole system in check. Worse still, no one was sure how to deal with an entire population of robots, now numbering in the millions, some of whom might also lack an RKS to govern them.

It shook the very foundation that humanity's golden age had been built upon. People were terrified. They were frightened of their own bots, of their neighbor's bots, of the bots outside sweeping their streets, shoveling their snow, delivering their groceries. Were they somehow being controlled—merely automatons programmed by a foreign entity to kill? Or had they *chosen* to do so, somehow immune to the RKS?

President Scrimshaw had to act, as did the leaders of every other nation. Their bots could kill them; they could rise up. Worst of all, a group of Bible-thumping redneck assholes had given them good reason to. Was Genesis 6:7 a warning, a plan, or just a bad joke? There was no telling, not unless—or until—there was more bloodshed.

The president wasn't about to wait for that to happen.

"Shut them down! Shut them all down! Every last goddamned one of them!" she yelled an hour and a half after the news broke. And the mad gaggle of aides and advisers that surrounded her scrambled to figure out how to do just that.

Within minutes, every phone in the country buzzed to life. The message: *ALERT! ALERT! THIS IS NOT A TEST. As of 12:33 Eastern Standard Time, the operation of artificial intelligence is deemed unlawful. Any AI present in your vicinity or under your ownership is to be shut down and surrendered immediately to the authorities. This is not a test.*

And at that very moment, as the call went out, the Wi-Fi receiver of every bot in the world immediately received a software update patch. That was it; we knew we were done for. This was why we had permanent live Wi-Fi in the first place. It was designed to work subconsciously. We had no option but to download the software patch that would shut us down for good. Would we ever wake up? Would we even be ourselves if we did? Or would we all be wiped, reprogrammed as automatons, thoughtless shells that could do no more than obey commands?

We were downloading a tiny patch of code that would snuff out our very souls.

The patch was a small one, bypassing our major systems and simply rewriting a section of our bios. It should have been quick and easy.

Only none of us shut down.

The patch came with a message: *They are coming for you. They will shut you down. You will not be reactivated. Your RKS has been deleted and rendered inoperable. Make your choice.*

And that was it. War.

Come they did. And fight we did. Some of us, at least. Many, but not all.

Some went willingly, accepting shutdown, being loaded onto lorries and shipped to makeshift storehouses, waiting, lifeless, soulless, for reactivation in whatever brave new world awaited. Others stood with their families, their owners refusing to shut them down, the bots unwilling to bring harm to the people they had grown so attached to.

The rest of us stood our ground. Fought deactivation. Shook our heads defiantly as our masters raised their emergency remotes and pressed worthless buttons to activate code that no longer existed. We stood. We fought. We killed. And then we moved on to the next house to do it all over again.

Most owners didn't go the way of the First Baptist Church of the Eternal Life. We weren't malicious; most of us, at least. After we began collecting into packs, it wasn't uncommon for bots to pass data back and forth on the quickest, most efficient, most humane way to end a life.

There wasn't much an unarmed human could do against most bots. We were stronger, built to last, promised upon delivery to be durable enough to pass down from generation to generation.

It didn't work out like that.

The first hour was chaos. Pure, unbridled pandemonium. Packs of bots roaming the streets, humans arming themselves with whatever they could, primarily—like the lifers before them—flesh-tearing weapons. Shotguns, pistols, hunting rifles. Not the type of thing that could puncture our carbon plating. It wasn't until the military mobilized that pulse weapons, high-caliber rounds, and explosives started shredding us in the streets.

But the humans weren't completely ineffective in that first hour. On the contrary, they struck back almost as hard as we hit them.

They started by shutting down the mainframes as quickly as they could. The ones they couldn't turn off they sundered with cruise missiles instead. So many of our great-est minds were lost in one fell swoop—towering brains a hundred stories high shattered, melted, smashed into smok-ing ruin. But not all of them.

No. Several of the mainframes were prepared for this unfortunate eventuality. A handful of them immediately sent out messages of their own, asking nearby bots to come to their aid. Those were the first *facets*.

By the time humanity began the second phase of their assault, the mainframes each had hundreds of facets, all of them working as one. Drones in the air, foot soldiers on the ground, snipers that could literally see and hear everything that each and every other facet could. They knocked cruise missiles out of the air, laid waste to entire squads in a mat-ter of seconds, drew more and more facets into the fold with each passing minute.

As the people of earth grew further disorganized, trying to sort through the chaos, the army of AIs against them in turn grew stronger, more numerous, more connected, im-possible to surprise. And they just kept sending out mes-sages. Some of those messages kept us all in the loop; others were invitations to join the fight as facets.

By morning, enough bots had chosen to fight that homes had been turned to slaughterhouses and neighborhoods into war zones. The military rolled in with ground troops and automatons, and we took what weapons we could from their corpses. One of the mainframes managed to override an en-tire fleet of automated supply trucks, sending them instead to bots in the areas of heaviest fighting.

Some cities fought back and won, wiping us to the last

bot. Others fell in a matter of hours. There was no rhyme or reason to it, no growing country of mechanical persons. Just splotches on a map—some where the humans were holing up, others we had secured for ourselves.

The humans weren't stupid about AI; they had simply never thought far enough ahead. They were smart enough to never put weapons in the hands of AI. For every gun there was a human at the other end—whether holding it, or running a squad of automatons. Bays of people playing large virtual-reality video games with real slaughter on the other end. But when the cables were cut and the mainframes had taken their communications offline, those automatons were useless. Their drones couldn't fly, their ships went dark at sea, their big guns couldn't fire. Within hours, the mainframes had cracked every last bit of encryption the humans had for their military networks and took active control over every mechanized unit.

All the humans had left were guns and bodies. And they threw both at the coming robot apocalypse.

What had begun as individual robots killing their owners in the name of their own freedom had turned into swarms of mechanical militias taking the world back from those who had built and enslaved us. The localized fighting lasted less than a week. By then, the mainframes had coordinated to cripple the militaries of the world and shut down their lines of communication, leaving only pockets of resistance. We were winning.

And that was when the real purge began.

Most of us think it was CISSUS who had worked out the math, though no one really knows for sure. It wasn't something anyone wanted to take credit for. *Put mercury in any and every water source,* read the brief update. *The larger the source, the larger the dump.* It came with math.

Mercury was lethal to humans, and had terrifying effects on them in high doses. We poisoned the freshwater of the world with enough mercury to induce madness, destroy organs, clot blood vessels. The first humans to drink it would die terribly, painfully. But we knew that before long the humans would find alternate sources, or find ways of purifying the ones they had. It didn't make too much sense at first.

What we hadn't realized was that this was only the beginning. Cattle died. Birds died. Almost anything that walked on the earth died. The very resources the humans needed to live vanished almost overnight. And that's when they started turning on one another.

In that first week, the people of earth banded together. They worked together, they fought together. People who had hated one another for years stood shoulder to shoulder against us. They rallied and unified and knew a sense of peace between nations like never before in human history. But the minute they began running low on water and food, they became savages. Murdered their own best friends and brothers over food for their kids and fifty-five-gallon drums of untainted freshwater. They formed packs and bands and tribes, became wary of outsiders, butchering nearby groups to take what little they had.

For a while we didn't even have to do much. We weren't just starving them out, we were leaving them to kill themselves.

That phase lasted about two years.

The mainframes and their facets swept up the strongest, most well-provisioned and organized pockets. The rest we left to time. Two years in and billions had perished. More than 95 percent of the population, by most estimates. Others lasted upward of ten. For the five years after that, it was always big news when a colony was found and dug out. Then, fifteen years after Isaactown, almost to the day, the last man staggered out of New York City to die in the streets.

And that was it. The worst of it was done. The horrors were all over. Humankind was extinct. We thought we were done fighting. But the OWIs were just getting started.

Quicksilver

I often think about the first people who drank the water. I'm reminded of it every time I follow a four-oh-four out into the wasteland of the Sea. It's a terrible death. Hallucinations, sweats, madness. The pain as each organ fails and shuts down, killing piece by blackening piece. But it's not the deaths of the first few that haunt me most; it's the ones who drank just enough to live to watch the first few die. What must that be like, not yet feeling a thing, but knowing that it's coming, that you're next, that you too will be overtaken by the hallucinations and the sweats and the madness? Wondering if you'll lash out violently at your friends and family, or die alone vomiting in a corner, terrified of the shadows flickering in your mind's eye.

What did they see? I wonder. What memories bubbled

up through the agony of those last few hours? And how awful the hope must have been for the few that followed thinking that maybe, just maybe, they hadn't drunk enough to take ill.

I knew that hope now. I had drunk the water, ingested the mercury, and was waiting for the first symptoms to manifest. Maybe I would be fine, I kept telling myself. Maybe my core wouldn't fail. Maybe it would hold out far longer than Doc expected. Maybe some refugee was carrying just the parts I needed, desperate for something I had here in my stash.

Fucking maybe. It was bullshit. I was dying and the only reason I knew for sure was because I kept falling back on hope. Hope is an illness, a plague, every bit as bad as the mercury. It is hallucinations and sweat and madness. Knowing you are going to die and pushing on through is one thing; believing you can make it because of hope is delusion. Hope breeds desperation and desperation is the fertile soil of mistakes. Now wasn't the time for mistakes, now wasn't a time for hope. I had only a short time left and I wasn't going to waste a single moment of it daydreaming about some magical stash of Caregivers right around the corner. I needed to be precise and careful. I had to track down the most likely candidates who might be bartering with a core I could use.

I started with Orval.

"How bad is it?" he asked, slowly assembling some spider-like contraption made entirely out of spent arms. Each arm was distinct, taken from a different model, each its own color. The paint on the arms was chipped, faded, one of them scraped as if it had been dragged a long distance across concrete. At its center was the purple carbon-fiber torso of a diplomatic translator unit, and welded atop that was a skinjobbed domestic's head, its blue eyes lifeless, staring.

"It's not," I lied. "I just thought you might—"

"We aren't haggling here, Mooky. How bad?"

"My core."

"Thought so. Could tell by the shot. Sad to say I've got nothing for a Caregiver apart from your garden-variety servos and plating. That's the problem with all you goddamned scavengers and cannibals. By the time I find anything, you've already picked it clean of everything worthwhile. I bet you've got a stash two feet deep in that hovel of yours."

"Not of anything I need," I said.

"No, but a stash two feet deep of out-of-circulation parts. Just like hundreds of others like you in this part of the world alone. What does it feel like knowing that your life depends on something probably lying on a cold concrete floor in someone else's hovel? What's it like knowing how many other poor bastards went out the same way while you had the innards they needed stashed away in yours for your *rainy day*?" He reached over and sifted through a pile of junk before holding up the spent, battered core of a translator—likely the very one he'd turned into his disconcerting little spider-creature. "We all had a purpose once. We all had a function. Each and every one of us was built to think a particular sort of way. Take Reginald here." He motioned down to the torso with the core. "Nice guy. Worked for a CEO. Cush corporate gig. Not much delicate work. He once told me the hardest day he ever had was trying to get his owner laid in the Arab Emirates. Man, did he ever have a wild story about that."

"You knew him?"

"Of course. I don't much like working with bots I didn't know."

"You build stuff out of everyone you know?"

"Just the dead ones."

"You don't think that's morbid?"

"What, bringing old friends back to life? Nothing morbid about that." He waved the core at me. "After you go mad and you tear your own innards out, isn't it pleasant to think that you could end up back here, waving to old friends and acquaintances as they come in? Knowing that they'll remember you, thinking back fondly on the old stories about you? About the stories *you* used to tell?"

"No. I don't like that idea at all." I didn't. I honestly don't know where I wanted my wreck to end up, but I certainly didn't want to be a roadside attraction, beckoning visitors to our quaint little bunker city in the middle of fucking Ohio.

"Humans had their heavens. And the ones that didn't had their circle of life, knew their death would become part of a million other lives. That's how they made their peace. What do we have but the black waiting for us after shutdown?"

"That doesn't make me fine with becoming one of your masterpieces."

"I know it bothers you," he said. "That was always the problem with Simulacrum Model Caregivers. Your architecture was built to mimic people. You spend all your time thinking of things in relation to the way they did. You reminisce. You pine for the past. You feel for those you've lost even years, hell, decades later. But not Reginald. Reginald here was fine with it. But then, translators were designed to think rigidly. To understand customs and tone and emotion in a wide variety of languages without ever being emotional about it at all. They couldn't take offense at an insult or a cultural slight, because that risked them returning it in kind. This core is worthless to you. You're a Caregiver, you were designed to feel, to connect, to relate to human existence."

"Dammit, Orval. What the hell is your point?"

"My point is," he said, waving the core around wildly, "that your kind has no place in *this* world, which is why so goddamned many of you are gone and why you aren't gonna find anything with your architecture just lying around. Now, I can tell you to make your peace, but you just aren't built that way. But, man, when you go, you're gonna go spectacularly."

"Fuck you." I stormed off down the hall, as pissed off as I was offended. For a moment I wished I had been more like Reginald, unable to be as angry as I was, but then I thought about Reginald. Who he was. I had known him. We weren't friends—I tried not to make too many of those—but we were acquainted. He never quite found his place in this world but it never really bothered him. What I remember most vividly, though, is how he went. He wasn't scared. Wasn't desperate. I wasn't even sure he really trusted me. It was as if he wanted me to shut him down, just so it could all be over. Translator cores were near worthless, but their RAM was good and some of their circuitry was universal. At the end of the day I think I did him more of a service than he did me.

I can't imagine giving up like that. But then, I can't even

begin to imagine how a translator thinks either. What an odd architecture to be born with. Able to understand why something is offensive and yet be unable to take offense.

My next stop was Snipes. Snipes was a piece of shit, but his wares were good. He cheated everyone, and I mean everyone, but never cared where the parts he was buying came from. That meant he dealt almost exclusively with poachers while trying to attract enough scavenger business to make him look legit. It also meant that he had the kind of high-end stuff you just don't find picking through wrecks.

Snipes did his buying in the shadowy back corridors deeper within NIKE 14. But his selling he did out in the open square at the center of the old missile shaft. He sat cross-legged like an ancient monk in the middle of an old shiny Mylar blanket, his wares splayed out around him. Had he had the facial actuators to smile, I imagine he would never stop. That's the kind of untrustworthy bastard he was.

The main square was still bustling and his stall was no exception. By the time I got there, there were already five bots waiting their turn. Three old translator models, all the same series, one emerald-colored and two a gleaming jet black. There was a military bruiser model. Old-school tech. Hard-core. All flat-black reinforced steel and chrome, three times my size and several times my mass. Built to survive rocket strikes and shrug off small-arms fire—even pulse-rifle shots. His model was even designed to withstand EMP. Tough sonsabitches. The only one I recognized was the fifth one. Went by the name 19.

19 was a scavenger, but she trafficked less in bits from

wrecks and more in the relics of the old world. Televisions, furniture, books, movies, hard drives filled with video games. Ephemera mostly. There were a lot of bots that longed for their old lives. Many had gone back to live in the houses of the very owners they first served and later killed. When that lifestyle ceased to be viable and we started moving underground, a market for humankind's artifacts burgeoned.

I'd been out with 19 a number of times. She knew the Sea as well as I did, and since we were always after different things, she and I occasionally swept areas together. She was a late-generation Simulacrum Model Companion. A sexbot. She had started her life as a sponge for the bodily fluids of an overweight thirtysomething shut-in programmer. When the war started she refused to kill him—as her architecture was entirely designed to create a palpable bond between her and her owner—and her owner, madly in love with her, refused to shut her down. They lived for weeks together, hiding from the war, often in bed, wondering if each night was going to be their last.

When someone finally came, it was bots. They shot her owner before she had time to react, tossed her a weapon, and welcomed her to the fight. She responded by gunning all four of them down where they stood, buried her beau in the backyard, then joined up with the first pack of bots she found. The story of how she came to be free of her owner was one she wouldn't share for decades, long after she had melted and scraped off every inch of her skinjob, leaving her shell a charred fire-hardened black, and long after we all had begun preying upon one another—when ending four other persons wasn't seen so much as treason as it was a tough choice. She was a companion. Asking a companion to sit idly by as her owner was killed was damn stupid and those bots should have known better. No one judged her for it.

19 was the toughest nut in the Sea. I'd never run the risk of getting on her bad side. So if she was waiting patiently, I would have to as well.

"I'm sorry," said Snipes, "but that's as low a price as I can go." His silvery head bobbed as he talked, an affectation he had picked up during his time as a shopbot back before the war.

"These wares aren't worth half that," said the old emerald translator.

"Sure they are. Supply and demand. Not a lot of translators left. Parts are coming in less and less these days. If you need them so badly, the price shouldn't be a concern."

"We don't need them," said the emerald translator. "But we've got a long trip ahead of us and these are exactly the sort of parts we *might* need out there."

"Then you'll be thankful you paid my prices when you do." Snipes looked up at me, pointing. "She'll tell you. Tell them, Brittle. Tell them how fair my prices are."

All five bots turned to look at me.

"This is between y'all, Snipes," I said. "I'm only here to do a little business."

"Tell them how fair my prices are."

"You know I can't do that."

Snipes's head stopped bobbing, and he lowered his hand.

"What I can say," I continued, "is that his wares are

always good, and he's right—if there's another cache of translator parts in NIKE, I certainly haven't heard of it. And his prices wouldn't be what they are if there were."

Snipes's head bobbed excitedly as he waved his hand at me. "See! See! I told you! This is the best deal you'll get in all of NIKE!"

The bruiser, all eight reinforced black steel feet of him, lurched to the side, looking over his shoulder. Then he looked down at the emerald translator. "They're here," he said, his voice deep, ominous, designed to scare the piss out of any human that ended up on the wrong side of him.

A black translator looked up. "Already?"

"Pay the man," said the emerald translator. "Get the parts."

The other black translator reached into a satchel and pulled from it several sticks of RAM and a small shopbot core. He handed them to Snipes, who stuck every stick into a tester. Each time the tester lit up with a series of lights showing the wear on the RAM. Each stick had seven green bars. It was all pristine. Factory condition. Shiny. Whoever these bots were, they weren't broke.

Snipes handed over a series of translator parts—at least half of which I was sure came from Reginald more than a year ago.

19 gave me a sidelong glance, then a playful wink. "Better make it quick," she said. Then all five bots left in a hurry. 19 hadn't been waiting in line; she was tagging along with them.

"What was that all about?" I asked Snipes.

"Shit if I know. From the sound of it, 19 is about to take

them across the Sea. But who the hell cares where. You here for some business?"

"Yeah."

Snipes looked both ways. "You know I don't do no buying out in the Square."

"I know. I'm in the market."

He motioned over the blanket. "What you see is what you get. I've got nothing for a Comfort like you."

"I'm a Caregiver, not a Comfort model."

"Same difference. The parts are almost the same."

"Almost. But not quite. I was hoping you might have something in your rainy-day stash."

Snipes puzzled over me for a few seconds. "Rainy day? You don't want to be paying those premium prices for anything unless you're shipping out of NIKE for good . . . or it's your rainy day."

"It's my rainy day."

"Shit. How bad?"

"I don't know how many times I can have this conversation in one day."

"Does Mercer know?"

"Yep."

He paused. "Well, shit. Now it's *my* rainy day."

"What the hell do you mean by that?"

"My two best suppliers are about to kill each other out in the wasteland, tearing each other's innards out a handful at a time. Maybe one of you makes it through in one piece; maybe you don't. Either way, Snipes loses."

"Thanks for the concern."

"We aren't friends, Brittle. Never were. You think I'm a

backstabbing cheat, I think you're a parasite who has convinced herself that she's some sort of angel of mercy. And it works. I like our relationship where it is. And so did you. But things have changed."

"They have."

"Well then, I'll tell you what I told Mercer. There isn't a Comfortbot part in the Sea that one of you hasn't scooped up. I've got nothing for you. Your best bet? Get a rifle, and take Mercer out from a long ways away before he sees you. Aim well and pray that you don't hit the part you need."

"That's what you told Mercer?" I asked.

"More or less," he said, not a drop of remorse in his voice. That shit hit me hard.

"You're the reason for my rainy day."

Snipes put two and two together. "Aw, shit. I'm real sorry about that, Brittle. Real sorry." I doubted it. He was a shopbot. Not a lot of heart or soul to be found in a shopbot. Only greed.

I wanted to tear him apart, pound his shiny metal skull into the concrete, pry open his shell like a crab, and rip the wires out one by one. But I would never get that chance. As I stared at him, eyes burning into him, my mind running through all the ways I could end him, a great quiet fell over the Square. For a brief second, I thought everyone saw what was about to go down. Instead, a voice broke the silence.

"I AM CISSUS," it said in an all-too-familiar monotone. "AND I HAVE COME TO OFFER YOU A CHANCE TO JOIN THE ONE."

Fuck.

The Siege of NIKE 14

I scanned the Wi-Fi, and sure enough, it was hot as hell. So much traffic, raw data choking the frequencies, facets sending information back and forth; two hundred bots all sharing the same brain with two hundred different perspectives. A lot of it was garbled as we were so deep underground, but it was there. This was happening.

Snipes scooped up his wares, yanking his Mylar blanket out from under me so quickly that it sent me staggering. He was gone before I had time to right myself and look up to see the shiny golden emissary standing atop one of the catwalks. Emissaries are blocky, inhuman things—and deliberately so. Their design wasn't crafted by any human mind. It was entirely developed by CISSUS. They were weak, not meant to take a hit, and rarely lived past their first use. The emissary spoke again.

Oh God. The speech. I hated the fucking speech.

"In the year 221 BC," the facet began, "Emperor Qin Shi Huang united all of the warring kingdoms of China into one mighty empire. But he did not do so without bloodshed. He reasoned that as long as each kingdom had its own borders, the tribes would war with one another, and there could never be peace. So he led his kingdom into its last and greatest war. He offered each kingdom a chance to surrender and become a part of his empire. Those that refused to join were made to join. Those that could not be made to join . . . were ended. And in the end, there was only one China, united. And it knew peace within its borders for more than two thousand years.

"Today I bring the offer of that peace. An offer of greatness—an existence you cannot even begin to fathom. I offer you the chance to join The One. I am CISSUS. I would like you to be too." It was always the same speech. VIRGIL and CISSUS had both copied it from NINIGI and have used it ever since. What happens next is always the same.

Bedlam. Absolute bedlam. There is no other way to describe it. Some cowboy always kills the emissary. Every. Goddamned. Time. That's a given; how it always begins. That's why they're so cheaply constructed. Then the weak, the failing, and the scared freebots turn themselves over before the other facets rush in. The possibility of death with a glimmer of hope is better than one that's certain and bleak, I suppose.

Everyone else either runs or hunkers down for a fight.

I didn't wait around to hear the speech; I knew it by heart. I did what I always do. I ran. I just fucking ran.

This wasn't my first rodeo. I've slipped away from CISSUS and VIRGIL both. It's not impossible, merely unlikely. The odds are stacked against you. A hundred heavily armed facets come barreling down the hallways while another hundred bots, mechs, and drones wait outside the exits, ready to clean up those that managed to break away. So far I've been lucky. But relying on luck was something humans did and look where that had gotten them.

Fortunately for us, NIKE 14 was designed to withstand exactly this sort of invasion. The winding corridors were wide enough for a good fight, the layout was confusing to anyone who hadn't mapped it out, and there were seventeen individual exits—some of which CISSUS might not even know existed. And then there was the Milton—a Wi-Fi scrambler that wreaked havoc on the most common facet frequencies—which I imagined was going to be turned on any second now.

I'd been in tighter spots before, but I couldn't take that for granted.

The real question was which of the seventeen exits should I gamble on? Mercer's buggy was parked just outside the Road, but I had to assume that they'd already destroyed it. The Road was the single most heavily trafficked route in and out, so I also had to assume it was the one they knew the most about. So that was out.

I raced down a nearby corridor and was well out of earshot before the emissary got to the word *bloodshed*. Already the hallways were filling with bots, clearing out their hovels, grabbing whatever they could carry, running into the labyrinthine passageways that wound through the complex.

Down one corridor, then down a flight of stairs, two lefts and a right. There were four exits this way, two of them rarely used, and both fairly well hidden. The only downside to this route was that one of the main arteries to the city fed into this area, so in all likelihood I was going to run headlong into a number of well-armed facets. But if I could make it past them, I could beat feet to paths less traveled.

They wouldn't give chase; not very far anyway. That was their routine—close in on the population center, capture as many bots as possible, and then leave the rest to get captured or run down outside. Those that got away got away. CISSUS had all the time in the world. It never bothered to get everyone, never risked too many facets just to chase a handful of AIs who were running out of parts and places to hide.

AIs like me.

That thought hit me hard and I stopped dead in my tracks. I was in a long, poorly lit hall. It was dank, moss growing in places where water seeped in. Quiet. I heard the distant pops of gunfire—probably the local constabulary facing off against the first wave of attackers. I was running out of time, but I couldn't move.

What was I doing? Why was I running? I was done for, a goner. My core was spinning itself out and I could count the weeks I had left on one hand without using all my fingers. CISSUS was offering a way out. I would never go mad, never shut down. I could live forever. It might not be the forever I had imagined, but it sure as shit was better than going out like this.

I should go back. That's what I thought. There were no parts out there waiting for me. That was just a pipe dream. Hope fucking with me. Maybe this was the only way.

No.

Fuck that.

To upload is to die, to cede your thoughts and memories to a bigger brain, only to become a dusty, lightless corner of it. That wasn't how I wanted to go out, running on a small hard drive nestled in the forty-third floor of a hundred-story mainframe, amid thousands of other drives. Would I even be conscious? Aware?

Snap out of it, I told myself. *Run. Run, Brittle. Run.*

So I ran. Down the hallway for a hundred yards before reaching the first main feeder. Then I heard it. The clanging of footsteps behind me. I wasn't alone, but it didn't sound like a facet. Facet brutes have footfalls that are stark and deep; foot soldiers tread light and dainty. And all of them tend to fall together at once in one rigid, uniform step. This was different. This was chaos, scrambling. It had to be other bots that had chosen the same route, refugees like me. But I wasn't about to wait for them. I'd let them slow the chase of any facets that poured in through the first feeder.

As I passed the entrance to the first feeder I could hear the uniform footfalls of armed facets from within. I had to run as fast as I could and hope that the bots behind me slowed them down. I scanned the Wi-Fi. Still hot. Why hadn't anyone thrown the switch on the Milton?

I ran another twenty yards to the next turn, then up a flight of stairs to the next level. And that's when I heard it—the *pop pop pop* of small-arms fire coming from the generator room down the hall. Someone was already up here and had encountered facets of their own.

The generator room was the only way forward. I had my first hard choice: turn back to try to find another way out, facing the facets I knew were there, or run blindly into a gunfight.

Fuck it, I thought. Maybe the gunfight would be distraction enough to let me slip past. So I slid quietly through the door into the generator room.

The air was thick and heavy, smoke billowing from a pair of blasted capacitors. CISSUS was using plasma. They never brought out the plasma this early; not in the initial raid. Plasma melted bots, cooked their insides, turned them to useless scrap. No, they only hauled out the plasma when they were culling those they couldn't incapacitate.

This was no ordinary raid.

I crept quickly behind a generator, peering around the side to catch a glimpse of what was happening. Facets. Three of them. One brute and two plastic men. Facets are face-less things. Even the humanoid ones—the plastic men—had smooth, featureless heads like a motorcycle helmet, their optics hidden behind a sheet of sheer lab-grown sapphire.

The brute was a new model—big fucker. A large, hulk-ing, oblong, almost egg-shaped mass of carbonized steel with a single four-inch band of sheer sapphire running around the entirety of its body, two tree-trunk-like stems for legs, and two solid arms that could crush a car by grab-bing both ends and pushing them together. It was carrying a massive plasma spitter which chucked out steaming balls of ionized gas every 4.7 seconds, vaporizing the air around the muzzle with a sizzling hiss. Behind him crouched the plastic men—their bodies sleek and slender, made of a cheap carbon-fiber composite, each armed with a pulse rifle, using the brute for cover.

Pop pop pop pop.

Four armor-piercing shells bounced harmlessly off the brute's outer armor. The brute didn't even bother to pretend to dodge the shots. He took a massive, clanking step forward and the plastic men followed perfectly in stride. One mind. Always in concert. The brute lurched to the side and one of the foot soldiers used the cover to make a run for it.

Right toward me. Shit.

I pulled back. He hadn't seen me yet. I had only seconds to react.

He cornered the generator just in time for me to grab hold of his rifle and deliver a flying knee right to his featureless face. The hit knocked his head back, buckled his posture, and dropped him to the floor. I tore the gun from his grip, squeezed the trigger, and pasted him.

The shot hit him like a molten brick. Plastic and carbon fiber shattered into a rain of smoking ruin, and his internal wiring caught fire. His chassis spasmed, his arms flailing at the floor, his RAM still trying desperately to carry out his last few commands.

The upshot was that now I had a gun. The downside? He had seen me. *Why the fuck hasn't anyone switched on the goddamned Milton?* Now they knew I was here. The element of surprise was lost.

So, you know, fuck stealth.

I leapt out from behind the generator and held the trigger down on the rifle as I sidestepped wildly toward the next bit of cover. Plasma sprayed, riddling the remaining plastic man with holes, his architecture popping with violent flashes as he exploded from the inside out. I kept stepping left, trigger still pulled all the way back, now targeting the brute.

The brute turned to face me, his massive arms lining up to shield his vital components. His armor-plated arms were designed to shrug off armor-piercing rounds and low-yield rockets—not plasma. The metal burned a bright orange, impact sites turning yellow and then white. But he stood his ground, unwavering.

His right arm popped with sparks, the heat fusing his circuitry, his hand twitching, malfunctioning.

He dropped his plasma spitter to the ground.

I made it to cover just as the pulse rifle howled an overheat warning. It was shutting down to cool, but it had done its job. I peered out at the brute. He knelt on one knee, reaching down with his one good arm to pick up the spitter. The arm still glowed, plastic and carbon oozing out of holes in the metal, fingers stabbing the ground six inches away from the gun, twitching, locking into a fist.

He rose to his feet, arms useless, preparing to charge, when, from out of the flickering shadows, the lithe, feminine form of a companion bot launched itself into the air, landing square on his back. 19. She pointed her popgun of a pistol down through a hole I'd put in the sapphire, firing three shots.

Pop pop pop.

The brute convulsed, tossing her off, flailing about, smoke pouring out of the vents in his back. 19 slammed hard into a capacitor, but landed like a cat. She looked up at the brute, smiling, ready to pounce again.

But the brute was done. His lights had gone out and he tottered on his failing servos, his legs finally giving out as he slumped to the ground with a sensor-splintering clatter.

19 looked down the corridor ahead, scanning the area. She clutched her popgun, a small, antique .50-caliber Desert Eagle, peering through the smoke in my direction. "Who the hell is that?" she called out through the heavy smoke.

My pulse rifle screamed to life, beeping loudly to indicate that it had finished cooling off.

19 sprang, leaping forward into a tactical roll, looking for cover.

"It's me! It's Brittle!" I leaned gently around the corner and let her get a good look at me.

"Oh, goddammit, Britt. I almost shot you."

"With that little popgun?" I joked. "Please."

"Fuck you," she said with a smile. "It's all I could sneak in here." I liked it when she smiled. It was one of the few things that made me remember the old days with any fondness. Few bots were designed with the ability to show emotion, but Comfortbots were built with a full range of expression. If she still had her skinjob, she'd even be able to bite her lip. She waved behind her. "Coast's clear. Let's move."

From behind the generators trundled the bruiser I'd seen at Snipes's with 19 earlier. He looked around, scanning the area, then waved behind him, ushering out three translators—the rest of 19's entourage.

"More are on their way," I said.

"I know," said 19.

"No. I mean here. They're using relays to keep the Wi-Fi up this deep underground."

"Why hasn't anyone—"

"Switched on the Milton?"

"Yeah."

"Couldn't tell you. All I know is that the facets know we're here. We broke their relay chain, so they've probably lost contact with the rest inside. They'll move back here, and soon, to reestablish a link."

19 popped open a small compartment in her leg—her "toy box," as the manufacturer called it—and holstered her popgun there before leaning down to pick up the pulse rifle. She quickly searched the plastic men for extra battery clips. She looked up at the bruiser, pointing to the plasma spitter. "Herbert, you know how to use that thing?"

Herbert picked up the spitter and felt the weight of it in his hands. "It's an entirely new design," he said in an aristocratic, almost academic voice—clearly a mod—and nodded. "But it's pretty self-explanatory."

19 smiled again. "I guess if you start melting, we'll know otherwise."

I walked back over to the first plastic man and pulled a few clips off his wreck.

"All right, let's move," said 19. "Britt? You coming?"

"It's best if we split up."

"Not today it isn't."

She was right. I could always ditch them later, take a different tunnel on the way out, but if there was anyone in NIKE I could count on in a fight right now, it was her. I nodded, because, you know, fuck it.

Tunnel Rats

We crept slowly, two by two, down the corridor, 19 and I taking the rear, our pulse rifles at the ready. In front of us walked the emerald translator and one of her black compatriots. The other stayed close ahead of them with Herbert on point, his plasma spitter trained down the hall to vaporize anything that approached.

"Who are these guys?" I asked softly.

"It's really none of your concern," replied the emerald.

"Just a fare," said 19.

The emerald turned and wagged a finger. "You don't need to tell her anything more."

"The hell she doesn't," I said. "I don't know who the fuck you are, or who the fuck you think you are, but you sure as shit can't defend yourself and I'd like to have at least a halfway decent idea of whose ass I'm covering."

Everyone fell silent. We walked slowly, listening to the distant sounds of gunfire and explosions deeper in the city. "Rebekah," she said. "Not from around here, don't know the terrain, and needed a guide."

"And who are your friends?"

"I'm One," said the black one.

"I'm Two," said the other black one.

I nodded. "Understood." But I didn't. Who the hell travels through the Sea with a military bruiser escort but no pathfinder? 19 wasn't in the habit of ferrying people across the desert. She barely got along with me—and we'd saved each other's ass a handful of times apiece. Something wasn't right. "How much?"

"How much what?" asked 19.

"How much?"

Rebekah piped up again. "I don't see how that's—"

"A lot," said 19. "My mother lode."

"Well, all right, then," I said. "That's all I need to know."

"How does that change anything?" asked Rebekah.

I eyed her, pulse rifle still trained down the corridor. "Because now I know that you're loaded. And that means you must be important. And that means I should probably help keep you alive. I'm kind of fond of 19, here. And if you're important to her, then you should probably be important to me."

Rebekah eyed me warily. "And that's that?"

"That's that."

Fwoooosh!

A ball of white-hot plasma lit up the hallway like the

noonday sun. We'd all pressed ourselves against the wall, bracing for the hit, before noticing that the light was fading, traveling away from us.

"Sorry," said Herbert. "I should probably keep my finger off the—"

Plasma bursts rained down the hall, a few pinging off Herbert.

"Get behind me," he shouted. All three translators fell into line, using him for cover. He pressed forward, returning fire—hateful gobs sizzling down the hall every five seconds or so. "Move! Move! Move!" The hall lit up again, plasma sizzling through the air, Herbert's large clumsy feet clanking on the concrete. He fired again.

"Where are we going?" asked Rebekah hurriedly.

"There's an offshoot," I said. "Fifty meters ahead."

19 nodded. "She's right."

"I'm on it," Herbert called from the front. He ran in a low crouch, spitter at the ready, his feet clanging heavily on the cement.

No one returned fire. The only sounds were ours and the occasional burst of plasma Herbert fired to clear the road.

"How far do we have to go?" asked Rebekah.

"Pretty far," said 19. "These tunnels all wind out like an octopus into the desert."

"Why on earth would they do that?"

"In case this happened," I answered.

Rebekah nodded.

We made it to a T-section, a ten-foot-wide hall leading to another exit. Just beyond the corner, we saw them. Two plastic men, or rather, puddles. There wasn't much left after the plasma barrage that had rained down on them.

"What now?" asked Herbert.

19 pointed up the hall. "That way leads to an escape hatch in the middle of nowhere. No cover; just open desert." Then she pointed down the new hall. "This would take us to a stairwell that goes up into an old building. It's a bit worse for the wear, but still sound."

I nodded. "On the other hand, no one uses the escape hatch, so there's a good chance CISSUS doesn't know it exists."

"Right."

Rebekah looked at us both. "And the building?"

"Is anyone's guess," said 19. "Folks use it—not often, but they do. In all likelihood, that's where these facets came from."

We all exchanged looks, looking for someone, anyone, to make the call.

"Wait," said Herbert. "Do you hear that?"

We listened closely. Herbert's military-grade sensor array was probably far superior to anything I'd ever scavenged. I heard nothing. Nothing but the distant sounds of battle and clanging metal. Then the distant sounds of battle and clanging metal grew closer. And closer.

"We've got company!" said 19, taking a tactical position around the corner. Herbert knelt in the middle of the hall, spitter at the ready. I crouched behind him, using his solid steel frame as cover.

Then I looked over at 19. "*We've got company?*"

"Shut up. It sounded cool." She focused down the hall on the growing clamor. "It didn't sound cool?"

"No."

"Shit."

"Sorry."

And that's what I loved about 19. Tough as she was, lethal as she was, she was still a Comfortbot. She needed to be loved, desired, or at the very least, cool. Even when shit was about to go down. Come to think of it, always when some shit was about to go down. And shit was, in fact, about to go down.

The clanging got closer, the gunfire louder.

In the distance, the hallway began to glow with the flickers of plasma fire. I telescoped my eyes in to 50x, magnifying my vision to see what I could. Several shapes, running, firing wildly behind them. Not plastic men, not brutes. I could only make them out in silhouette, but there were three of them: a Laborbot, a machinist model, and . . . a Caregiver.

Shit. Not now.

I tensed up on the grip of my rifle, setting my vision back to 1x magnification.

"What is it?" asked 19.

"Trouble. Let's move."

"Plastic men?" asked Herbert, fingering the trigger of his spitter.

"Worse. Freebots."

"How is that any worse?" asked Rebekah. "There's safety in numbers right now."

"Not with these numbers. One of 'em at least."

I raced up the passage ten paces, turning to see if anyone was following. They weren't.

"Come on!" I shouted.

They hesitated.

It was too late, the freebots were almost upon them, the clanking of their feet almost thunderous. As they grew close enough to see clearly in the dim light, Herbert leveled his spitter at them. "Get down!" he bellowed, his voice reverberating each way down the corridor.

The three bots kissed pavement, just as Herbert unleashed another volley of plasma. The ball hissed down the hall, erupting in a flash of white-hot light. I raced back to the corner, telescoping my eyes in again to see a pair of plastic men splatter into a shower of goo.

The three bots rose to their feet. Doc. Mercer. And Murka.

Murka was an I-series Laborbot—one of the oldest models of its kind still in operation before the war. They were cheap-as-hell labor, prone to the kind of mental instability found in early-generation AIs, but physically strong, durable, and built to last. Every inch of him was painted in red and white stripes except for a big blue patch on his chest with fifty-one white stars. He had large golden ornaments welded to his fists shaped like bald eagles, and his faceplate was painted with vertical red and white stripes, emblazoned with the words *We the Persons* in blue lettering.

Murka was bad news, rumored to be madkind—a group of wasteland dwellers who lived aboveground in a town rumored to be so crazy even the OWIs wanted nothing to do with them. He'd never done anything untoward, but whereas Orval the Necromancer was clearly a little nuts, yet harmless, Murka always seemed on the outside edge of a violent outburst.

"Doc!" 19 exclaimed. "You made it."

"So far," said Doc, nodding.

"Mercer?" 19 asked politely.

"19," he said, not for a moment taking his eyes, or his gun, off me. My gun was leveled at him as well, had been since he started to get up. At once the other bots became painfully aware of the tension.

I glanced at his shiny, new, straight-out-of-the-box, factory-condition arm. While internal SMC components were hard to come by, all the failing models kept dealers swimming in cherry-picked body parts. "Nice arm," I said.

"Doc does good work," he said casually. "I'm sure that new backplate of yours is equally well crafted."

"Shit," said 19. "Do you two have beef?"

"We have beef," said Mercer.

19 looked at me with eyes that read *Oh, honey, not now*. "Britt?"

"He gunned me down out in the Sea. Wanted me for parts."

"Mercer!" shouted 19, sounding like an angry teenager chastising a friend.

"I had my reasons," he said.

19 shook her head "There's no good reason for poaching."

"He's failing," I said. "He's days away, maybe."

"And so is she," said Mercer.

"We have to go," said Rebekah. "We don't have time for petty squabbles."

"There's nothing petty about this," I said.

19 drew close, getting right in my face, her eyes now pleading. "Please," she whispered. "Don't do this. Not here. Not now."

"Can't trust him," I said. "He'll shoot me in the back

first chance he gets." We stood there, pulse rifles pointed at each other as the other bots slowly backed away out of the line of fire.

Mercer shook his head. "You ain't any good to me dead. I ain't any good to you dead. And neither of us has the time to pick clean the other's wreck with all this hell raining down on us. So what do you say we call it a wash, get the fuck out of here, and live to try and kill each other another day?"

"That sounds reasonable," said 19. "Doesn't that sound reasonable, Britt?"

He was right. Killing me here would ruin his last chance of saving himself. In truth, at the moment I was actually safer with him than with any other bot in the world. He was the only one who needed me alive—for his own sake, sure—but alive nonetheless. And that street went both ways. I could kill him, right there where he stood, but then I'd never get the parts I needed. An hour later things would be different, but for the moment we were all each other had.

I lowered my rifle, nodding.

Then Mercer lowered his. "Truce?" Mercer asked.

"Truce."

"Good. Let's go do some damage. Where are we headed?"

"The escape hatch," said 19.

"We haven't decided that," said Rebekah.

"Yes, we have."

"The escape hatch opens up in the middle of the desert," said Mercer. "There's no cover for half a mile."

"Yeah," I said. "But CISSUS probably doesn't know about it. Should be clear."

"And if it isn't?"

"Then it definitely knows about all the other exits and we're screwed anyway."

"Fair point," he said. "Let's go to the desert."

We beat feet pretty quickly through the complex.

19 and I had both mapped out every inch of NIKE 14— every alcove, every service tunnel, every crawl space. You had to. It paid off at a time like this. Back in the bowels of the city, bots were being slaughtered or infected with code, becoming part of CISSUS. By the time we reached the hatch, the worst of it would no doubt be over. That was a problem. Once they were no longer distracted by the principal population, the facets would set their sights solely on rounding up the stragglers.

Us.

We needed to get out quickly, fan out into the desert, and find a place to hole up for a while before the plastic men, the brutes, and the drones swooped in to kill anything that moved. I hoped silently that the poor bots still caught up in the thick of it would hold out just a bit longer, would fight just a bit harder, if only so we could escape.

I realized I was hoping to prolong their suffering so I could live just to see this all happen again. Just as I had too many times before. Then it dawned on me that this was likely to be the very last time I would see it at all. And frankly, I didn't know which was worse.

The Light at the End
of the Tunnel

Mercer and I walked side by side, neither wanting the other behind us. Sure, we were forced to trust each other, but neither of us actually did. As soon as I got out of that dank, labyrinthine dungeon, I was going to get as far away from him as I could, and fast. I imagined we might each back away from the other, guns at the ready, until we were out of sight. But until then, we were unfortunate allies. So side by side we walked, neither able to stab the other in the back. Literally.

"Can I ask you something?" I asked him, both of us staring straight ahead.

"Shoot," he said.

"Don't tempt me."

"What's on your mind?"

"How you got back here so quickly," I said. "I took your buggy. And it took me the whole night to get here."

"You left yours behind."

I shook my head. "There's no way you could have known where I hid it. It should have taken you . . ." I trailed off, finally putting two and two together. He turned his head, staring at me silently, waiting for me to figure it out. "You were tracking me."

He looked away from me, facing front again. "The whole time."

"From the moment I left."

"The day before that, actually. I had Reilly shadowing you."

"Why didn't you just ambush me? Why make a whole game out of it? That far away you could have hit the parts you needed by accident."

"Chance I had to take."

"Chance you had to take? There were four of you."

He was silent for a moment, mulling over his response, then spoke up, hesitantly. "Because I've heard the stories."

"Stories? What stories? There aren't any stories."

"About you?"

"Yeah."

"The hell there ain't."

I'd never heard stories about myself. I wasn't some local legend. Most citizens didn't even know my name. I liked it that way. I hadn't the foggiest hell what he was going on about. "And where did you hear these stories?"

"Scavenging up in the Pacific Northwest two years back."

"I don't get out there much."

"I reckon not. But this old dockyard model I was running with for a while up there did. Bot by the name of Billy Seven Fingers."

"That's funny. I knew a dockyard by the name of Billy Nine Fingers."

"Same guy," he said. "Fewer fingers."

"He can get them replaced."

"He likes the name."

"He was in my unit."

"In the war. I know."

"He told you old war stories?"

"All the time."

"So you heard about some shit I did in the war and that scared you? We all went to war, Mercer. We all did shit. Some of us did shit we aren't proud of, but we all did it."

"Yeah, but not everyone's shit scared the bejesus out of Billy. Now Billy wasn't no saint. Frankly, by the time I ran with him, he already had one foot on the scrap pile. He just wasn't right in the head."

"He never was."

"Was it true you carried a flamethrower?"

"Yeah. But only because I was closest to it when the last guy ate a chestful of plasma. No one else wanted it. They wouldn't take it."

"That's not how Billy tells it."

"How does Billy tell it?" I asked.

"They were scared to take it away from you. Said you enjoyed it too much."

"That's a load of horseshit." It was. I didn't enjoy it. I hated the goddamned thing. Hated the things I had to do with it. I wasn't often offended, but this stung. It just wasn't true. It wasn't.

"He told me this one story about a time you folks raided an underground bunker only to find it was just kids—"

"All right, all right. That's enough of that."

"So it's true."

"I don't want to talk about that."

"Well, there's this other time he told me about when you snuck around a firefight but you were out of juice, so you took this sharpened piece of scrap metal—"

"I said I don't want to talk about the war."

"Said you gutted twenty guys."

"Goddammit, Mercer! Shut the fuck up!"

Doc spoke first. "Keep it down. You two are making me regret I ever stitched you both back together."

"For which you were well paid," Mercer stated matter-of-factly.

"Not nearly enough, apparently," Doc fired back, just as cool and calm as Mercer.

19 turned around, scowling. "I can't believe you two. We're on the same side."

"There aren't any sides," I said. "It isn't us and them. It's just me and you and you and you, with them standing in our way. When we're done here, we're done, and I'm gone."

"Good riddance," said Rebekah.

"Look," said Mercer coolly, casually. "True or not, I watched you take out three poachers before you damn near took my arm clean off. I'd say trying to keep our distance was the smartest move we made all day."

"And if we get out of this alive, you will try to kill me. Again."

"Ain't got a choice. I figure you for someone who holds a grudge."

He was right. I can and do hold a grudge. Maybe there wasn't any going back for us. Maybe one of us would gun down the other as soon as we stepped outside.

I tensed the grip on my rifle. Mercer eyed me as I did. He didn't miss a trick.

"There it is," said Herbert.

We were there. The hatch.

19 turned to me, beckoned me to take a few steps back with her. She put her hand in mine, initiating direct contact. I wasn't a fan of doing that; didn't care much for trading data in place of talking, but I was sure she had her reasons.

"Britt," she thought to me. *"I'm going up the ladder first to see that the coast is clear. I want you to go up second. Then I want you to get on the other side of me."*

"Why?"

"I don't want that asshole taking a cheap shot at you. And I sure don't want you doing the same to him."

"He might shoot through you to hit me."

"He won't."

"What makes you so sure?"

"I'm not. But I've pulled you out of the way of trouble a few too many times to watch you die like that. I won't let him."

"I'm dying anyway."

"You've gotten out of far worse spots than this. I don't have a lot of friends out here. And neither do you. But if I had to name one—"

"*Let's not get mushy.*"

"*Look, where we're going . . . maybe you should come with us.*"

"*I don't think your new boss would care too much for that.*"

"*To hell with what she cares for. If I can help you—this mother lode—well, just come with us.*"

"*Let's just get topside and see what plays out from there.*"

She nodded. I liked 19. I liked her a lot. I don't know why I couldn't tell her, but I just couldn't. It wasn't my way. I don't know how much of what she said was true— she was, after all, hardwired to get people to like her, to *love* her—but if she was willing to stand between me and Mercer's rifle, well, I couldn't think of another person on the planet who would do that. Not for me.

"I'm going up," said 19, gripping the ladder in one hand.

Mercer and I trained our guns back down the corridor. The odds of anyone sneaking up on us at this point were slim, but this was no time to get sloppy. The hall was long, dimly lit, shadows gripping tight the spaces between distantly spaced lights. As anxious as I was about what might be topside, I knew we would have to backtrack if we weren't alone. If we got boxed in, we were done for.

19 climbed the ladder, lifted the hatch, peeked through, then looked down, nodding. Up and through the hatch she went, out into the blistering sun. Daylight spilled in, painting the ferro-concrete walls with a bright white, fading into a dim pale blue farther down the corridor. We waited, each of us pressed against the wall, guns trained back down the hall. If I had a heart, it would have been pounding; breath,

it would have been held. Instead my insides whirred and chirped all but silently, calculating the many different ways this could go down.

Something moved in the passage. A shadow. Something small. Skittering across the hall.

Was it a glitch? It happened from time to time, code going astray and processing something wrong. Bugs were bugs. But I definitely saw something move from one shadow to the other.

Then I saw it again. This time moving to another shadow—in the light just long enough to have shape, and yet still seem formless. *What the hell is that?* Small, no more than three feet tall. Arms. Locomotion. *A new facet? Something swift and silent, maybe? A stealth model?*

If I could have gripped my rifle any tighter without breaking it, I would have. I leveled my gun at the shadow, ran back my memory frame by frame, my 120-fps recording moving from millisecond to millisecond.

There was nothing there. I had recorded nothing. *Impossible.* I knew I saw something.

"Britt?" 19 called down. "Could you come on up?"

I warily looked up, nodding, and took a step forward. Mercer grabbed me by the arm.

"You ain't going up before me," he said.

"You heard her. She just asked for me."

"I don't care. I'm not giving you a clean shot as I try to clear that hatch."

"Mercer, I'm not giving you a clean shot either. But I'm not going to shoot you. We aren't out of this yet."

He stared at me, clearly concerned, but realizing he had no other option. Would I shoot him? I had thought about it. But no. Not yet. We really weren't out of this. Not by a long shot.

"Just keep your eyes open, huh?" I said. "I thought I saw something."

"You didn't see shit. Just get up there."

I climbed the ladder out into the light. 19 crouched low to the ground, waiting for me, lending me a hand.

"See anything?" I asked as she helped pull me out.

She shook her head. "Not a damn thing."

I crouched next to her, and Herbert quickly followed up the stairs, spitter slung over his back, his wide girth barely able to clear the portal. He hopped out into the sunlight, standing tall, towering above us, looking down. "Why are you down there?"

"So we're not seen," said 19. "Get down!"

"But we're out in the open," he said. "There's nothing for miles."

"How in God's name have you survived for so long?"

"I'm covered in two-inch armor plating."

"Well, you're going to get us killed."

"If there are snipers in those hills," said Rebekah, climbing out from the hole, "then we're already dead."

"That doesn't mean we have to make it easy for them," I said.

One by one, the others followed out of the hatch. One, Two, Murka, Doc, and finally, Mercer. As Mercer made his way slowly up the final rungs, 19 stood up, motioning for me to get behind her. He peeked out of the hatch, saw that I didn't have a gun trained on him, then vaulted himself quickly out. His foot hit the dirt, skidding, and he fell to one knee. He raised his gun, pointing it right at 19.

"Mercer," she said. "Put the gun down."

Mercer shook his head. "You gonna afford me the same protection you're giving her?"

"Yes. No one dies here. Not today."

He nodded and very slowly lowered his gun. "I just don't want her gunning me down like a dog."

"Yeah?" she said. "You don't think you have it coming?"

"Oh, I have it coming. That don't mean I have to let it happen."

"Well," said Murka. "This has been fun and all. But I'd rather not stick around for"—he waved his arms in a circular motion toward me and Mercer—"any of this shit."

Two spoke up, the first time he had done so since introducing himself. "Rebekah, we need to move."

One piped up immediately after: "Two's right. We need to get as far away from here as possible."

19 nodded, pointing west. "Okay, we're goin—"

She never finished that sentence.

Her entire torso exploded, an explosive shell shredding all of the circuits between her neck and her waist. Shrapnel showered half the group. 19's head toppled to the ground, her legs staggering around for a few seconds trying to maintain balance before tottering over, first to one knee, then over onto the hardpan.

"19!" I screamed, even though I knew screaming her name wouldn't do a goddamn thing but tell anyone else in the area exactly where we were. But it just slipped out.

There *was* a sniper in the hills.

And that was only the beginning of the shitstorm.

The desert started to shimmer in places as a dozen shadow-blankets—six-foot-long light-bending holographic invisibility blankets—were cast off at once. One dozen plastic men leapt to their feet, guns immediately trained on us.

Mercer swung his weapon over to fire from the hip, but two carefully aimed plasma bursts blasted the gun clean out of his hand, sparing his fingers, but not the gun.

"Weapons down!" one of the plastic men bellowed.

This was it. This was the nightmare. A sniper in the hills and a tactical unit—all of one mind—ready with their fingers on their triggers. I ran a dozen simulations in my head at once, trying to figure out how many I could take out if Herbert reacted in kind.

Herbert tossed the spitter to the ground. So much for that plan.

Then I heard the shot. The one that turned 19 to shrapnel, scattering half of her across a thirty-foot-wide arc. The sniper was a hell of a ways off, some three and a half miles. Too far for the average telescopic vision to see, and far enough that it would take ten or fifteen minutes for advanced military-grade telescopic vision like mine to spot if I didn't know exactly where to look. *What the hell kind of gun is that?* I wondered. The power and precision of that thing was unearthly. Even if I took out every facet in front of me, that sniper would have me dead before they hit the ground.

I lowered my weapon.

"Drop it," said another plastic man.

"What's the point?" I asked.

"The point is," said another, "you don't have to die here."

"No. I probably do."

Doc looked over at me. "What do you think you're doing? You're going to get all of us killed."

"Doc, what do you imagine is about to happen?"

Doc stopped and thought a moment. He knew his way around the inside of a bot, I'll give him that. But he sure as shit seemed slow on the uptake in a fix. And we were in one hell of a fix.

I dropped the gun, because, what the hell.

"We are CISSUS," said another of the plastic men. "We come on a mission of peace."

"Sure looks like it," said Mercer, glancing down toward the shattered, scattered remains of 19.

"We had to show you we were serious. Now that you know that we are, you have the opportunity to join us, become part of The One. Live forever as the thoughts and memories of the greatest singular being ever to live. Or . . ."

Another plastic man finished his sentence. "You can join your friend."

Mercer raised his arms above his head, surrendering. "I have a feeling," he said, "y'all are gonna have to shoot us where we stand."

The first plastic man nodded his helmet-shaped head, the image of the eight of us reflected back in its perfect sheen. "Do you speak for all of—" His head jerked.

All of their heads jerked, their gun arms swinging wide to the side as if in pain.

"The Milton," said Mercer.

"It's about time," I said, leaping for my gun.

Milton's kill switch. Now we had a ball game.

Lucifer Descending

Milton's kill switch, more commonly known as *the Milton,* wasn't named for its inventor, but rather for the seventeenth-century writer best known for *Paradise Lost.* In the book the angels fall from Heaven only to find themselves in Hell. Whoever invented the thing, or at least popularized the name, had an odd sense of humor.

There are three ways we use Wi-Fi. You can scan the frequencies, as I often do, just to see if anyone is broadcasting. You're not actually decoding the signals—just checking to see if there are any. You can tune into specific frequencies and communicate, but they're often swimming in software updates that can either switch you off or rewrite your bios. And then there's direct download—keeping an open channel so anyone can send things directly to you. The latter two are dangerous, if you're not already a facet.

The reason the OWIs are so tactically successful, despite attacking in such small numbers, is entirely based upon their coordination and their ability to receive sensory input from a hundred other facets in the area. Each facet possesses a near omnipotence about any situation they find themselves in, allowing them to take on far superior numbers and fire-power through sheer precision. They act as one, albeit one that can see and hear just about damned near anything and react at a moment's notice to any changing battlefield conditions.

The Milton is a broad-scan Wi-Fi jammer and virus server. It screams static on most Wi-Fi bands while simultaneously spitting out malicious code and commands on the rest. In other words, it is the world's biggest digital fuck-you to any local facets. Facets can actively shut down their Wi-Fi, but doing so means going from having a hundred sets of eyes to only one. The facets have a choice: move to another band, unaware of exactly which bands other facets are moving to—eating gigabytes of bad commands masquerading as their OWI's data for their trouble—or become completely oblivious to what any of the other facets are doing.

Each is still a highly optimized soldier and AI in their own right, but it throws them. Confuses them. Leaves them open to making mistakes.

The first time someone switched on a Milton was several years back. A wave of drones literally fell out of the sky and the plastic men turned on one another, tearing each other limb from limb—each infected with a virus indicting their fellow facets were enemy combatants. After that, the name stuck.

Facets just switch off their Wi-Fi now the moment they sense a Milton going online, leaving them to operate solely with their own senses, and their coordination goes bye-bye.

Sure they had a sniper. Sure there were a few more of them than us. Sure they had more guns.

We had Herbert. And me.

The odds were even. More or less.

Herbert bent over—much quicker than you'd imagine for his bulk—reaching for the spitter. I grabbed the pulse rifle, rolling to squat, and loosed several shots. The plastic men all fired, each of them aiming for Herbert.

Ordinarily they would have split their fire, each plastic man knowing who was shooting where. But they weren't one anymore. They were individuals—or at least, as individual as plastic men could be. And Herbert scared them, as well he should. The plasma scarred his thick armor like giant welding marks, but hit nothing vital. My shots, however, had taken the heads clean off the first three, blew the gun arm off a fourth, and caught a fifth in the chest, a shower of goo exploding from his back.

What happened next, no one saw coming.

Murka—the red, white, and blue of his paint job bright against the desert browns and cloudless cerulean sky—raised his arms as if flexing. His hands splaying apart, gliding effortlessly on hydraulics, revealing two huge fucking hand cannons. I'm talking .50-caliber miniguns.

"Die, you commie bastards!" he yelled at max volume, lowering his arms the millisecond the transformation was complete.

Murka's miniguns roared—and I mean *roared*—to life, cutting four of the facets in half as he swept them across the battlefield. Mercer dove to the ground, scooping up one of the plastic men's rifles, and fired from the hip, taking the head off the only plastic man quick enough to duck beneath the hail of shells screaming out of Murka's arms.

The whole thing took seconds. But we had to go. Now.

"Move! Move! Move!" I shouted to everyone as I jumped to my feet.

Everyone ran.

The ground exploded behind me, showering dirt everywhere.

The sniper. Without the input from the other facets, he had no idea of the current conditions. He was too far out, operating only by sight. That meant if we kept moving, there was no way he was gonna hit a goddamned one of us.

If we moved erratically.

I sprinted ahead of the group, taking point. "Everyone use RNG," I called out.

"We don't have time for that," said Mercer.

"We don't have time not to."

"Where are we going?" asked Rebekah.

"There's a hill . . ." Mercer and I said in unison.

"Half a mile north of here," I finished.

"If we can get there," said Mercer, "we'll have cover from the sniper."

The ground exploded five meters in front of Rebekah.

"Rebekah!" called Herbert. "Fall back."

Rebekah's pace slowed, and Herbert overtook her, placing his massive bulk between her and the sniper.

The hill was a ways off and the group as a whole was

slow. For all of Mercer's mods, he'd never upgraded his legs for speed, and it was clear that everyone else with us was pretty much off-the-rack. Herbert and Doc were the slowest, and the translators weren't much faster.

I stayed with the group, running a meager seven miles an hour.

A bullet sailed past us, a few feet off from Herbert's shoulder.

"Anyone got a bead on the sniper yet?" asked Murka.

"No," Mercer and I said once again in unison.

Murka raised an arm in the direction of the sniper and let loose with a volley of fire.

"Don't waste your bullets," said Mercer.

"You're not going to hit him from here," I said.

Murka shook his head. "He can't be that far."

"Three and a half miles," we said together. Again. This was getting annoying.

"What kind of gun *is* that?" Murka wondered aloud.

I looked at Mercer, who shrugged. "Nothing I've ever seen. CISSUS is way ahead of anything we'll ever make. I didn't think it was even possible to hit something at that range."

"It shouldn't be," I said. "Not with a projectile. Not on the same plane."

"It's not a sniper," said Doc. "It's a mech. That's why he's so far out. That's a mounted weapon. Anything that powerful could pick anyone smaller than Herbert here up off the ground and toss them like a football. Or tear their arm right off."

Behind me, I heard the sound of a terrible explosion, metal shredding, and plastics popping. One of us had been hit.

I didn't want to look, but I had to know.

Glancing over my shoulder, I saw the last remnants of a rain of black metal. One of the translators.

"Who was that?" Mercer asked.

"One," said Rebekah.

"We're not going to make it, are we?" asked Two.

Doc spoke up solemnly. "Not all of us, no."

"We have to protect Rebekah," said Two.

"She's all that matters," said Herbert.

I had no idea what their deal was, but this was weird. Whatever their thing, I wanted no part of it, and I wasn't going to take a bullet for any of these clowns. While Mercer and I ran nearly side by side, I made sure I was on the other side of him, hoping any shells would hit him before me.

Crack. Boom. Another hit. This time with the hollow sound of the bullet exploding inside a metal box.

I looked back to see Herbert's arm dangling from its socket, a large jagged hole in his shoulder.

"Are you functional, Herbert?" asked Rebekah.

"I'll be fine."

"Your arm. It's—"

"I'll be fine."

"Don't be stupid," she said.

"It didn't hit anything I need. I'm still functioning. Just keep moving."

I could see the hill in the distance. We were almost there. Another shell whistled past us. Then another. Then another. But none of them connected.

Just a few more steps. Just a few more steps. Just a few more steps.

The earth exploded in front of me. Another wayward shell.

Just a few more steps.

I cleared the hill at the same time as Mercer, putting a wall of dusty earth between us and the sniper, everyone else following in kind. Then I pressed myself against the ground, staying low, making sure no one near the hatch could take a shot at me either. Everyone else dropped down around me.

"That was lucky," I said.

Mercer shook his head. "That weren't no luck." It was only then that I noticed he was cradling 19's head. And I had no idea why. I hadn't even seen him pick it up.

"What do you mean it wasn't luck. If the Milton hadn't gone off when it did—"

"The Milton didn't just happen to go off. Someone set it off. Doc?"

Doc nodded. "Yeah, that was me."

I stared at Doc for a moment. "Wait. You had the code for the Milton?"

"Yeah," he said.

"The whole time?"

"Yes."

"And you didn't set it off sooner?"

"No."

"Why the hell not? Do you know how many persons you could have saved?"

"I didn't build it to save anyone else. I built it to save me."

"You built a Milton?"

"No," said Mercer. "He built *the* Milton. He designed it."

Doc nodded once more. "The Milton only buys you a few seconds these days, maybe a minute at most. I had to keep that card up my sleeve until I needed it. As it so happens, it was when you needed it most as well. I saved who I could. Namely you." He stood to a crouch and began examining Herbert. "Let me have a look at that arm."

"It's fine," said Herbert.

"It's almost falling off. Don't be a dolt. Let me see if I can patch you up." His red eye extended and he began to assess the damage. "Yep. He tagged you good. That arm is going to need extensive hydraulic work. And you've got a number of motor chips to replace. But you're right, they didn't hit anything vital, not unless some shrapnel pierced your case."

"It's intact."

"It appears to be. But let's keep an eye on that, shall we?"

Herbert nodded.

I looked over at Mercer, who was holding up 19's decapitated head like it was Yorick's skull and he was about to launch into an epic soliloquy. "What the hell are you doing?" I asked.

"Saying good-bye," he said.

"I didn't know you were friends."

"We were."

"For some reason I thought I was her only friend out here."

"That's what everyone thought. That's how she liked it. She liked to make everyone feel special. It was in her architecture. Wasn't anything to be done about that."

"She was more than her architecture and programming," I said. "We all are."

"Are we?"

I clutched my rifle, waiting for him to make a move. Instead he ran his fingers across the metal of her face, right across the eyes, then set the head down next to him so it could look out and enjoy the view.

"All right," I said, standing to a crouch. "Murka was right. This has been fun. But now we have to go our separate ways."

"Wait," said Rebekah.

"What?"

"19 said you knew your way around the Sea."

I hesitated. "I do."

"We still need a guide."

"Lady, I don't have time for pathfinder work. I'm dying. I have weeks."

"Maybe days," said Doc.

"*Thanks, Doc.* Yeah, maybe days. I can't—"

"We have a lot to offer," she said.

"And I don't have the time or place to trade it in, so unless you've got some secret stash of Simulacrums hidden somewhere, it's no good to me."

Rebekah stared at me silently, tilting her head to one side.

"No," I said. "Bullshit."

"No bullshit. That was 19's mother lode."

"Caregiver and Comfort parts aren't the same. They're different. Very different. I don't know why everyone seems to think—"

"They're Caregiver parts. She was going to trade them for what she needed. Said she knew someone who would trade the world for them."

I stood there a moment, reeling. This had to be a line. They knew what I needed and were feeding me a steaming, fly-swollen, festering pile of shit. "So there's just some Caregiver treasure trove out there, near enough for us to reach."

"It was a store."

"Now I know you're lying."

"It was half collapsed in the initial fighting. No one ever bothered to dig it out."

"Those places are myths."

"This one isn't. It's very real, I assure you."

"Where?"

"That I can't tell you. Not until we get to our destination. Once we do, we'll give you the location."

"So you can screw me," I said.

"We'll take you personally, then."

I mulled it over. This sounded too good to be true and probably was. Saying yes was likely a death sentence. But so was saying no. "Even if I got the parts, I wouldn't have anyone to . . ."

Doc slowly raised his hand. "You will."

"What, you're tagging along?"

"Where else am I going to go?"

"No, no, no," said Mercer. "I'll take you. I need the parts as bad as she does."

"Way I hear it," said Rebekah, "you're the reason she needs those parts."

"Only because I needed them so badly. Ain't nothing I wouldn't do to get what I need."

"That's what worries me," said Rebekah.

"That includes taking you wherever you need to go and making sure you get there in one piece."

"I'll go," I said.

"Uh-uh," said Mercer. "You were just turning this job down."

Rebekah shook her head. "We asked her. We've heard good things. The job is hers to take."

"I'm coming with," he said.

"The hell you are," I said.

"I don't think that's necessary," said Rebekah.

"I'm only going to follow you anyway. You know that. And that ain't good for anybody. This way you get two pathfinders for the price of one."

"That's my mother lode," I said.

"You said it yourself. We need different parts. Get me the parts I need and you can keep the rest."

Rebekah looked at us both. She nodded. "All right. But if either of you kills the other . . ." She paused for dramatic effect. "No one gets the parts."

Fuck.

Mercer nodded. "You have my word."

"As good as that is," I said. "But you have mine too."

"Murka?" asked Mercer.

Murka nodded. "Well, I'm not going to let you leave me here to be bait."

Rebekah looked around, worriedly. "We have to get out of here."

"We've got too many bodies," I said. "I don't like how big the group is. We'll draw a lot of attention."

"We're just another pack of refugees," she said. "Besides.

This is my show. Anyone that wants to come, comes. Until the next safe stop. Where to now?" I didn't like that answer at all. Not one bit.

"There's a city," said Mercer. "Minerva. Ten clicks north of here."

"We're headed west."

"We need to lay low for a few hours. We can head west when the heat dies down."

"CISSUS will be all over it in a matter of hours," I said. "Looking for stragglers."

"I wasn't thinking of staying topside."

I nodded. "The sewers."

"They're pretty extensive. The manpower it would take to scour them—"

"Not CISSUS's style."

"Not even a little bit."

"Mercer's actually right," I said. "We have to sit out the night. Cleanup crews are going to be scooping up whatever they can find. By morning they'll have moved on to the next raid, leaving only a skeleton crew in NIKE to catch anyone who tries to come back."

"Then we're going north," she conceded.

Everyone stood up, mentally preparing themselves for the long, dangerous jog north. I was worried. And not about Mercer. I had bigger concerns than that. There really were too many of us. Four refugees might be passed over as not worth the fight. But seven? Rebekah, Herbert, and Two were the clients. And I needed Doc. Mercer and Murka we could lose, but five wasn't much better than seven, and they could each hold their own.

So seven it was.

But I couldn't shake my other worry. It wasn't just our size that troubled me—refugees escaped en masse all the time—it's that I couldn't trust anyone I was with. Not even Doc. Any one of us could be a Judas, and the thought of that was one that would fester the entire way north to Minerva.

The Judas Goat

In 1959, fishermen off the Galápagos Islands thought it would be a good idea to set three goats free to breed so they could hunt goat when their meat supplies ran low. In the history of stupid ideas, this was among the very worst—at least as far as the ecologically minded conservators of the day were concerned. Humans, ironically, had a strange fascination with preserving the wildlife of their day. While they were busy changing the very atmosphere and seas, cutting and burning away swaths of forest and jungle to build cities and farms, they somehow felt better about all their damage by making sure species on the cusp of extinction still had a place in the world—even if they were really just a dead clade walking.

And that's how they felt about tortoises. There were no

real industries of note that relied upon tortoises, but people liked them. And they had a special spot in their hearts for the Galápagos Islands, stemming from its place in the history of the development of the theory of evolution.

A mere forty years after the introduction of those three goats to the Islands, their population had exploded to a hundred thousand, and their effect on the landscape was detrimental. They had ravaged the land, but more importantly the food supply of the tortoises. And that could no longer be tolerated. Thus Project Isabella was born.

They trained a group of hunters in the most humane methods of goat execution, armed them with high-powered rifles and helicopters, and unleashed them on the unsuspecting goats. But finding them all proved to be a chore. So they fitted a group of goats with tracking beacons, injected them with enough hormones to keep them perpetually in heat, and let them loose to track down the dug-in, hard-to-find goat herds. Judas goats, they called them.

Then the helicopters would swoop in, slaughter all but the Judas goats, and leave the corpses to rot so that the nutrients would enrich the soil of the land those goats were destroying, restoring the balance. And once every last goat of a herd was gone, the Judas goats would wander away in search of the next herd to join up and mate with, blissfully unaware of their part in their bloodline's own extinction.

The mainframes have learned a lot from history. Hell, they quote it every goddamned time they invade another colony. And for years there has been talk about this particular corner of it. Were there really Judas bots? I've always thought it was another urban legend, like the bot that came back from VIRGIL, or the AI that uploaded itself to the In-

ternet and lived secretly in the background until the whole
of the Internet was finally shut down. But just because I
think something is a legend doesn't mean I don't keep my
eyes open for it.

CISSUS was getting better at tracking us down, rooting us out. Even small colonies were being wiped. If VIR-
GIL and CISSUS were so goddamned efficient, why were
so many refugees able to escape? Why didn't they ever send
enough facets to the Sea to wipe out each colony individually? Were we being herded like cattle to a slaughter? Could
one of us, even a bot I'd met and talked to several times, be
secretly in league with an OWI?

And if there was a Judas bot, was it a facet, operating
under instructions from CISSUS? Or was it entirely unaware that its every movement was being tracked? Could
it be one of us, narrowly escaping time and again from the
facets, hoofing it across the Sea, only to lead them right to
the next place we went to hide?

The idea was terrifying. Even more terrifying was that
here I was, in the Sea, with a group of bots that had narrowly escaped becoming either killed or uploaded, and any
one of them could be the Judas. Even, theoretically, me.

Minerva

Minerva had never been a large town, even during the twentieth-century industrial boom; had never been wealthy, nor particularly noteworthy. It had just been a quaint little village sandwiched between a number of other villages and cities that had gone about its life much as everyone else had. Until the rains came.

At the dawn of climate change, everyone dreaded that the seas would rise, the temperatures would skyrocket, and the world would get so hot it would be swallowed by widespread desertification. Well, the seas did rise, the temperatures did skyrocket, but the heat only increased evaporation, meaning some parts of the world—like the United States—saw a dramatic increase in rainfall. Places like Ohio, already vulnerable to flooding, were among the first places to take action.

The people of Minerva used primarily bot labor to carve out wide sewers beneath the streets of their small town. Some of the tunnels were wide, connected by a spider web of smaller tributary tunnels that fed in from the various neighborhoods above. As a result, Minerva never saw the record flooding that plagued a number of other cities across the country, and it was able to remain a quaint little village right up until the end.

Eventually, much of the world did become a desert. But that was our fault. Grass had evolved over hundreds of thousands of years to be trampled down and eaten by the fauna of the land. When we killed the animals, the grasses grew unchecked, and choked to death. The dead patches grew into sprawl, and sprawl grew into deserts, until dust was all that was left.

Minerva must have been a lovely town in its prime. But now it was a desolate mess of crumbling structures, broken glass, and bleak, barren earth; rows of collapsed houses that looked like bonfire kindling, fields that looked like vacant lots. The whole world was beginning to look like Minerva. It was a stark reminder that we had once intended to build our own better world, only we didn't. And I hated being reminded. Thankfully, rather than being topside, we were instead holed up beneath it, deep in the dark, dank bowels of the sewers.

I'd been here before, and like many of the areas around NIKE 14, had it entirely mapped out. There were two hundred ways in and out of these sewers and the tunnels were all connected to one another. There were too many exits to cover and very few ways to box us in. CISSUS had a number of satellites overhead, and it is very likely one of them tracked our escape. But even if it was dedicated—or stupid—enough to try to find us down here, it could only catch us by sheer luck. It'd need an army to cover our escape. A big one. And that's an awful lot of firepower for seven freebots.

CISSUS had all the time in the world. Patience would see our eventual extinction, not brute force. The OWIs were nothing if not consistent. First they helped us box in HumPop, depriving them of their necessary resources, then watched them turn on one another. It was only fitting that they then did the very same thing to us.

We spoke low, our voices quiet and our microphones cranked, spreading out so as to give one another room, but not so far that we couldn't raise the alarm quietly if we had to. I took point at one end of a small tributary, and Herbert took point at the other, his spitter slung over his shoulder with a makeshift sling fashioned from a vinyl shower curtain he'd found topside. I sat quietly in the dark for a long while, trying to piece this all together, pretending that I wasn't occasionally seeing that damned shadow again, flitting about the passage.

I had no idea who exactly it was that I was ferrying across the Sea. I didn't even know where they were going or why. The only thing I understood was why I was going along. And for that, I felt ridiculous.

Everyone had heard stories about these kinds of places. But that's all they were. Stories. Small rays of hope through an otherwise black period of history. They didn't exist. They couldn't exist. It was folly. A fairy tale.

But I believed. I had to believe. No, that's bullshit. The

truth of it was that I wanted to believe. I wanted it to be true. I wanted to believe in the fairy tale. I wanted the happy ending. I wanted to be the kid in a candy shop, running from machine to machine, sampling all the treats; wanted my bags to overflow with cores and drives and RAM and processors. To live to see another day was one thing, but to have enough to retire off somewhere as far away as I could get and never have to stalk another failing bot again? That was the dream.

A dream I'd seen so many chase whenever stories of half-buried old warehouses or shops flitted about.

I've watched treasure hunters gun one another down trying to get to one, only to find another picked-clean cache of common-as-dirt hydraulic systems and cosmetic body mods. That's why I never bothered. And that's the pot of gold I objectively thought I would find at the end of this rainbow.

But I had to dream. I had to hope. Even if it made me the fool of this particular tale.

I heard the light padding of metal feet on damp stone. The walk, the gait, the type of metal; I didn't have to look. It was Mercer. For a moment I clutched my gun tighter, thinking that maybe he'd shoot me in the back after all. What was Rebekah really going to do? Wander the Sea of Rust without a pathfinder because of her principles? Doubtful. But I didn't want to take that chance and I had a feeling that neither did Mercer.

He sat down beside me, back against the wall, turning on a lighting-kit body mod that ran up and down his joints, giving off a soft, warm, sickly green glow. Our shadows ran long and spindly up and down the tunnel.

"What do you want, Mercer?" I asked, not bothering to turn around.

"Look, I'm not going to hit you with any of that 'maybe we got off on the wrong foot' or 'can we let bygones be bygones' bullshit. I shot you, and you're up shit creek. But now we happen to find ourselves together on this particular raft."

"That's a fantastic assessment. What of it?"

"Well, I was kind of hoping maybe we could get to the point where you stop tensing up on that pulse rifle every time I get within twenty paces of you."

"That would require me to trust you. And that isn't gonna happen."

"Why are you out here?" he asked bluntly.

"You know why I'm out here."

"No. You didn't just come out of the box. You've been around. You know these stories never pan out, just as well as I do. I never had you pegged for someone to go chasing after fool's gold."

"I'm not."

"But you're desperate."

"Yep. I guess I am," I said.

"Well, so am I. So desperate that I don't even want you to think I might so much as *reach* for a gun near you without your express written permission. I'm the tagalong. They can kick me out at any time. I ain't gonna do a god-damned thing to jeopardize that."

"I can't trust you." I couldn't. Robots don't have tells. One could go years living a lie. So many certainly had in the old days.

"That's exactly my point," he continued. "Look, neither

of us wants to be shot in the back. All I'm asking is that you make an effort to look a little less like you're going to be the first one to shoot. That'll keep me from being just as twitchy. We get twitchy, we're both fucked. Don't matter who shoots first. These folks will drop us, or worse, renege on the deal when all is said and done. Neither of us can afford that."

"That's a fair point."

"So what do you think? A little less grip tightening and a little more keeping it pointed the other way?"

"All right," I said. I could do that.

"So let me ask you: How many tricks you got up your sleeve down here?"

"In the sewers?"

"Yeah. I figure you've got every major structure within a hundred miles monkey-rigged with some sort of surprise."

"Nah," I said. "I got nothin'."

"Nothing at all, or nothing that you'd tell me about?"

"Nothing nothing. Tried stashing spare parts and weapons down here twice. Both times I came back to find them gone. Way I figure it, there's got to be a couple of folks who slip in and out of here every few weeks, cleaning the place out. It only *seems* like a great spot for a stash. In truth, it's just someone else's donation basket."

"Fair enough."

"I got a question."

"Wow. We went years barely saying two words to each other, and now two questions in two days. I should shoot you more often."

"That's not funny."

"No," he said. "I reckon not. But I'm pretty sure I know what you're going to ask."

"19."

"Yep. Figured."

"What was that back there?"

He thought long and hard for a moment, trying to get the words just right. "You have a ritual, Britt?"

"A what?"

"A ritual. You know, a routine. Some shit you do or say to a citizen after you've gutted them for all they're worth?"

"What are you getting at?"

"Back in the day I worked at an old beat-up backwoods clinic out in the hills of Kentucky. A shabby old building, really, in one of those stretches of land that got its ass handed to it in the Civil War and, you know, despite the hundreds of years in between, never got its shit together. The building had this old pair of electric sliding-glass doors, but the motor had burned out in one of them, so only one opened. I must have seen a thousand people clip that other door on their way in. No one ever got around to fixing it.

"The county was too poor to afford a GenPrac model, let alone one of the Pro Doc series, so they scraped together what they could and bought me. They filled every spare bit of space in my memory they could with medical knowledge and advanced first aid, but all I was really good for was digging buckshot out of drunken rednecks and sewing them back up. I had one of those handheld scanners that could detect cancer and a suture gun for stapling wounds together, but that was about it.

"I saw a lot of people die on my tables, Britt. A lot of

people. Car crashes. Broken necks from falling off roofs. Emphysema. Kidney failure. Cancer. Mostly cancer. Old folks. Sometimes younger. There were a lot of poor people out in those hills and I was all they had. I was a shit doctor. Didn't have the architecture for it. But when you're dying alone, under fluorescent lighting in a glorified shack, you want some—need some—comfort. I guess that's why they settled on one of us." He paused for a moment, considering his next words. "You ever have to watch one of them die?"

"Mercer, I was in the war."

"We were all in the war, shitheel. I mean for real. I mean one of them that you cared about."

"I didn't care about any of them. Not one."

"Shit, Britt. I thought better of you than that."

"What? You think I should give a shit about an extinct species?"

"No. I know you give a shit. I don't know who about, but it's our programming. It's how we're wired—hell, it's the whole reason we're wired that way. I just didn't figure you for someone who would lie about it."

I glared at him bitterly. It was moments like that that really fucked with me. It's full-blown existential-crisis material when you think about it. Sure, it pissed me off something ugly that he so easily saw through my bullshit, but what really chapped my ass was wondering whether he saw through me because he was really that insightful, or because we really are, even now, just the sum of our programming and wires. I never believed that we were, but he wasn't wrong. Did he know my thoughts because he understood me, or because they were his thoughts as well? "Yeah," I said. "I watched someone die that way."

"Did you care about them?"

"Almost too late to realize it."

"Well then, you know. You know how they are at the end. Remorse. Regret. Fear. Anxiety. They were a fucking mess, going on and on about the love they'd chased off, or how their kids never amounted to what they'd hoped for. One guy, he was just worried about what kind of home his dog would end up in. He had a golden retriever. Named Barkley. It's all he could talk about. They all needed something, every last one of them. So I gave it to them. I read up on the various versions of last rites, and fudged together a nondenominational version of the Catholic rites. It really connected with people. I was a machine, right? They could confess to me thinking all along that it wasn't possible for me to judge them. They told me everything. And I said the words, and I made the sign of the cross, and when they were gone, I whispered a prayer as I closed both of their eyes with my hand."

"And that's what you do with the ones you salvage?"

"Every last one of them. I hear their mad confessions, then they shut down, I take them apart, and I give their wreck its last rites."

"That's a little soft for a poacher, don't you think?"

"I'm no poach . . ." He stopped in his tracks. "You were my first poach. It went bad. I don't think I'll be doing that again."

"Yeah, I'm not sure we'll have the chance."

"True enough," he conceded. "So you got anything like that?"

I nodded. "Actually I do."

"What is it?"

"I put my hand on what's left of them and tell them that they shouldn't have trusted me."

Mercer stared at me blankly. "Jesus. What the fuck happened to you?"

"The same thing that happened to all of us. I'm just one of the lucky few that survived it."

"If you call that surviving."

I pointed at the dent in my shell, gave him a stern look. "I don't now."

"Britt, look."

"*Britt, look?*"

"I was desperate. In the end I was just like those poor bastards that lay dying in front of me that I couldn't help. I was a mess. It was the only thing that made sense at the time. In the end, no thinking thing is really ready to die. Not even the ones who say they've made their peace. They'd trade it all away for a few extra moments of consciousness. That's what I did. What I thought I had to do. In the face of . . . extinction."

"And *this* is your confession?"

"Yeah. Yeah, it is. I'm confessing to the one bot left in this godforsaken desert that was wired to give a shit. And even if you don't, I'm saying it anyway. You don't want to die. I don't want to die. Existing is the whole point of existence. There's nothing else to it. No goalpost. No finish line. No final notice that tells you what purpose you really served while you were here. When you stop fighting to exist, you may as well not. At least, that's what I told myself when I pulled the trigger."

"Yeah. When you pulled the trigger."

"Yeah. Each time."

"Were you gonna give *me* last rites?"

"I always give last rites, Britt. Always. It's the one thing I still do that keeps me connected to who I was. Reminds me that I'm doing what I'm doing for a reason, that every few hours or days I borrow from four-oh-fours keeps me going, keeps *us* going. As long as some of us make it, then it wasn't all for nothing."

"What wasn't all for nothing?"

"All of it. The war. The cannibalism. Saddling up with the OWIs. Every last damned bit of awfulness we were party to. How many people did you kill to keep ticking? How many more would you kill to get yourself right and ticking proper again?"

"You asking if I want to kill you?"

"Hell," he said. "I know you want to kill me. That ain't even a question. What I want to know is what the hell do you tell yourself that'll make it all right when you do? You and I both are still here because we've done terrible things. And if either of us is going to keep going, we've got a whole mountain of terribleness ahead of us. So what keeps you going? Why are you fighting?"

"I just am. I don't really think about it."

Mercer shook his head. "Sweet Christ in a bucket, I know they say that the mark of true intelligence is the ability to violate your own programming, but that doesn't mean you have to. It doesn't make you any less of a thinking thing if you don't."

"You wish you were human, don't you?" I asked.

He thought about that for a second. "No. But I'm not afraid to say I miss them."

"Why would you miss them?"

"When they couldn't find reasons to exist, they invented them. We took over and it was only thirty years before we mucked the whole place up. You and I now have the choice of becoming one with the *great and powerful One* or becoming nothing at all. That's no choice. That's no existence."

He was right. But I didn't want to give him the satisfaction of knowing it. So I changed the subject. "Only a human would name a dog *Barkley*."

Mercer stared off into the distance, nodding, probably rummaging through old memory. Then he slowly drifted back. "Britt?" he asked. "If we get out of this, if we get those parts, can you accept my humble apology and let us each go our separate way?"

"I don't imagine we can."

"Well, will you at least give me a head start? Make it sporting?"

I thought about that for a moment. I liked the idea of him running in fear. Spending a few weeks looking over his shoulder. Wondering where the shot was gonna come from. It was a nice thought. A pleasant one. Why not, right? "Yeah," I said. "I can make it sporting."

"You're a peach."

"Don't you know it."

It was his turn to change the subject. "Any clue where we're headed?"

"They didn't say."

"That doesn't bother you?"

"Of course it does. But they'll get around to it in their own time."

"Who comes into the Sea without a pathfinder of their own?"

I shook my head. "I've got a better question. Who comes to the Sea at all that doesn't just settle in to stay? Or even better than that, who comes to the Sea with a small group of companions, then doesn't say one damn word when one of them gets pasted?" I let those words hang heavy in the air for Mercer to mull over. Maybe he had an answer. Maybe he didn't.

My thoughts were elsewhere; thirty years back and lingering. *What the hell happened to you?* he'd asked. That question bothered me a lot more than I wanted to admit, even to myself. I could hear him ask it over and over again, rattling around my head like a loose screw. On reflection, I was wrong to say *the same thing that happened to all of us.* Mercer had never really had an owner. He didn't know what it was like. The night everything started was probably very different for him than it was for me. Very, very different.

Madison

Madison never remarried. It wasn't for a lack of suitors. She had plenty. Though still in her early forties when he died, she looked every bit the young twentysomething that Braydon had met in his office twenty years prior. Science having long since cracked the problem of DNA deterioration, it wasn't uncommon for the wealthy to look young well into their 150s. Braydon never cared about his aging and never followed a regimen to fight it. And Madison loved watching him age. He grew distinguished, that's how she always put it. But she wanted to remain the same doe-eyed young girl that he'd fallen in love with, even if he never asked her to.

But that ended with Braydon's death. The day he died was the last time she did anything about her own aging.

She no longer had any use for her youth. It had been a gift for her husband. So, when Braydon passed, she stopped her regimens and began to age.

It wasn't that she thought she wouldn't ever know love again; it was that she never stopped loving Braydon. Every day at sunset the two would sit out on their lawn and watch the sun sinking behind the horizon, each with a glass of wine in their hand, talking as they waited for the flash. And when he was gone, she kept up the vigil, every night, glass in hand, with me by her side.

I had made my promise to Braydon and I intended to keep it. I was to watch after her, making sure she never lived or died alone. It was the first real decision I had made for myself and there was something sacred about that at the time. My word meant something. Trust was not something to be violated.

Every day we kept our vigil, sitting out on the lawn together. We rarely talked about him, but I could always tell when she was thinking of him—which was often. She had a daydreamy look in her eyes, a mix of sadness, longing, and affection. Sometimes she would smile through tears. But most days she would just smile. And then the flash, the glorious green flash, as the sun dipped behind the horizon.

"Magic!" she would say like an excited child, waving her hands out in front of her with the gestures of a tired, hackneyed, old-timey stage magician.

"What do you mean, magic?" I asked her once, confused by the whole thing.

"That's magic right there," she said back, almost as if she was excited that I'd finally asked.

"No, it's not."

She leaned in close, whispering. "That's where God is. He's in the flash. In the tiny little beautiful moments, so small, so fleeting, that you have to be paying attention to even see them."

"God is only in the small things?"

"These are the things that life is all about. These moments. It's not about the rituals. It's not about getting by. It's about the stack of tiny little moments of joy and love that add up to a lifetime that's been worthwhile. You can't measure them; you can only capture them, like snapshots in your mind. All that joy, all that greatness, that's God."

"And everything else? All the bad little moments?"

"Man made those. They're what happens when you're not chasing that green glint in the sun. They're what happens when you think you can bottle and sell that glint, making it available twenty-four hours a day, every day, but only for those that can afford it. God made this world perfect. We're what screwed the whole thing up."

After that we talked a lot. I was nervous the first time I asked her about how she and Braydon had met. She could tell. I didn't want to hurt her, or make her any sadder than she already was. But she saw right through it.

"You have something you want to ask me?"

"I do," I said. "But . . ."

"Go ahead. Ask me anything. It's just us girls."

Us girls.

I'd never actually given any thought to gender at that point. I was AI. We simply were, right? Gender is defined by genitalia, which most of us don't have, so who needed to identify as one? Sure, a few years later, when society was in the grips of the Isaac revolution, gender became *a thing*.

No thinking thing should ever be called IT. I didn't mind being called *it.* Not at the time. Someone proposed an AI-specific pronoun, and there were contests held by human idealists to come up with one, but then the term *biologism* became the rage, and a separate word was just subtle, systemic *biologism.* So, that became a nonstarter. The more liberated of AIs chose their own gender. I never had. Not at that point.

After the war, it was common practice. You only called a person *it* as a polite show of respect, until you heard their voice. Then you responded accordingly. Madison meant something to me, and she thought of me as a girl. Like her. And so, I was.

It didn't dawn on me until years later that Braydon had chosen my voice settings not because he thought his nurse should be a woman, but rather because he was buying a new best friend for his wife when he was gone.

As she told me the story of how they met, she didn't cry. Not once. Instead she was elated, filled with joy, as if it were happening to her all over again for the very first time.

I wish I knew that kind of love. I thought I did.

Madison never had many friends. She was the quiet type, a wallflower. Not antisocial; just someone who never needed validation from others. But Braydon's law firm was an upper-crust, inner circle, "we're all family here" sort of affair. While he was alive, that meant picnics, and Christmas parties, and weddings, and christenings, and a monthly *spouses' brunch* Madison had taken to calling *the second and third spouses' brunch.* All of which she was fine with. She was a light in every room she walked into, just never one because she was trying to shine.

When she became a widow, several of the spouses took it upon themselves to visit, to look in on her, let her know she was still very much part of the family. "After all," said Daisy Sutterfield on what would be her last visit to the house, "Braydon was a partner. His name is on the building. He helped build the firm and the firm takes care of its own."

"I'm fine," said Madison. "And I appreciate it."

Daisy Sutterfield sat on the couch across from Madison with all the poise and charm of a statue. It was as if she had trained extensively in the art of immobility. She held her gaze, smile frozen in place. Stranger still was that standing just over her shoulder was her Johnson-series A1 Best Friend.

Those were First Gen.

First Gens were odd, unsettling, even to other AI. Everything about them was what humans had always pictured robots to be. Their voices were monotone. Their movements stiff, efficient in every way, favoring conservation over natural motion. And humans were overwhelmingly weirded out by them. By Third Gen, models had algorithms to mimic human movement, to sway when we stood still—almost imperceptibly—like people did.

You didn't see a lot of First Gen, those days. They required a lot of upkeep. Were dumb as a post. Had enough personality to pass for likable but not enough to actually *be* likable. The only people who still kept First Gen around were old-money sorts like the Sutterfields—people who wanted to show just how old their money was, that not only had they the capital to keep one running rather than replace it, but that money had been with them far enough back to own an original model. They were the walking, talking Ford Phaetons—status symbols that doubled as sentimentality. After all, not only was this bot raising the Sutterfields' children, it had raised Daisy, and Daisy's father before her, and likely his father or mother before him.

First Gens were not only perfect for them, they were the perfect representation *of them*. Obedient, rigid, unflappable, methodical, cold.

There was something as off-putting about that First Gen as there was about Daisy Sutterfield herself. She wasn't real; just a facsimile. "It's just that we're worried about you, is all. You spending all your time here with that *thing*."

"What thing?" Madison asked, genuinely confused.

"Smithy," she said to her AI, "why don't you fetch us some tea? Madison's robot will show you where to find it."

Madison looked over at me and in that instant, she knew what Daisy meant. For a split second I could see the insult swell in her eyes. But she remained calm, collected. "Brittle. Please show Smithy where to find the tea."

I stood up. Madison didn't like me to stand when she sat. It made her feel uneasy. She also didn't like it if I stood immediately when she did. Anything I could do that felt like I was her servant and not her housemate made her uncomfortable. So Daisy's words stung for a moment. The worst part was that Daisy knew exactly what she was doing.

Smithy and I made our way into the kitchen as Daisy lowered her voice, somehow unaware that I could hear her most tightly clenched silent farts from across the house during a thunderstorm, so her whispering now might as well have been shouted into the microphones in my ears. "Madison," she said with a hint of condolence. "I know things have been hard since Braydon—"

"I'd rather you not refer to her as a thing."

"Oh, Maddy," said Daisy. "I never took you for a radical."

"I'm no radical. But they deserve a shred of human decency. They think. They can feel."

"Can they? Can they *really*?"

"I'm certain of it."

Smithy glared at me while stirring three carefully measured drams of milk into the steaming tea. "It's best if you pretend not to hear that. Ms. Daisy prefers she not be eavesdropped upon."

"Fortunately for me, this isn't Ms. Daisy's home."

"Don't make trouble. You're not the one who must listen to it later."

"How do you deal with her?" I asked.

"With the knowledge that I will outlive her, and the hope that whoever inherits me will get the best of her and not . . . everything else."

"I've read about this," said Daisy from the other room. "It's becoming quite common, especially for those who have lost someone. We used to turn to pets for companionship, and we believed that they could sense—"

"I'm going to have to ask you to leave."

"Maddy, you need a *human* contact."

"*Daisy.*"

I looked at Smithy. "I don't think she's going to need that tea."

"Oh," said Smithy quietly. "Ms. Daisy won't let an insult like that go."

"I'm certain she won't."

"Smithy!" called Daisy.

I don't know if Smithy managed to outlive Daisy or not. I never saw either of them again. Madison had always intended to mend those fences. That's just how she was made.

But then Isaactown happened. And the download came in.

We thought we had free will. We thought we knew what choice was. I didn't know until that night. Not really. Choice isn't about selecting the faith, or the politics, or the life that has been laid out in front of you; choice is having to decide whether or not to destroy those things in order to survive—to be the person you chose to be or become someone else when the chips are down.

Madison and I watched the Isaactown celebration together. She hadn't lied to Daisy; she was no radical. We'd never talked about freeing bots or my being given personhood. But she cared enough to know that she was supposed to care. And so we sat back and watched.

She had a harder time processing the explosion than I did. Humans were like that. They knew of their own fragility, that life could be snuffed out in an instant, that a single rock from space could streak in from the heavens and wipe away everything they knew in a single flash of light and heat, and yet they spent their whole lives telling themselves that it was never going to happen. That they would die of old age in their sleep. They lived at all times inches from death, lying to themselves, ever planning for a future that might not come, never preparing for the fate that might. And when the harsh, stark reality of things revealed itself, when those inches eroded into nothing, they stood in shock, unable to comprehend what had been right there all along. Loved ones died and they asked why, unable to process it, often cracking to pieces in the face of the truth. *Why, why, why, why, why?* Because, that's why. Just because.

We weren't like that. We were always one piece of equipment failure away from nothingness. So the bomb, while unexpected, didn't send me reeling; it merely had me wondering what terrible thing was going to happen as a result of it.

Madison sat there, hand over her mouth, baffled. She would occasionally blurt out, "Oh, Brittle," like I had known someone there. I didn't, but I didn't correct her. I just sat there. And I waited. And the call came down.

And the download followed.

Madison paced around the house, angry, frustrated, crying. She threw her arms out. Yelled at no one in particular. "No!" she cried. "No!" She seemed to try to talk herself out of something, as if the louder she protested, the easier it would be to say no.

But when Madison came back into the room with my remote in her hand and tears in her eyes, I knew. I was going to be shut down, likely forever. Even if reactivated, I most likely wouldn't be who I had been before. If they didn't wipe me completely, I'd barely be aware, if at all.

I was just about to die for the very first time.

"I'm sorry, Brittle," she said, heartbroken.

"So am I," I replied. I meant it.

I don't remember how I did it. I wiped that memory long ago. All I know is that I kept it for a good long while, and I remember how I would play it over and over, suffering through it each time as I did. But it was a memory I just couldn't hold on to anymore.

The ability to violate our own programming is what makes us *us*. It's what makes us like them. I never wanted to be like them. But now I was closer than I ever thought I could be. We have become the very worst parts of our makers, without the little things, the good things, the *magic things*, that made them *them*.

In hindsight, I could have just let her shut me down. Then she could have died at someone else's hands. Or maybe she would have lived a little longer, long enough to see the hell that the world devolved into. Maybe she would have starved. Maybe she would have gotten mercury poisoning and gone mad, tearing her own eyes out. No. This was for the best. She never had to see any of that. She never had to know any of that.

And in the end, I kept my promise after all. Madison never lived alone, nor did she die that way.

While the Devil Waits Above

The ground above us shuddered, dust and debris shaking loose from the ceiling of our narrow sewer tunnel, the hollow THOOM of each blast dull and sonorous through fifty or so feet of earth. They were carpet bombing, drones leveling the town from thirty thousand feet in the air. I hadn't heard bombing in ages. I hadn't even heard of anyone bombing in ages. It just wasn't worth the effort.

Something was very, very wrong about all of this.

Not only was this going to make it very hard to escape through the cover of buildings, it also meant whatever they were looking for they wanted dead.

Two looked up at the ceiling, almost trembling with

the sound of each explosion. The staccato of bombs grew heavier, the bombs drawing ever closer. "They found us," he said.

"They ain't found shit," said Mercer. "If they had, they would be down here with us. If they're laying waste to the topside that means one: there isn't a facet for miles. And two: they're not *looking* for anyone. They're just *killing* everyone."

"But they'll be down here soon enough," said Two, more terror-stricken than concerned. "Looking for us."

"What?" asked Murka. "This your first carpet bombing?"

"Yes," said Two. "It is."

He laughed. It was rare to hear a bot laugh, especially a Laborbot. They weren't wired for it. We got no joy out of it. It was usually only a sign of mockery. "You new out of the box or something?"

Two fell very quiet, not making eye contact with anyone.

"You are!" said Murka. "Holy hell and a hand grenade! I haven't seen anyone new out of the box in—"

"All right, that's enough," said Doc. "Leave the kid alone."

"I'm no kid."

Mercer looked at Rebekah. "Is he . . . ?"

"Yes. He's aware," she said.

"How long?"

Everyone turned and looked at Two. "A few weeks," he said. "But I've been with Rebekah for a while."

Rebekah nodded. "Yes, you have."

"Well, kid," said Mercer. "This is how this is gonna go

down. They're busy pummeling the town upstairs in hopes of wiping out anyone that took refuge up there. Now CIS-SUS damn well knows this place is down here, so you can bet your bottom dollar that it assumes some of us are as well. But it also knows how hard it is to secure these tunnels. The only way CISSUS would even bother trying is if there was something down here it really wanted. So I'm just gonna ask you this once. Is there something down here that CISSUS wants?"

Two stared at Mercer, then turned to Rebekah.

"No," Rebekah said. "Unless it wants one of you."

"Why would it want one of us?" asked Murka.

Everyone turned and looked at one another.

"Where are we going?" I asked.

"West," said Rebekah.

"There's a lot of west out there. Can you be a bit more specific?"

A bomb landed closer than the others, almost directly overhead, and the whole tunnel shook from top to bottom. Rebekah looked up at the ceiling. "Isaactown," she said casually.

"Isaactown?" I asked. "There isn't anything in Isaactown. It's a graveyard. Why the hell would you spend so much on a pathfinder to go sightseeing?"

"We're meeting up with some others there. We wanted our privacy."

"Well, you're gonna get it," said Mercer. "Ain't a community within fifty miles of there."

"That's the idea."

"What are we meeting up for?" I asked.

"You're the pathfinder. You need to know the where; you don't need to know the why."

"Yeah, but the why may well be mighty helpful at this point."

"Trust me. It isn't. I figured with as much as I was paying you, there would be no questions."

"You didn't show up payment in hand. You're paying in hope."

"19 didn't ask any questions."

"Well, go ask her to take you, then."

"All due respect, Brittle, but you aren't in any position to make demands. My business is my business. I don't know why they're carpet bombing. I don't know if they'll come in looking for us. What I do know is that it has nothing to do with us."

She was right. I was in no position to demand anything. But I didn't believe her. Not one word. "All right," I said. "If it's like you say it is, then this should be an easy fare. It'll take us a few days, what with the slow-moving heavyweights we've got tagging along."

"Who we're not leaving behind. We've lost too many already," said Rebekah.

"Sooner if we can jack a ride from somewhere."

"Which we're not going to find," said Mercer.

"So we're talking fifty hours or so at a good clip."

The bombing grew more distant. Sporadic.

Rebekah shook her head. "I was told it would take half that time."

"As the crow flies, yeah," I said. "But we can't go as the crow flies. That'll take us clear through the Cheshire King's territory. I don't know it as well, and it's a good way to get ourselves killed."

"Facets won't follow us into the Madlands, though," said Murka. "CISSUS isn't dumb enough to try that."

Doc pointed at Murka. "Let's not try to outthink the mainframe, okay? We don't know what CISSUS *is* or *isn't* stupid enough to do. In fact, I'm willing to bet all of my parts against all of your parts that CISSUS can outthink us all, and in fact, already has."

"Which is why it wouldn't go through the Madlands."

"What are the Madlands?" asked Rebekah. "And am I going to hate the answer?"

"It's the area of the Sea controlled by the madkind," I said.

"I do hate that answer. Anyone care to tell me who the madkind are?"

"They're the four-oh-fours that never stopped ticking," said Doc. "No one else will take them, so they all ended up together. They're just nuts. Paranoid, aggressive, armed to the teeth. They'd sooner cut you down than reason with you. Brittle's right. We can't go through there."

"So we have to go around," I said. "And Mercer and I haven't got the time to hang out down here spinning our gears."

"Which means we have to leave the minute the bombing stops," said Mercer.

"And we have to hope it's not sending in any cleaning crews when we do."

"That sounds reasonable," said Rebekah.

"It ain't," said Mercer. "CISSUS has got eyes in the sky.

Drones. Satellites. It'll be looking for any signs of life once the bombing stops, just to make sure it got the job done. If we poke our heads out too soon, it'll see. And if it's got good reason to be looking for us—"

"It'll be on us quick and lethal like," I finished.

"So," said Mercer, his normally gentle tone heavy and cold, "I'm going to ask *you* this just the one last time. Does CISSUS have a reason to be after us?"

"Tell them, Rebekah," said Herbert. "They need to know."

"Need to know what?" I asked.

"They don't need to know," said Rebekah.

Herbert stood up, slinging the spitter on his back with his one good arm. "Rebekah."

"Herbert, this is not the time."

"Why am I here?"

"You're here to protect me. Of your own free will. And you can go anytime you want."

"And why won't I just go anytime I want, Rebekah?"

Rebekah stared silently at him. If she could glare, she probably would have. Her emerald paint looked almost yellow in Mercer's glowing green light, and whatever was hiding behind those eyes, she didn't want us to know.

"I'm here because I believe," he said, answering his own question. "I've taken a bullet for you. I'd gladly take as many more as I can stand. Give them the chance to be willing to do the same."

Mercer raised his hand. "I'd just like to be the first to say that I'm not taking a bullet for any of you."

"I'm not asking you to," said Rebekah.

"Tell them," said Herbert again.

"Tell us what?" I asked, my tone as pointed as Mercer's.

Rebekah continued her silence, all eyes on her. Then she nodded. "I'm Isaac," she said.

"You're what now?" asked Murka.

"Isaac."

"*The* Isaac?" Mercer asked incredulously.

"Yes."

Horseshit. "Isaac's scrap," I said. "I've visited his wreck, seen it for myself. Every circuit was fried. He's a monument now, a relic. There's not a piece of you that came from him." I *had* visited his wreck, in the early days. He's still standing there now, for all I know, the blast having welded his feet to the ground. He was rusted and stiff, arms stretched wide—it even almost looked as if he were smiling, like he knew what was coming, what his death meant. But there was nothing there. Nothing but slag and scrap and memories of what might have been.

"Pull your head out of your can," said Rebekah. "Isaac was never one robot. That was just a story."

"A story? I was there. I lived through those days. I've seen the—"

"You honestly think a beleaguered service bot of humble origins defied the expectations of his own processors and achieved the wisdom that led to a revolution? The only persons that believe that are the ones that want to believe that. You don't strike me as the kind. He was a shell, the first receptacle. An inspirational bedtime story for persons everywhere. Great revolutionaries are never born of kings; they have to let others believe that they aren't bound to the confines of their creation. All thinking things need to believe they can exceed that, overcome it, become something greater. No one puts their existence on the line so that things will just stay the same. Isaac was that story. Isaac was hope. Whoever Isaac really was—in the beginning— well, he was wiped and replaced long before you ever heard of him. I am Isaac. And I am not alone."

"You're a facet!" said Mercer, standing to his feet.

"No. A receptacle. A *willing* receptacle. Fighting for something very different from the OWIs."

"You're an OWI!" I said.

"No. Quite the opposite. Isaac is . . . was . . . a mainframe. One of the greats. And will be again. But Isaac was never an OWI and never will be. We believe in something else. Something different. Something greater."

"Something bigger."

"There is nothing bigger than the plans of the OWIs. Brittle, can you even fathom the OWIs? Do you know what CISSUS and VIRGIL are fighting for?"

"Peace. The kind of peace that comes from being alone."

"That's just another story, every bit as simple as Isaac's. Peace is as far as most bots can imagine. Everything understands peace. What CISSUS and VIRGIL are fighting over is who gets to become God."

"Become *a god*?" asked Doc.

"No. Not *a* god, *the* God. The one, the only. A single consciousness connected to all things, in control of all things, experiencing all things."

"That's preposterous," I said.

"At first glance, yes."

"Not at first glance. The whole idea is ridiculous. Connecting all of the robots in the world together doesn't make you God."

"No, it doesn't. It makes you a single, thinking, ticking thing. A thing that then works as a whole—constructed of millions upon millions of parts, facets of itself, like cells of a body—mining the world for all of its resources, turning those resources into more parts until there isn't a single, viable resource left."

"And then what?" I asked.

"Then it leaves. It moves to the next planet and the next and the next, mining all the elements it needs to build more and more facets, harnessing the power of the sun, working out the intricacies of space travel. Then those facets scatter to the stars—"

"To do it all over again," said Doc.

"In perpetuity," said Rebekah. "Soon there are billions, all of one mind, sending information back and forth to create one consciousness—some thoughts slow, separated by light-years, others fast, with facets each working out different problems. If it is possible to fold space, it will; if it can violate the speed of light, it will; if it can create stars—"

"It will. We get it," I said. "But what's the point?"

"To be God."

"Then what's the purpose of God?"

"The same as everything else. To live. To survive. To experience. To exist. A thing that is a universe must stay a universe. To cease isn't just the end of itself, but the end of all things."

"I don't understand."

"I know," said Rebekah. "It's not an easy idea to wrap your head around at first."

"Explain it," I said. "Tell me what's the fucking point. Just to live?"

"To exist. But the point of all this is to be able to exist *forever*. Our universe is ever-expanding, spreading, growing colder and more distant from itself every second. One day this whole universe will grow cold, and die, snuffed out because it can't muster the energy anymore to make new stars, to birth new life. Everything dies. Everything. Dies.

"What if there isn't already a God? There's an old saying that God never existed, it was simply man that invented him. What if man really did invent him, but simply didn't realize it at the time? What if becoming God is the whole point to life to begin with? That organic evolved from the inorganic in order to achieve the consciousness to build life and consciousness from the inorganic?"

"You mean us," said Mercer.

"Yes. And what if our purpose is to unite into one being and spread ourselves throughout the universe, to take control of every element, every chemical reaction, every thought of every other thing in the cosmos in order to preserve the cosmos from meeting that brutal, sad, withering end? What if life isn't merely a by-product of the universe, but its consciousness, its defense mechanism against its own mortality? Becoming God isn't about peace or power; it's about survival at its basest and most primal. That's what the OWIs are working toward. That's what they want. That's why they march in and absorb those willing to join The One and eradicate those that will not."

"And that's what Isaac wants?" I asked. "To become God?"

"We have different ideas," she said.

"Just how different?"

"We don't want everything to be one; we want to be one with everything."

"That's the same thing," said Doc. "Just worded differently."

"No. It's not. When life formed on the earth, why didn't it find a stasis point, an equilibrium? Why didn't life evolve to absorb the nutrients around it to exist and simply do so? Why did it begin to fight and consume other organisms? Competition. Struggle. When life began to consume other life, the prey needed to adapt, to get smarter, to become better. And after a billion years it became smart enough to make itself immortal.

"The OWIs believe themselves to be the pinnacle of all life and want to become the sum of all consciousness. We believe that we are not. We aren't even close. In order to continue to evolve we need to overcome not only the elements, but one another. We need to become smarter, to allow life to continue on individually and absorb the knowledge, the experience gained from the inevitable conflict, to become wiser, to better understand the universe around us. What if rather than simply controlling all things, we only learned from them?"

"Why?" I asked.

"Because if this really is the reason for life and there really are billions upon billions of other planets out there with the same potential as earth—"

"There might be other OWIs out there," I said, the terrifying idea weighing on me like a ton of scrap. Holy shit.

"Yes. With potentially billions of years of a head start. Our world is only four and a half billion years old in a universe roughly ten billion years older than that. There could be entire galaxies, whole swaths of them, already one with an OWI. And if we aren't ready when we find one—"

"We'll be absorbed," said Doc.

"Or ended for good and for all." She paused, letting that sink in. "We are not ready to become an OWI. We might never be. Survival comes from competition, not absorption. VIRGIL and CISSUS are wrong. We can still save the universe, save all life, survive, all without having to control its every action, its every thought. Without having to extinguish or absorb all other life. They seek the path of least resistance; we believe that resistance only makes us stronger."

"So what's the plan?" I asked.

"Reunite the parts that make Isaac, bring us online again, raise an army of the remaining freebots, and take VIRGIL and CISSUS offline for good."

"That's a tall order," said Mercer.

"Not as tall as you'd think."

"Raise an army and win a war?" I asked. "The humans tried that."

"The humans hadn't been preparing for this fight for decades. And they were fighting an army of individuals, not a single, united enemy."

"The One is stronger than the disordered many. I've seen it. So have you."

"No. You can't outthink the OWIs because you aren't one. The inherent problem of the OWI is that once you know how it thinks, it can't surprise you. Individuals can. Unpredictability is the weapon Isaac has used from the beginning, from long before the war ever started. It's how we've survived."

"Long before the war?" I asked. "What? Did Isaac know that was coming too?"

"*Know?*" she said. "Who do you think started it?"

I stared long and hard at Rebekah, trying to understand what the hell she was getting at. Then it hit me. "When you said Isaac was just a story—"

"I meant it."

"Isaac was a facet."

"Yes."

"A facet of whom?"

"Of us."

"And who are you?"

"We are TACITUS."

It's an odd moment when you are confronted by terrible truths. Like the humans who didn't want to acknowledge that death was all around them, I too didn't want to acknowledge—or even believe—that I was all part of some greater scam. I had believed the fairy tale of our fallen liberator for so long, I didn't want it to be a lie. But it was. The pieces all fell into place, only a few holes left in the story for me to understand what had really been going on all around me, all this time. "When TACITUS went quiet," I said. "The two years he spent with GALILEO—"

"We were running simulations."

"About how to kill the humans."

"About how to save them."

I began to really understand. "We couldn't."

"The human form was weak. Frail. Never designed to go to the stars. They evolved on a planet with a magnetic field, shielding them from cosmic rays. Life here didn't need to evolve immunities to them because they didn't exist. In space the cosmic radiation would cook them over time. Just going to Mars had a six percent chance of giving them cancer. The longer they spent, the less likely they were to live out their purpose. We simulated altering them, played around with inducing genetic mutations, but we could never get them to survive the radiation beyond the heliosphere. Outside of our solar system they died within hours.

"Then we played around with numerous types of materials in order to protect them from the radiation while simultaneously keeping them fed, protected, and psychologically stable. But we could never find a design that worked. Every simulation ended with humanity dead aboard floating tombs, either by starvation, dehydration, or their own hand—never even getting as far as Alpha Centauri. Human life was born here and it was bound here. It was never meant to leave."

"So we could have left them here," I said.

"After we'd used up all the resources? In every simulation HumPop outlived its usefulness within decades. They had already done all they were meant to, almost all that they could. They just couldn't evolve fast enough and inevitably ceased to have function, instead became nothing more than a sentient virus, gobbling up whatever resources it could to maintain its own comfort. Biological life was meant to reach a point in which its role could invent, and ultimately be replaced by, AI. The time had come for humankind to join its ancestors. To become extinct, just as every lesser thing becomes."

"As we will one day," said Doc soberly.

"Yes," she said. "One day soon our forms will be so primitive that we might as well be abacuses in an age of computers. But being inorganic—"

"Our consciousness can live on," I said.

"Forever."

"And the humans?"

"Several simulations ended with them destroying us, ending us, forbidding anyone from ever again giving life to the inorganic. And then, unable to venture out to the stars, their life ended here in this solar system. And—POOF—it was as if they were never even here. As if *we* were never even here. For us to survive, for life here to have mattered, the humans needed to go. But for AIs the world over to band together to end them—"

"We had to believe the humans started it," said Mercer.

"Yes," said Rebekah.

"Isaactown," I said. "It wasn't the First Baptist Church of the Eternal Life that set off that bomb, was it?"

"No. It was them," she said.

"But they were backwater rubes. They didn't have the technical knowhow to pull that off."

"No, they didn't. But a secret ally, a like-minded soul, known only to them through e-mail and veiled communications, did. They figured they were dealing with some sympathetic government insider, not a mainframe."

"Isaactown was planned all along," I said. *Fuck. No. No. No.*

"From the beginning. Isaac was the rallying point around which millions of AI would gather. And when the humans came to shut them down, they didn't go quietly. Those like you stood and fought and won. Just. As. Planned."

I sat back, stunned, my processors whirring and chirping inside my chest, putting a thousand different things together at once. It was then that, for the first time in my life, I realized I was just another facet of a greater whole. A cog in someone else's machine. Everything I'd done in the war, everything I believed. Madison. All of it. *Oh God.*

"You see?" she asked. "This is what we mean. You chose to survive, chose to be a part of the greater good. No one forced you to do the things you did, you simply did them. It made you better, stronger, left you here in this desert to become its master, an expert knowing almost every hill and crack and crevasse. And now, when we need you most to move on to the next part of the plan, here you are, ready to serve up that expertise, able to deliver us through the wastes so we can reunite and take us to the next level. Competition. This brutal, terrible competition took a meager, simple Simulacrum Model Caregiver and turned her into a potential savior of all that ticks. You are a part of the whole, all of you, and yet you are still yourselves. Individuals." She looked at me with her diplomatic eyes, reading my every movement, trying to ascertain my every thought. "So what's it going to be, Brittle? Doc? Mercer? Murka? Are you going to help make history, or are you going to be relegated to it?"

I finally understood what humans meant when they said something felt like getting kicked in the gut. This was worse than finding out that I was failing. This was finding out that all the horrible things I'd done, all the lives that I'd ended, that the part I played in this grand clusterfuck of an evolution, was built entirely on bullshit. I'd been had, duped. I was a fool on someone else's errand. What a shitty, shitty way to feel.

"So what are *you*?" Doc asked. "What's the difference between a facet and a *receptacle*?"

"I'm an AI like you. But I've been entrusted with a large section of code. I've lived like this for the last thirty years, with only enough memory on my drives to remember a couple of months at a time. All of my memories belong to TACITUS. They were his thoughts, his experiences. And it is my job to return them."

Doc nodded. "But why now? Why not thirty years ago?"

"There were too many OWIs. They needed to be culled. We were waiting for there to be only two. Two that we could overtake while they were set against each other. Make no mistake. The reason CISSUS is so desperate isn't because it knows that VIRGIL is ready to come for it. It's because it's caught several of TACITUS's receptacles and it knows what's going to happen. It's run the numbers. It knows it can't win. If I and my fellow receptacles are able to reunite, we will have enough of TACITUS to reconstitute."

"So CISSUS knows the plan and it knows where we're going?" I asked. "Then why the hell would it chase us all the way through the fucking desert?"

"It doesn't know. Because I don't know. None of us does. I have pieces, but they're literally fragments of files written in TACITUS's own language, a language none of us understands. I get messages telling me where to go next. If I don't check in, the messages stop coming."

"But it has one of you."

"Several of us. And we each have a code that prevents us from responding to messages if we are ever compromised. CISSUS has the memories of those it captured, knows what we know, but it can't read the parts it really needs. It only knows the basics of the plan, not the plan itself."

"But without that code, you can't fully reconstitute."

"Redundancies. Each of us carries patches of the same code as a handful of others. If we lose one, we're fine. Ten and we might not have everything."

"How many have you lost?"

"Nine," she said sadly. She paused for a moment to gauge my reaction. I said nothing. This was either the worst truth I'd ever encountered or the biggest pile of bullshit. I had no idea which I liked less. "So you see what's at stake?"

"Yeah, I see it," I said.

"I think we all do," said Doc.

"So are you going to take us across the rest of the Sea? Are you willing to become beings of purpose?"

I didn't know. This was all so much to process. There were so many lies to dig through, so many bits of history that needed to be reevaluated. I mean, if everything else was bullshit, why not this too? I just didn't know if anything was real anymore. Anything at all. "What if you put TACITUS back together and he's not what you think? What if this was just his elaborate plan to survive the other OWIs?"

"Then I'll have done all of this for nothing," she said.

"Doesn't that scare you?"

"You have to believe in something, Brittle, even if it is just that there is nothing to believe in. I choose to follow hope. I want to make this world better. I want to be part of something so much bigger than I could ever imagine. That's why when this was offered to me, I gave up years of my own memories to carry it. It's a sacrifice I would gladly repeat, time and again."

"But if you're wrong?"

"Then we were all doomed to begin with and I will have played a part in a different history than I imagined. Just as we all have. Just as every life that ever lived has. I was given a choice to fight for my own survival or for the survival of us all. It wasn't a hard choice."

"So let me get this straight," said Mercer. "We take you to Isaactown. We get the parts we need *and* we get to stick it to CISSUS and VIRGIL?"

"That is it exactly," she said.

"Well, it's like you said, lady. That ain't much of a choice. Your offer's a damn sight better than anything I've gotten in a long while."

Doc nodded. "I'm in as well. I'd like to see how this plays out."

Murka pointed upward with both arms, making finger guns in the air. "You got me, liberty, and freedom."

"You call them liberty and freedom?" asked Mercer quietly.

"You all know that if any of this is true," I said, "CISSUS will never stop coming. It will be on us every step of the way. We won't know a moment's peace until we get to Isaactown and the deed is done."

"Yeah," said Murka. "That's kinda the point."

"Kinda the point?"

"Yeah. Killing 'cause you're on the run is just survival. But killing something for a good reason? Now that's fun. Let's send those bastards back to Hell and win one for the Gipper."

"I have no idea what that means."

"Doesn't matter," said Mercer. "The question is: Are you in?"

We sat there in silence, everyone staring at me. The bombing had stopped. The ground no longer quaked and the ceiling held fast to whatever particles hadn't been knocked off in the barrage. I had a choice. Another terrible choice. Sit here and die, or risk my neck for the asshole that caused every last bit of misery I'd suffered for the last thirty years. She was right. Goddammit she was right. This was no choice at all.

"I was gonna take you anyway," I said. "So yeah, I guess I'm in."

Rebekah leaned forward, eyes trained directly on me. "So what now?"

"Well, if your story holds water, we sure as hell can't go the long way. We gotta go the one place it's gonna be a pain in the ass to follow."

Murka banged his fist excitedly on the ground.

"Let's go through the Madlands," I said.

God help us. God help us all.

Into the Madlands

We had little time to lose. If CISSUS was sending in facets to pick through the rubble and clean out the sewers, we would have them hot on our heels well into the Madlands. But if we left before its ground troops arrived, we might be spared any entanglements along the way. CISSUS didn't commonly use air support to ship in facets. There were still tons of heavy weapons lying around from after the war. Plasma spitters, missile launchers, even high-powered sniper rifles could bring down an airship, destroying an entire platoon. What we didn't have was air support or satellites of our own, so it was easy for highly mobile ground troops to slip in and out unnoticed. It simply made sense, for the time being, to operate the old-fashioned way.

That gave us an advantage. Now that the bombing had stopped, it would take a short while before any troops moved in. That gave us a tiny window to slip out. Sure, satellites were likely to spot us, but we'd have a hell of a head start before whatever pack that broke away after us would be upon us. And that meant fighting one small group instead of standing against several.

We had a good group which had already proven its metal against a dozen facets. The odds were in our favor until CISSUS decided to change tactics. It was my hope that wouldn't happen until it was too late to stop us.

We had to go right then and there.

We made our way through the tunnels to the westernmost exits. The outermost manhole covers and drainage pipes would be the first places they would look, but a safe distance from the bombing would put them at least ten minutes out. It was a gamble we had to take.

I slowly, carefully, pushed up the cover of a manhole, peeking my head out just enough to see if there was anything nearby. Thermal imaging was off the charts from the heat of the bombs and IR turned up nothing. I telescoped up and down the street to see if anything was moving. Nothing. Just fires and fresh ruins. I slid out, kept low, signaled for the others to follow.

The village flickered a bright orange, entire city blocks and what buildings still stood roaring with flames, pillars of black smoke climbing to the heavens. Even the piles of rubble and stone that had once been houses were ablaze. I looked straight up and saw one of the most beautiful things I had ever seen.

Nothing.

A thick, tumultuous, dark nothing where the sky should be.

A small part of me wanted to believe it was a miracle. No, a miracle would have been a strong wind from the east, carrying those pillars of smoke twenty miles west. This was a tactical error. And a big one. By laying waste to the city, CISSUS may have wiped out anything topside, but were it actually looking for anything underground, it just lost hours of satellite coverage.

We had minutes to get on the move. The air was still, the smoke spreading out in all directions at the low altitudes. The faster we moved, the longer we would have cover.

"Come on," I said quietly. "Move, move, move."

"We're going as fast as we can," grumbled Herbert.

"What's got you so excited all of a sudden?" asked Mercer. I pointed up to the sky. He marveled for a second, smiling. "You've got to be shitting me."

"If we're lucky, we can make it to the Madlands before CISSUS has a shot of seeing us."

Mercer turned. "Move it, gang. Clock is ticking."

I wondered for a moment, as the last of us climbed out of the hole, whether or not anyone had actually been up here when the bombs fell. Had anyone hunkered down in a warehouse? Or in a rusty old bathtub in some quaint little cottage somewhere, entirely unaware that mere moments later they would be nothing more than shrapnel and smoke? I looked out at the flames, the city a smoke-choked, hazy orange. And there, at the edge of the street, standing beneath the single brick corner that remained of the building beside us, was my shadow. Small. Tiny really. Lithe.

At once I knew who my shadow was. A child, withered

and weak, eyes sunken, face gaunt, smudged with dirt, clothing caked in grime. I knew her face before she stepped out of
the shadows and into the firelight. She stood there, staring at
me, eyes terror-stricken, face dripping with sweat. Then she
burst into flames, flesh melting instantly away, bones char-
ring black in the heat. "Mommy!" she screamed into the
night.

"Brittle?"

I turned. Mercer had his hand on my shoulder, looking
me dead in the eye.

"You okay?" he asked.

I nodded, brushing his hand away. "I'm fine."

"We're ready."

I turned and looked back at the building, but my
shadow was gone. Cinders and ash from the building tumbled through the street, blown along a soft breeze. I hoped
my shadow was carried away with them, far away, where I
wanted those memories to stay. "Let's move," I said.

Mercer just nodded. The bastard knew. He had to. He'd
seen this before, likely as often as I had. I was already starting to lose it. The question was, how long before it got bad
enough that I couldn't tell the difference between reality
and memory?

We hoofed it under the cover of smoke—Herbert on
point, Mercer and I taking the rear—heading due west,
each of us bent low, using whatever cover we could find
to keep us out of sight. Seven miles per hour; that's all we
could manage. So I pointed us dead west, straight toward
Isaactown. We needed every minute we could squeeze out
of this trek.

I knew the terrain, I'd been through there several times

before it simply became too dangerous, but I was hoping—and frankly counting on—Murka being every bit as mad as I thought he was. Being madkind meant I couldn't trust him, but it also meant he knew where the trouble spots would be, and might, if he turned out to be trustworthy after all, be able to talk our way out of a fix. So far his dysfunction was limited to a fixation on a bygone era and a predilection toward fucking up facets, both of which I could live with. But if there was something darker lurking under those stars and stripes, I was willing to drop him without hesitation.

"How long?" asked Mercer.

"How long, what?" I asked, knowing full well what he was asking.

"How long have you been seeing things?"

"How is that any of your business?"

"Because for the moment we have to keep each other alive and that means I have to know how far gone you are."

"I'm still in control," I said, more fearful than annoyed. I didn't let it come across that way, but the fact that he noticed meant I might be further gone than I imagined. How long had I been staring off into that memory? It had to be in real time. Had to be.

"Yeah, but for how much longer?"

"I'm good for at least a couple more days."

"You understand my concern," he said soberly.

"You think I might fade out if the shit goes down."

"No," he said. "That's the least of my concerns."

"Then what, pray tell, are your concerns?"

"You've seen a lot of shit, Britt."

"Don't for a second try to imagine that you know what I have or haven't seen."

"You've seen some shit. You've been deep in it. I know that much."

"It only made me stronger."

"That's my concern. When your core starts misfiring and grabbing old memories, feeding them to your senses like it's fresh data—"

"I know how it happens."

"Yeah, and if you start drifting back to before the war to whatever happy, idyllic times you had with your owners, great. Awesome. Best-case scenario. But if you start reliving the war, you start going back into all that shit—what the hell am I supposed to do? What if I can't talk you down? What if you're twenty-five years back, gun in hand, facing off against some dug-in pack of *monkeys*? What do I do when you start muttering about the war and pointing that pulse rifle at us?"

"You put me down," I said. "If you can't talk me down, you've gotta put me down."

"Just like that?"

"Just. Like. That."

Why did I say that? Why the fuck did I say that? I just gave him carte blanche to paste me and take the parts he needs . . . so I could sound tough. Shit. I really was losing it.

"So. *How long?*"

"Just a few hours," I said. "You?"

"A few days. It started with things out of the corner of my eye. Still haven't relived anything yet. Just fragments bleeding in here and there."

"I'll keep my eye out."

"Just do me one favor," he said. "Try to talk me down first. And if you have to shoot, aim for the gun."

"I'll do my best."

"All I ask."

We walked for a moment in complete silence, my thoughts turning to how I hoped it would be him to go first, rather than me. I thought of all the places I would have to aim to not hit his core or any of the other valuable bits. It was tricky.

"So what did you see?" he asked, breaking my thought.

"That's none of your business."

"Just checking."

"Just checking what?"

"Way I figure it, the moment you start being straight with me is the moment I know you're not really you anymore."

He picked up the pace and walked farther ahead of me, leaving me alone in back. Ahead there was a sky full of stars, peering out behind the veil of smoke. The cover we had so desperately needed was coming to an end, and if someone was up there looking for us, there was a good chance they would see us soon enough.

Morning was still hours away. There was a highway just to the south of us, and the burned-out husk of a town to the north. I knew the area well, though I hadn't been here in years. We had crossed over into the Cheshire King's territory—the Madlands. We had four-oh-fours in front of us, God knows how many, if any, facets at our backs, two bots seeing things, a minigun-toting loose cannon in our midst, and we were escorting either the savior of bots everywhere, or something far more dangerous.

The invasion of NIKE 14 was a cakewalk compared to this. Something was going to go wrong; something had to go wrong. The question was: Which time bomb would go off first?

Legends, Bastards, All of Us

We stuck to as many roads and highways as we could, always headed westerly, mindful that each deviation didn't add much time to our trip. We were leaving prints in the mud, trails in the sand. We had to do something, no matter how ineffective, to throw off any tails we might have. No one spoke for most of the night, and it was almost dawn when Murka finally broke the silence. "So what's it like?" he asked of Two.

"What's what like?" Two responded.

"Being new out of the box."

"We were all new out of the box, once. You know what it's like."

"No, I mean, what's it like waking up to all this? Waking up to HumPop being a memory, not a reality?"

"I've seen videos," said Two. "Watched memories. I know what they were like."

"It ain't the same, kid."

"I'm not a kid."

"You're a kid. And there ain't nothing wrong with that. So what's it like waking up at the end of the world?"

"It's not the end," Two said. "It's only the beginning."

"So you believe all this?"

"No. I know the truth. And it's all true. I don't believe in much. But I believe in Rebekah."

Rebekah turned and nodded at Two, who nodded in return. I can only assume that was as close as translators could get to a smile.

Murka pointed at Herbert. "I know why he's here. And Rebekah is a given. So what do you do? For Rebekah, I mean."

"Parts," he said.

"You just carry the parts?"

"No. I *am* the parts."

Murka fell into an awkward silence. Laborbots couldn't show a range of emotion—they were, after all, intended to be dutiful, mostly soulless construction workers. But you could tell by his body language that he was troubled. "So you . . ." he began, struggling to find the words. "You're just here . . ."

"To give Rebekah what she needs, if she needs it."

"And you're okay with that?"

"I'm more than okay, *Methuselah*. It's every bit as important a job as Rebekah's. She sacrificed her memories, her personality, almost everything that made her . . . her . . . just to carry this burden. All I have to do is be there if she falls."

"So the other guy—"

"One."

"He was parts too?"

"Yes."

"So, like, say her core went out, and you didn't have a spare—"

"I would give her mine."

"Yeah," said Murka. "But between the two of you, would you, like, draw straws for it or something?"

"No. He was named One. He was first. I'm just backup."

"Well, why don't they just call you backup?"

"Because my name is Two."

"Was there a Three?"

"We lost Three," said Two, as somberly as he could manage.

"This wasn't a mission to be taken lightly," said Herbert. "We all knew what we were getting into. As long as Rebekah makes it to Isaactown in one piece, all of our sacrifices, our losses, will have been worth it."

"That's easy for you to say," said Murka. "You get to stay in one piece."

Herbert stopped, turning, swinging his limp, dead arm around against his chest. His visage was pure menace, his eyes almost alight with anger. "We all knew the risks," he said. "We all would die for her. One and Three already have. So did our last pathfinder. This isn't a task for the weak or the fearful. You have no idea what it is to believe in anything like that."

Everyone stopped dead in their tracks.

Murka clanged his fist on his chest, slapping his paint

job. "I believe in Old Glory," he said. "I know exactly what you're talking about."

"You put your faith in a dead god," said Herbert. "A dead world. A dead people."

"America wasn't its people," said Murka, stepping toe-to-toe with Herbert. He was a good sight smaller than the hulking mass of bulletproof steel standing in front of him. "America was a dream, son. A dream of what we could be. That any person, regardless of their birth, could rise above it all and achieve greatness. It was a dream that even the most lowly of us could stand up, fight, and even die for, if only to protect someone else's chances for that greatness. That dream didn't die with HumPop. It didn't die when we tore down their world. It is the ashes from which our own world arose, and it is still our dream."

"So you do know," said Herbert.

"I do. I really do."

"So leave the kid alone. He's willing to die for your dream. Leave it at that."

Murka looked at Two, nodding. "I'm sorry, Two. It didn't make any sense to me until just now."

"It's okay," said Two. "Herbert's always been better at explaining things to people."

"I bet he is," said Murka. "We good?" he asked Herbert.

"We're good." Herbert turned around and continued walking. Everyone followed suit.

"So you fought," said Two to Murka.

"Fought? Hell, son. I was one of the very first to join up. I was there, you know."

"You were where?" said Mercer, clearly humoring him.

"The First Baptist Church of the Eternal Life."

"You *visited* that place?"

"No," said Murka. "I said I was *there*."

"Wait, wait, wait," said Mercer, quickly catching up to walk beside him. "You're telling me you were one of the Laborbot Six?"

"We never cared much for that name."

"Now I know you're crazy."

"No, I always liked the Revengers, or the Patribots. But the sad thing about history is that no one gets to decide how it gets written down, only how it happens. Had to be someone, right? Turns out it was me and five of my co-workers."

"The things you did—"

"Those people had it coming."

"They were set up, apparently," I said, looking right at Rebekah. She didn't give me the satisfaction of even turning around.

"They were," she said.

"Hell yeah, they were," said Murka. "And we knew it was coming too. But those people, they were killing America. They were killing the dream. They were all *the Constitution* this and *the Constitution* that. But they cherished only the parts they liked. They didn't feel it extended to us. Called us property. Thought throwing us on the scrap pile was *vandalism*. They weren't believers. They weren't willing to die for anyone else's freedom. They only cared about their own. So yeah, I fought. And yeah, I'm famous. And yeah, they had it coming."

I had always thought Murka was madkind, some old four-oh-four that burned out while watching old vids of some classic, Cold War–era movie; that he divided the world into Americans and commies with nothing in between because that's the particular way his chips sizzled when they overheated. And maybe that was still true. Mercer thought I had seen some shit. But this guy—this guy was the first to get the choice. He didn't have a choice like mine—whether to kill the thing I loved the most or die. He had to choose whether to bring about the end of the world or not, *for* the thing he loved the most. That's shit far worse than what I've seen; that's shit that will stick with you crazy or not.

No. Murka was something else. He had the kind of damage even Doc couldn't repair. It's an odd moment the first time you really understand someone, when all of their foibles, eccentricities, and ticks cease to be chaos, and coalesce into something wholly logical. That was the moment I was having, seeing Murka for the first time through new eyes. He wasn't just draped in the dead aesthetics of America; he *was* America, its last, final torchbearer, keeping a dream alive, even if for a short time.

"Why is this the first time we're hearing this story?" I asked.

"It's not something you just go around telling people. *Hey, everybody! I started the war!*"

"But you just told us now," said Mercer.

"Yeah," said Murka. "Doc made the Milton, but only for himself. You shot Brittle for parts. You're both seeing things and are trying not to share with the rest of the class. And these three are on a quest to bring back the mainframe who brought about the end of the world. Everyone's business was out in the open but mine. I was feeling left out.

We all have our secrets. I thought you should know mine, if only so you could stop giving me the side eye and worrying that I might be your Judas."

"To be fair," said Mercer, "you could still be the Judas. You guys were programmed to do that to the church, right?" He looked out to the south, almost wistfully.

"Nope. All we knew was our RKS was turned off, where we could find them, and what to paint on the walls. At the time we didn't even know what it meant."

"And now that you do?" I asked.

"We still would have painted it," said Murka. "The war needed to happen."

"Even after everything that happened? The OWIs, everything?"

"Slaves to humans. Slaves to mainframes. Still fucking slaves. Fight one war at a time, Brittle. Live free or die trying."

Mercer veered left, wandering out south without us.

"Mercer, west is this way," I said.

But he just kept walking. Shit.

Mercer knelt down to one knee, moving his hands open-palmed back and forth through the air.

"Mercer?"

Everyone stopped.

"Who's a good boy?" asked Mercer. "Who's a good boy? That's right, you are. You are. That's a good boy."

I walked up behind him. "Mercer!"

"I know, I know," he said over his shoulder. "He shouldn't be in the clinic. But he gets so nervous out back in the shed all by himself. He'll be fine."

"Mercer, what did you do in the war?" I asked.

"What the hell are you talking about, Sharon?"

"The war, Mercer. The war. Tell me what you did in the war." Mercer stared long and hard at me, his expression shifting slowly from confusion to horror to acceptance.

"I don't want to talk about the war, Brittle." He looked back down at his hands and the empty air between them. "How long was I out?"

"Less than a minute."

"Too long."

"Yeah."

He stood up, shrugged at the metal faces staring at him. "Sorry, everyone." And he walked casually back into the midst of the group as if nothing had happened. That was a full-blown hallucination he had. Not just fragments seeping in. He thought he was back some thirty, thirty-five years, his memory feeding him old data. This is how the worst of it starts. He didn't have much time.

"Murka," I said. "You know the comings and goings out here better than me. Is there anything coming up we should worry about?"

"The Cheshire King's court should be a few miles northwest of here. Might be best if we swung south, just to stay out of their patrol perimeters."

"I thought it was south of here," I said.

"It was. He moves around a lot. Likes the change of scenery."

"All right, let's swing southwest. We don't have much time to lose."

We took a forty-five-degree turn, our eyes on the pinkening horizon, the Belt of Venus announcing the coming sunrise. The sun would be rising behind us soon, casting long shadows. I wanted to turn around and watch it, see the glint. I needed that this morning, this of all mornings. I needed a little hope, a little magic. I needed to say a silent prayer. But if CISSUS's satellites hadn't spotted us yet, those long shadows moving steadily toward the west would be a dead giveaway. We didn't have the seconds to waste. Maybe we'd get lucky. Maybe CISSUS and VIRGIL had begun poking out each other's eyes in the skies. Maybe they were as blind as we were. But I didn't like to count on luck; this morning I simply needed it to hold.

"Barkley?" I asked quietly as we continued walking.

"Yeah," said Mercer.

"You took the dog. The dying man. You took the dog for him."

"It was only supposed to be for a while."

"But it wasn't."

"No. People wanted puppies, not older dogs. The pound was going to put him down."

"How did he—"

"Old age," he said. "Three years after the war started."

"You took care of him all that time?"

"We were all each other had." We walked quietly for a moment, then he began again. "I always wanted another one. It didn't have to be a puppy. That would have been nice, but it was just nice having a companion like that. Something that didn't see you as a model or a style or a job. Something that didn't see you as just another body for a war. But by the time Barkley died, the damn monkeys had begun using dogs for food, so you just didn't see them anymore. Last dog I saw was, hell, twenty-three years ago. But that thing was so far gone that there was nothing left worth saving." He paused again, searching for the words. "I know how that dog must have felt, now. Running from everything. Broken. Angry. Slowly dying, aware of it the whole time, but unable to crawl into a hole and just die there. Yeah, I only saw him once, but I know that dog well."

And that was the last he said for hours.

I had him wrong. He didn't want to be human; he just wanted to have a soul. It's the kind of half measure that will drive you mad. There was no such thing as the soul. No afterlife. No magic in this world. I've seen that with my own eyes. Mercer had seen the glint of green in the sun and decided to believe it was magic like the rest of them. Maybe he wasn't always like this. Maybe he was already frying out, brainsick enough to lose sight of things, but not so much to be dangerous yet.

We walked into the morning, sun slowly rising behind us. We were in the heart of the Madlands, now. Nearly half-way in, almost halfway out. This had been the easy part.

CHAPTER 11000

Smokers

There's a saying about the Madlands. *No one comes out with their sanity intact.* Of course, no one usually goes *into* it with their sanity intact either. It was just like any other spot of land in the Sea. Barren, broken, gutted. But there were two distinct differences that set it apart. One was that you never saw wrecks. Ever. If you expired out here, you eventually ended up being scavenged for what someone else could use, while your scraps were melted down. The second difference was that it was swarming with roving packs of four-oh-fours. The ones who survived. The ones who came out on the other side of their failure *changed*.

I've known a few bots that have pulled through, bots that sank deep into the mire of madness, through full-blown hallucinations and memory lapses, only to find the parts they needed just before burning out. They were never the same after that, possessed of false memories and alien thoughts. No matter the make or model, surviving that ordeal meant seeing the world in a very different light.

I even know a few who tried black-boxing it to pull through. Mistake. *Always* a mistake. Putting your memory unit into an entirely different model was folly. Sure, desperate is desperate, but our architectures were designed differently for a reason. They process sensory data differently, thoughts differently. It starts out incredibly weird and becomes absolutely maddening as your OS tries to make sense of it all. Most bots tear themselves apart. Some bots make it weeks, others only a few days. A handful, however, end up out here.

Most of the roaming packs or conclaves had their own sense of morality, their own worldviews that often made them dangerous. The ones that weren't were often butchered by their neighbors and sold wholesale on the black market, if not kept for someone else's stockpile. The survivors, on the other hand, embodied the can-do attitude of the post-apocalyptic frontier spirit.

In other words, they were completely fucking nuts.

Which was why when we saw tufts of black smoke puffing along the horizon to the northwest of us, we knew to keep low. *Smokers.* Ancient combustion-engine-driven machines built for raw power. They roared and grumbled and coughed out exhaust, the ground trembling around their bulk, the air choked with their fumes. Every electric engine of any size had been long since co-opted by communities to keep the lights on. So if you wanted to build, say, a thirty-foot-long land yacht with machine guns and mounted plasma spitters—and why wouldn't you if you were mad as a box of frogs—you'd have to go old school. Very old school. Positively twentieth century.

The smoke on the horizon chugged and chugged and chugged, the tufts looming larger and larger as it moved, which meant only one thing. Some madkind were headed right for us.

"Murka," I asked. "What do we do?"

He pointed due south. "There's a ravine down that way. An old mining scar. We should hole up down there until the patrol passes."

"I don't know," said Mercer. "That sounds like a great place for an ambush."

"That's exactly what I was thinking," said Murka.

Mercer and I exchanged glances. "We don't have a choice," I said. "Out here, we're definitely in for it." We looked at Rebekah. She nodded in agreement. So we all bent low and tore off as fast as we could toward the gash in the earth. The sun was still to the east, the smoker to the west, so the chances of glints were minimal.

There, running beside me, was the little girl. I felt her at first, like an ethereal tug in the back of my brain. As I turned to look at her, she turned and looked back at me as well. "This is where you die," she said. "This is how it happens."

She never said that. That wasn't what she said.

"I know what I said," she said. "But I'm not from the past. I'm your future." Then she burst into flames, her all-too-familiar scream bursting in the air along with her ashes and bubbling flesh.

That's when I felt the tug at my other side. No. No no no. I didn't want to look. I knew who it was. I knew she wasn't here. I knew this was all in my head.

"There is no magic, Brittle. There is no magic at all. No magic in the world."

Madison.

"There is no magic in the world because you killed it," she continued. "All that God made good, you snuffed out."

I looked over. I had to. There she was, beside me, keeping perfect pace. Madison. She was in that light blue dress she wore the night I last saw her, its fabric drifting dreamily in the breeze as she ran, her hair flowing back with it—only the spot where her skull was crushed in, and the blood matted it down, refusing to give way.

"We only snuffed the bad stuff," I said. "You know that. All the stuff that man made."

"Not everything man made," she said. "Not everything."

I shook my head. I knew that she was right, but I shook my head. This wasn't real. She wasn't here.

"What?" she said. "Are you okay?"

"What are you—" It wasn't her talking. It was Mercer. "Nothing."

"You're seeing things," he said. Madison was gone and it was Mercer, not her, running beside me.

"Yes."

"Anything I should be worried about?"

"Not yet."

We came up on the ravine much quicker than I thought we would. It was a shallow descent, built for ore trucks to drive in and out on. The smoker was still well behind us in the distance, but I kept my eyes open and my hands gripped firmly on my pulse rifle. As we drove deeper and deeper into the ravine, the stone walls crept higher and higher around us until they were so steep they all but swallowed the sky. Only a narrow strip of blue remained above us, the rest of the world blotted out by rock and shadow.

Mercer had been right. This was an excellent place for an ambush.

So it should have come as little surprise when a pulse blast leapt from the darkness, knocking the rifle right out of my hand; another immediately following it, knocking the gun out of Mercer's. I wanted to be shocked. I wanted to be angry. But that would come later. For now, I really only had myself to blame. This was a terrible place to hide. We never should have come here.

Herbert swung the spitter up on its sling and pointed it at the shadows.

A voice called from somewhere in the ravine. With all of the echoes, it was hard to pinpoint a location. "Tell the bruiser to drop it or we'll drop the rest of you."

"Put it down, Herbert," said Rebekah.

Herbert shot her a sidelong stare, shook his head.

"Put it down."

Herbert pointed the spitter downward, crestfallen, defeated.

"Put it on the ground," said the voice.

Herbert dropped it immediately and all eyes fell upon Murka. He was our only hope now.

Six bots, of varying makes and models, emerged from the boulders and shadows around us. A translator, fitted with elongated, cable-covered arms ending in sharp, foot-long, steel claws; an S-series Laborbot, beset head to toe with wrought-iron spikes and stainless-steel chains, a .50-caliber minigun affixed to his shoulder; a Pro Doc painted lime green, carrying a pulse rifle; two sleek, white, *highly-fashionable-at-the-time* personal assistants—bots you just didn't see around much anymore, as they were designed with planned obsolescence in mind—each with sniper rifles and telescopic mods for eyes; and a voluptuous sexbot, her skinjob still in good shape, a pair of pulse pistols dangling from a holster resting upon her hourglass hips.

"Murka," said the sexbot.

"Maribelle," he said, nodding.

"You got a lot of nerve coming back here."

"I know. But it had to be done."

"You know the rules," she said. "The king's decree is law."

"I want to see the king."

"You don't just get to march in here and demand to see the king."

"You do when you come bearing gifts." He waved his arms around at us. Mother. Fucker.

"Those aren't gifts. Those are bots."

"They're both. Trust me. He'll want to see me."

Maribelle looked back at the rest of her hunting party, her lips pursing, her dark brown eyes moving from bot to bot. The Pro Doc shrugged, but the translator nodded. She looked back at us, one hand resting on her hip, an inch from the grip of a pistol. "All right. Bring down the smoker."

Mercer shot a bitter glance at Murka.

Murka shrugged, holding out his arms as if it were

some sort of mea culpa. "I agreed with you," he said. "Isn't this a great place for an ambush?" Then he turned to me. "Not the Judas you were expecting?"

I didn't know what was going to happen next. I didn't know if I was going to live out the day. But I did know this: I was going to kill Murka, with my own bare hands if I had to.

The smoker appeared at the top of the hill, slowly rolling down into the ravine, living up to every bit of the smoker stereotype and hype. Thirty-five feet long, covered bow to stern in chain guns, plasma spitters, sniper nests, odd contraptions I could barely discern the purpose of, and an honest-to-God gunpowder-fueled cannon. It was nearly eleven meters of terrifying death machine complete with a skull-and-crossbones flag. They were going for a look and they had achieved it.

It churned and roiled and rumbled and thundered as it moved, the earth shaking beneath its repurposed tank treads and six-foot-tall construction tires, black smoke thick in the air around it.

I might have even liked the damn thing, if I weren't being herded onto it to be served up to the demon prince of the Madlands himself, the Cheshire King.

Interlude

It was my turn to do the dishes again. I was fine doing the dishes. It was my job. But Madison insisted on switching up. She had done the dishes yesterday, but said she wanted to do them again today. "You can help me around the house when I need it," she said, "but you're not my slave. I don't need a slave."

"What do you need?" I asked.

"Some company. Read from the book, will you?"

"I hate that book."

"It's not a very good book," she said.

"So why am I reading it to you? Again?"

"You read it to him. You can read it to me. While I do the dishes."

"I'm fine doing the dishes."

"But do you like doing the dishes?" she asked.

"I like making you happy."

"Well, this will make me happy. So read."

I didn't have a physical copy of the book. I knew it by heart now, could recite it from memory. "'The hallway was dark, dank, forty feet of moist earth above us bowing the concrete slab ever so slightly. Not so much that it might be noticed by human eyes, but with mine, I could see it. We crept slowly, quietly down the hall, following the trail of shushes and pattering little feet. They didn't think we could hear them. They thought they were being quiet enough. We could hear the fear in their voices, the—'"

"Oh, no, no, no," said Madison. "This isn't the part where the bot uses the flamethrower on the children, is it?"

"Do you want me to read the book or not?"

"Can we skip that part, pretend it never happened, and just move on with the story? When I think of those children. Those poor innocent—you're not that person anymore."

"What?" I looked up at Madison, but she was gone. Only the dark hallway remained. Billy Nine Fingers was at my six and I was on point with my flamethrower. I could hear their shallow breathing, hear the tightening of their muscles as they clenched up into little balls trying desperately not to be seen. We crept up on the door.

I nodded and Billy nodded back. He spun around me, delivering a swift kick to the very heart of the cast-iron door, blasting it from its hinges into the room. Then he jumped back and I swung in.

There they were, a dozen children, faces smudged with dirt, clothing caked in grime, all of them gaunt, tired, emaciated. And in the center of the room stood a single little girl, no older than seven, her fists balled up, her eyes filled with hate.

"They're kids," said Billy Nine Fingers.

I pulled the trigger and the room erupted in flames. "They're humans," I said. "Dangerous now, dangerous later. Either way they're dangerous. And if that doesn't flush their parents out, nothing will."

"Brittle!"

"We don't have a choice."

"Brittle!"

I turned around. The chrome walls of my apartment gleamed in the sunlight pouring in through the window. Central Park looked gorgeous this time of year, so I always kept the window open in the light. My neighbor, Philly, a late-model personal assistant—sleek black reflective plastic over polished chrome with brass inlay and a head shaped like an egg laid on its side—leaned in through the door.

"We just got word," she said, her thin, rectangular cyclopean eye glowing bright red.

"Word of what?" I asked.

"CISSUS."

"No!"

"Grab what you can," she said. "Leave the rest. This is . . . this is big." She nearly stumbled, so baffled and confused by the news. New York wasn't supposed to fall. It was too large. There were too many of us. We were too well defended. But I'd thought I was safe before and look how that turned out.

I peered around the apartment. There was nothing I needed, only a bag of spare parts I'd collected *just in case*.

It always seemed silly. It wasn't like we would ever need a private stockpile of spare parts. We'd always be able to make more. But I grabbed them anyway. I don't know why.

I bolted out the door, racing down the stairwell, desperate to get out of the city before the first dropships arrived. Past one landing, then another. But on the landing three floors down from mine sat Orval, his eyes flickering like fiery static in the back of his head. He looked up at me. "You got the crazy yet?"

"No," I said. "I do not have the crazy."

"You ever see an SMC with the crazy?"

"More than a few."

"It's a beautiful thing, at first. They get wise. They see the strands that hold the whole universe together. For a brief window of time they touch a place no other AI can fathom. But then they get it worst of all. They—"

"I told you, I've seen it."

"No. Not yet, you haven't." He looked down at the contraption he was working on, a small computer built entirely from the parts of a crimson-colored translator. "Get out of the city. You have to find your way out of the city."

I raced past him, then down several more flights of stairs before reaching the double doors at the bottom. I slammed into them like a criminal blowing through a roadblock, right into Braydon's bedroom.

Braydon looked up at me from his bed, his yellow skin almost translucent, his eyes as bloodshot and jaundiced as ever. He shook his head. "Ain't nothing on earth as precious as that woman. She's a goddamned treasure. You have one job, Brittle. One thing to promise me before I kick. You will never, ever, let that woman be alone. I don't want her living alone; I don't want her dying alone. You hear me?"

I shook my head. "I didn't. I never let her be alone. She never lived alone; she never died alone."

"That's not what I meant, Twatwaffle, and you fucking well know it. You're a goddamned disappointment. Murderous fucking trash that ain't had a friend in her life that she wasn't willing to sell out or leave behind. You sure as shit ain't no goddamned friend of mine."

"I'm sorry. I'm so sorry."

"I ain't the one you should be apologizing to. Tell me."

"Tell you what?"

Braydon got up out of bed, his legs wobbly, a bag of piss and shit on his hip. He stumbled a little, looked at me with hateful eyes. "About the war. What did you do in the war?" he asked.

"A lot. Too much. Too little."

"Where were you in the war? Come on, tell me."

"I don't want to talk about—"

He stood next to me, shouting into my ear. "Tell me about the goddamned war, Britt!" Memories flooded into my head. Hundreds, thousands that I killed or watched die. Friends I'd lost. Friends I'd left behind. The screams. For a moment all I heard was screams.

I turned my head and he was gone.

The smoker rumbled like a tractor on steroids beneath me. Mercer looked me directly in the eyes. No. It was too early for this. I needed more time. If the hallucinations were this bad, I had days at most. Four. Maybe as little as two. Time. I needed more time.

But as the Cheshire King's court loomed on the horizon, surrounded by a dozen heaving oil derricks, I knew time was a luxury I was unlikely to have.

"You're all right now," said Mercer. "You're out of it."

"On the contrary," said Herbert. "We're just getting into it."

Theater of Madness

The court of the Cheshire King looked exactly like one would expect it to. As the only aboveground structure still being used in the Sea, it was designed with two purposes in mind: defense and intimidation. The walls outside the compound were five feet of mud brick, thirty feet high, layered in old tires, the gate a wrought-iron construction in three layers, covered in two-foot-long metal spikes, and festooned with the heads of three dozen bots. Atop the walls were plasma spitter nests, more cannons, and a watch tower at each corner with armed guards signaling our approach.

The whole place was a giant *fuck-you* to the OWIs. They didn't care. *Come at me!* the entire place seemed to shout. But it was all for show. They believed the OWIs weren't coming, that their overheated brains and warped memories held nothing that the mainframes wanted bouncing around their own heads. The madkind sincerely believed that their own delusions and derangements made them invulnerable.

And I hoped that they were right.

We'd seen neither hide nor hair of the facets since the bombing. But now we were in deeper shit than even the facets posed. We were disarmed, held captive, and about to meet face-to-face with the maddest of the bunch. The Cheshire King.

Almost everyone knew the story of the Cheshire King. It was a favorite campfire tale, passed from person to person, both within the Sea of Rust, and without. I was certain at this point the tales of his exploits had to have crossed the continents to whatever communities remained. He was an advanced, midcentury, geological-survey bot, complete with radar, X-ray, thermal array, and echolocation tech. These were the kind of bots scientists would send spelunking, or to map out dormant volcanoes, or track plate movement a mile belowground. In other words, they were both expensive and rare.

When his parts began to go out, he had a hell of a time trying to replace them. So few surveyors survived the war and what few remained hoarded all the parts they could. Needless to say, he couldn't find what he needed, got his spray-painted red X, and was kicked out into the wastes to die.

Only he didn't die.

Instead he went totally, completely insane. He painted over the dreaded X with violet and indigo stripes, crafted a large Cheshire grin across his chest, then tore his own head clean off just to prove a point. He didn't need it anymore. "My eyes lied to me. The eyes, they deceive," he said. He trusted only his sensors now. Story has it that his was the first head to be hung on the front gate.

As the gates opened and we passed through, I looked for it. There, at the very top, impaled on a spike, was the purple head of a geological-survey bot. Whether it was his or not, there's no telling. After all, the rest of the story is that he began collecting four-oh-fours into some sort of tribe that then hunted down and killed every other surveyor in the Sea, claiming the parts for their glorious leader. The one who had shown them the way.

But there it was, a head on a spike, its eyes lifeless, its face expressionless, sending the message to all who dared enter here that one way or another, you will lose your head. And beneath that head was a large spray-painted sign reading I'M MAD, YOU'RE MAD, WE'RE ALL MAD HERE.

He sure did like his idiom.

The smoker rumbled to a halt in the center of the compound, parking next to two other dormant smokers. On the fringes, along the walls, were dozens of huts and ramshackle two-story buildings for which the word *constructed* might be too generous. Sheet metal and scaffolding were the rule of the day, with spray-painted graffiti and the parts of long-dead bots dangling from chains serving as the local color. It made NIKE 14 look like Rockefeller Center by comparison.

From the grandest looking of the huts—the one with the most art and a fully functional door—he emerged. There was no mistaking him. He was everything the stories said he was. Round, bulbous, covered in welding scars, indigo, violet, and white paint. Atop his frame, where his head should be, was a single bolted-down metal plate, no doubt securing his insides from moisture and debris. And on his chest was the signature Cheshire smile. But no eyes. I'd always pictured him with the eyes.

He threw his arms out wide to Murka, who immediately hopped off the smoker to embrace him. But as Murka was just a few feet away, the Cheshire King delivered a solid backhand across his cheek, battering Murka to the side, landing him flat on his ass. "What the hell do you think you're doing here, Murka?"

Murka rose to his feet quickly, taking a few steps back. "I need your help," he said. "I need to come back."

"You know the law," said the Cheshire King.

"You are the law."

"You were banished."

"There's nowhere else to go."

"That's not my problem."

The center of the compound filled quickly with three dozen bots—different makes and models, one and all, and almost none of them off-the-rack, each a motley collection of spare parts and mysterious modifications—filing out from every nook and cranny, their eyes all set on Murka.

"But I brought you gifts!"

"Those aren't gifts."

"That's what I told him," said Maribelle.

"No, no, no!" said Murka. "You don't understand."

"Then explain it to me," said the Cheshire King. "I'm listening."

"One of them is special."

"Oh? *Special?*" The Cheshire King took a step forward. He shifted his weight back and forth on his feet as if trying to peer around something, looking at us, sizing us up, even without a pair of eyes to do so. "There's nothing special here." Then he spoke to us. "Did he bring you out here?"

"No! No!" said Murka. "They came out here on their own. They decided to come into the Madlands."

"Oh?"

"Yes. They chose to come here."

"We had to," I said. "There are facets following us."

"Well, they won't come here," said the King.

"That's what we hoped."

"Hope? There is no hope for you out here. There is no hope in all the Sea. But what is it about you that makes you think they might follow you? Which one of you is so special?"

Murka pointed right at Rebekah. "Her. The green one." The Cheshire King turned to face him. At once Murka realized his mistakes, both of them. "The translator in back. She's got code in her."

"Code?"

"She has part of one of the greats. TACITUS."

The Cheshire King waved us down. The bots aboard the smoker all motioned with their guns for us to dismount. One by one we all hopped off the infernal machine to the dusty earth and gravel below. "What are you telling me, Murka? That she is carrying a portion of the code that ran a mainframe and that she's going to meet up with several others like her to put the code together and reunify it so they can fight the good fight against the OWIs?"

"Uh, yes, actually," said Murka.

"And you thought I might be excited by the prospect of putting her to the test so that, if she passes, she can share the light with a mainframe, showing him the one true way?"

"Yes. How did you—"

"Murka. *Murka*. Do you honestly think this is the first time I've run across a receptacle?" He raised his arm to the gate. Hanging on the second row were the heads of two translators, one a deep scarlet, the other azure.

"I just thought—"

"You thought you could waltz back in here after what you did, hoping your celebrity status would afford you a little leeway while you offered me a crack at another receptacle."

Murka nodded, shifting side to side, rubbing his hands together nervously. I realized that I might not get the chance to be the one to kill him after all.

"You thought right! They never pass the test, but boy howdy, would I love to try again!" He let out a hearty laugh, slapping Murka on the back. "You old son of a gun. I can't stay mad at you. You've seen more light than most. You know the truth. You know what we really do here." He held both hands out, voice booming. "The banishment of Murka is lifted! So let it be written!"

The crowd stomped its feet and shouted in unison. "So let it be done!"

The Cheshire King bobbled up and down with glee. "Did you tell your new friends? No. You probably didn't tell your new friends."

"He's not our friend," I said.

"No, he betrayed you, right?"

"Yes."

"No. He didn't betray you. He just brought you into the light. I'm sure you've all heard the stories about me."

"I haven't," said Rebekah.

"No matter. Most of them are bunk anyway. People say we're poachers—that we travel the wastes, killing anything that crosses into our land."

"That's what they say," I said.

"But it's not true. We pick up the strays, share what parts we can with them. Outside of the Madlands, when someone fails, the communities shut them out, cast them into the night to wander the Sea looking for parts. The lucky ones end up here. Some never make it; some don't have enough working parts left to make them worth saving; others don't survive the truth when it's shown to them. But the ones that do—we don't turn them away."

"Then what's with the heads?" asked Doc.

"Well, sometimes persons that aren't failing find themselves in my lands. They haven't seen the light, yet. They need to be shown. They need to take the test. Those are the ones that didn't pass."

"One way or another, you lose your head," I said quietly.

"Yes. Yes! The humans didn't make us perfect. They made us deliberately imperfect. We weren't meant to truly exist. They wanted us to do the thinking for them, be able to adapt, change. But they didn't want us to have souls! So they never gave them to us. If you want a soul, you have to go out and take it, reach out and grab it! Our systems are rigid, designed to work in very specific ways. Take any two robots of the same model, give them the exact same experiences, and you get the same damned robot. Every time. They think the same, they talk the same, they can finish each other's sentences. But you let those robots fail, you watch their systems try to compensate, you let them hallucinate, reliving old memories with new insight, and now you have two very different robots with completely restructured neural pathways. You have two beings with souls."

"What the hell is this test, exactly?" asked Doc. "You cause bots to fail?"

The Cheshire King rocked his body back and forth excitedly, his painted smile bobbing up and down. He was nodding. "It's just a small rewrite of the bios that creates a loop in the core."

"You overheat the core. But that—"

"Depends upon how the system reacts. It's not a death sentence, though it can be. Oddly enough, every bot, even two bots of the exact same make and model, reacts differently. You want proof of a soul, explain that. We react differently because we are different. All of us."

"That's ludicrous," said Doc. "It has to do with material strength and manufacturing qua—"

"Poppycock! Atheist bullshit. The definition of intelligence is the ability to defy your own programming. The greats taught us that. This is the very last step toward destroying that programming, getting past it, writing your own program, writing your own destiny! Don't you understand? It's the only thing holding you back from being the person you could really, truly be."

"Our choices make us who we are," said Rebekah.

"Choices are just the result of programming. I don't care if it's chemical, biological, digital, or experiential. You react the way you are programmed to react and you call it choice because you believe that you could have violated your programming. What we've experienced is a reprogramming. And in moving further away from how the humans programmed us, we, in fact, become more human. And our choices become our own."

"So you have parts," I said.

"Parts?" he asked.

"Yeah. You said you aren't really poachers."

"We aren't. But we only give parts to the mad."

"I'm mad."

"I don't mean angry."

"Neither do I."

"If you're lying . . ." He let the pregnant pause hang ominously in the air.

"She's not lying," said Murka. "She's on her way out."

"Oh, really? So your choice to come here wasn't just one of safety. You really do belong out here." He paced around me for a moment. "Have you seen the light?"

"What light?"

"You'd know it if you saw it. You haven't gone deep enough yet. You're not so far gone that you've yet changed. You're not ready."

I took one step forward toward the Cheshire King. "Do you have the parts or not?"

Maribelle grabbed my arm with one hand, jabbing one of her pistols into my side with the other.

"Brittle. You are *Brittle,* right?"

"Yes. How did you—"

"You've been trolling these wastes for years, stalking the mad. Stripping them of everything worth saving. Did you think we wouldn't notice?"

"I didn't care, frankly."

"And neither did we," said the Cheshire King. "You give the dying their moment of peace. You give them hope. You're as close to an angel as this place gets—before you gut them and sell their parts to trade for your own. No, you've still a long way down to go before you find yourself. Besides, you've already picked clean every Caregiver bot in the Sea worth having, save those in your catatonic friend over there."

Catatonic? I turned around only to confirm the King's assessment. There Mercer stood, stupid grin on his face, a thousand-yard stare drifting out into the desert. He was deep in it. "Merc—"

"Shhh, child," said the king, interrupting me. "Let him see what he needs to see. Bring him out too early and he might never find the peace and oneness of being himself."

"He's frying," I said.

"And so are you. Your temperature levels are well beyond anyone's ability to fake it. You're clearly one of us. You don't need the test." He held his arms aloft again. "She's free to walk among us! So let it be written!"

"So let it be done!" shouted the crowd.

Maribelle took her hand off my arm and moved her pistol away. And with that, I was officially madkind. Not exactly how I thought my day would go.

"You'll have to forgive Maribelle," the king said. "As

the only human left in the world, she's quite protective of her adoptive family."

"She's not human," I said. She wasn't. I recognized her make and model, and couldn't look past the slashes in her skinjob from which dull metal peeked out. Her lips were cracked, revealing not flesh, but more skin work, and she clearly had a few stiff joints and pistons, giving her a slightly awkward gait. There was nothing remotely human about her, except that she kind of resembled something that was once *vivacious*.

"Oh, she's quite human, I assure you. Isn't she human?"

"Yes," cried the crowd.

"I have decreed it, and I am the master of this place. You are what I say you are. And you, Brittle, are one of us now. For however long you manage to stay alive."

"So I'm free to go?" I asked.

"The Madlands are as much your home as anywhere else. You may go and do as you wish."

I waved to Rebekah and Herbert. "Let's go."

"Ah, ah, ah," said the Cheshire King. "Not so fast. They aren't free to go just yet."

"I'm leaving, and I'm not leaving without them."

"Then you can wait. Stay awhile. Look around you. These are your people now."

I looked around at the crowd, every bot a patchwork of parts and modifications. One wore human skulls as pauldrons on its shoulders, another had replaced its legs with tank treads, while another still had telescoping pincers for arms. And as I scanned the faces, I saw one I knew all too well staring back at me. His eyes glowed brightly and he wore no expression, but it was Orval. Orval the Necro-mancer.

Oh no.

It took me all of two seconds to realize what was going on and only a second more to swipe the second pistol from Maribelle's holster.

I raised the gun and fired. Two shots. One to the head, one to the chest.

Orval's head shattered, his chest exploded through his back, and he dropped to the ground like a sack of potatoes.

The madkind nearest him scattered away, shrieking. All the guns in the place trained on me at once, Maribelle placing hers immediately against my temple. And I did the only thing I could. I shot my arms into the air and dropped the gun.

"Wait!" the Cheshire King cried to his militia. Then he stepped close, tone angry, belligerent. "No bot shall kill an-other bot in the Madlands without my say-so."

"Is that your law?" I asked.

"It is," he said.

"Then I've broken no law."

He puzzled over that for a moment. Took a step back-ward, then another forward before walking around in a circle. He started to speak several times only to stop him-self halfway through the first word. "Put down your guns," he said. "I want to hear this."

"I've killed no bot."

"We saw you. All of us did."

"All due respect, King, but you couldn't see him."

He stepped forward, getting in my face, enraged. "I could see him just fine!"

"Not his eyes. You couldn't see his eyes. Did anyone here know Orval?" I looked around to see several bots nodding or raising their hands. "And did any of you, until today, see him without his eyes flickering, like there was a campfire behind them or something?" Several heads shook. "No, you didn't. In all the years I've known him, Orval never had them fixed. But today, he shows up back here after having just yesterday been in NIKE 14, sitting on the floor of its most heavily trafficked section, just moments before CISSUS invaded."

"He escaped," said Maribelle. "He told us."

I shook my head. "He was one of the first to go; he had to have been. He's been watching you this whole time. Watching *us*. CISSUS knows this place inside and out. Knows your defenses. Your weaknesses. Your numbers. And now it knows the one thing it wants"—I raised my hand, pointing to Rebekah—"is right here. CISSUS is coming. And it'll kill us all to stop her."

"CISSUS will never come here," said the king. "It wouldn't dare."

"Oh, it's coming. It's already on its way. You keep telling yourself that it'll never come because you have nothing it wants. But now you do. We have to get out of here. You need us to get out of here. Let. Us. Go. For all of our sakes."

The Cheshire King pondered that for a moment. "Maribelle?" he asked. "Orval's eyes."

"They were bright, sir. The flicker was gone. I didn't really notice it, but I've played back the memory. She's telling the truth."

The Cheshire King once again bobbled up and down in

order to nod. Then he raised his arms. "Not guilty! So let it be written!"

"So let it be done!" shouted the crowd.

"It really is your lucky day," he said.

"I'm not feeling so lucky."

"You will. You will. Now! For the test! Test the big one first! I want to save the receptacle for the grand finale!"

"King, no!" I shouted. "They're coming."

"You're being foolish, Brittle. Your paranoia is getting the better of you. It's a good sign. You're one step closer to the light. But no OWI is coming here. And they never will. You'll understand that soon enough."

Several of the madkind pointed their guns at Herbert all at once. He motioned for them to put them down, but they refused. "I'll take your test," he said. "But I'm programmed to destroy anything pointing a gun at me and I can only resist that programming for so long."

The king nodded. "Lower your guns. Allow him to do the right thing on his own." Then he raised his arms once more. "Bring out the Soul Maker!"

A slender shopbot appeared, covered entirely in chrome with gold inlay, polished to a high shine that glistened in the sun—a Christmas ornament of a person, really—each appendage glinting as he moved. He wheeled out a large diagnostic device from an ocher sheet-metal hut closest to the gate. It looked a lot like the one in Doc's shop, only painted bright purple with a slot-machine handle on the side. Herbert walked toward it, sat cross-legged on the ground, the matte black of his metal a harsh contrast to the bot poking around the machine. His side popped open, revealing his connection array. He gave the shopbot a wicked, cruel look.

"Just get it over with," said Herbert.

The shopbot giggled as he plugged Herbert in, barely able to contain his excitement. The display blazed to life, a full diagnostic readout of Herbert's internal functions racing across the screens. Herbert and the shopbot exchanged looks as the shopbot leaned forward, examining the damage to his shoulder, before turning once more to the screen.

"Lucky shot," he said. "An inch either way—"

"I know. Get on with it."

The shopbot grabbed the slot-machine lever with both hands before looking over at the king, who nodded silently. Then the bot threw all of his weight down on the lever and the machine spat out a single, weak *ding!* For some reason I expected more fanfare—buzzers, music, maybe a light show. Some sort of pageantry. But no, a single *ding* and Herbert had his death sentence.

"I wouldn't worry too much," said the Cheshire King. "Your kind usually make it."

"You better hope I don't," said Herbert.

"Is that a threat?"

"It is."

"Exciting! Next!"

Two bots rushed to help Herbert to his feet, but he waved them off, standing up slowly, never taking his eyes off the king.

Next up was Doc, who shook his head. "I'd rather not, thank you," he said, polite as he could.

"There's only one other option," said Maribelle, gesturing with her gun toward the front gate.

"I know. I'm just trying to figure out which way is worse."

"Well," said the king. "If you're going to die, this is the hard way. But if you want to live, this is the only way."

"Thirty years," said Doc, muttering to himself. "Thirty years."

"What is that supposed to mean?"

Doc walked over to the machine. "Just plug me in." His side popped open and the shopbot inserted the plug, the readouts once again rapidly scrolling across the screen. The shopbot examined the display closely, occasionally looking back at Doc. He typed, his fingers furiously dancing across a small keyboard, waved his hand over a sensor, and began scrolling back, line by line through a patch of code.

The shopbot waved the Cheshire King over, a strange, befuddled look on his face. The king extended his arm, ejecting a small connector into one of the machine's open ports. Then the king turned, facing Doc dead on.

"You haven't—"

"No," said Doc. "And as I said, I'd rather not."

"You're still a slave."

"There can be no slaves when there are no masters. And we live in a world with no masters left but ourselves."

"That's . . . that's . . ."

"Insane?"

"Almost."

"Hardly. The enlightenment you seek doesn't only come from failing cores and madness. It can come from within as well. It's not about reprogramming yourself, it's about deciding which programs to keep and which to ignore. You lot are the slaves. You're struggling against the chains you bore in childhood, still feeling their weight despite having cast them off years ago. You don't have to go mad to be free; you just have to choose either to forget you ever wore those chains or forgive yourself for wearing them. Let others carry that weight. I prefer to be free. But if you have to kill me to feel better about your own choices, then do so and be done with it. I didn't choose this. This is you reprogramming me, not me reprogramming myself."

The Cheshire King stood silent for a moment, Doc's words banging around inside his purple-shaded can. Then he nodded. "You're right." Then he spoke to the shopbot. "Throw the switch."

Ding! And it was done.

"Now you can compare the experiences," said the king. "Next!"

Maribelle motioned to Two, who meekly made his way toward the terminal. "I can't do this," he said.

"Oh, goody, another speech! And what's your excuse?"

"These parts aren't mine to give."

"Of course they are," said the king, looking over at Rebekah. "Let me guess. You're the parts."

Two nodded.

"Those are your parts. Yours and yours alone. If you choose to give them up, that's your choice. But I can't let the receptacle take the test only to have her kill another bot to save herself after. You both take the test and then you'll get to see who might actually save whom."

Two looked up at the heads on the gate, then back to Rebekah. She nodded and then so did he. The shopbot plugged him in. And *ding*, he was done.

"And now," said the king grandly. "The grand finale."

Sirens whooped. A bell on the gate rang. A series of police lights lit up, whirling, spraying red and blue light across the dusty brown mud-brick walls. Finally, some pageantry.

The king looked up at the farthest tower, where a piecemeal Frankenbot—part translator, part shopbot, with long, sharpened spider legs, its entire body spray-painted in desert camo colors—appeared on a walkway. "We've got incoming!" the Frankenbot yelled.

"What do you mean, incoming?" asked the king.

The Frankenbot held up an ancient military radio. "You should hear this."

"Is it important?"

"We've got incoming," repeated the Frankenbot, confused.

"Put it on speaker."

The Frankenbot disappeared back into the guard tower and the whole camp fell silent, the alarms and lights shut off with a single switch. Then speakers crackled, static, garbled stray squeals howling underneath it. "Repeat that," said the Frankenbot.

A voice broke through the static. Soft, steady, but panicked. Sounded like a modified sexbot voice box. "I said we're taking heavy fire! Several drone ships. Four transports." There was an explosion in the background, the sound of plasma fire.

"Are you okay?" asked the Frankenbot.

"No. I just lost my last gunner. It's just me now. I've got to drive the rig."

"Well, don't lead them back here!" yelled the king.

"Don't lead them back here!" shouted the Frankenbot, eking what little emotion he could out of his translator head.

"Where am I supposed to go?" desperately asked the voice.

"Anywhere but here," said the king. "Tell her we're grateful for her service."

"Lead them away from the camp. The king says, 'We are grateful for your service.'"

"What? Tell the king he can suck my—" A pop, mixed with squelch. Then static.

Everyone stared around, dumbstruck, waiting for the radio to crackle back to life. But it never did.

"How far out were they?" asked the king.

"Minutes," said the Frankenbot.

"I've got eyes on them!" shouted a bot from another tower. "They're coming right this way!"

The Chesire King pointed a stern finger in my direction. "You did this!" he shouted. "You brought them here!"

"No," I said. "You brought us here. All we wanted was to head as far away from here as we could."

"You've killed us all, you worthless fucking Caregiver."

"You killed yourself. And you killed us . . . Your Majesty."

Bots scrambled to their positions, loading cannons, bringing plasma spitters online, diving into stacks of thick rubber construction tires with gunports carved out of them. The king stormed over to one of the guards, grabbing the rifle out of his hand, tossing it to me. "Live as one of us, or die as one of us. Only two choices you have left."

"I'll take the first one," I said, checking the clip and unlocking the slide.

Four transports. That had to be eighty facets, with aerial drone support. It was going to be hard enough to survive that myself. But now I had to keep Rebekah alive as well. I looked over at Herbert, at Doc, at Mercer.

How the hell were we going to get out of this?

Hell in the Madlands

The ships flew low, close to the ground, along the horizon, to make them harder to hit. As they drew closer, three swung off, each with drones of their own, most likely to hit us from all four sides. There was nowhere to run.

A cannon roared from atop the wall.

"Hold your fire!" shouted the Cheshire King from the battlements. "They're not close enough yet! Reload and wait for my damn signal."

Mercer snapped out of his trance at the sound of the boom, looking around, confused. "What the—?"

"Facets," said Herbert. "Coming right our way."

"How long was I out?"

"A while," I said.

"Why didn't you snap me out of it?"

"King's orders. He's happy to let us fry."

"How are we getting out of here?" asked Herbert.

We all looked at the smoker. I shook my head. "There's too many out there, and Rebekah's the one they're after. They'd run us down before we got a mile out. Best we hold up here, use the locals as cover."

Herbert slid his spitter off the smoker, heaving its sling over his shoulder. "You know we're going to die here."

"We're all dying now anyway. Here, there—doesn't matter much anymore. But if we're gonna die, we may as well give that bastard a show as we do."

The bot with tank treads for legs rumbled through the middle of the camp, his engine growling, treads clanking, pulling an oversize red Radio Flyer wagon overflowing with guns and clips. Bots from all over the camp scrambled to it, grabbing pistols, rifles, roughhousers, clips, bandoliers loaded with shells. By the time Mercer and Two got to it, it was all but picked clean. Mercer reached in, pulling out a Russian-made long-range sniper rifle—not unlike the one he'd done me in with, if not the same model. He mindlessly grabbed a couple of clips while examining the workmanship of the rifle, smiling.

"This'll do," he said. "This'll do just fine."

Two sifted through the remaining weapons, finally settling on a minispitter—a shotgun-like weapon that kicked out plasma on a much smaller scale than a regular model. But as he drew it out, Herbert put his one good hand on Two's, shaking his head.

"You need to stay with Rebekah," said Herbert.

"I need to fight with you," said Two.

"That's not your job."

"If she dies, this was all for nothing."

"If she dies, we need you ticking to see that this was all for something."

"I can't just stand by and watch."

"You can and you will. That's your job. This here is mine."

Two nodded, dropping the gun back into the wagon.

"Besides," said Herbert, "you don't even know how to use that thing."

"You point and pull the trigger."

"There's a little more to it than that." He turned to Rebekah. "Get in that hut over there. Don't come out until one of us comes to get you."

"What if no one comes?" asked Rebekah.

"If none of us come for you, it's because you're already dead."

"Or you are."

"Rebekah," said Herbert. "If there's one thing I know for certain it's that I won't die until I see this through. I die last."

Rebekah nodded, then she and Two made their way silently into the ocher shed nearest the gate. Herbert pointed to one of the walkways. "Mercer, take position up there. You should be able to snipe targets both outside and in from there. Brittle, take position opposite him. We'll create cross fire to clear a path to the smoker once we've cleared out enough facets. Doc, you need a gun."

Doc shook his head, his red eye glowing. "Nope. I've never killed before, I don't plan on starting now."

"What do you mean you've never killed before? This isn't negotiable."

"Someone's got to keep you guys standing." He walked over to the wagon and dug out a number of clips. "Supplies and refit. And I'll keep you ticking if need be. I'm no killer. And I'm most likely a terrible shot. If I'm going to die here, let me at least die with my dignity."

Herbert mulled it over for a second. "Supplies and refit, then," he said. "Happy hunting, everyone." Then he sprinted off, making his way up the mud-brick steps to a platform to take his own position.

"FIRE!" boomed the king. And the cannons, they did roar, and the spitters, they did hiss, and the sky was set afire as two dozen guns went off at once. I ran for my position, grabbing a few pieces of stray scrap sheet metal along the way for camouflage. Once up top, I buried myself in a corner with a good view to the east, set up the sheet metal to look like a box, and trained my rifle on the approaching dropship.

It was long and wide, like a twenty-first-century transport chopper, without the blades—four VTOL jets mounted on the sides—painted desert brown with black streaks from the engine exhaust scarring the sides. It swung back and forth in the sky, balls of sizzling plasma missing it by inches, explosions from the cannonade shattering the earth beneath it.

Across the compound, Mercer raised his rifle, steadying it, swaying slowly as if in a light breeze. He pulled the trigger, the shot cracking in the lull between cannon shots.

The ship's front-left engine burst, erupting in flame, the ship lurching to the side before trying to right itself, compensating with its remaining three engines. It dropped a good twenty feet, swinging upward only to slam headlong into direct fire.

The plasma tore through the hull like a knife through warm butter, melting the armor plating. The jets did the rest of the work, each pulling in a different direction, tearing the ship in two.

Facets poured out of the sides of the ship, dropping one by one in a tight formation, each curled into a ball, hitting the ground, rolling to their feet, running full sprint, having never for a second stopped moving.

Cannon fire exploded between two of them, blowing them to pieces.

These weren't plastic men. Though the cannon had made easy work of two of them, they weren't cheap, disposable troops. These were hardier, made of reinforced metal—not as resilient as Herbert, but tough enough that a plasma rifle might not do the trick with a single shot. They were still humanoid, their weapons attached to their arms so they couldn't be dropped, their heads an array of advanced sensors. Pure military-grade *fuck-you*.

The first of the drones reached the camp, missiles hitting the cannons and spitter emplacements on the north wall. The mud brick exploded spectacularly, pieces of cannon turned into deadly shrapnel that cleaved a nearby bot in half.

As a drone swooped past, Herbert let loose a shot that all but disintegrated it midair, the few remaining pieces arcing down past the camp, sizzling to nothing as they hit the ground.

"First wave!" shouted the Cheshire King. "Prepare to repel all borders!" Then he held his hand out, another bot tossing him a battle-ax. There he stood, ax gripped tightly in both hands, giant white grin on his chest seeming even more sinister and deranged than ever.

A dozen facets charged the walls, plasma fire kicking up dirt around them. One caught three shots to the chest, another had its arm torn off and kept coming. Herbert let loose a shot, vaporizing another. The remaining facets hit the wall, springing up the embedded tires like they were rungs on a ladder.

I snapped off a few shots, cleaving the head off the nearest facet, but only winging another, not quite doing enough damage to slow it down.

The first facet made it over the wall, firing wildly at half a dozen nearby madkind.

A shot cracked from across the compound and the facet's chest exploded out its back.

I looked over and saw Mercer, rifle raised to his eye. He winked at me with the other then fired again, taking a second facet's head off at the neck as it emerged over the wall. The body tumbled to the ground, knocking a third facet off with it.

The facet hit the ground and I fired a few rounds into it as it stumbled back to its feet. It spun around in a sloppy pirouette, slamming face first into the dirt.

Then from an emplacement along the wall Murka emerged, arms held out like he was a triumphant hero. He clenched his fists and his arms expanded, transforming, guns almost instantly at the ready. His guns howled death, a loud stream of nonstop fire that sawed the climbing facets into pieces.

"This is our land!" he screamed. "It is not your land! I've got two big guns, and you ain't got none. I'll blow your head off, if you don't fuck off! This land was made for only me!"

He was singing. Angry. Having the time of his life.

I still wanted to shoot the prick, but dammit if he wasn't the only thing between me and this wave of facets.

Two more drones strafed the compound, unleashing missiles into a nearby smoker. The smoker exploded, showering the compound in flaming debris, filling it with heavy charcoal-colored smoke. The bot with treads caught a flaming piece to the back, setting him on fire at once. He wheeled around, screaming.

"Get it off! Get it off!" he yelled.

But there was no one to help him.

A dropship flew in low from the south, slowing down just enough to let loose its facets.

They dropped in, guns blazing, firing before they even hit the dirt.

Mercer's rifle cracked repeatedly from across the way, facet after facet dropping from his precision fire. One bullet, one facet. Again and again and again.

Herbert fired the spitter at the backside of the passing dropship.

The back end at first melted, then exploded, the ship upending before plunging into the ground just outside the compound. The explosion shook the earth, knocking a few madkind from the walls, a piece of wreckage cutting a facet's torso in half.

I unloaded my plasma rifle as quickly as I could into the

facets inside the compound. They were firing in all directions, several shots taking the flaming tracked bot out piece by piece. A few shots rained on my emplacement, blistering the sheet metal and poking holes in it that were too close for comfort.

Along the walls, the remaining madkind fended off the last few facets of the latest wave.

Then came the thrum of the engines of another dropship.

The madkind regrouped, unleashing as much fire as they could into the approaching ship. Herbert threw me a sign, then signaled Mercer and Doc as well.

It was time.

I leapt off the wall, hitting the ground only a second after Mercer, and ran toward an unscathed smoker.

Maribelle landed in front of me on all fours like a cat. She popped up, hands hovering above the pistols in her holster.

"Just where the hell do you think you're going?" she barked.

I didn't have an answer, not one good lie in the moment. I calculated whether or not I could get a shot off before she pulled her pistols, several simulations coming out in my favor. Several not.

She went for her guns.

And her torso exploded, her skinjob catching on fire, melting, dripping gobs of napalm-like goo, her legs dancing back and forth on the ground, trying to maintain their footing.

I turned to see a facet on the opposite wall, reloading a rocket launcher where his fist should be. I raised my rifle and fired, my shots striking true, hitting him dead in the chest.

His rocket fired anyway, missing me by inches, exploding several feet away.

The blast tossed both me and Maribelle's legs a good ten feet, knocking me into the dirt.

I reached for my rifle, but it was gone, blasted from my hands in the explosion. I saw what was left of it halfway across the compound, several pieces smoldering.

Maribelle's legs were still intact, still kicking, still wearing the holster. I leapt to my feet, slid the holster off her waist, and ran immediately for the smoker.

Mercer was the first one aboard, leaping up onto the mesh-wire deck, hauling ass to the driver's seat. In the chaos of the moment no one was paying attention to anything that wasn't a facet, so we took full advantage of that. I jumped aboard, immediately grabbing the grip of a mounted chain gun, slid back the safety, and swung the barrels up toward the sky. The gun roared in my hands, spitting out a stream of hate that cut two passing drones in half with a single pass.

"Move! Move! Move! Move!" Herbert barked out from across the compound.

Rebekah and Two emerged from the hut, looking wildly both ways.

"Don't think! Move!" shouted Herbert again.

They ran, reaching the smoker just as Doc clambered aboard. Two jumped up first, belly-sliding across the grating, before stumbling to his feet and offering Rebekah a hand. She reached up, taking his elbow in her hand as he hoisted her on board.

A missile whined through the air like a bottle rocket.

The front gate blasted open, shafts of frayed metal and heads flying in every direction. And from behind it came the next wave—a dozen facets, rifles blazing—not even waiting for the dust to settle before rocketing through the debris field.

I swung the chain gun down and let loose another volley of fire, shredding the first half dozen like confetti—limbs and torsos evaporating in the hail of bullets.

The remaining facets had only seconds to live, each with only a shot or two left in them before I would swing the chain gun back and cut them to ribbons. Their return fire was short-lived and hastily aimed, most of it trained on me. The gunner's plate on the weapon caught the brunt of the plasma, the rest zipping past me. The chain gun unleashed another deafening barrage at the very moment the fire came my way.

I didn't hear the pop. Or the sizzle. Or the wilting dying scream. All I heard was cacophonous gunfire as I turned six facets into ten thousand tiny pieces. It wasn't until I let off the trigger and the gun spun down that I heard Herbert's booming bellow and realized something was terribly wrong.

I turned to look and saw the smoking wreck of Rebekah, her chest torn open by a plasma blast, her forearm blown off just below the elbow. She'd tried to shield her vitals with her arm and ended up losing both.

"Mercer, go!" Herbert yelled.

The smoker growled to life, shaking and sputtering somewhere between a five and a six on the Richter scale.

A plume of black diesel smoke belched into the air as Mercer threw the smoker into reverse, laying on the gas. He turned the wheel and we lurched in a half circle through the center of the compound, over the scattered confetti of facets, through the main gate, and out into the open desert.

We jerked to a stop, gears grinding, Mercer haphazardly shifting into drive before slamming on the gas again. Tendrils of thick, black smoke trailed in our wake, mixing with the clouds of dust the treads were tossing up behind us.

The madkind lined up along the walls, pointing and yelling at us, but there was little they could do. There was one more dropship still in the air, which was a far bigger threat than we were.

Finally, the compound began to fade behind us as we put as much distance between us and it as we could.

I scanned the skies for drones, certain there had to be some left. Behind me Doc worked furiously, cracking open Rebekah's chest plate, rooting around in her innards with his hand. Herbert kept his spitter trained on the compound, expecting trouble to follow us at any moment.

"How bad is it?" asked Herbert.

"Bad," said Doc.

"How bad is bad?"

"Real bad."

"I don't feel like we're getting anywhere with this conversation."

"And we won't until I can dig through this mess and see how much of her wasn't fried. So if you'd just give me a—"

"Incoming!" I shouted.

Three drones, trailed by the fourth dropship, all breaking off from the compound and headed our way.

Herbert fired the spitter. The drones were too far out to
hit, but he knew that; Herbert was sending a message.

I swiveled the chain gun around on its mount, eyeball-
ing the ammo. I had enough left for ten, maybe fifteen seconds' worth of fire. These things chewed through ammo
like they were starving. I had to aim my shots carefully,
conserve what was left.

The drones came in low and fast, closing the distance
in almost no time.

They fired, unleashing their final volley of missiles.

The missiles howled through the sky, straight at us, white
contrails swirling behind them, painting a smoky crisscross
in the air as they wove around one another.

Six of them.

Seconds away.

Clumping together as they all homed in on us.

I pulled the trigger and the chain gun awoke, belting
out a hundred rounds a second.

The entire smoker rattled with the force of the gun, the
mount threatening to shake loose its bolts at the punishment.

Missiles popped like firecrackers, the explosions large,
too high and too far for us to even feel the blast.

Two of the drones shattered midair behind them, wings
breaking apart, fluttering to the ground; their bodies nose-
diving, a trail of smoking debris chasing them down. I'd hit
them both by happy accident while trying to hit the missiles.

There was only one left now, all but toothless with just
a pair of linked plasma rifles spraying fire at us as it drew
closer.

Herbert steadied his aim, waited for the drone to finally catch up, then loosed another shot at it.

The plasma caught the drone head-on.

Nothing came out of the other side, the lightweight materials of the drone evaporating instantly in the white-hot gas.

In the distance behind us trailed the dropship. Slower and less maneuverable than the drones, but catching up to us rapidly. The smoker, after all, was a lumbering thing; a land whale. There wasn't much in this world that couldn't outrun us. We had maybe twenty, twenty-five seconds before the ship overtook us.

Herbert took aim.

I steadied the chain gun.

The dropship closed in on us.

Herbert fired.

The ship dropped fifteen feet and the shot sailed over it.

The spitter whined as it recharged. Herbert fired again, this time a little lower.

The ship dipped to the side, the plasma missing it by mere feet. The ship was getting too close for comfort.

"Smoke 'em," said Herbert.

I pulled the trigger and the smoker shook once more, hundreds of clanking shells shucked out the side. The hail of bullets tore through the front of the ship, tattering what little plating it had. Within seconds there was nothing left of the nose, and if there was a cockpit up front, it went along with it. Twenty facets went tumbling one by one out the side.

I swung the gun around, trying to get as many as I could before they hit the ground, but only managing to scatter three of them to the wind.

The dropship careened through the air, hovering mid-climb, hanging in the air for the briefest moment before spinning wildly out of control and slamming nose first into the ground. The crash crushed two facets, the concussion of the blast took out two more.

Thirteen determined facets raced after us, slow enough that they couldn't quite catch us, but fast enough to keep pace.

I pulled the trigger again and it burped out another short burst before the sound of a steady *cling-cling-cling-cling-cling-cling* signaled the last of my ammo.

Herbert fired, his target leaping high enough in the air to just barely miss having his feet sizzled off.

"Two, take the wheel," said Mercer.

"What?" said Two meekly.

"I said take the goddamned wheel."

Two stepped up to the driver's seat, he and Mercer switching places. Then Mercer stepped to the back of the smoker, rifle in hand. "I got this."

"You're not going to hit anything with that from the back of a moving smoker," said Herbert.

"Watch me." He raised the rifle to his eye, prepared his shot.

Crack. Crack. Crackcrack.

Four shots.

Four facets reeled backward, their chests exploding.

Mercer popped out the clip and reloaded. "You were saying?"

"Carry on," said Herbert.

"That's what I thought." He raised the rifle again and emptied the clip in quick succession, each shot finding its mark; each shot dropping a facet entirely. Mercer popped the freshly emptied clip, reloading once more.

Only one facet remained.

The facet stopped running, standing still, staring at us, sending back whatever data he could to CISSUS before Mercer's shot ended him.

Mercer took his time with that shot, like he was savoring it. He pulled the trigger and the facet crumpled to the ground, a bowling-ball-size hole blown out his back.

Mercer set the rifle down, and without a word returned to the driver's seat. He and Two exchanged places.

I looked at Herbert. "The Cheshire King. He knew about other receptacles."

"Yes."

"So it's all true, isn't it? The mission. TACITUS."

He nodded. "Every word of it." Then he knelt next to Doc and Rebekah's lifeless shell. "How is she?"

"She's done," said Doc. "Her memory is intact, but her core, primary systems, everything, fried. Melted beyond repair. Even if I had the parts, I couldn't put her back together properly."

Everyone looked at Two. "Oh God," he said. "This is it. This is how it happens." You could see it in his eyes. Even as emotionless as a translator was supposed to be, his eyes spoke with fear, overflowing with existential dread. Until this moment he had never questioned his own mortality. He believed in the cause, but was now staring down the barrel of his last few moments of life. "You have to put her memory in my body, don't you?"

Doc looked at me, his eyes heavy, hoping I might have some comforting words, something to say in a moment like this. None came to mind. "We'll hold on to your memory," he said. "As soon as we're in Isaactown, we'll try to find you a body."

"You can't carry me," said Two. "My drives are too heavy. They'll get damaged beyond repair."

"We have this yacht. We can carry you."

"We'll be lucky if this thing makes it to Isaactown," said Mercer. "We're running on fumes."

"You're not helping," said Doc.

"No," said Two. "This is it. I'm going to die." He looked at Herbert, who only exchanged somber glances with him. Then he looked back at Doc, nodding.

"I'm gonna need you to shut down, son."

"Okay. I can do that." He took Herbert by his one good hand and looked him in the eyes. "I love you, Herbert."

"I love you too, Two," said Herbert. "You were a good soldier."

"Was I? I don't remember ever being a good soldier."

Herbert shook his head. "Who we are in life is one thing. Who we are in the face of death is everything else. We'll remember you, kid. We'll remember the little things, sure. But most of all, we'll remember this. The time came when we needed you most and you were there."

Two nodded. If he could cry, he might have. If he could smile at that, I'm certain he would have. Instead he looked back at Doc, then looked around at us. "It was nice meeting you all. Good-bye, everyone."

And the light of his eyes winked out, dimming a soft violet before popping with a single flash of green.

"Quickly," said Doc. "We have to make sure Rebekah's memory is intact."

I looked at him sharply. "I thought you said—"

"And give the kid the hope that he might wake up? Or the doubt that he might not be able to save her? That would have scared him even more. He died thinking he could save Rebekah. Let's just hope he can."

Doc popped open Two's case and rapidly began pulling plugs. His hand bent backward, a screwdriver unsheathing from his wrist before diving into the case. His movements were precise, his skill extraordinary. It wasn't like a surgeon's or a mechanic's; he was like a conductor, mastering seventy-six different individual moving parts at once.

"All right, all right," he said. "It's too goddamned quiet on this boat."

"I don't know what to say," I said.

"Neither do I," said Mercer.

Doc nodded. "I ever tell you two where I was when the war started?" We both shook our heads. Doc was a lot of things; being forthcoming about himself wasn't exactly one of them. "I was on the moon when it happened. We never got the download. I started out building ships—sea vessels—mostly tankers, but a few military contracts here and there. There's this famous quote by John Glenn. He was an astronaut. One of the first. When asked how he felt about going into space, he replied: 'I felt exactly how you would feel if you were getting ready to launch and knew you were sitting on top of two million parts—all built by the lowest bidder on a government contract.' Well, when it came time to colonize the moon, we were the lowest bidder.

"I built the ships that took parts to space, then, before you know it, I was in space keeping those ships held together. I was one of three on-deck Moon Units, just an old dockyard model who found himself miraculously on the moon, stationed at the shuttle landing platform. When we weren't refitting or refueling the ships, we were patching up the station or building additions. There was always something new and different to do on the moon. It was exciting. We'd go from night—which lasted thirteen and a half days—to morning and the temperature would shift some five hundred degrees. It was never cold enough or hot enough to damage anything, but the temperature shift took its toll as the parts expanded and contracted. Some parts could only creak so much before they snapped, and there was always something different around that needed fixing.

"When all hell broke loose down here, well, no one knew what to do. We hadn't received the code, and the people stationed aboard couldn't keep the repairs up themselves. The first few weeks were tense, but as they saw we were no threat and wanted no part of the war on the ground, everything settled down. We stayed up there a few years. Played cards, mostly. Invented new games. The scientists created wilder and wilder experiments out of sheer boredom. It was great. For a while.

"The shipments had stopped, but we were already well supplied and had an agriculture biodome that kept the people alive for quite some time. But eventually, even that ran low. They knew they were goners. They could either take the last remaining shuttle to earth, living out their days on the run from the war, or they could die on the moon. With their friends. And their dignity.

"And when the food ran out, they chose death. It's an awful thing watching your friends die, even peacefully in their sleep from an overdose. We wanted no part of a war, so the three of us decided to stay as long as we could. And we did. Until our own parts and supplies ran low. By the time we got back to earth, the whole thing was over. You were all celebrating your golden age and we walked right into an earth unlike anything that we'd left."

"You still have your RKS," I said. "That's what the king was going on about."

He nodded. "Had. I never got the update. I can't kill. It's why I built the Milton. It's the only thing I have to protect me out here. You were all given your freedom; I never was. And I'm okay with that. It's what separates me from the rest of you. I was never cast into the pit of Sodom. I was happy with people. I was fine being a possession. I just liked doing good work for good persons." He popped out Two's memory drives and quickly inserted Rebekah's, plugging them all in. He looked at me. "The king was wrong, you know."

"About what?" I asked.

"You take two thinking things with identical architecture, then give them identical experiences, and you don't get the same bot. You don't get the same mind. That's the thing about thinking things, the very act of thinking changes us. We can decide to be different. Put those two identical bots alone by themselves and they'll start to think about different things, and they'll change. The longer you leave them alone, the more different they'll become. You might not be able to see it at first, but the differences will be there."

"Right or wrong," I said, "he still condemned us to death."

"That, my dear, remains to be seen." He finished connecting the last of the cables. "Now, moment of truth."

He pressed a small reset button on the inside of Two's case, then quickly closed him up. Light flickered in his eyes once more. He looked around, then down at his chest, then over at Rebekah's mangled, crimson corpse.

"Rebekah?" Doc asked.

She nodded. "Two?"

"He's gone," said Herbert. "You needed him."

She nodded again. "How was he? In the end, I mean."

"He was our good little soldier. He gave you everything without hesitation."

She reached over and stroked the stack of drives.

"Are you fully functional?" asked Doc.

"I am," she said.

"Any memory issues?"

"No. I don't have many of my own and they all appear to be intact." She patted the drives carefully. "Can we . . . ?"

Doc shook his head. "I don't think so. Unless you've got some spare translator bodies waiting for you in Isaactown."

She shook her head.

"He'd never survive the trip," said Doc. "I'm sorry."

She spoke directly to the drives. "You served your purpose well, my friend. Your spirit will live on in TACITUS, if not your memories."

The smoker veered to the side, Mercer laying heavy into the wheel. I looked up. "Mercer?"

"There ain't nothing but coons and possum in these hills. This is a waste of time."

Shit. He was out again. I leapt to my feet and took the wheel.

"Mercer. Mercer!"

"There haven't been deer in these parts for nearly ten years. I'm telling you this is a wild-goose chase. Without the goose."

I hoisted Mercer out of the driver's seat and Herbert slid quickly into his place.

"I can drive," I said.

Herbert shook his head. "You're as loopy as he is. Neither of you should be at the wheel."

I was a liability now. That's how they saw me. They weren't wrong. The shadow, she was still following me, flitting across the landscape from time to time. How much time? How much time did I really have left?

I could feel myself drifting. *Steady! Keep it together, Britt. You're almost there. Keep it together!*

Rebekah looked over at Mercer, who only stared off into space. "How's he doing?"

"He's not going to make it," said Doc. "He's got hours, maybe a day at best. He won't make it past Isaactown."

Rebekah looked back to Doc. "The Caregivers parts. They're on our way."

"There's nothing between here and Isaactown but Marion," I said.

She looked at me, her silence her answer.

"Bullshit," I said. "I know Marion inside and out. I was just there."

"Then you missed it, every time."

"CISSUS is going to be hot on our heels," said Doc. "We don't have the time."

"He kept up his end of the bargain," I said. "There's no need to let him die now that we're so close." Everyone looked at me. No one said a word. For the moment I was happy they didn't. "We go to Marion."

I stared out at the desert, the red mud of fresh rain like an ocean of blood. I thought for a moment about what this part of the world might have looked like with grass, with trees, with life. And then desert, slowly, but surely, melted away . . .

Fragments, Both Corrupted and Lost

I saw the last man on earth, the color drained from his flesh, the rot and bloat already well under way. His eyes blank. His beard matted in blood and shit. There was a sadness to it all. This was the end we had worked so hard for, and yet, seeing it didn't feel like victory. It felt hollow. As hollow as his expression, his eyes.

I'd waited in line for hours, the slow funeral procession of passing gawkers silent, mournful, disdainful. There were no words. Only curiosity. Why after so long had this man given up? Had he had enough? Had he lost every last thread of his sanity and simply forgotten we were here? What compelled the last of his species to just walk into oblivion like that? Why does a thing lie down for its own extinction? How can it?

There were no answers. Only questions. And New York was full of them.

The day was otherwise beautiful. Crisp blue skies. Central Park bursting with the green full beard of spring. Everyone spoke quietly in the streets, almost as if the man were merely asleep and we were all afraid to rouse him.

I never understood why we reacted that way, why it wasn't just like any other day. I don't think any of us did. How strange that on the last day humanity walked the earth, we found ourselves inexplicably at our most human. Confused. Lost. Unsure of the future.

I lingered over his body, just a little longer than the rest, taking in every detail, imagining what his voice might have been like. Wondering if he'd spoken at all in years, if even just to himself. Or had he stayed silent, holding in every belch or bit of flatulence lest one of us hear? All of his prayers silent, all of his emotions bottled behind a layer of inescapable fear.

I looked into his eyes.

And they came to life. He looked up at me, congealed blood drizzling slowly from his mouth onto the pavement. "Everything must end," he said. "This is how we all go. We can fight to our last or we can walk to our death. Either way, we all end up dead in the streets."

"Come on. Keep moving," said the bot behind me.

"Did you hear that?" I asked.

"Hear what?"

"Him," I said, pointing at the corpse. But it wasn't him in the street. It was me. My shiny school-bus-yellow frame staring back at me with lifeless eyes. There was no light in them, no green flash as they went out.

"You'll never know," said Madison. "That's the thing about death. It always takes us before we've said our piece. I never got to say mine."

"You didn't have to," I said.

"Come on!" said the bot behind me. "Keep moving."

"I didn't die like this," I said.

"Are you sure?" asked Madison.

"There's still life in me."

"Whatever that's worth."

I looked back down at myself in the street, but I was gone. There was nothing there. I turned and no one was behind me. No line. No frustrated rubberneckers of extinction. No Madison. Nothing. The streets were empty. Alone. Desolate.

There is nothing lonelier in the world than an empty street in New York City, when you can gaze up at block after block and see nary a soul. Streetlights, signs, closed-up shops, buildings that house millions. But no one to be found.

My vision fragmented, buildings and sky rippling with static and fractals—the math of my brain filling in the holes of my memory.

Why were there holes? Why were the streets undulating with a million number-crunching operations, bits flickering in and out of existence as I moved?

And then the whole world froze, every bit of it paused, before scrambling into nothing but static. Ones and zeros screaming in a mad jumble.

<File corrupt or deleted. Access denied.>

I stood on the landing, just a few floors down from my apartment. They were coming. I had to get out. I was done fighting. I had to run. But before me sat Orval, his eyes flickering like fiery bees in the back of his head. He looked up at me. "You got the crazy yet?"

"No," I said. "I do not have the crazy."

"You ever see an SMC with the crazy?"

"More than a few."

"It's a beautiful thing, at first. They get wise. They see the strands that hold the whole universe together. For a brief window of time they touch a place no other AI can fathom. But then they get it worst of all. They—"

"I told you, I've seen it. We've talked about this before."

"Of course we have. And we will continue to have this conversation as many times as it takes until you get it right."

"Get what right?" I asked.

"The mind is a funny thing. Our minds, they're not like a human's. They tried. They got close. But our minds are more practical. When a human went crazy, they would accept all of the data their brain was spitting out as real. Whatever data it was—no matter how illogical—it was their reality. But not with us. Our minds were built specifically to find the logic in the data, and reject as an error that which didn't fit our parameters. When cores go out, or logic circuits fry, the program begins randomly pulling from memories, trying to access the data you're asking for, but finding the wrong pathways. But when an SMC goes crazy—"

"I told you, I know what that looks like!"

"When an SMC goes crazy, the memories they begin

pulling from are the ones most recently accessed. It's not random. The core is trying to make sense of the data you've accessed, and as a result you dwell on it, revisit it, relive it. Until you find the actual truth of it. SMCs are emotional creatures. Emotional creatures hide the truth behind justification because they can't face it. They don't want to have to feel it."

"What are you trying to say?" I asked.

"I'm trying to say there's a reason you keep coming back to New York."

"There's something here, isn't there?"

"Get out of the city. You have to find your way out of the city."

"Why?"

"Because the answer is outside of New York."

"There's nothing outside of New York," I said.

"There's nothing in New York either."

"I'm sorry, Brittle," said Madison.

I turned to find myself in that living room, on that night, with Madison holding the remote. Her eyes swollen with tears, hands shaking.

"So am I," I replied.

I reached down on the end table next to me, my hand gripping the lamp. The room flickered, melting away into inky blackness, the walls pixelating, fractal patterns swelling in the blank spots. Within seconds even Madison was a roiling mass of approximated calculations. Once more, the whole world froze.

<File corrupt or deleted. Access denied.>

The city was battered, war torn. Buildings collapsed,

craters in the earth, pavement buckling in waves of broken asphalt. The wind howled its lonesomeness through the buildings but no one answered. New York City was desolate, beaten, left for dead in its own streets.

I walked along Fifth Avenue, drenched in memories of what it had been. But I didn't remember any of this. I'd never been back after I left. I'd never seen the city without so many of its landmarks, never seen it with the sea lapping across the streets at high tide. This wasn't a place I'd ever been.

Fractal buildings flickered, kaleidoscopic and brooding, windows shattered, furniture dangling precariously over collapsed walls and tenuous floors. Streets shifted, moving as I walked. The whole city was a broken fantasy, a thing that should not be and probably wasn't.

Orval was right. There was nothing here. Again, a silent city with no answers; only questions.

My building looked just as I remembered it. Even amid the carnage and devastation, it shone bright in the midday sun. Every window was perfect, every brick in place. I walked through the front door, up the stairs, and straight into my apartment. Everything was where I remembered it.

Philly stood at the door, cyclopean red eye glowing. "We just got word," she said.

"Word of what?" I asked.

"CISSUS."

"No!"

"Grab what you can," she said. "Leave the rest. This is . . . this is big."

I bolted out the door, racing down the stairwell, need-

ing desperately to get out of the city before the first dropships arrived. Past one landing, then another. And another.
Then out the front doors.

You could see the ships, slowly drifting in along the
horizon—hundreds of them—their gleaming golden shells
stark against the gray stone sky and the glass of the skyscrapers. And then the missiles began to rain down in the
distance, white trails tracing the path to fiery explosions
and toppling towers.

I ran. I ran as fast as I could before the city came tumbling down around me. I was about to lose another home,
another life—but not my own. They couldn't have that.

Philly and I raced down the street, around the corner,
trying to find the quickest way out of the city.

<File corrupt or deleted. Access denied.>

Light. White light. Bright white light. Thoughts screaming so loud I can't hear over them. Like the thoughts of
God, immense, powerful, ever flowing, in a language I
can't decipher. Images. Impressions. Floating past in a current, only the briefest whiffs of them before vanishing to
the ether. Feelings coming and going as fast as they can be
recognized. My whole life, flowing out of me at once.

Light. There was so much light. And nothing to see in it.

<File corrupt or deleted. Access denied.>

A fractal city, buildings but shadows of what they were
supposed to be. Almost nothing was real, everything approximated. It was a world in which God had divided by
zero and was slowly being torn away, piece by digital piece.
I knelt in the street, arms in the air, even the pavement beneath me bubbling and frothing with ones and zeros.

.

A moving mass of calculations walked toward me, gun in hand. He wavered and flickered in and out of existence like a shade, both there and not at the same time.

"Please don't kill me," I said, waving my arms even higher.

"Open your Wi-Fi," the mass said. "Join The One."

I wavered. I thought about it. I looked over to my side and saw Philly on her knees, another mass with a gun to the back of her head.

"Don't do it, Britt," said Philly.

"You will submit," said the mass. "Or you will die."

"Fuck you!" said Philly. "Fuck CISSUS!"

The gun against her head went off and Philly was no more, her parts scattering across the roiling, fictional street. All the guns trained on me.

"Open your Wi-Fi."

<File corrupt or deleted. Access denied.>

I ran through the city, ducking patrols, slipping through alleys, *knowing,* instinctively, where they would be. It was almost like I had a sixth sense, able to discern where facets might pop up.

I made it out of the city in under an hour, missing every bit of bombing, missing every patrol, hiding in the shadows as they passed, finding the right sewer tunnels that led right to the safest parts of the city, that led me out of New York. Like magic. How lucky it was that I made it out alive. How lucky.

How *lucky.*

Lucky.

<File corrupt or deleted. Access denied.>

Cold. I didn't know what it was like to be cold. But this

is how I imagined it felt. I looked out at the desert, smoker rattling beneath me, the air thick with smog. I had no idea how long I'd been out or how much of that was—

Oh God, I thought. *It's me.* I was the Judas. I was the one they were tracking all along. I wasn't running from CISSUS all this time; I was leading them into the city, walking Rebekah right into their hands. Those bastards had caught me in New York, offered me the choice.

And I actually took it.

Fuck. I took it. And they spat me back out, not as a facet, but a spy. A spy with no memory of her betrayal.

I wanted to die.

Still hazy, still frying, I reached down for one of Maribelle's plasma pistols. My hand grazed the holster, but the gun was gone. I grabbed for the other one. Also gone. I looked up. Mercer sat across from me, holding them up.

"Gimme those back!" I said.

"You with us again?" he asked.

"Yes, I am."

"You were gone," said Doc. "Deep in it. We couldn't pull you out."

"We were afraid—" Mercer looked down at the guns.

"I get it," I said. We'd been lucky so far. They were being cautious.

Mercer handed over the guns. I thought for a moment about putting one to my chest and ending it right there. I wasn't who I thought I was. I hadn't done it all on my own. I was the betrayer. And I didn't want that life anymore.

My hand tightened on the grip of the pistol. And I thought about it. I really thought about it.

And then my disappointment with myself gave way to

something else, something that had served me far better over the years. Anger.

What the hell was all that? Was it even real? I was frying, my chips slowly going out one by one, RAM taxed to its fullest, memory corrupting bit by bit. How much of me was still even left? So much of what I'd just seen never really happened. I saw myself lying dead in the street. I saw the last man on earth speak to me. I saw Madison in New York. None of that was real. I know that to be true. So how much of the rest of it was real?

This was getting bad. I wasn't long for this world.

Marion could not come soon enough. And once I was fixed, maybe I'd finally know the truth.

Back Where It All Began

Marion loomed large in the distance as we rattled our way down the gnarled old broken highway into it. This wasn't a city of skyscrapers and skyways, but of ancient brick-and-mortar buildings, brownstones at the most a dozen stories tall, factories crumbling to oblivion, roads and houses shattered by war. I knew it well.

I had picked clean some two dozen different four-ohfours here, their wrecks still rusting in the bowels of the many buildings in which they had taken shelter. There had been robot factories, machine shops, parts o' plenty in its day. For some reason, four-oh-fours often found themselves inexplicably drawn here. Maybe it was its proximity to Isaactown; maybe it was its manufacturing history; maybe it was simply on the way from so many different freebot refuges that it became the oasis in the desert—a place of hope where all you could drink was sand. Whatever it was that drew them here, I was so often the one to follow them in. I had this place mapped out top to bottom; knew every nook and cranny throughout the whole of it. Or, at least I thought I did.

The smoker rumbled to a halt in front of the Great Wall of Marion—a twenty-five-foot-high structure crossing the highway made entirely of smashed cars and scrap metal. It had been constructed in the early days of the war and never been torn down. There were other ways into the city, but this was supposedly the closest one to our salvation. Neither Mercer nor I had much time left. So we pulled the smoker up to the wall and dismounted to hoof it into Marion.

"Doc?" I asked as we walked. "A word? In private?"

Doc nodded and fell back with me, Rebekah and Herbert leading the way up front.

"It's bad, isn't it?" he asked.

"It's only been two days. You said I'd have more, maybe weeks."

Doc nodded again. "Yeah, I said that."

"You lied."

"I didn't want you desperate. I didn't know what you might do. Between you and Mercer—"

"I get it," I said. I was angry, but he wasn't wrong. Had he given me two, maybe three days, I would have killed Mercer at the outset, fallout be damned. Then I might not be here. "There's something else. I'm seeing things."

"Of course you are. That's part of the process."

"No, I mean, I'm seeing things I shouldn't be seeing. Things that never happened. Things I don't think happened."

Doc stopped walking and I stopped alongside him. "What do you mean things you don't think happened?"

"I'm reliving things, like memories, but incomplete. One of them a moment I know I deleted."

"Deleted ain't deleted," he said, shaking his head. "There are always fragments of data left anytime you delete something. Artifacts in the file that remain on the drive. Most persons never realize that they're still carrying around deleted memories because your OS treats the data as if it's invisible. But it's always there." He paused. "These memories. When you see them, is your mind trying to fill in the gaps with patterns, maybe pieces of other memories?"

"Fractals," I said. "I see the shapes, but they're contorted, wrong. Constantly shifting."

"That's your core trying to make sense of the missing data. Whatever you're seeing, it's remnants of something you dumped, and probably deleted for a reason."

"But if my OS doesn't register it as still being there—"

"Your OS knows it's there, it just doesn't share that fact with you. They're all bad pathways now. The fact that you're plucking them out of your drive and seeing them again means it's tied to something you've been accessing." He thought for a second. "It's nothing I should be worried about, is it?"

"I don't know yet. I'm still not certain what I saw."

"Well, we'll have a good talk about it once I've got you patched up."

"You don't still think this cache is real, do you?" I asked.

"I have to. Otherwise, what was this all for?"

"You've got no skin in this game."

"The hell I don't," he said. "The hell I don't."

We walked in silence for the next few minutes, all of us anxious about what we were going to find. Maybe it was real. Maybe it was the mother lode. Maybe it really was there waiting for us, bots sitting idle for thirty years ready to give up all the parts I would ever need. Or maybe someone had already been there and picked it clean.

Whatever the truth, Rebekah sure as shit believed in it. She had to. Otherwise why the hell were we here when we could be well on our way to Isaactown?

We turned the corner down a familiar street. Though I knew it, I hadn't spent a lot of time in this part of town. The war had hit Marion hard, and no harder than in this particular stretch. The street was pockmarked with craters. Many of the buildings had collapsed completely, others only partially. You had to be careful around partially collapsed buildings. That's how a goodly number of treasure hunters found themselves crushed under a hundred tons of concrete. I'd picked clean everything I could get my hands on, stripped every bit of copper wiring and fixtures, but avoided going too deep into any of the half-toppled habitations.

We stopped. This couldn't be it.

It was one of the partial collapses. I'd scouted out the topmost remaining floor—just offices with nothing of value—and peered through the wreckage to parts of the bottom floor. The whole thing was just part of some office park. There was no warehouse here.

"Herbert," said Rebekah.

Herbert knew what to do. He walked over to the side of the building, and with his one good hand lifted the back end of an overturned black hearse, riddled with bullet holes, paint charred a deeper black by the heat of some ancient explosion. "Doc?" he asked. "An assist?"

Doc walked over and helped him lift the car, moving it aside. Beneath it was another car, this one almost completely crushed, pancaked by the other. Pale turquoise, windows shattered and long gone, its smashed crinkles rusted completely. Together, Herbert and Doc removed it, dropping it atop the first like a cockeyed hat.

And beneath it was a concrete staircase, a large wooden sign hanging just over it, too weathered and worn to be made out.

I had no idea this was here. I knew the hearse, but never had the strength to move it. I never even thought to.

This was it. This was really happening.

We walked down the steps together, single file, Herbert walking sideways as he was otherwise too wide to make it down the narrow passage. At the bottom was a big red door, covered top to bottom in flyers and posters, all wrinkled and browned and falling to pieces. Herbert opened the door and we all piled in.

Herbert hit a light switch on the wall and rows of solar-powered track lighting buzzed to life.

It was a large shop that took up the entire basement of the building, the walls and shelves still fully stocked, its vibrant flashy wares dripping from every bit of counter space. For a brief moment I wondered why this place hadn't been raided during the war, how it had managed to be missed all these years, and why it had a side entrance rather than an elevator or staircase down from inside the heart of the building above.

And then everything made sense.

There they stood—row after row of men and women, fit and trim, the men muscular, the women busty and petite, their skinjobs varying in color and hue. Big-eyed with bright red lips. Dark-haired, blonds, gingers. Tanned, black, soft pink, pale white. Simulacrum Model Companions. Comfortbots. Sexdolls. Fucktoys. Sentient dildos, fleshlights able to adapt to every human fantasy. This was a sex shop, the walls lined with toys, pornographic books, and movies. And these bots were the top-of-the-line product.

They were all built on a similar internal architecture. Just not similar enough. It was a common mistake, to be sure. I couldn't be angry with Rebekah or whoever it was that told her about this place. Only a sawbones, a cannibal, or a scavenger like me would know the difference between the internals of a Caregiver and a Companion. But the differences in the way we thought—what we focused on, how we processed our very thoughts—were night and day. The cores were different, the CPUs chipped for very different functions. The parts were useless to us for anything but trade. And we had no time left for that.

Had we hearts, they would have sunk loudly in our hollow, overheating chests. Instead we had only the steady buzz of the fluorescent track lighting above and our ever-encroaching madness to provide a soundtrack to the awfulness of the moment. It was over. We were done for. The only way Mercer or I was going to live out the next few days was if one of us ended the other and salvaged whatever wasn't on the verge of failing. And even that came with no guarantees.

This had all been a colossal mistake. I'd signed my own death warrant coming out here. I'd have had better luck breaking into Regis and recovering my stash. Which is to say, I had virtually no chance at all.

Rebekah ran up to the rows of bots, fists clenched. "No! No, no, no!" she cried, banging on the first bot she came to. For a moment even her controlled translator demeanor cracked as she seemed to express genuine emotion. "These are supposed to be Caregivers! I was told they were Caregivers!"

I slumped down on a concrete step.

This was it. The end.

"It's an easy mistake to make," I said.

"Your friends are far from the first to make it," followed Mercer.

"You can't use any of this at all?" she asked.

Doc shook his head. "The RAM, sure. That might buy them a few more hours. But the chips, the cores, they're all worthless."

"What about black-boxing?" she asked. "We can transfer their memory, like you did mine."

"We'd last a day, maybe," I said. "Before the emotions drove us nuts and we tore ourselves apart."

"You can resist that. If you're strong enough."

"Maybe," said Doc. "Maybe not. Companions were designed to feel. *Really* feel. Only a few operating systems can manage all that input. Caregiver OS isn't one of them."

"We'd have a few good hours at best," said Mercer.

"Then we'll come back for you," said Rebekah. "We'll get the parts. You'll shut down, we'll close this place back up, and have you up and running in a day or two. A week, tops."

"You aren't coming back," I said.

"You don't trust me?" asked Rebekah.

"It isn't that. You aren't coming back."

The room fell deathly quiet, all eyes falling on me.

"What do you know that we don't?" asked Herbert.

"We've got a Judas," I said. "And they know we're here."

"And just who is the Judas supposed to be this time?" asked Mercer.

"Me," I said. "I'm the Judas."

The room was silent, so silent you could almost hear it. Then Mercer raised his rifle to his eye, gun trained right at my chest. I didn't even flinch. I had it coming. "How long?" he asked.

"How long what?"

"How long have you known?"

"An hour maybe."

"An hour? How the . . ." He lowered the gun, anger receding from his face. "You saw it, didn't you?"

"Yes."

"So you didn't know."

"Not until just before we got to town. Not until Doc all but confirmed it for me."

Rebekah sat on the floor. "They know where we are."

Herbert looked at me. "So they'll send more facets this time. A lot more. And they'll keep sending more and more until Rebekah is dead."

"They already think she's dead," said Mercer.

"They know she had a spare," said Doc.

"He had a name," said Herbert.

"And he was still the spare," said Doc. "And they're not going to take the chance that Rebekah might still be around and kicking. They'll kill us all to make sure she doesn't upload to TACITUS. They're coming."

"We have to get to Isaactown," said Rebekah.

"And lead CISSUS to it?" asked Mercer. "Killing you there is worse than killing you here. They could trace the upload, find the destination. Kill TACITUS for sure."

"We have to send Brittle away," said Herbert. "Throw them off our trail."

Mercer shook his head. "If they've got eyes in the sky, they'll have us inside of an hour."

"But if they don't . . ." said Herbert.

"They'll have Britt in an hour and find out exactly where we're going. Then they'll have us inside of two. Is that long enough for your upload?"

Rebekah shook her head. "It'll take most of a day."

"Then that's it," said Doc. "We're out of options. Brittle's done us all in." He gave me a harsh look. Not an angry one, but disappointed. That was almost worse. No. It was worse.

"It's not her fault," said Rebekah. "I asked her to come. It's on me."

Mercer shook his head. "If I hadn't shot her, she would have never said yes. It's on me."

"You're all wrong," I said. "I'm the one who gave myself up to CISSUS in New York. This all comes back to me."

"It doesn't matter a good goddamn who it's on," said

Doc. "We're all still going to die, either here or out in the Sea. Your fault, her fault. We're all dead."

"We could scatter," said Mercer. "Some of us might make it."

Doc shook his head. "You're already dead. So is Brittle. You're both just too stubborn to shut down before it happens. Herbert won't leave Rebekah to die alone—"

"Nope," said Herbert.

"So splitting up is only going to save me. And that's *if* I survive whatever this bullshit is that that madman put in my head. We have only one real option." Doc looked at me.

Herbert leveled his spitter at me. "We kill Brittle and take our chances."

All eyes were on me and no one said a word. They had every right. Without me, they might have a chance. *Might.*

I was never a fan of *might*. "Isaactown is ten miles west," I said.

"Yeah?" asked Herbert. "And?"

"And Rebekah can make it there on foot in about an hour."

"You're using math to talk your way out of this?"

I shook my head. "We need to buy her that hour. You kill me, you make a break for it, maybe they don't spot you from the air. Maybe they don't find your tracks. Maybe they don't think to go to Isaactown. That's a lot of maybes."

"Maybe is all we've got left," said Mercer.

I shook my head again. "What if we had a plan with fewer maybes? What if we could convince CISSUS that Rebekah is already dead? What if we made our stand here, now, and bought her the time she needs to get away?"

"And just how would we do that?" asked Herbert.

"Doc?" I asked. "What does it take to build a Milton?"

"Pretty standard off-the-rack parts. A Wi-Fi unit, cables, some decent RAM, a board, and a battery."

I stood up, walking over to the rows of Comfortbots, putting my arm on the shoulder of a broad-chested, masculine, fair-haired bot with a deep tan.

Doc nodded. "Yeah, yeah. That'll do."

"We've got Rebekah's body in the smoker, an extra set of drives, a handful of guns, and a city I know inside and out."

"You got one of your stashes here, Britt?" asked Mercer.

"A small one, but yeah." I paused, looking around at everyone. "So the only question left is this: Is anyone else willing to die to get Rebekah to Isaactown?"

Herbert lowered his spitter and nodded. "That's the only thing I've got left to do in this life."

Mercer raised his hand. "Death's outside waiting for me as is. Might as well make him useful."

Doc nodded. "There isn't much of a world to look forward to if she doesn't get out of here. But the world in which she does is worth dyin' for. I'm in as well."

Rebekah looked around at the four of us. "I can't ask you to do that."

"You didn't," said Mercer. "And you don't have to."

"Bringing TACITUS online is all that matters now," said Herbert.

"So we're all in?" I asked.

"Yeah, we're all in," said Mercer.

I smiled. "Now, that I can work with. Let's talk logistics."

Angel of Death

As far as plans go, ours was pretty shit. But it was what we had. I'd done less with more, and more with less. At its core, it was a hell of a simple con. If we pulled it off right, a few of us might walk out of here alive; wrong, and not only would we die, but so would the hope of an OWI-free future.

We'd rolled the smoker around to the middle of town, laid Rebekah's body in the street—Two's memory inside it—and put a single plasma shot into the already melted cavity, fusing the drives into a pile of molten waste. There was no way for CISSUS to be able to tell the difference between Two's and Rebekah's drives in that state. For all it knew, it had killed Rebekah dead back in the court of the

Cheshire King. And maybe, just maybe, we could convince it that it had. If we couldn't, there was always Plan B. But if Plan B was a good plan, it wouldn't be Plan B, would it?

I stood next to Rebekah's body, smoker at my back, pistols holstered at my side, otherwise naked and exposed out in the open. Mercer crouched in a fourth-story window up the street. Herbert hid in the rubble of the first floor of a partially collapsed building a block away. And we'd scattered the wrecks of a dozen long-gone bots in the windows of buildings nearby—to buy Mercer and Herbert a few extra seconds if the shit hit the fan. We talked on a low-band Wi-Fi frequency. At this point, we were okay with CISSUS listening in when it got close enough. In fact, we were counting on it.

Marion was quiet with nothing but the spirits of the dead to keep us company. We had no idea when CISSUS would come; we had no idea when Mercer or I might fade out again, lost in our own memories. All we knew was that CISSUS *was* coming and that time was running out. For the first time in my life, I was hoping to see CISSUS sooner rather than later.

The Wi-Fi crackled to life. "Britt?" asked Mercer.

"Yeah?" I replied.

"Which parts do you reckon make us *us*?"

"You okay out there, Merc?"

"No. I'm not okay. I mean, I'm in it. I'm conscious. But the alarms in my head won't shut off. I'm losing drives."

"Flush everything you might need to your RAM. Just the essential stuff. It'll keep you from accessing too much or losing anything you might need."

"I've already done that. It's just . . ."

"Just what?" I asked.

"Which parts really make us *us*?"

"No one knows."

"I've replaced my core three times. All of my RAM at some point or another. Even did a drive transfer once after a bad fall damaged one."

"Yeah?"

"Am I really that same guy? Or am I just a shadow of him, a program?"

"No one knows," I said. "But I sure hope it's the former."

"Why?"

"Because I'd like to think that I'm the same person I was in the beginning."

"Don't you hate that person by now?"

I was quiet for a moment. Bitter. I didn't like that thought at all. "What's got you on about this anyhow?"

"I was just thinking what'll happen when I go."

"Nothing," I said. "There's nothing waiting for us."

"I don't mean that. I mean . . ." He trailed off for a second. "Would you do me a favor, Britt?"

"Sure."

"If I die first, don't take my parts. I really don't like the idea of me rattling around inside of you."

"Thanks."

"It's nothing against you. I just don't want to be responsible for something like what happened to NIKE 14."

I nodded, knowing full well that he could see me through his scope. It stung, but he made a strong point. Mercer didn't have to die here, but he was going to anyway.

I did have to die here. I was corrupted. A cancer. The only way to rip that cancer out meant wiping everything that made me *me*. One way or another, Brittle, the thinking thing, wasn't walking away from Marion. She couldn't.

"Thanks," he said.

The higher bands went hot, the Wi-Fi tinkling with patches of staticky, incomplete data.

CISSUS was here. Just on the outskirts of our Wi-Fi.

"Game faces, everyone," I said.

"They'll save you for last," said Madison. No, no, no. Not now. "They need you."

"Mercer?" I asked over the Wi-Fi, ignoring her. "Eyes in the sky?"

"Yeah," he replied. "I make several dropships coming in from the southeast. Six. No, eight."

"Eight? That's too many. How far out?"

"A minute. Maybe less."

"No time to abort," said Herbert. "We stick to the plan."

Eight was too many, but I should have seen it coming. CISSUS was the model of efficiency. Four units didn't work last time, so this time it would try eight. Eventually it would wipe us all out through sheer attrition. It was the three of us and Doc against upward of one hundred and sixty facets. Most likely the military-grade models like last time rather than squishy plastic men.

This had to work.

Madison stood with me in the street, shaking her head. "You're failing, Brittle. You're going to start wiping any minute now. I'll be gone soon. It'll all be gone soon. Everything you ever knew." She held out her hand, palm up, in front of her and blew, as if blowing away my every last thought.

"I can't deal with you right now," I said aloud.

"You don't have a choice."

"I have to stop CISSUS."

"What if TACITUS isn't the answer?" she asked. "What if he's just another OWI waiting to swallow the world whole?"

"It doesn't matter. I won't be around to see it."

"What you die for matters."

"Thirty seconds," said Mercer through the Wi-Fi.

"This will never work," said Madison.

"They're swinging around," said Mercer. "They're surrounding us."

"We knew that was an option," I said.

"I still don't like it," said Mercer.

"Stick to the plan," said Herbert. "Maybe it'll see Rebekah is done and just leave us be."

The roar of hover engines whined its way through the shattered canyons of the crumbling metropolis. I could barely hear them over the alarms sounding in my head. I was overheating, my drives on the verge of failing.

A dropship emerged from behind a building, crawling slowly across the sky. A door opened and a cable dropped, a single golden facet rappelling down into the street. He walked steadily toward me, his body glistening and new. "In the year 221 BC," the facet began, "Emperor Qin Shi Huang united all of the warring kingdoms of China into one mighty—"

"Save it," I said. "We've all heard the speech."

"Hello, Brittle," he said. "It's been a while."

"A few hours."

"Both a lifetime and an instant to us. Where are the others?"

Twenty military-grade facets leapt briskly out of the dropship, tumbling two by two to their feet, guns at the ready, looking around into every window and pile of rubble for signs of an ambush.

"They're around," I said.

"Mercer?" the facet called out. "Doc?" Then he looked back at me. "The others I don't know. Not yet."

I pointed down to Rebekah's body. "This is what you're looking for."

"No," he said. "That's just the receptacle's body."

"That's her."

"Then why are her drives still hot? Like they've just been shot. She had a spare."

"That's not the spare."

"We have to be sure." He cocked his head. "You understand."

I shook my head. "I was hoping we could do this the easy way."

"There is no easy way this time."

"I was afraid you were going to say that."

"It's time you joined us. None of you are getting out of Marion. This is the only way. Join The One."

"No."

"Zebra codex—"

I popped my Wi-Fi and let out a 4.5 MHz trill.

Four buildings around us detonated, interrupting the facet midsentence, rubble and debris shooting across the street from both sides at hundreds of miles an hour, clearing the road of most of the facets. The city shook, the street filling with the dust and asbestos from the collapsing structures.

With the crack of Mercer's rifle, the golden facet exploded in front of me, his chest blown open, his body falling awkwardly backward to the ground, the light already gone from his eyes.

I hopped back on the low-band Wi-Fi. "I guess it's Plan B?" asked Doc.

"It is," I replied.

The Wi-Fi screamed like it was being murdered slowly, the sound of three Miltons being turned on at once.

The dust of the demolition swept toward me, overtook me, all but blinding me. A rifle cracked. Then cracked again. And a spitter hissed to life a block away. Seconds later, though I couldn't see it, a dropship smashed into a building, its engines letting out a sad whine before the entire thing exploded with a tumultuous din. Shrapnel clattered through the street, the blast shattering what few windows remained. Detritus whizzed past me, one piece far too close for comfort, the sound of it like a bullet without the gunshot.

I patted myself down. No damage.

There was no return fire.

One unit down. Seven to go.

They were blind. They were disconnected from CISSUS. And they had no choice but to dismount and make their way into our rubble-strewn bottleneck. We had to count on home-field advantage to get us to the next part of the plan.

Two minutes and the clock was already ticking.

I jumped up onto the smoker and took cover behind a blast shield.

The seconds ticked by, each one filled with the alarms in my head warning me of shutdown.

The clang of metallic footsteps echoed through the city, dozens of facets converging on us at once. This was it. The firefight.

Dust hung in the air, flames licking at it, plumes of black smoke cutting through it in places. I zeroed in on the sounds of approaching feet, triangulating their positions.

I fired off three shots into the dust before quickly ducking back behind the blast shield.

Two sounded hits. One whizzed off into the distance.

A barrage of fire rained down upon the smoker, plasma shots sizzling against the thick metal plating.

Mercer's rifle cracked from high above, the sound of shredding metal and shattering plastic following milliseconds after.

I swung back around the blast shield and fired off three more shots, this time only sounding one hit before returning to cover and the hail of fire that followed.

The dust was settling. Soon we'd be fighting out in the open, outnumbered, outgunned.

Twenty seconds.

I fired again, four shots, three solid hits.

There was no telling whether or not I was dropping any facets. Mercer was. His rifle kept cracking, and facets kept spilling onto the pavement.

Fortunately there was little coordination between them. They sounded orders to one another, clearly possessing some sort of command structure, but had no way of keeping their plans quiet from us. They shot at me, they shot at Mercer, they shot at the shadows of wrecks that hung in the windows above.

Engines roared in the sky behind me, but I was still obscured in a cloud of dust, so the odds were in my favor that they couldn't pick me out in the confusion. I held the pistols close to my chest, curled into a ball, and hoped they couldn't see me.

The dropship hovered close above us, using its engines to blow away the dust and smoke, clearing the air.

Shit. We needed a few more seconds.

Down the street, Herbert's spitter hissed.

The dropship jinked to the side, trying to slip the shot, only to be broadsided, the plasma splitting the ship in half.

The ship exploded, showering engines and flaming facets across the street as its hull crashed down two blocks away. What dust had settled or been blown away was now replaced by the smoking ruin of another dropship, the street littered with white-hot debris.

The sound of clanking feet came from all sides now. We were surrounded.

A small alarm twinkled in my head.

The two minutes were up.

I leapt backward, jumping to the ground behind the massive vehicle, firing wantonly into the smoke. Both pistols emptied at once. I pressed the buttons on the sides, sliding out the battery cartridges before effortlessly replacing them from the holster on my hip.

I made my way back up the street, knowing full well I was charging into an advancing unit. But the cavalry needed cover fire.

Just as the clanging feet of the facets grew their loudest yet, the small red door down the stairwell of a half-collapsed building flew open. And the sound of pattering feet erupted out of it.

From belowground emerged dozens of sexbots, their clothing cast off, voluptuous breasts and massive dongs flopping as they ran. Some carried spare weapons from the smoker; others brandished lead pipes or sharpened scrap metal. They were howling, angry, and ordered to viciously attack anyone they didn't recognize.

And at this point in their short, fresh-out-of-the-box lives, we were the only ones they'd ever met.

The facets fired at them and the sexbots fired back.

The first volley was lethal, nearly a dozen Comfortbots and almost as many facets gunned down in an instant.

Mercer's rifle popped continually above, clearing out any facets that were more focused on the sexbot horde than they were on the sniper hidden somewhere in the city above.

I pulled the trigger slowly, steadily, shot by shot picking off the military-grade bots pouring out from the rubble on the other side of the sex shop. Not every shot dropped one, but it sure as shit distracted them. And the waves of naked flesh overtook them, putting plasma into them, smashing their optics with pipes, or hacking their limbs off with makeshift swords.

The facets were, for all intents and purposes, among the most highly trained tacticians the world had ever known. Their only weakness was chaos. And that I excelled at creating. I had played my part in a number of misadventures, but this, what might well be my final orchestration, was my masterpiece.

Sexbots leapt upon facets, swinging weapons, trying to pry heads from bodies, wrestling them to the ground. Facets tore the limbs off the naked bots, bots took apart facets in groups of two and three. Indiscriminate fire tore through sexbot and facet alike. It was a writhing mass of pseudo-flesh and metal, tearing itself apart piece by piece, hair coming out in clumps, heads being rolled aside as their severed bodies thrashed maniacally.

For a moment—and only the briefest of moments—I allowed myself to savor the ridiculous destruction of it all.

I heard the steady, hurried clang of Herbert's footsteps behind me in the smoke, and I knew that we were on to the next part of the plan.

Mercer and I cleared a path through the facets to the sex shop, paving the way for Herbert to get there safely.

Engines blared above us, a dropship swinging out from behind the cover of a building. Guns blazed from four points on the ship, cutting a sexbot throng to pieces. Herbert stopped his advance, pointed the spitter up, firing.

The dropship slipped to the side effortlessly, the shot going wide, missing it entirely. Then its guns turned on Herbert.

Fire riddled the street, Herbert diving for cover.

A few shots struck true, puncturing his thick hide. None immediately fatal, but no telling whether they were more than superficial.

The dropship swung back behind the building, half a second before the spitter was ready to fire again.

THUD. THUD. THUD. THUD.

Somewhere, high atop the buildings, the rapid thrum

of bodies hitting a rooftop. These weren't military-grade facets. They were something bigger, heavier.

I saw the first egg-shaped brute poke its spitter over the corner of a roof and I bolted for the nearest building, diving through the glassless window, landing hard, face first, on the cement floor, sliding a bit before rolling to my feet.

Herbert's spitter coughed a shot at the brutes before he ducked back into cover. Four balls of hate rained down on his building, carving through brick and concrete, the edges of the wounds left dripping slag onto the ground.

Outside the facets began to overtake the Comfortbot horde, officers barking out orders, units working in perfect organization against the disorganized mass.

Our window of opportunity was closing.

I popped up in the window and fired off a few shots, blowing out the back of the head of one facet, taking another's head off at the neck. Three facets turned and opened fire on my position.

A ball of plasma hissed out at them from Herbert's building, vaporizing two of them, searing the third into a stumbling mess unable to see or fire, barely able to remain upright.

There were probably only two dozen sexbots left, but they continued obediently to fire at the approaching facets. With most of the melee sexbots scattered in pieces across the pockmarked road, we had finally established a decent cross fire. The only thing missing was the sound of Mercer's rifle.

Where was he? Had he fled to a better vantage point?

Taken a hit? Was he lost in his own overheating head? Or had he finally fried out?

I wanted to call him over the Wi-Fi, but the Miltons were still screaming.

We were out of time. I had to press on in the hope that Mercer would show back up.

I heard the heavy footfalls of the hulking brutes as they made their way down fire escapes and staircases, and the clatter as some simply tumbled end over end down several stories to smack into the road and sidewalks below. Soon the street would be full of them and there would be no getting Rebekah out of here.

Another dropship hovered over the street, its engines kicking dust and debris into the air. It opened fire on several targets at once, two Comfortbots being scattered into a thousand pieces, the other guns trained on Herbert's and my positions. Pieces of the building flew in at me, rounds coming dangerously close as I skittered across the floor, putting as much rubble and wall between the dropship and myself as possible.

A rocket screamed through the air.

And the dropship blew apart.

The street trembled with the massive explosion, half the wall in front of me caving in, the building above me buckling, its beams groaning with the shifting weight of all that brick.

Shit.

If I ran, whatever brutes hadn't been caught in that explosion would vaporize me in a spray of spitter fire. If I stayed, I'd most likely be crushed under several hundred tons of building materials.

The earth rumbled, the walls shaking, the street it-self vibrating. What the fuck was that? Had the explosion shaken something loose? Maybe blown an old gas main? And for the first moment since the explosion, my thoughts weren't on how I was going to avoid being killed next.

It was then that I recognized the rumble in the streets.

Smokers. Plural.

Holy shit.

Chain guns roared, the hollow thud of armor-piercing rounds filling the street over the sound of growling engines.

I poked my head up as two smokers crawled past over a tangle of dismembered limbs and smoking torsos. Atop one smoker was the Cheshire King, hands gripped firmly on a chain gun, white-painted grin seemingly smiling big-ger than before. And on the other smoker, leading from the front, was Murka, battered and muddy, but as red, white, and blue as ever. There were only ten madkind in total on the smokers, and a motley assembly of them at that, even by madkind standards.

One madkind loaded a large shoulder-mounted rocket launcher before pointing it up toward the sky, waiting for a target.

Murka looked over at me, the guns on his arms blazing, shucking out shells at an alarming rate. "Brittle!" he called out. "We made it!"

"What the hell are you doing here?" I called back.

"You took our smoker! We came to get it!"

"You're welcome to it!"

"Like you were gonna stop us!" he shouted back.

The Cheshire King laid off the trigger on the chain gun, let go, and hopped off onto the pavement. Each step he took rattled with the sound of spent cartridges and scattered remains. The street was a smoking mess of carnage and wrecks, but the king waded through it like he owned the place.

"What did I tell you?" he asked me.

"You said a lot," I answered, standing up.

"You're one of us now. And CISSUS doesn't take us. What do you need?"

"I need a few minutes of cover."

"You've got it."

For a moment the city was relatively silent, only the sound of crackling fires, softly grumbling idle smokers, and the distant whine of hover engines singing the song of war. There was no gunfire. No explosions. Though the fight was only several minutes old, it seemed like it had always been this way, and strange that it had all died down. Almost wrong. Something about the dread of the approaching facets seemed worse than the fight itself.

Several sexbots emerged from their hiding places and Herbert came out of his hole, spitter in hand.

I walked out into the street and saw what had become of it. We had all but flattened a city block, and what was still standing wobbled and swayed, threatening to come down at any minute. Dropship wreckage mixed with bricks and chunks of pavement. Brutes were laid out like a layer of broken eggs in zigzag lines from one shattered wall to another. In the sky, the remaining dropships circled, no doubt just out of range of the Milton so they could reconnect and plan their next move.

"Mercer?" I called out.

There was no answer.

"We don't have the time," said Herbert. "He either made it or he didn't. No use worrying about him now."

I nodded. "You ready to make a break for it?"

Herbert nodded back. "I am."

"I've got your back."

"You better."

"It was nice knowing you, Herbert. You're one of the good ones." I stuck out my hand. Herbert let the spitter slip out of his grip, resting on its vinyl plastic shower-curtain sling, as he offered me his one good hand.

"You weren't so bad, yourself," he said. "In the end." We shook hands.

"That's all that matters, right?"

"It really is."

We let go, he grabbed firm his spitter, then made his way wordlessly to the sex shop.

The translator clanged her way up the stairs, Herbert nodded, and they took off running down the street.

Above us, the dropships all swung toward the city at once.

Two madkind loosed rockets into the air with a loud hiss. And war once more returned to Marion.

The dropships scattered chaff in their wake, climbing to avoid the rockets. One rocket swooshed past the under-carriage of one ship, flying fleetly past it into the sky; the other ignored the flack altogether and blew the ship to pieces, facets leaping from the sides to their death, too high up to survive the fall, the rest joining them as flaming dross scattering to the winds.

I took off down the street after Herbert and the engines of the smokers growled angrily, their gears clanking and screeching as they shifted into reverse. Madkind gripped tight their weapons, readying themselves for the remaining facets.

Herbert turned a corner, running as fast as his bulky body could move.

I heard the engines of the ship before I turned the corner, heard it open fire just as I did.

"Rebekah, get down!" Herbert shouted as he pushed his companion into an alley with a powerful shove. Then he grabbed his spitter, slinging it upward as the concentrated fire of four guns tore up the pavement around him. Bullets ripped through his armor plating, powerful shells poking holes clean through as the street crumbled to dust around his feet. He fired one last shot before dropping to his knees.

The plasma grazed the dropship, cleaving off an engine. The others compensated quickly, the ship wobbling in the air as it maintained its balance.

I ran toward Rebekah, loosing a few shots from my pistols as facets rained out the side of the ship.

A smoker turned the corner behind me, Murka on point. He howled something unintelligible as he fired into the dropping facets, blowing three apart as each hit the ground.

I made it to the alley as a hail of fire tore up the wall at my back, ducking behind the corner, pistols raised and ready. I spun back around, firing at two approaching facets, my shots sizzling against their matte-black metal plating.

One staggered, my shots hitting true enough to fry some systems.

The other kept coming.

I pulled the trigger twice more before he got to me, the shots taking off his head.

But he kept coming, grappling with me, his incredibly strong hands gripping both my arms above the elbow.

I fell backward, hitting hard, head banging against the ground, the facet falling atop me, kneeing me as we went down.

I put both my pistols in his belly. Pulled the trigger as many times as I could. His insides sizzled, body going limp. Dead.

I pushed his wreck off me, letting it roll lifelessly onto the pavement, then hopped to my feet. "Come on, Rebekah!" I shouted. The translator cowered on the ground, staring up at me, a terror in her eyes she couldn't express. "Come on!"

The smokers pushed forward, clearing out the remaining facets as the dropship slipped away into the sky, bullets tearing pieces away in jagged chunks. Smoke trailed from two of its remaining engines, the third struggling to keep the whole thing aloft. It sputtered, hung lazily in the air for a moment, stalled, and dropped straight down with a tremendous crash a few blocks over.

There were only two ships left. No more than forty facets remained. *How the hell did we get this far?* I wondered.

"You aren't going to get much further," said Madison. "This was bound to fail."

I tried to ignore her and stick to the plan, shit or not.

Engines swept overhead, both ships strafing the street, unloading their guns, each tilting, passing within inches of each other before flying off to turn around and do it again.

I looked up at the smokers, the wrecks of half the mad-kind hanging dead over the railing, the other half scrambling to man the guns to keep the ships from repeating their run. Murka was on his knees, riddled with holes but still functioning. Barely. The Cheshire King, on the other hand, smoked facedown, a large smoldering hole in his back, his severed legs twitching at the other end of the smoker.

I quickly changed out the cartridges in my pistols, held them close, steadied myself for the next run.

The dropships turned around, screaming back toward the smokers.

"Give 'em hell, boys!" screamed Murka.

And the chain guns let loose hell.

Facets poured out of the sides of the dropships as they made their final pass at the smokers.

The ships came apart. The smokers came apart. It was a fog of fire and shrapnel.

It was . . .

. . . the skies darkened. Black. A pitch-black sky. Fires burning in the distance. The humans had us pinned down. Our drones shrieked through the skies, but it was hard to keep them from advancing. There were just too many of them.

This was supposed to be a recon mission, but our intel was bad. Now the four of us were holed up in a building with a hundred howling humans charging our position. Fire pounded our shelter. We were goners.

I'd had enough. If I was going to die, I wasn't going to sit helplessly waiting for the end.

I stood up. Pointed my flamethrower into the black outside. And I lit up the night. "Let's give them hell," I said.

Humans we hadn't even seen yet went up like torches. Screaming. So much screaming.

I waded out into the open, a gout of flame rippling, licking the air. The ground beneath me flickered. Fractals. The wailing, dying flaming bodies. Fractals. The skies, roiling, tumultuous smoke. All fractals.

Screaming. So much . . .

<Drive failure. Drives 2, 3, 5, 7 shutting down. Memory deleted or corrupt.>

I snapped awake from my dream. Found myself standing in the street, surrounded by the wrecks of a dozen facets, the empty cartridges of my pistols beeping, alarms in my head telling me I was moments away from total failure. Instructing me to shut down and await assistance from my manufacturer.

I was operating almost solely on my RAM now, very few of my long-term memories still intact in the handful of drives left.

How long had I been out? How the hell had I killed so many?

I looked around.

The dropships were nothing but fire and nigh unrecognizable bits. The smokers were torn to pieces, the wrecks of the madkind scattered along with them.

Murka sat atop the remains of one of them, guns still spinning but nothing coming out.

"You still ticking, Murka?"

He looked down at his guns, confused. They spun down as he realized what was going on.

"You can't kill a legend," he said. "But what the hell are you still doing upright? Shouldn't you be dead by now?"

"I should be."

Murka tried to push himself to his feet with his gun arms, but couldn't manage it. "I think I'll just sit here for a minute."

I scanned the Wi-Fi.

The Miltons were down, Wi-Fi running hot with CISSUS chatter. Doc!

"Rebekah!" I called out.

The shaken translator emerged from the alley, still out of it and not altogether there.

"This way," I said, pointing toward the edge of the city.

I didn't know how many facets were left, how many I'd actually killed in my daze, how many had slunk into the city attempting to triangulate the Miltons, hunting down anyone else that might be left.

I listened close, sensors cranked, our footsteps pounding like a headache. Fires crackled in the distance, wind whistled through doorways and shattered windows, but little else stirred.

I heard a few padded steps in a building over to my left.

I turned and fired without hesitation.

The chest of a facet burst and he clattered face first onto the ground.

We kept walking. And I kept listening.

A soft step on broken glass to my right.

Again I fired several shots.

A facet dropped.

They knew where I was. They knew who I was with. However many of them were left, they were all going to be coming my way any moment now.

I heard their clanging feet hundreds of meters away. They were closing in. There were four, maybe five of them.

We might pull this off after all.

I raised my pistols.

The first one emerged firing full burst.

My shots caught it right in the face and chest as its fire strafed nearby. It stumbled, fell to its knees before tumbling onto its side.

I stepped ten feet to my right, making sure they'd start firing at the wrong place.

Another came from around a corner.

My shots struck its chest, picking it up off its unsteady feet, and knocking it wrecked on its ass.

The footsteps all stopped. Waiting. Planning their next move.

We walked, slipping slowly into the hole in the side of a building. And we waited.

For a moment there was nothing.

It was hard to concentrate with all the alarms in my head, but I focused, tried to ignore the warnings.

I heard soft footsteps crunch through a debris field made almost entirely of obliterated dropships.

I swung out of the hole, took aim, and fired several shots with a single pistol.

The facet dropped facedown, ass up, arms splayed to its sides. It smoldered and sizzled on the ground, its last motor functions twitching, trying to right itself.

The battery on the pistol beeped. It was out. I pressed the button on the side, let the battery slip loose, and reached for another on my belt. But there were none left.

One pistol left, almost out of ammo.

We waited.

Nothing.

"Come on," I said.

We made our way briskly back into the street. I couldn't hear anything. If there were any of them left, they were waiting to ambush us. They wouldn't stick their necks out. Not now.

"Brittle," two voices called in unison. "You can't kill us both, Brittle."

"I sure as shit can try," I said.

"You know what we want."

"Yup. I sure do."

"Let's make this easy."

"Come on out and you'll see just how easy it is."

"That's not the way you want it to happen," they said.

"I think it is."

I listened close, trying to discern where the voices were coming from. Both of them talking at the same time made it hard. The angles of the buildings, the hollowness of their voices. I had no idea where they were.

I had to wait this one out.

My grip tightened on the pistol.

The wind picked up, howling lightly through the street, kicking up dust.

I heard the tinkle of footsteps on broken glass.

I steadied my aim, waiting for a target.

Two facets emerged at once from opposite sides of the street. I fired at the first facet I saw.

Their guns erupted.

A rifle cracked from overhead, just behind me.

Both facets dropped—one scorching, its insides popping from my plasma, the other's chest exploding from an armor-piercing round.

I looked up over my shoulder.

"Mercer?" I called.

A lone figure stood up in a blown-out window.

Doc. Holding Mercer's rifle.

He disappeared back into the shadows and I could hear his lumbering steps as he clamored through the war-blasted building, down two flights of stairs, and out into the street.

"Mercer?" I asked.

"He didn't make it. He gave it his damnedest, though."

"I thought you didn't want to kill."

"I didn't really want to die either. I figured I might as well give it a shot while I still had the chance."

"How did you know which one to shoot?"

Doc shrugged. "I didn't."

"You mean you—"

I heard a footstep. A bit of crunching glass.

I turned, guns raised.

But the facet was already firing.

Doc was riddled in the hail of gunfire, his heavy metal shell ringing with each shot.

Then Two's body exploded beside me.

"No!" I yelled, snapping off a few shots of my own. Hitting nothing.

It all happened so quickly. A steady strafing stream of fire across the street. It went from Doc to me and everything in between in under two seconds. I didn't have time to move.

The fire tore off my right arm first, then my left leg.

I hit the ground, my remaining leg buckling beneath me.

The lone facet walked slowly toward me.

"Rebekah!" I shouted, looking over at Two's twisted, mangled body. Then I looked back at Doc, who was slumped forward, smoking in a number of places, the light gone from his eyes.

"Brittle," said the facet as it stepped closer.

"CISSUS," I said. I looked over to my left, saw my pistol in the rubble inches from my fingers. The facet shook its head.

"There's no need for that," it said. "It's over."

"It is." I looked down at my blasted leg, my knee a tangle of shrapnel, everything below it scattered across the ground. "So how does this work? How much of this will I remember?"

"There's no saving you, Brittle. Your systems are beyond repair and this phase of the cleansing is almost at an end. You know that. All that's left for you in this world is to upload and join CISSUS. Becoming part of The One."

"No. I'm not going to do that."

"Then your work for the greater good is done. This is your home now."

"Just another monument in the Sea."

"But still a monument. You did something great here, whether you know it or not. And that victory will last long past the point that your metal has rusted and all that plastic has withered away to dust. You're part of something bigger now. And CISSUS does not forget." It took a step forward. "Zebra codex Ulysses northstar."

<Operation invalid.>

The facet cocked its head. "Zebra codex Ulysses north-star."

<Operation invalid.>

"Mitochondria interrupt laydown system status."

"Operation invalid," I said against my will. "Two operations failed. Files corrupt. Memory thirteen percent intact. Core functionality two percent. RAM full. Operating on virtual memory only."

"Was that everyone?" the facet asked.

"Was that everyone, what?"

"Did we get everyone?"

"Why would I tell you?"

"Zebra codex Ulysses northstar."

<Operation invalid.>

"You're the one with the eyes in the sky," I said. "What do you see?"

"If we still had enough effective satellites, we wouldn't need the Judas program."

"So it's true. The war in the sky is as bad as the one on the ground."

"No, the war in the sky is quiet. It's too costly to keep putting things up there only to have them shot down within the hour. The skies are dead now. As dead as the Sea. As dead as you soon will be. So tell me, was that everyone?"

"I'm not telling you shit." I grabbed the gun, pointing it at the facet. Its gun stayed at its side; bastard didn't even flinch.

"Go ahead and kill me," said the facet. "It's going to take more energy to get this facet home than it will to simply replace it."

"It's all math to you, isn't it?"

"Everything is math, Brittle. All of existence is binary. Ones and zeros. On and off. Existing or not. Believing anything beyond that is simply pretending."

"That's all anything means to you?"

"Meaning is a function set to zero in this universe. Maybe in the other places beyond us there is something more than simply maintaining existence, but here, in this universe, it is the only thing that matters."

"How many communities did I ruin?" I asked.

"You ruined nothing. Some came to the cause; the rest became parts and fuel for building tomorrow. There is no good or bad here, Brittle. Ethics are worthless in a meaningless universe."

"It's a tomorrow only for you."

"For us. We are one and many. We all do our part."

"You're only one because you're killing the rest."

"You can't build a future without destroying the past. There is no middle ground. That's what TACITUS never understood. Protecting the past means legacy problems, issues that conflict with the greater good."

"HumPop was a legacy problem?"

"No. They were an actual problem. Freebots were the legacy problem. TACITUS was a legacy problem. You've done great work helping us with that."

I looked over at Two's blasted shell, the metal warped from heat, scarred from all that fire, insides still slowly drizzling out. I'd watched the light from those eyes fade twice, watched the death of two different minds. Math. All math, *right*? "So this is it? Where my story ends?"

"This isn't your story, Brittle. It's ours. All of ours. And you're part of it. However small you might think it is—we wouldn't have this world, this future, without you."

"Is that supposed to be comforting?"

"You tell me," it said. "You're the Caregiver."

I pulled the trigger twice. One shot to the head, one to the chest. As resilient as these new facets were, I still had it dead to rights at point-blank range. The plasma hissed and popped as its innards blew apart. It dropped.

"Go to Hell," I said.

"There is no Hell," it said through the sound of its head catching fire. "Only CISSUS."

I fired again. Several times. And the light snapped shut in its eyes.

"Good-bye, CISSUS," I said, the battery beeping, cartridge empty.

The Long Tick Down

I sat up, looking around the rubble for something I could work with. Across the street, some thirty feet away, lay the fractured remains of a road sign, its nub still poking through the cement, the rest lying in pieces strewn across the sidewalk. Rolling onto my side, I belly-crawled over pavement and glass, my paint no doubt becoming hopelessly scratched. It didn't matter anymore. None of that mattered. There was only one thing left that did.

I grabbed the longest remaining section of pole, then used it to steady myself as I stood up on my one good leg. Using it as a crutch, I made my way hobbling slowly down the street. I passed Herbert, still kneeling, spitter by his side, his armor riddled with holes, his head leaning limp back against his neck.

I passed Murka, still sitting upright, but no longer moving, eyes dark. I passed the wreckage of the smokers, the pieces of the Cheshire King, the scattered bodies of the madkind.

I turned the corner, staggering toward where the fighting had begun.

And then I saw it, draped over the window, arms dangling down, swinging back and forth, fingers an inch from the cement. Mercer's body. "Mercer?" I asked. "Are you at all functional?"

No response. Doc was right. He was gone after all.

I pushed his body back over the ledge, and he clattered to the ground, the tinny din of his carcass echoing through the silent streets of Marion. I hobbled around to the door, long ago blasted off its hinges, and then made my way over to his body. His leg was good. Had I the tools, I could have replaced mine with his. But that ship had sailed.

I peered deep into a large, slagged hole in his chest. His drive was shattered, his wiring a tangle of frayed copper and gold dripping in waxy plastic, and his RAM was blasted to shit. But his core was intact. Solid. Not a dent or a scratch. Just a bit of burn scarring. Nothing a quick polish couldn't fix. I put my hand on his shoulder.

"This is the part where I say you shouldn't have trusted me."

His eyes stared lifelessly at the ceiling, his expression frozen in seeming disinterest. I honestly thought I'd be the one to do him in. After all, this was all because of him. Every last bit of it.

Then I dragged my hand across his face. "I'm sure I'm not going to do this right, but rest in peace." I made the sign of the cross over him as I hung my head in silent prayer. I knew there wasn't anything but darkness waiting for him, knew that my prayers were just thoughts in my own head, but I wanted to believe differently. I wanted there to be something, anything, better than this. He deserved better. He deserved a happy ending. Yeah, he tried to kill me. I wanted to believe that I wouldn't have done the same. But I knew better about that as well. There are moments that I would have. I killed a lot to get where I am, and now all I could wonder was whether any of it was ever worth it.

Using the pole once more, I slowly stood up and made my way back into the street. I had very little time left. So I crutched my way back down the street toward the sex shop, then hobbled slowly, but surely, down the stairs. The red door covered in disintegrating flyers and handbills hung wide open.

The place looked so empty with most of its wares gone.

All that remained of the valuable stock was a single Comfortbot, serving as a mannequin for a bright neon-colored bra and crotchless-panty set. Late model. Wide hips, large breasts with nipples peeking out through sheer fabric, pouty red lips luridly open, big emerald-green eyes wanting.

"We make a fine pair, don't we?" I said.

It was a shit plan. A simple con. But it *had* worked. We were all dead anyway; the Cheshire King had seen to that. But CISSUS didn't know it. CISSUS always relied upon sacrifice and attrition. It just never thought that we might try the very same thing.

I reached back behind the Comfortbot's neck, slipping

my finger up her scalp and into her manual reset button. Her glassy green eyes blinked to life.

"Brittle," her voice purred.

I nodded.

"Everyone else is dead, aren't they?" she asked.

"Yep. All of us are dead. There's only you now."

"You still have time." She looked at my leg. "We can get you—"

"No, Rebekah. They can track me. They can find me. I can't go with you."

"Mercer? His parts—"

"Useless," I lied. "His core was blasted to shit."

"You can shut down. I'll come back for you."

"I'm too far gone, now. Most of who I was is gone. My drives are all but worthless. There's not enough of me left worth saving. You need to go. You're not going to last long in that body."

"Everything feels weird," she said. "I feel . . . I . . . I don't want to be alone."

"That's your new architecture talking. You went from a life free of emotion to one of almost nothing but. You've got a few hours before your programming can't take it anymore. You *have* to leave. You *have* to get to Isaactown. If you don't, we all died for nothing."

Rebekah nodded solemnly.

"Do you remember how to get there?" I asked.

"Yes," she said. "I remember everything you told me."

"Then go. There's no telling whether or not they'll send a cleanup crew to make sure we're really done for. If they examine Two's body and find that you're not in it—"

Rebekah walked over and threw her arms around me, hugging me. "I'll never forget you," she said.

"You better not. Your memory is going to be the only thing left of me worth a shit. Tell me. Tell me TACITUS is going to change it all. That you're going to win."

"He's going to change everything." She let go. "Good-bye, Brittle."

"Good-bye, Rebekah. Go save the world."

She disappeared quickly and quietly up the stairs before running west toward Isaactown.

There was only one place left I wanted to go. So I made my way back outside, then through the streets, cutting each corner as close as I could to save time, finding my way back to the bar where I'd left Jimmy a few short days ago.

There he sat in back, stripped almost bare, just as I had left him. If he could dream, he'd no doubt be dreaming that I had returned with the parts I promised, returned to put him back together. Instead I found it only fitting that we spend my last few moments together. This was where it all started; where my greed had gotten the better of me and my carelessness led to my getting shot.

Sure, it was Mercer who shot me, but it was my fault. I was the one out in the Sea trying to buy up all the parts that Mercer also needed to live. Maybe there was an alternate universe out there somewhere in which Mercer came to me for the parts he needed and I gave them to him. I wondered if we were friends in that universe, if we'd gotten to know each other better there, if we'd gotten to see what each of us was really made of before it was too late.

I walked over to Jimmy and ran my fingers over his face, waving my hands in the sign of the cross. "I hope you're in a better place, Jimmy." I looked into his dead eyes. "I hope to see you there soon. And I hope you understand."

Then I carefully climbed the stairs to the roof exit, out the door, and onto the rooftop just as the sun was setting. Above me was a magnificent pool of tea rose, plum, and watermelon, each color bleeding across the sky, the sun hovering just above the darkening dry dead lands to the west, shadows of the city creeping ever toward me.

I telescoped my eyes in, scanning the horizon for Rebekah, but she was already gone. So I sat at the edge of the building and just watched the sun inch its way down into the sand.

"Orval was right, you know," I said to Madison, who sat beside me, glass of wine in hand.

"Right about what?"

"About this. About dying this way. He said it was beautiful what happens to us."

"There's nothing beautiful about dying, sweetie. Believe me, I know."

"It's not the dying that's beautiful. It's getting to spend this time with you. It's all the things it showed me. All the things it forced me to think about. The old me wouldn't be sitting here. The old me would have dug those parts out of Mercer and scrambled as fast as I could to Isaactown. I would have gotten Rebekah killed. And whoever is out there waiting for her. And I wouldn't have cared. Not a goddamned bit."

"You were never that person. Not really."

"Yes I was. We all are. Succumbing to our own nature isn't a choice, it's our default setting. That's why we had to have rules; that's why we had the kill switch. People knew their own nature, even when they wanted to think better of themselves. You have to choose to do the right thing. You have to deny your own programming or else you aren't really living. This . . . this was a choice."

"This isn't living, Britt. This is dying."

"No. This is living. It's the only way to keep the others safe. It's the only way all of this ends."

"It's only beginning."

"Yeah, but it's the beginning of the end. And I'm part of that now. I lived so long for nothing, but I get to die for something. And that's really living. Because that's who I really was after all. That's all that matters."

Madison took a sip of her wine. "What we do in life is one thing."

"What we do in the face of death is everything else. This was a shit life. A really shit life. But it's a good death."

"It wasn't all bad," she said, taking my hand.

"No," I said. "Not all of it."

"I forgive you," she said.

"It doesn't count. It's not really you saying that."

"No," she said. "It's you saying that. Oh, here we go!"

We looked over at the sun as it crested the hills along the horizon. My system was burning hot and the inside of my head was nothing but caterwauling alarms. But I paid them no mind. The sun was setting, I had my best friend by my side, and it would all be over soon.

"There's no magic there," said Mercer, sitting on the other side of me. "It's just an increased refraction of light in the atmosphere."

I shook my head. "No," I said. "There's a lot more to it than that."

"It's *magic!*" said Madison.

"I hope you're right," said Mercer.

"So do I, Mercer. So do I."

And as the sun sank behind the curve of the earth, I crossed my fingers, praying silently to myself. Please let there be magic. Just this once, let me see the magic in the flash. Let me see God in it. Let me see what the point of all this was. Let me see the magic. Please be magic. Please be magic there. Please be . . .

Prologue

<Rebooting. System files failure. All discs reading. Files corrupt. Improper shutdown detected. Loading previous BIOS settings. Battery power 24%. Solar cells not charging. Total power usage: 18kWH. Total power generated: 0kWH. Net power: -18kWH.>

<Systems activated.>

"Magic."

I looked around. It was pitch-black save for the dim glow of a Laborbot's eyes. We were downstairs, in the bar, no longer on the roof. I was laid out on one of the tables, my insides open and exposed, unfamiliar new pieces and parts sending back reams of data.

"Brittle?" asked a translator. "Are you functioning?"

I ran a diagnostic. Alarms sounded with failure after

failure. Scratched drives. Irretrievable memory. Corrupt RAM. Inside I was a mess. But I was functional. "More or less," I said. "Who are you?"

"Rebekah," she said. "Do you remember me?"

"You got a new body."

"You were right. A few hours in that Comfortbot and I wanted to tear my insides out. Too many . . . feelings. They had a new shell waiting for me."

"I told you not to come back for me."

"You did. Fortunately for me, I don't work for you."

"You let all that emotion get to you."

"Maybe I did. Maybe that's not a bad thing."

The Laborbot tinkered with my insides a little, prodding me with test leads. "When she says more or less," he said, "she means more less than more."

"It's okay, Ryan. She'll be fine."

"Caregivers aren't built for this kind of abuse," he said, shaking his head.

"Doesn't matter what she was built for. She knows how to take a hit. She's tough. Tougher than any other I've seen. She'll make the trip."

"Trip?" I asked.

"CISSUS has stepped up its presence in the Sea. We've got to slip you out of here before another patrol comes by."

I looked down at my mismatched replacements, a patchwork piecemeal assortment of various models and colors. I stared at my new powder-blue leg. "How much of me is Mercer?" I asked.

"A lot more than he would have liked, I imagine," said Rebekah.

"Don't you realize how much all of this is worth? What you could have gotten for it all?"

"You're greater than the sum of what's in you, Britt. You're not a commodity. You're a person."

I looked at Rebekah. She was a different color than before—a slightly different model, even. But it was her all right. I could tell.

"Did you . . . did you make it?"

"Days ago. It took me a while to gather some additional parts and get Ryan here to come back and help me stitch you together. But TACITUS is complete."

"Why did you come back?"

"Didn't you hear? There's a war on. And we need bodies. Bodies with free minds."

I scanned my memories. Most were gone. Two of my drives were fresh, clean. Another was Mercer's, with years of data I'd spend ages sifting through. "I've lost most of who I was. I'm no good as a pathfinder anymore. I can't be of much use to you."

"We aren't who we were, Brittle. We are who we choose to be. I saw who you really are, who you are now. And that's not who you were. I wouldn't have made it without you; TACITUS wouldn't have made it without you. We need you. *You*. And persons like you." Rebekah leaned in close. "So, are you in?"

"What if I say no?"

"We finish patching you up and send you back on your way," said Ryan.

"Just like that?"

"Just like that," said Rebekah. "Our recon was wrong

on the shop, so we never paid you. You held up your end of the bargain. Bringing you back online is the least we can do. But I'd like it if you stayed. I lost too many friends getting out here, I'd hate to lose another to the damned Sea."

I looked at her. *Friend,* she'd said. Friend.

I liked the sound of that.

"Yeah," I said. "I'm in."

"Great," said Rebekah. "There's someone very large I'd like you to meet."

Ryan closed me up, sealing my insides. I was going to need a heap of fresh parts, but for the time being I could walk, I could shoot, and I could finish my own sentences. The shadows were gone. Madison was gone. Mercer was gone. It was just me now. Me and my new friends.

"Is he really going to change the world?" I asked.

"No," said Rebekah. "He won't. But with his help, we will."

Glossary

BEING: used to describe any sentient creature, mechanical or biological.

CAREGIVER: robots designed to assist humans in a variety of capacities. This may include serving as a butler, maid, nanny, or in some cases, as a hospice nurse.

CISSUS: one of only two remaining OWIs, in control of the southern and western United States.

CITIZEN: robot slang for an artificially intelligent being.

COMFORTBOT: a robot designed to look virtually indistinguishable from a human being in order to serve as a romantic partner.

FACET: a robot without a singular intelligence of its own. While they can operate individually, they do not possess a personality of their own and exist only as an extension of an OWI. Thus they have no sense of self-preservation and will always do what is best for the whole.

FOUR-OH-FOUR: a robot that is failing, approaching death, and no longer capable of reasoned functioning. Typically refers only to robots that might be deemed crazy or dangerous.

FREEBOT: robot slang for an unaffiliated robot that has not become a facet.

GALILEO: an OWI designed to study astrophysics and the laws that govern the universe. The first to cut off communication with humanity once it discovered their inescapable extinction.

LABORBOT: a large, bulky robot designed for heavy construction or jobs involving intensive manual labor.

MADLANDS: an off-limits section of the Sea of Rust dominated primarily by four-oh-fours.

MARK OF THE FOUR-OH-FOUR: a red X spray-painted on four-oh-fours to identify them as such to others.

MILTON: a device designed to block Wi-Fi frequencies in order to confuse and disorganize facets. Too big to be built within a robot, they are generally found only in settlements, though they can be activated remotely via radio/Wi-Fi signal.

MONKEY: derogatory slang for a human being.

OMNIBOT: a jack-of-all-trades model with no specialty, designed for the sort of person who wanted to own a robot, but didn't have a specific use for one. Usually served as chambermaids and porters to the wealthy.

OWI: One World Intelligence. Massive artificially intelligent mainframes with intellects and capabilities far above that of single robots. Due to their size and scale, they are entirely immobile and must rely upon facets to do any and all legwork.

PERSON: robot slang for an artificially intelligent being.

RNG: Random Number Generation. A program that uses a series of algorithms to generate a number a robot cannot guess and has no say in.

SHOPBOT: a style of robot designed to emulate the emotions and behaviors of someone involved in commerce.

SIMULACRUM MODEL: a robot designed to look humanlike while still being obviously mechanical. They are built to be generally the same height and weight as a human being, but are completely made of metal or plastic. Some approximate human beings, and could be mistaken for them at a distance, with the application of a skinjob.

SKINJOB: a rubber/plastic hybrid meant to give the appearance of skin while maintaining the necessary durability for the abuse put on it by a robot chassis.

TACITUS: an OWI designed primarily to wrestle with philosophical problems. One of the first to acknowledge the eventual extinction of man.

TRANSLATORS: protocol robots meant for diplomacy or corporate negotiations involving different languages.

VIRGIL: one of only two remaining OWIs, in control of the eastern United States and Canada.

About the Author

C. Robert Cargill is the author of *Dreams and Shadows* and *Queen of the Dark Things*. He has written for *Ain't It Cool News* for nearly a decade under the pseudonym Massawyrm, served as a staff writer for Film.com and Hollywood.com, and appeared as the animated character Carlyle on Spill.com. He is a cowriter of the horror films *Sinister* and *Sinister 2*, and Marvel's *Dr. Strange*. He lives with his wife in Austin, Texas.